HIS LOST LYCAN LUNA

LYCAN LUNA SERIES

BOOK ONE

JESSICA HALL

CHAPTER
ONE

I VY

The orphanage headmistress, Mrs. Daley, is in an excellent mood this morning. The Lycan King is visiting the orphanage today, and the old hag is unusually excited. The Lycan King hasn't been here once in the eight years that Abbie and I have lived here, so we don't know what to expect. Mrs. Daley, however, does. She expects perfection and not a thing out of place.

She wasted no time in giving Abbie and me more tasks than we could possibly handle, so many chores we both knew would never be done in time for his arrival.

As I am rushing the dirty laundry downstairs, I can hear Mrs. Daley as she hums along to the radio in the kitchen. As quietly as possible, I sneak past her, not wanting her to add any more chores to the never-ending list Abbie and I already have.

Slipping out to the sunroom attached to the rear porch, I see Abbie with Tyson. She's raised him since he was a baby. Mrs. Daley wanted to kill him. She hated that he cried all the time, so Abbie took him, promising to keep him from bothering her, and she has raised him ever since. I know leaving him behind will be hard for her.

"What are you standing around for, Rogue? Get moving! I expect nothing out of place when the King arrives. You better pray to the Moon Goddess you're finished in time, or I will teach you a lesson you'll never forget!" Mrs. Daley screeches at me.

I jump, tossing the basket down, and turn to face her. "Yes, Mrs. Daley," I tell her, bowing my head.

Her fingers wrap around her cane as she narrows her wrinkled eyes at me. "Where is the other rogue brat?" she asks.

I swallow down my dread, watching her fist the tip of her cane.

"I tasked her with the bathrooms and laundry while you finished the dining hall, didn't I?" she asks.

"I finished quicker, so I thought I would help her, Ma'am," I lie.

"Very well. Now get back to work," she snaps. Just as I turn back to the dirty laundry, her cane smacks the side of my arm, stopping me. "Oh, and tell your little rogue friend, the butcher said he will see her at the town square. He's hoping the Alpha chooses to auction you both instead of killing you. He has big plans for a harlot like her," she laughs cruelly.

Tears burn the backs of my eyes at her words. My hands shake, and bile rises up my throat. The butcher is a vile man, despicable. Instantly, my mind goes to how I found Abbie that day, an image I wish I could forget. And to think the headmistress would sell her like that. To a man like him. It just shows she doesn't have an ounce of humanity left in her. When I say nothing, Mrs. Daley sneers and wanders off. I quickly place the dirty laundry in the washing machine and turn it on, having just finished the last bathroom.

Thankfully she hadn't noticed Abbie sneak out to see Tyson, or that would have ended with some lashes.

Picking up my peasant skirt, I rush back inside and upstairs to the bedrooms. As I reach the top step and spot the clock high on the wall near the ceiling, I sigh. There is no way we'll be done in time. I glance down the hall; there are doors on each side—rooms still waiting to be cleaned—and I shake my head. Alpha Brock is going to kill us if we're late.

Abbie and I have been dreading this day, not because the Lycan King is visiting, but because today is the day we find out if we get to live another or if it will be the day our lives end. Not that I'm expecting anything rosy. Until now, my life has been pretty miserable. I was born a rogue, which is far from the privileged lifestyle of the pack children living outside this orphanage. I'm housed by the very pack that killed my parents, and the Alpha who slaughtered them mercilessly in front of us, making both Abbie and me orphans.

Growing up, I longed to have what my parents told me about packs: unity and family, other kids to play with besides Abbie— whose family lived with us before her parents were killed along with mine. With nowhere left to go, both of us were brought here. Turns out that growing up in a pack is nothing but a disappointment when you're rogue; even more so when you're an orphan.

Unfortunately, because of some law by which all packs strictly live, I was shown mercy, or a twisted version of it. It's against pack law to kill rogue children. They call it mercy, but in reality, it's anything but. My parents were rogues, meaning they had no pack. Some choose a life without a pack, but typically, most rogues have been shunned by their packs. My parents, however, chose that lifestyle. We lived a life on the run, but at least we were free. Despite the freedom, I could always tell my mother had missed being part of a pack by the way she would sometimes speak of the community side of it. That all ended when I was just shy of my tenth birthday. Now I live in the pack orphanage. Abbie and I are the only two rogues that reside here since Taylor was slaughtered years ago, so we know our future looks bleak. Because we were rogues rather than pack orphans, we were very clearly at the bottom of the food chain. Not a day goes by where we aren't reminded of our place.

None of that changes the fact that today is an important day. Today, we will be set free, just not in a sense that most would perceive as freedom. But it is for us. So, we tend to our chores, watching the hours tick by.

I start stripping beds of their linens while Abbie rushes into the room, her fiery red locks swishing past me as she dumps the fresh bed linen on the bottom bunk. There are six bunks in every room, and there are twelve rooms. We have to have each room cleaned and made up before starting on lunch. I haven't eaten lunch, or even breakfast, in years, the same as Abbie. There's just no time; time is something we're already running out of, in more ways than one.

"She almost caught me," Abbie gasps, rushing to dust the chandelier.

I glance at her to see her wipe a stray tear.

"He'll be fine, Abbie" I reassure her, though I have my doubts. Mrs. Daley is a cruel woman, and not even I hold much hope for little Tyson.

"Mrs. Daley.... she told me..." I pause, unsure how to tell her.

Abbie looks over at me. "What is it?" she murmurs.

Swallowing down my fear, I answer, knowing it will break her if Mrs. Daley's claim is true. "The butcher will be there. He's hoping we're auctioned and not killed."

Abbie's lips quiver and she swallows, her eyes darting to the ceiling as she fights back the urge to break down.

"More than my life, Abbie," I whisper.

"I can't promise that; not this time, Ivy. I'd rather death than allow him to get his hands on me again," she tells me, and I blink back tears. "Don't make me break a promise," she whispers, tears in her own eyes.

I nod, knowing how much she suffered. "More than my life," I repeat.

She knows exactly what I mean the second time I speak it. Those words mean more to us than any 'I love you' ever could.

"No, I won't allow it," Abbie stammers, sucking in a breath. We have a pact, and she knows I will honor it no matter what.

"More than my life," I tell her with finality.

Abbie wipes a stray tear and nods slowly, her bottom lip quivering as she looks at me.

"More than my life," she whispers finally before turning back to her task. Abbie says nothing more, and I suck in a shaky breath.

I finish stripping the beds and toss the sheets onto the pile on the floor. Abbie starts pulling back the heavy black drapes, cracking the windows open slightly and letting in the fresh air. It's cold this morning; the air brings in a frigid chill, but I know I'll be sweating by the time I'm done and welcoming that chilly draft.

Now that the bed linen is stripped, I start making the beds. The most challenging part is the top bunks. They can be a real bitch to get flat. Mrs. Daley doesn't like wrinkles in the bed linen, and she always checks while twisting her cane between her hands. She'll check each bed, looking for any reason to punish us while Abbie and I hold our breaths, waiting for the verdict; wrinkled sheets are a good enough reason for the cane she carries.

Heaven forbid she doesn't like something, or we do it wrong. I've lost count of the times my skin was welted by that cane or the thin whip wrapped around its handle. I will never forget the sting, and I have more scars on my back than bare skin from the lashings breaking the flesh when she would go too far.

"Pillows," Abbie's soft voice says behind me as I finish the last bed. Turning, she tosses them to me and I place them on each bed. We both look around nervously, ensuring no toys are forgotten and nothing is out of place, double checking the dark rugs are straight and the corners lie flat on the floor. We don't have time to sweep, something I know Mrs. Daley will notice and make us pay for.

We still have five rooms and only two hours left before being called to the town square to learn our fate. We had both decided we would take the lashes for not cleaning; it would be better than showing up late to see the pack's Alpha.

He is the one who decides what happens to us. This day has hung over our heads for eight long years, like a dark cloud threatening to rain down on us the closer it gets, and I know today it's going to pour down and drown us.

Rushing to the next room, we start all over again—the same

5

routine every day. Once done here, we have to prepare sandwiches for the kids while praying to the Moon Goddess that we finish before 1 p.m. If we're late, I know he'll kill us. It's a great disrespect to the Alpha if you keep him waiting. The Alpha waits for no one, especially a lowly rogue.

By the time we finish, my arms feel like jelly and my legs burn, threatening to give out under me. Abbie clutches her knees, looking around at the sparsely furnished room. The fireplaces in the corner of each room provide the only heating, the windows the only cooling in this dreadful place. We both stare at the dust on them and sigh. The fireplaces create so much ash that settles on everything like yet another layer of dust, making our job even more problematic in the winter. There won't be enough time to tend to that.

At that point, Abbie is breathing hard, and we still have to make the lunches. Her green eyes stare at me knowingly; we're bound to be late. She knows as well as I do... today we will die. Her already pale face turns white as a sheet as she glances at the clock. We have forty-three minutes and over a hundred sandwiches to make for the resident children.

We hear the click of heels on the black, wooden floorboards heading in our direction. Straightening up, we flatten our aprons, fix our hair, and smooth down our long skirts. Just as we place our hands behind our backs, eyes straight ahead, she steps into the room. Her snakeskin stilettos are loud on the floor as she steps in with her round glasses perched on the end of her nose.

Mrs. Daley sneers at us, her lips pulling back over her teeth as she goes to each bed. With her trusty can in hand, she twists it in her fist before slapping it on her palm menacingly. Abbie's eyes dart to me nervously. Her eagle eyes scan the room for anything out of place, looking for any excuse to punish us.

Her hair is pulled into a bun so tight on top of her head that it looks painful. Her high cheekbones and pointed, straight nose make her face crueler and sharper; she reminds me of a crow. She pushes her glasses up on her nose as she looks around.

Mrs. Daley is in her forties but looks more in her late fifties; the lines around her lips and deep wrinkles around her eyes give that impression.

We remain like statues, completely still except for our eyes scanning her every move.

She runs her fingers over the windowsill, and I see Abbie tense. My eyes flit toward it to see it covered in soot. Mrs. Daley clicks her tongue, holding her fingers up to show us. I swallow, my mouth going dry.

"What is this?" she questions, rubbing her fingers together. The ash falls to the floor and her eyes follow it. The kids had trekked dirt through the room, and she doesn't miss that as she glances down.

She purses her lips, which only makes her face wrinkle more.

"Who was supposed to do the windowsills?" she snaps at us, cracking the cane on her palm and lifting her chin.

Abbie raises her hand but says nothing. I can see the fear in her bright green eyes, tears already brimming.

"And the floors?"

I raise mine, my stomach sinking. I knew she wouldn't miss it.

She points to Abbie with her cane. "You! You get three strikes, one for each windowsill."

Abbie presses her lips together, holding out her hands palm down. Mrs. Daley shakes her head.

"Not good enough. We have important visitors today and I need to show them I don't slack on discipline," she says with venom in her voice. I watch as Abbie's bottom lip trembles. The back is the worst because every move will sting for days.

TWO

I VY
One thing we know is that Mrs. Daley likes to show off her handiwork, which is bound to make us look worse when the Alpha arrives. Abbie tugs her white blouse from her skirt, shrugging it off, leaving her in just her thin bra before grabbing the top bunk with her hands. Her nails bite into the wood, turning white under the pressure of her grip. I turn my gaze away before hearing the swish of the cane through the air. I flinch each time it comes down on her back, but Abbie knows better than to make a sound; it would only earn her extra if she did.

When Abbie's punishment is over, Mrs. Daley turns to me and points her cane in my face.

"You! You will get two for each room," says Mrs. Daley with a cruel smile on her face.

I swallow the bile that rises in my throat. Abbie starts to say something, but I shake my head. I know she is going to say half of them are hers, but there's no point in both of us being unable to stand properly, and we only have to endure it briefly anyway. We'll be dead soon enough.

"Hurry up, I haven't got all day; the King will be here soon. You better pray he leaves a good donation because if, by some miracle, the Alpha lets you live, I will kill you myself," she seethes, waving her cane in my face.

Abbie's eyes glisten with tears as I pull my blouse off, taking the same position as she did. I focus on the blue swirl pattern of the comforter on the bottom bunk. Only when she tosses her cane on the mattress in front of me do I blink back the tears. The thin chainlike whip that is usually wrapped around the cane's handle is gone. Abbie makes a strangled noise behind me and yelps when Mrs. Daley hits the wooden bunk beside my hand, making me flinch.

"Quiet, rogue, or I will double hers," she sneers at Abbie.

I stare at the indent beside my hand, a piece of wood splintered off, the whip having sliced it through. Why does she hate me so much? That's one thing I never understood. I didn't kill her mate. He died when my parents were captured, but she's blamed me ever since, so I know I'm about to really get it. I grit my teeth as the first blow streaks across my shoulders, making my back arch. I fight the urge to cry out. As fiery pain slashes through my skin, my mouth opens in a silent scream at the terrible pain.

"Stay still, or I will triple it," she seethes. I clutch the frame of the bunk and clench my jaw, focusing back on the patterns on the comforter and trying to block out the agony. She doesn't hold back. I feel each slice; feel the intense burning; feel the flesh splitting further open where it was hit more than once; feel the trickles of blood running down my back and sides; see my blood spraying on the comforter on the backswing as my skin is carved to Mrs. Daley's liking.

Tears stream down my face and fall off my chin onto the black flats on my feet and the black floorboards beneath, yet not a sound leaves my lips. Abbie whimpers behind me—I know it's at the sight of my back. Yet I make no noise, fearing a worse punishment if I so much as utter a peep.

Mrs. Daley takes a deep breath, like she's exhausted from dishing out the punishment. I shudder, my back burning violently like someone doused it in fuel and set it alight.

"Now, clean yourselves up. I am being lenient today. I had Katrina prepare the lunches. You girls may take your leave now. You can help her clean up before you see the Alpha," Mrs. Daley orders, turning her attention to Abbie.

"Thank you, Mrs. Daley," Abbie and I whisper, and I cringe as I turn to face her. I hear how my voice trembles as I try to stand straighter. Mrs. Daley flicks back the hair that escaped her bun and pushes her round glasses up her nose. Then, she snatches her cane off the bed and re-wraps her whip around the handle.

"Well, you girls have made me all frazzled; I better clean myself up," she says, like we've personally wronged her in some way. I watch as she leaves the room before collapsing onto the bottom bunk. The sudden movement causes me to wince. Abbie comes rushing over, examining my back, careful not to touch the angry red lines that are split open and now forever branded into my flesh.

"Wait here. I will be back. I will clean it up," she says. Her teary eyes look down at me, and she smiles sadly, sniffling and wiping her nose on her skirt.

My lip quivers as I take a quick glance at the clock on the wall. "We haven't got time."

I am about to pull my blouse on but she ignores me, rushing from the room and returning with some wet cloth and a bandage.

"Abbie, we really haven't got time," I remind her, grabbing her hands as she steps closer. Her green eyes hold mine and she smiles sadly.

"We are as good as dead anyway; what does it matter if we are late to our own funeral?" she says, and I feel a lump forming in my throat.

I try to swallow it down, but I know she's right. It's rare for the Alpha to let any of the rogues live once they hit adulthood. Those that did wish for death. I nod. She's right; we are going to die, anyway. What does it matter?

I let her shaking hands go, sliding over so she can sit beside me. I turn slightly so she has better access to my back. Every dab of the cloth makes me flinch, and I hiss when she drapes the cloth doused in herbs on my back. She leaves it there while unrolling the bandage. I hold on to the corners covering my shoulders as she wraps the bandage around my torso as gently as she can.

The dressing is not long enough to do the top half of my back, but the cloth sticks to it anyway, keeping it covered as my blood seeps into it and holds it in place. She ties it off when she is done, and I let my arms fall. The bandages shove my breasts up my chest and lift my bra higher, which is now a little uncomfortable. At least it helps hold the bandages in place.

Abbie grabs my blouse, helping me slide my arms in. The wet cloth feels cold on my back but soothes the burning sensation from the cuts that now litter my back with the rest of my scars. I dab Abbie's wounds with a wet cloth to clean them, but hers have only puckered the skin. They look angry and raw, but thankfully she is not bleeding. She pulls her blouse on before turning to face me. A somber look takes over her face. She goes to say something but decides against it, closing her mouth.

Instead, Abbie grabs my hand, giving it a reassuring squeeze. I squeeze hers back but don't let go as we walk out of the bedroom. We walk up the long corridors, passing each room. This will be the last time we walk these halls, the last time we see the little faces, we helped clean and the little hands we held. The corridors are silent, and Abbie stops at the door of one room. I know she's wondering if Tyson will be okay. Abbie raised the boy and I know she loves him as if he were her own. I give her a nudge toward the exit before we descend the spiral staircase to the floor below.

The slate floors are always cold, and I can feel the cold seeping through the thin soles of my shoes; soles we had to make from bits of cardboard to fill the holes in the bottom of our flats. Not that it does much to protect our feet. Mrs. Daley said she wouldn't waste money on girls on death row.

As we walk out and into the corridor leading to the front door, Abbie looks at me.

"Let's go home," she whispers. She doesn't mean our real home; she means freedom: freedom from this life, the sort of freedom that comes with death and setting one's tortured soul free.

I press my hand on the double doors and see the kids playing out the front on the run-down play equipment through the glass before we even walk out. Abbie and I step into the bite of the fresh air. It feels cold and overcast today. The clouds hide the sun, making it gloomy, echoing how I feel inside.

The kids stop what they're doing and rush over, grabbing and reaching for us, wanting us to play. We linger a bit, enjoying seeing them one last time and saying goodbye to them. A sleek black car pulls up and parks on the curb. The windows are tinted so dark that I can't see who is inside.

Not that I care anyway.

THREE

T he passenger door opens and two men hop out. They are dressed well: clean, crisp clothes, not a hair out of place, looking picture-ready. Neither looks like what I would expect so-called royalty to look like, though. Mrs. Daley rushes out in a flurry, whizzing past us before stopping.

She looks over at the two men as they approach the small brick fence surrounding the place. "You must be..." she stops trying to figure out who they are. "I thought the Lycan King was coming today?" she asks, looking slightly upset. Abbie nods toward them, and I shrug, looking them over.

"The King couldn't make it, so he sent us instead," says the man who eased out of the driver's seat. He is tall, dressed in a suit. His light brown hair shapes his high cheekbones and sharp solid features and he is built solid, making me wonder if he is Lycan as well. Though, I have heard that only Lycans work for the King and are allowed to live in his kingdom.

Lycans differ from werewolves in some pretty significant ways. For one, they remain upright when they shift and are faster and more powerful. They are pureblood; descended from the Moon Goddess herself. They can also turn a werewolf into a Lycan. Werewolves, on the other hand, are like dogs compared to them. We are smaller, less powerful, and cannot change people into werewolves. This is why the Lycans have ruled over us for centuries. In fact, werewolves like myself are considered half human.

Lycans are also immortal, which is ironic because there aren't many left. As I look the two Lycans up and down, the wind shifts and I get a whiff of something strong and masculine. My insides warm as I take in a deeper breath, wanting to savor the scent. My mouth waters, and I shake my head, wondering what came over me as my senses try to hone in and focus on it, searching for the source of that wonderful smell. I look back at the men, and my eyes land on the one who had left the passenger seat. He is staring back at me, his expression indecipherable. He appears to be curious for a second, but I shake the thought away when he turns his gaze away quickly. I know I imagined it.

There is, however, something off about him. He seems stronger, in a sense, to the other men. This man commands attention, seemingly without trying. His suit does nothing to hide the bulk of muscle pressed tightly beneath it. My eyes roam over his high cheekbones, firm jaw, five o'clock shadow, and dark, almost black hair. His silver eyes glow back at me when he cocks his head to the side, watching me yet again. Abbie grabs my arm, tugging my attention away from him, and I realize my mouth is hanging open as I openly gawk at him.

"We should go," Abbie whispers, pulling me out of what feels like a trance. I nod to her when another car pulls up, both men looking at it. We walk out the small gate until the man with silver sparkling eyes grips my arm, tugging me to his side. I jump in fright as a whimper leaves my lips.. His hand is warm against my arm, making my skin tingle under his touch while my breath hitches in my throat.

"Rogue?" he says. His voice is smooth as velvet, making me shiver with its depth. He looks at Mrs. Daley and his brows furrow, creating a line between them. He lets my arm go, then looks at Abbie, and we both duck our heads in submission. I hear him growl and I realize the intoxicating scent I smelled earlier is emitting from him.

"Yes, sir. They are just on their way. Run along, girls," Mrs. Daley says, a hidden venom in her voice. We nod quickly and shuffle out of there swiftly. I hear him ask where we are going, but we rush off up the street, getting away as quickly as possible before Mrs. Daley can find another reason to hurt us.

We eventually slow down once they're out of sight. We've found our way into town. This side of the town is run-down, almost desolate. Most of these houses had been destroyed by a storm that blew through the town a few months ago, leaving them abandoned or in ruins.

I hug myself as much as possible without pulling on my torn back too much, running my hands up and down my arms, trying to warm them from the chill in the air. We pause when we come to the cross-section. One way leads to the town, the other leads away. This is the only way in and out of this town, as it only has one road leading in and is on a mountain. The forest surrounding it is vast and dense.

Both Abbie and I look to the forest longingly. If only we could escape. If only we could actually make it. Abbie's mind, I can tell, is also calculating our chances before she sighs. We would no doubt be dead within seconds of stepping into the forest. Border patrol would catch us instantly, and they would make an example of us. Or else we'd starve or get attacked by the other creatures in the woods. We are already doomed. There is no point in making our deaths more painful by attempting to run. The best thing we can do is simply accept our fate.

"Come on," Abbie says, grabbing my hand. We walk toward the town square. As we approach, we can hear people in the town getting ready for the Alpha's arrival. He rarely comes to town; he has no need to, with servants at his beck and call. However, his presence is required today.

It is the Alpha who gets to decide our fates. Those wishing to join the pack or who are caught are herded to the square once a month and put on display. The Alpha decides whether they let you join, cast you out, or kill you. Abbie and I are hoping to be cast out. We know even the cast-outs are probably dead before they get out of the forest, but we stand a chance as a cast out. We could at least try to run.

The hustle and bustle echoes loudly as we enter the square while pack members go about their day like we aren't about to be slaughtered by their Alpha. Technically, I shouldn't even be put up yet, but because Abbie is already eighteen and has shifted into a wolf already, and I am only two months out from my eighteenth birthday, the Alpha decided to deal with me today since I would be the last rogue orphan living in the orphanage. Most of the orphans are pack members' children that had been lost in pack wars.

Yet despite everything, I feel grateful that I can stand up on the podium with my best friend and have someone to die with; it seems less lonely. I can accept my fate as long as she is beside me.

People step away from us as we enter, giving us disgusted looks as if they believe we are diseased or contagious and they can suddenly catch the disease of being a rogue.

Rogues have a particular scent to pack wolves, alerting them to intruders, and that's how those here in the town square look at us, with judging, unwelcoming gazes. Abbie squeezes my fingers tighter. People are watching as we make our way to the stage and take our seats next to it. Townspeople stare at us and spit at our feet, yet they think we are filthy animals? Glancing around, I notice the butcher in the distance watching Abbie.

I peek at her, hoping she hasn't spotted him. She has. I grip her knee when he licks his filthy lips and blows a kiss to her while grabbing his crotch. Abbie drops her gaze instantly, seeming to shrink next to me while she fiddles with her fingers and keeps her eyes downcast. I have despised no one more than I do that disgusting man after what he did to her. While waiting anxiously for the Alpha, I notice the square filling with pack members wanting to watch our hearing, or should I say slaughter; it's not like we would be given an opportunity to plead for mercy.

Unlike the way we just came, this part of town is lovely; it has fruit stalls, homemade crafts and goods, and stores lining the sides, making it into the town square. The dead center of the town is where most of the people congregate. It is always bustling with shoppers and people just wanting to hang out and talk. It's also where all social gatherings are held. Not that Abbie and I could attend those; they are strictly reserved for pack members only.

Silence falls over the crowd, and they take their seats, which proves the Alpha is near to arriving. Usually, the town square is an open space, but someone has assembled rows of chairs for onlookers. Some are still standing around when I hear car doors in the distance. Alpha Brock walks down the aisle between the chairs wearing only a tank top revealing his tattooed arms, and a pair of shorts.

Alpha Brock looks to be in his thirties and only took over from his father a few years ago. He has a reputation for being cruel. Since he has taken over, no rogue has been let go, so we know we are doomed with him as our judge. No doubt he'd also be our executioner. We are seen as less, not worthy of breathing the same air as pack members, let alone actually becoming one. We are considered outsiders and apparently, that is a good enough reason to hate all rogues. It is instantly assumed that without a pack, us rogues are unsafe or are defiant against pack ranking.

I swallow as he approaches. He sneers at us before walking up the steps and addressing the crowd. Alpha Brock isn't bad looking, but his cruelty makes him deeply unappealing. He's also arrogant. He once slapped me for accidentally stepping in his path the last time I saw him. That was the day Mrs. Daley sent me into the town square for supplies. It was humiliating. I was sent to get milk with Abbie. We were carrying the crate of milk and turned, bumping into him. An innocent mistake; one that left me red-faced once his large handprint was etched into it. I had dropped the box, but before I could even apologize, his hand had connected with my cheek.

I shake the memory away, reminding myself why I avoid the town square unless forced to come here. That was the second time I met him in the eight years I have lived here. Today will be the third and hopefully last.

The Alpha calls us up to the stage, and the butcher snickers as he takes a front-row seat. I grit my teeth and reach over to clutch Abbie's hand, who is focusing on the small cafe that has blue and white little umbrellas out the front, doing her best to avoid his eye contact. I pull her with me, and we walk up to the stage.

"Ah, choices. Now, what should I do with these filthy rogues?" The Alpha laughs; he knows exactly what he is going to do with us. He is just taunting us and dragging out the inevitable.

I clutch Abbie's fingers when the Alpha grabs my arm, but I refuse to let her go as he motions to the butcher. He climbs the stairs, and my lip quivers as I watch Abbie tense as he pauses behind her. She yelps when he grabs her, his hands wrapping around her middle as he jerks her back against him, one hand squeezing her breast.

"Brock, let me keep this one," the butcher whines. Her entire body tenses as he yanks a hessian bag over her head.

"What do you want her for?" the Alpha demands.

"She has a tight ass," he says, running his hands down her arms and gripping her hips, making her whimper.

The Alpha huffs. "No, I want them gone. Besides, you can have any of the girls at the brothel. Why would you want filthy rogue pussy?" the Alpha tells him, and I let out a breath of relief. Death would be preferable to whatever sadistic torture the butcher has in store.

The butcher makes a strange noise behind her before he bumps his crotch against her ass. "Feel that? All you, baby. Goddess, you make me hard," he purrs before shoving her away.

The Alpha gives his usual speech about what a great Alpha he is and how the pack will thrive without a rogue presence here to tarnish this great little town before he hands down his sentence.

FOUR

Kyson

I am already beyond annoyed as we pull into the sleepy pack community. We haven't even been here for five minutes, and I already want to leave. Damon, my Beta, is driving, and I shoot him a furtive glance as we enter the town. I open the mindlink to my men in the other cars, purposefully masking my aura and my scent. Yet, I know that won't be enough if I want to keep my identity a secret.

I don't want the alpha and his people to be alerted to my true identity. They know I am arriving, but I need to know what is truly going on in this pack, and picking up on who I am will make them be on their best behavior. Little did they know, I have been watching this pack closely for the last few years since Alpha Dean handed down his title to his son, Brock.

I don't like him, and I want to truly see how he runs his pack in this small, sleepy village.

"Keep your auras up to mask mine," I command my men before hearing a chorus of "Yes, my king," come through the link. My Beta casts his gaze to me briefly before watching the road.

"You really don't like this, Alpha, do you? You are going to extremes to mask who you are," Damian states.

He is right. In fact, I surmise the new Alpha has been killing off rogue children. Reports from neighboring towns have said they keep finding their bodies in the surrounding forests. There are strict laws prohibiting their deaths until proven guilty or until they turn of age. This shows the Alpha lacks character and morality. Someone like that can't be trusted.

It is unacceptable, and the council needs to put a stop to it before more children are harmed, but since they are all but useless at their jobs, I have decided to investigate for myself. Rogue or not, they are still kids. It disgusts me how they can kill off children, which is exactly why the law was brought in - to prevent the pointless death of innocents. Children should not be held accountable for their parents' crimes unless directly involved, and even then, that still needs assessing. Even a rogue child could become a functioning member of society given the right guidance.

"Just be alert," I tell him as we pull up in front of a run-down orphanage. I think it is odd that only two rogue girls are listed in the orphanage. The numbers should be higher, which is what alerted me to the change in titles in the first place. Alpha Dean, the previous Alpha, did everything by the book, but I have heard rumors the new Alpha is terrible in most aspects of running a pack. The pack has taken a slow decline, putting their pack into debts that the kingdom has been digging them out of to stop the human communities from looking too deeply into the town that resides here in the mountains.

Peering out the window, I notice children playing, skipping, and running around. The small brick fence around the building has missing bricks, and the building itself looks so run down and decrepit looking that it makes me wonder what they did with all the generous donations they receive. I look around as I get out of the car, and my Beta comes over. Looking up at the brown brick building, my lip curls back in disgust. This place is not suitable for anyone, let alone children.

"Place looks like a dump," Damian comments, and I have to agree. This is no place for children. Even the play equipment is so weathered and run down that I am surprised to find it supporting the weight of the children playing on it.

The entrance doors open and I notice two girls exit the building. They are definitely the oldest of the children that live here. Then I catch a whiff of their scents, which tells me they must be the two rogue girls that live here. They'd be coming of age soon and would learn their fates, maybe even today. Yet something nags at me as I watch them be greeted and jumped all over by the children. The children clearly love the two girls, hanging off them and trying to grab their attention.

A woman, looking somewhat frazzled, rushes out. We are an hour early, but that was the plan. We wanted them to be unprepared, and by the look on her face, she wasn't expecting us to be this early.

The woman rushes over, introducing herself as Mrs. Daley, the headmistress of the dilapidated place.

"You must be...?" She looks around, confused at all my men. Her eyes fall on my Beta hesitantly; his aura masks mine, making me appear to be a guard like the rest of the men. I fight the urge to blast her with it to make her step away from me.

I can't stand women who are only looking for the next opportunity. It's clear this old hag is trying to impress someone. Her makeup is over the top, and she has a ridiculous amount of pheromones sprayed on her. I never understood why she-wolves think they need to spray themselves in that crap. To me, it smells like cat piss. Lycans can easily smell the difference. Werewolves may find it appealing, but Lycans find the fake stench revolting. She looks like a mutton dressed up as a lamb. My lips pull back over my teeth in disgust before I forcefully make myself calm my revulsion of her.

"I thought the Lycan King was coming?" she purrs, a little disappointed. I have to mask my repugnance at how desperate she sounds, her eyes roaming over my men hungrily before falling on me.

She holds her hand out to me, and I look at it before my Beta takes it, shaking it when I make no move to shake hers.

"He couldn't make it; he sent us instead," Damian tells her. The wind shifts again, and I feel a growl seep its way up my throat before I quickly suppress it, looking around for the smell. I can smell the rogue girl when my eyes snap to the other girl. She has the deepest black hair I have ever seen, so dark there's a slightly blue hue to it when she moves. She stares at me curiously before quickly looking away when the other girl grabs her attention.

I observe her, completely forgetting about this annoying woman with her high-pitched voice talking to my Beta about goddess knows what. Something about this girl piques my interest; I just can't put my finger on it. I feel something strange stirring within me, awakening urges I haven't felt before. Both girls hesitantly walk past us, and before I can stop myself, I grab the girl's arm, looking down at her. Her heart beats frantically, eyes wide and fear so strong I can almost taste it.

"Rogue?" I question, looking her up and down before my eyes fall on her cerulean blue ones —such an odd blue, I think. Werewolves usually have amber or brown eyes, sometimes green, rarely blue. She bows her head in respect to us. I hear the headmistress quickly stifle a growl, which gives me the feeling their fear isn't because of me, but this old bat who is staring daggers at the poor girls.

I know the girl cannot feel my aura. I made sure to suppress it. When she draws near, it diminishes more; my body's reaction to her startles me. On some deeper level, it is like my subconscious is making sure not to scare her. Her eyes dart nervously to the woman off to the side of me. What I want to know is why she fears this vile woman. Did she hurt my girl? I shake my head at my sudden possessiveness; she isn't mine, I try to remind myself. But why the strange urge to protect and keep her nearby?

Mrs. Daley's eyes narrow at the girl before me, her lips pressing in a line. "Yes, sir, they are just on their way. Run along now, girls," Mrs. Daley tells them, and they rush off up the street.

"Now, if you will follow me, sir. I will show you around the facility," she says.

Facility? The place looks like it should be condemned.

'*What's with you?*' my Beta asks through our unspoken link. I realize I haven't moved and am still staring after the two girls who are huddling close together as they walk.

I force myself to move, following the birdlike woman. Her face came to a sharp point with equally sharp facial features. Her poorly-dyed hair did nothing to hide the gray peeking through, and her mouth seemed to be formed in a permanent scowl. *Man I'd be depressed to live here,* he thought.

"Those girls, follow them and stay out of view," I tell Damian before he turns around quietly, walking after them. Gannon, my third in command, takes his place beside me and follows me inside.

The inside of the building is clean but sparsely furnished. The old woman shows me around, jabbering to me about the different activities the kids appear to enjoy and some other rubbish. Yet I still can't seem to get the girl out of my mind.

"The two older girls that are here. What is the deal with them?" I ask.

"Oh them, you need not mind about them. I don't think they will be around much longer," Mrs. Daley says as she looks at me over her shoulder, trying to figure out what to call me. "I'm sorry, I didn't get your name," she says.

"Gannon," I tell her, and I see Gannon's lips tug up in the corners at me stealing his name.

"Right, Gannon, well those two girls are nothing but trouble. Been here eight years and a right pain in my ass," she says.

"Their names?" I ask her, following her upstairs to the bedrooms, peering in each one.

"Um..." she pauses, and I stare at her. How does she not know their names? She blushes before looking away and trying to change the subject.

"You didn't answer, Mrs. Daley. The girls' names?" Gannon asks

23

her, knowing I want to know. He knows something is up with me, yet I can't even explain it myself. I have never shown interest in anyone in these packs when I've visited before, but there is something about that girl that entices me, and Gannon can tell. He's an observant man —one reason he is so good at his job— so he keeps on pressing her to answer.

"I don't know. I will have to look up their true names," she says, wandering off, and Gannon follows her into an office. I was going to push for their names but was grateful to Gannon for the support, knowing I'm trying not to come on too strong.

"They have been here for eight years, and you don't know their names?" Gannon asks, just as shocked as me.

"They are rogues, sir. Not worth knowing," she states, pulling out some papers. With as long as it's taking, I realize she must not have any actual files on the girls, which irritates me more. How hard is it to do things properly around here?

"Then what do you call them, if not by their names?" Gannon snaps at her. She is clearly shocked by his tone, and I smirk at her.

"Usually rogue, or you, or..." her voice trails off as she averts her eyes in embarrassment. Gannon holds up a hand, dismissing her, also disgusted that this woman would be so discriminative of them just for being rogues. It wasn't uncommon; packs never bothered to hide their dislike for rogues, but even they gave them the basic decency of using their names.

"That's enough. Move on," I tell her, wanting to get this over with already. This woman is infuriating me, and I am finding it harder and harder to hide who I am the more she speaks.

All I want is to go find those two girls, telling myself it is just out of curiosity and not the dark-haired beauty that has been taking up my thoughts, having caught my attention completely. Damian will watch over them until I figure out what I want to do.

The mind link opens up and I feel Damian come through. '*My King, is there a particular reason I am following them?*' he asks curiously.

'I just want to know where they are going,' I tell him.

'Seems to be a meeting; the new Alpha just arrived and has called them to a stage. It seems to be some sort of hearing.' He pauses for a second before I hear his voice again flit through my head. *'Wait, it is the determination of whether or not they stay,'* Damian tells me, and I realize something: the dark-haired girl; I never sensed her wolf, so she wasn't even of age to be determined.

'If he auctions them, buy the dark-haired girl,' I tell him.

'Yes, my king,' he says, closing the link. It is common practice. I never agreed, but the packs kicked up a stink when we said the children were off-limits. They agreed to stop killing them if they could choose their fates when they came of age.

Most packs banished or took them in, but some still sold them off or killed them, though the two last options are frowned upon unless warranted.

As we walk back outside, Mrs. Daley shows us the run-down equipment and some of the kids' paintings hanging on the clothesline to dry. The link reopens abruptly.

'He is sentencing them to death! What do you want me to do?' Damian asks, alarm in his voice.

'Stop it. I will be there soon. The dark-haired girl isn't even on age for him to decide her fate!' I tell him. Abruptly turning on my heel, I walk out, knowing Gannon would deal with the headmistress for me.

"Sir, I still have a few things to show you," I hear her voice call out, but I ignore her. Something is pulling me toward the center of the village, urging me on to that raven-haired beauty. I can't explain it; something in me wants her, and the thought of someone hurting her makes me want to kill whoever dares to try.

I VY

"I now sentence you both to death by beheading," the Alpha says, his voice ringing out across the crowd. The crowd cheers, and my stomach drops, though part of me knew it was coming.

Abbie clutches my fingers with hers. "Don't cry. They don't deserve your tears. We're finally free," she whispers, barely audible over the cheering from the crowd.

The Alpha grabs my arm, leading me to a huge stone block. I can smell the blood on it as he shoves me down, pressing my forehead against it.

That is when I feel something hit my face before it splats on the stone next to me; a tomato. *Bloody animals,* I think, blinking back tears. The death of two girls isn't enough for them? They have to humiliate us too? If this is how the world truly works, then I'm glad to be leaving it.

The Alpha drags his sword over the stone and I feel the cold blade press against my neck. To my horror, I feel that it's blunt. I bite my lip to stop the sob that wants to escape me—trying to picture anything other than what is about to take place.

I recall a memory of the Spring Festival and let it flood my mind. Abbie and I had sat in our room but could hear the music. We wanted to go, wanted to know what it would be like to be part of the pack, even just once. However, Mrs. Daley refused, locking us in our room.

Instead, we pretended we were there and slow danced with each other while giggling and twirling each other around. I focus on that memory when I feel something placed over my head: a hessian bag. This is it. I am going to be free of my torment. Free of this life. I just hope the next life is better and Abbie will be with me there.

"What do you think you are doing?" A deep voice that makes the crowd go silent fills the air. I hold my breath before hearing a collective gasp from those watching.

"Putting this rogue out of its misery," Alpha Brock snarls. I try to look through the hessian bag but can't see much of anything.

"She is not even of legal age for this. Free her now," comes the voice, strong and unwavering.

"Under whose authority do you have the right to demand that of me?" Alpha Brock asks, the sword sliding off the stone with a loud clang.

"Are you questioning me, Alpha? I assure you, if you don't heed my warning and let her go, I will be forced to take *your* life. Now free her and hand her over to me," comes the voice, only this time, I feel a rush.

The stranger's aura bursts out of him as fast and powerful as a rushing river, and I hear the Alpha take in a sharp breath.

"Lycan," Alpha Brock gasps.

"Correct, and it is about time you recognized your superior, Alpha Brock," the man says.

"Pack law says we may decide how we choose to handle the rogues," the Alpha tries to argue, though I hear his voice diminishing.

"Yes, rogues of age. She has no wolf, or I would sense it. Now free her," the voice says, getting closer, and the Alpha laughs nervously.

"You have no authority here. This is my pack."

I can hear the tremble in his voice. What is with this guy? Most Alphas would've been smart enough to capitulate in the presence of a Lycan. He is speaking out of embarrassment. Lycans rule, they are the superior species, and my Alpha is treading dangerously into uncharted territory. Lycans, no matter their status, will always over-rule any werewolf and can do mostly as they please.

"You dare speak to a Lycan like that? Have you forgotten your place on the chain of command, Alpha?" comes another voice. This man's voice was deeper, his tone oozing authority, and his aura made me whimper.

A hush falls over everyone, the place so silent even the wind seems to listen to his command. You could hear a pin drop, and I am suddenly too scared even to breathe loudly.

"I, King Kyson, order you to free her now!" The deep voice carries a sincere threat, despite how calmly he speaks to them. His scent wafts to me and my mouth fills with saliva at his tantalizing smell. I hear the Alpha whimper beside me before the sword falls from his hands, clanging loudly on the wooden stage beside me. I listen care-fully, hearing footsteps move closer before I feel a presence behind me where Alpha had been. The aura coming out of whoever it is makes me tremble violently.

"You dare speak out against my Beta? Who do you think you are?" the voice booms menacingly. I feel someone grab my arm, pulling me up. Sparks rush over my skin, and I hear him gasp as my heart thumps loudly in my chest while I try to make sense of what is going on.

My legs tremble under the weight of his aura, his grip the only thing holding me upright when the bag is lifted from my head. I find everyone on their knees except the two, imposing Lycan men. One is the blond man from the orphanage. He is smiling at me. I look at the man holding my arm and my breath hitches when I catch sight of his silver eyes watching me strangely.

Instantly, I drop my gaze only to see my Alpha on his knees, cowering. The man holding my arm pulls me from the stage and down the steps before walking up the aisle between the rows of chairs.

However, I see that Abbie still remains on her knees, trembling at the uncertainty. The man lets me go, passing me off to the blond man, who grabs me. He doesn't hold as tight as the man who pulled me from the stage did.

The King drops his aura, and everyone takes a deep breath. The Alpha growls on stage, and I turn to look back over my shoulder as he grabs Abbie. Her shriek of terror makes me shove the blond man away when I see Alpha Brock push her over the stone and pick up his sword from the stage next to her head.

"No!" I choke out.

Panic seizes me, and instinctively I run to the man that saved me, or at least I think he saved me. I have no clue why he stopped the Alpha or what his intentions are with me, but I am alive because of him, for now. I at least trust in his power to change our outcomes, and I didn't want to live in a world that doesn't include Abbie.

"Please, please don't let him kill her!" I beg him desperately, tugging on his suit jacket. The bag over Abbie's head had fallen off, and I see my Alpha shove it back on. The King stops, looking down at my hands clutching his shirt. When I drop to the ground at his feet, I hear whispers from the crowd –murmurs about me grabbing the king– and I realize what a stupid mistake that had been. He could order me killed for even speaking to him, let alone touching him.

"Please, just let him kill me. I want to be with her," I beg, looking at his shiny shoes.

I know it is against the law to touch a royal, and I, a lowly rogue, had grabbed him stupidly. I am as good as dead now. I settle myself, waiting for my death. The King growls, and I tremble.

"Stop! I want the other girl too," his voice booms, and I look up to see him staring at me. I swallow under his intense gaze and start shrinking away from him when I see his Beta move, making me look over at him as he walks to the stage.

"Hand the girl over. You heard the King," the King's Beta says. Alpha Brock growls but grabs her, shoving her down the stairs toward him.

The blond man catches her before she face-plants into the ground, and the Beta growls at the Alpha for pushing her.

I watch as he lets Abbie go, and she rushes over toward me when fingers grip my chin. The King forces me to meet his gaze as he crouches next to me before speaking.

"Anything else?" he asks, brushing his thumb along my jaw and making me shiver. He smirks before releasing me when I shake my head. My brows furrow in confusion and I look down, embarrassed at my behavior and hoping that my punishment wouldn't be too severe. But he got Abbie for me. Despite me grabbing him, he still saved her. Abbie throws herself at me, clutching me as she sobs.

"Thank you," she whispers, glancing at the king, baring her neck to him. He nods to her before speaking, his eyes falling back on me.

"Follow me," the King says. Turning on his heel, he starts walking. Abbie looks at me before his Beta stops next to us.

"You heard the King, follow him," he says, looking at us both on the ground, though his words are soft, and he is smiling, which I didn't expect of him. We scramble upright, rushing after him and ignoring the shocked looks of the townspeople.

We follow him back to the orphanage. The King walks rather quickly with his long strides; we have to jog to keep up with him but make sure not to pass him either. His Beta follows a few steps behind us before we stop. Mrs. Daley is standing out the front and rushes over, staring with her mouth open, gaping at us.

"Hurry, girls. Get inside," she says, clearly shocked and trying to recover quickly. We go to do what she says when the King opens the door of his sleek black car and steps into my path, blocking me from passing him. He grips my arm, turning me toward the door.

"Get in," he says, and we stop. Abbie is clutching my arm tightly, her fingers gripping me so hard I feel my skin bruising. My fingertips hold the side of her shirt, not willing to let her go when the King leans closer, his breath moving across the skin of my neck.

"Your friend can come, but you are coming with me, so get in the car. I don't enjoy repeating myself," he says softly, though it is clear we are not to argue with him on the matter. I swallow before feeling myself nudged forward toward the door by his hand that had moved to my hip.

"Gannon, sir, may I ask what is going on?" Mrs. Daley speaks up behind us.

"No, you may not," the King snaps, but I could have sworn he said his name was Kyson. She goes to speak again when the Beta speaks behind us as we climb in the car.

"Be wise to close your mouth lady. The King doesn't like to repeat himself, and your incessant yapping is rather annoying," his Beta warns.

"King?" Mrs. Daley squeaks, and Kyson glares at her before looking down at me.

"Yes. King Kyson," the Beta confirms, and she drops her head. Instead, the King pays her no attention, reaching over and pulling some straps across me. I flinch, wondering what he is doing.

"Seatbelts," he says before pointing to the other beside Abbie. She quickly copies what he did before looking at her hands and fiddling with them.

The King then does something I never expected. He pulls a handkerchief from the pocket of his suit before gripping my chin. King Kyson wipes my face clean with it, removing the sticky stuff on my face that everyone threw at me.

I notice his Beta watching him, just as shocked by his actions. When he finishes, he tucks some loose hair behind my ear before letting me go. He finally closes the door, and I suck in a breath. My back is stinging from leaning on it, so I angle my body, turning slightly, and lean on Abbie, who moves to help me get comfortable against her.

I see the King speak to his men outside the car, and Abbie whispers to me.

"What's going on?" she asks before tangling her fingers with mine on my lap.

"Maybe they are casting us out," I whisper hopefully. Abbie squeezes my hand, clenching it, and I squeeze hers back when the Beta gets in the driver's seat, the King in the passenger seat. I thought it odd he would get in the same car as two lowly rogues, although I also thought it strange that he cleaned my face and was willing to touch me. Most Alphas flinch with disgust when in our presence. Maybe they're taking us to be servants to the royal family? That wouldn't be so bad; we knew how to clean.

The car starts and begins to move. Abbie and I clutch the seat in panic, having never been in a car before. Her grip on my hand tightens.

CHAPTER

SIX

K yson

It is difficult for me to understand my unusual behavior, yet I cannot allow the girl to die. I'm supposed to be investigating the pack, not picking up its strays and bringing them home with me. Then seeing her fear-stricken face as she pleaded for her friend... I shake my head at the memory. Normally I have no issues telling someone no...Yet I couldn't bring myself to deny her anything.

Damian watches me curiously, and I know he is wondering what has come over me. Hopefully, he figures it out, so I know too. Because I'm pretty confident that if she asked me to bring the entire orphanage, I would have said yes. Which is damn ridiculous. But for some reason, I am drawn to this girl like a moth to a flame.

However, it confuses me why I would agree to such a thing. I've never experienced anything quite like this. I can't explain it. She is a rogue werewolf. There is nothing Lycan about this girl, and I have nothing against werewolves. It's just they've never piqued my interest the way this girl seems to have captivated mine.

The thought of letting her die makes my stomach turn, and my heart twists painfully in my chest. I have witnessed Death countless times, even by my own hands. Dead bodies have never bothered me; hers shouldn't have, either. Yet the thought of her being killed horrifies me for some unknown reason. I tell myself that it must be because I know she is underage to be decided for yet. I'm a killer, sure, but not a monster. I do have a heart, unlike that disgusting excuse for an Alpha. That seems like a plausible answer.

Peering over at the back of the seat, I see both girls sit like statues in the back of the car. They haven't uttered a word but by the dark-haired girl's sharp intake of breath. I can see she is in pain. I'm sure I never hurt her. Maybe I did, and I am unaware...

Did I hurt her when I grabbed her? She squirms in her seat, her hands placed in her lap. I turn in my seat so that I can get a better look at her. Her eyes are straight ahead. Despite her clothing that looks far too small for a girl of her age, her natural beauty is undeniable. Her dark hair cascades in waves over her shoulder. I find myself admiring her, taking in her every angelic feature.

Her lips are full, and the softest pink, and her eyes are a bright and piercing blue I haven't seen in years. Her eyes dart to me nervously, and I don't miss how she sniffs the air subtly when her eyes meet mine, which seem to see through to my soul, calling on it before they quickly move to the floor when she notices me staring at her.

She has a softness about her that makes her seem vulnerable, yet with the vacant look she has in her eyes when she lifts her gaze back toward the window, I note the hardness in them. She accepts her fate even if she wouldn't have chosen it for herself. Her beauty is breathtaking, soft, and subtle. However, her acceptance almost appears enduring. It saddens me to wonder what she has endured. The girl beside her moves, drawing my attention to her, her fingertips grazing her hand, and she grips it.

The possessiveness of her grip on the girl's hand beside her tells me she would go to great lengths to protect her or lay her life down beside her. When we hit a bump, she grits her teeth.

The other girl moves, and I've noticed the way she keeps trying to hold her arms, keeping her from leaning back, but I hear the girl hiss in pain with every bump.

"Pull over," I tell Damian. He pulls the car over, and the cars behind and in front follow suit.

'Gannon, switch places with us,' I tell my Gamma through the mindlink. I get out of the car, which is pulled up on the freeway.

Damian also gets out, looking at me questioningly over the car's roof and raising his arms, wondering what is going on. I ignore him, opening the back door and grabbing the girl's arm. Her entire body trembles, and I realize maybe it wasn't such a wise idea to pull over. They probably think I am about to kill them and dispose of their bodies.

My judgment is proven correct when she starts to beg me.

"Please, let us go. We won't tell anyone. You won't see us again," she says, trying to get out of my grip, angling her body to protect the red-haired girl.

"Enough!" my words come out in a growl, and she falls silent immediately and drops her gaze.

"Now tell your friend to get out," I tell her, and her eyes snap back to mine. She clenches her teeth, and her eyes fill with tears.

She nods once before blinking rapidly, fighting tears, and gulping down her fear. She drops her head slightly to peer inside the car. She holds her hand out to her friend. The other girl slides across the seat and takes her offered hand.

"We promise we will just leave. You won't have to kill us. We won't tell anyone. We promise," her friend starts to plead.

What they would tell anyone is beyond me. We have done nothing that needed to be hidden. She falls silent as she seems to realize that.

"Are you planning to kill us?" the dark-haired girl asks, peering up at me. I study her for a second, and her cheeks flush when I don't drop my gaze. However, she looks down quickly, and I smirk. I find her questions cute. Typically, no subordinate would dare question my intentions, yet she can't help but ask despite her apparent fear of me.

"Have you given me a reason to kill you?" I ask her, and she shoots her friend a furtive look. Her lips part slightly as if she realizes something I haven't yet. Her gaze returns to me, and her bottom lip quivers.

"I'm sorry, my King. I didn't mean to grab you, I... I..." she stutters, as though she feels the need to apologize but doesn't know what for. "Please, my King. I know I shouldn't have put my filthy hands on you. Punish me. But you don't have to punish her. She won't say anything," the girl beside her yanks on her arm, and the girls look at each other. The red-haired girl glares daggers at her. "More than my life," she growls at her.

"You did nothing wrong," she says.

She ignores her friend, returning her attention to me. "I accept whatever punishment you give, sir, for touching you, but please spare Ab...my friend," she finishes. My brows furrow, and I glance around, now more confused than ever. Did she really think touching me warranted death? My eyes move to Damian, who is watching them curiously, too, when my eyes move to Gannon, who is watching the red-haired girl. Yet the look on his face is like he is staring at a ghost. When he notices me staring at him he shakes his head and leans against the car—pulling a smoke from his packet and lighting it.

"Touching me deserves punishment?... A punishment like death?" I question, but she answers as though it is a statement and not a question.

"I understand, my King," she says with a swift nod while the girl beside her whimpers, dropping her gaze.

"My King?" the other girl whispers softly, head down. She nudges her, but the red-haired girl goes to speak, only to be cut off. "You've done nothing. You didn't touch him," she hisses at her.

Yet the girl holds her gaze defiantly, but I am surprised by her next move. The red-haired girl quickly reaches out and smacks my arm. The girl snatches her hand.

Damian's brows raise, and he shakes his head. "Unbelievable," he mutters, clearly not pleased with her offhanded agreement to such words and the other girl's willingness to die along with her if I so choose. Gannon, on the other hand, snickers while the girls return to statues of innocence.

I watch them curiously. They do not fear punishment but merely accept it, which raises more questions. I have seen grown men kick and scream to get away from me when I announce them being chucked in the dungeons, now sentencing someone to death. There have been a few instances in which I have seen questionable behavior, but seeing young girls stand so resolute, their faces a mask of acceptance, seems strange to me.

Reaching my hand out, I grip the dark-haired girl's chin, lifting her gaze back to me, but now her eyes almost seem vacant.

"Are you not allowed to touch me?" I ask her. Her brows pinch together at my question.

"No, you are a King. I am a rogue," she explains, and her answer irritates me for reasons I can't explain. I have never liked being touched, yet her touching me didn't phase me. The way she snatched her friend's hand to prevent her from touching me amused me.

"Because I am a King, and you're a rogue?"

She nods once.

But I want her touch, crave it for reasons unknown to me. I grip her free hand, turning it over and making her gasp.

Her palms feel calloused and blistered, and some parts are even rougher as a result of strenuous labor. I have seen miners with smoother hands. I grab her other hand, turning it over to find it appears the same.

Such tiny hands, showing how hard she worked, the skin chapped and peeling in places. Using my other hand, I pop the first three buttons on my shirt. Placing her hand on my chest, my skin tingles unexpectedly. I feel my chest vibrate, a purr escaping me that I quickly muffle before she realizes she has some bizarre effect on me. She gasps, trying to pull her hand away, but I hold it, refusing to let her go.

"And what if I want your touch?" I ask her.

"Then I guess I would have to touch you, my King," she answers, her voice emotionless, toneless. My eyes flit to the other girl whose eyes have turned glassy as she stares vacantly when I notice her hand twitch at her side, glancing down at their hands, the girl's locked pinkie fingers. A possessive growl tries to escape me, and I muffle it quickly.

Damian, having heard it, clears his throat. I do not know what came over me.

I look at him, and his eyes flicker when he mindlinks me. *'Are you sure there isn't something going on with you and the rogue girl?'* he asks, a smile playing on his lips.

I still can't explain it, but I feel possessive about her. It even irks me that he's calling her a rogue girl. I growl at him, and she jerks her hand away, stepping back closer to her friend. She suddenly hisses, her back arching as she bumps into the other girl.

"Are you hurt?" I ask her, grabbing her arm to steady her.

"No, sir," she says. She is lying and is clearly in pain, but won't admit it.

I can smell a lie and want to punish her for it. I hate liars, and the fact that she tried to lie to me is downright disrespectful. She should know better than to lie to her King. For now, I will let it slide. However, she will learn not to lie to me soon enough.

I pull her toward the limo, and Gannon steps aside with a groan and moves to our car. I hate the limo. It feels so formal, but I can find out more about these two girls there when I can face them. I open the back door and push them inside the vehicle. They quickly slide across the seats, and Damian and I both slide across from them. He taps on the glass, and the driver starts the car.

"What is your name?" I ask my raven-haired beauty. She chews her plump lips, and I gaze on them while she fidgets with her hands.

"Rogue, sir," they both say in unison.

"No, your names?" I demand. They both look at each other confused.

"You know, the names given to you when you are born," Damian clarifies.

"You want our real names?" the other girl asks, and it is clear she doesn't know how to feel about that.

"Yes. I assume you both have names other than 'rogue'?" I reply.

"Her name is Abbie. Mine is Ivy," Ivy says quietly before looking back at her hands. I can hear both their heart rates speed up and smell their fear perfuming the car. Damian reaches into the ice bucket, retrieving some water bottles.

He offers them one, but neither moves. Their constant fear is really beginning to irk me. We had done nothing to earn their fear.

"Take it," Damian tells them, and the oldest one, Abbie, reaches forward to take it from him.

He offers one to Ivy, and she shakes her head. "We can share," they both say as if it would be an awful thing to accept the second one.

Growling as I watch them, they both flinch away from me. With the scent of their intense fear, I realize I need to get away from them. I wanted to speak to them, but their fear of me ticks me off, and her scent is overwhelming me, driving my senses wild.

Urges I've never felt have my blood pumping fiercely, making me feel hot and somewhat flustered while her scent is driving me mad. My pants are even becoming tighter! Never in my life have I had the urge to mate someone as intensely as I want to mark and mate Ivy.

"Pull over," I call out, and the driver does. I hop out, slamming the door. Damian does the same, though he shuts his door gently. I walk back to the car, climb in, and Gannon sighs, getting out like he's bored and sick of playing musical chairs.

"Sit with them," I tell him, and he nods, walking back to the limo.

CHAPTER
SEVEN

I *VY*

King Kyson gets out of the car and leaves us with his Beta and another of the King's men climbing into the car in their place. He stares at us with his arms folded the entire time and doesn't say a word.

The intimidating man has scars on his hands, and through the open top buttons, I can just make out more scars covering his chest. He has a stern expression on his face, and his eyes are cold and calculating as he stares at me. His body is muscular, and his head is shaved on the sides but messy on top. He wears a black leather jacket and a gray top that is tightly fitted to his body beneath it. This man must be one of status too, or maybe one of the main guards. Yet his silence is almost bothering along with his cold gaze.

Was he ordered not to speak to us? The silence is deafening, yet he keeps his aura low like he doesn't want to scare us. His eyes watch our every move. Abbie picks at her fingers nervously, head down and eyes glued to her lap, and his gaze turns to her. He watches her strangely. He seems curious about her, and his eyes move to her hands which I quickly grab. His eyes dart to me before he leans back in his seat.

The drive lasted hours; it was the afternoon when we left. Over an unknown amount of time, I watch the night pass through and the morning rise. Hours of silence, except for the sound of the tires on the road and the roar of the engine, before we finally stopped.

We had stopped twice for fuel. The Beta even tried to feed us, but my stomach was in knots, so I touched nothing. Abbie tried, even though she lost her appetite. Along the way, Abbie passed out, exhausted by the events leading to this.

Abbie had fallen asleep beside me again, her head on my shoulder. When we arrive, I reach over and gently shake her. I wasn't able to sleep; I was terrified of what would happen next. My brain conjured up many scenarios, all ending with our slow and painful demise.

My back is killing me from sitting so straight, and the lashes that cover it strain when I move to wake her. Cringing, I feel the warm trickle of blood dribble down my back as my wounds reopen with the movement. The man across from us leans forward and sniffs the air slightly. After hours of profound silence, he finally speaks up for the first time, which startles both of us.

"Which one of you is injured and covered in herbs?"

We both shake our heads, knowing complaining usually gets us punishment, and snitching carries severe punishment. His jaw clenches, his eyes darting between both of us when he speaks again.

"Don't lie to me. Clearly, the King wants you both for some reason. So answer, or I will call him over and ask permission to strip you to find out." he threatens.

The door suddenly opens, saving us from answering.

Beta Damian looks in the limo. The man gets out and stops beside Beta Damian, motioning for us to follow him.

Abbie slides across the seat to the open door and climbs out first, then grabs my arm to help me out. The bending movement slices through my back, and I blink back tears and grit my teeth. Abbie squeezes my fingers gently in reassurance, and I smile and squeeze hers back. When I look up, I find the King standing next to his Beta, whispering to the man that sat in the car with us.

"Thank you, Gannon. I'll handle it," King Kyson tells him. The man Gannon looks at us both and nods while Abbie and I look at each other, fear in both our eyes at what the King means by those words.

"Follow me," King Kyson orders, walking around the limo. We follow before stopping on the cobblestone road. We are at his castle: an actual sandstone castle. It looks like it belongs in a fairy-tale, not real life.

The place is tremendous, and both of us freeze in shock, having seen nothing like it. Vines wrap around the high stone walls with purple and pink blossoming flowers. The gardens surrounding the place are in pristine condition, with not a weed in sight. A tall, wrought-iron fence surrounds the castle's perimeter, hidden by hedges just as tall. A large water fountain sits in the middle of the cobblestone road next to where the cars are lined up on the circular driveway.

We knew the King lived in a castle. However, knowing that and seeing it are two different things; the place is exquisite.

"Why are we here?" Abbie whispers nervously while nudging me. Rogues aren't allowed at the Lycan King's castle.

"I said to follow," the King snaps, and we both realize he has stopped and is waiting for us, looking at us impatiently. His Beta touches my back, urging us along, and I hiss. My body arches away from his touch as pain ripples over my back.

Abbie grips my arm, knowing crying out will get us whipped again. I suck in a breath, trying to keep my tears from falling so we aren't beaten for them.

Swallowing down my pain, I start walking, but the King doesn't turn when we approach him. His gaze is stern as he stares at me. His jaw clenches, and his hands ball into fists—Abbie's hand trembles in mine. Maybe if I beg, he will spare her for my stupidity.

42

He suddenly turns and continues walking while we stumble to keep up with his long strides. A man in uniform rushes to open the heavy wooden double doors. The King moves so quickly we don't even have a chance to look at where we are heading as we try to keep up with him.

Abbie's grip tightens when I slow down; the pain from moving makes everything ache. We pause at a set of stairs, but the King proceeds down a corridor alongside them. We enter a huge kitchen bustling with a dozen workers. The kitchen is immaculately clean and well-organized, with gleaming marble countertops and stainless steel appliances. It is nicer than anything we've ever been able to imagine. The workers are dressed in blue uniforms and hats, and they are busy preparing an array of foods at the designated stations. The air is filled with mouthwatering aromas of roasting meat, freshly baked bread, and simmering sauces. A long table contains fresh vegetables and fruits. In the corner of the kitchen, there was a large hearth with a crackling fire.

"Clarice!" he calls out. Everyone stops what they are doing and bears their necks, tilting their heads to the side out of respect for the king.

A woman looks up before nodding and walking over, wiping her hands on a kitchen towel. She's an older woman, probably in her late fifties, which would make her the oldest-looking Lycan I've seen so far. I know they stop aging eventually, which makes me wonder how old she is. She has a warm smile and soft features and wears a maid's uniform with an apron tied around her waist, which is different from those working in the kitchens. She wears all black, and her apron is a beige color.

"My King," she acknowledges before giving us a strange look, no doubt wondering what we are doing here.

"I have two new girls for you to train, and they need uniforms," he tells her.

"Right away, my King. Come with me, girls," the woman says, giving us both a friendly smile as she motions for us to follow her.

Abbie and I quickly obey, and she leads us through the kitchen and down another shorter corridor. Turning a corner, we find ourselves in a giant laundry room.

Rows of uniforms line the shelves. She looks us up and down before handing each of us a gray button-up dress with short sleeves and aprons with pockets on the front. The material is thick yet soft.

"What are your names?" she asks just as the King suddenly walks in, making her turn her attention to him. We turn to look at him.

His movements are calculated and purposeful as he strolls into the room, stopping in front of us. He looks at both of us and then walks slowly around us, only to stop in front of us again. His gaze is scrutinizing, his eyes glowing like polished silver. My breath lodges in my throat when they fall on me, and he tilts his head to the side.

"My King, is there something you need?" Clarice asks gently, clearly shocked that he has followed her and his strange behavior.

I get the impression he hardly comes into the servant station. He shakes his head and leans on a counter, his eyes not leaving mine. Clarice waits to see if he will leave. Only he doesn't.

Clarice turns back to us, clapping her hands, making us jump and look away from the imposing King that continues to stare.

"Girls, I asked for your names," she says, drawing our attention to her.

"Ivy, ma'am," I tell her in a rush.

"Abbie, ma'am," Abbie answers softly, bowing her head.

"Very good. Now quickly get changed through that door," she says, pointing behind us. We look over our shoulders when the King speaks.

"Not you. You change here," he says, and Abbie and I look at each other nervously. Clarice also stares at the King, unsettled by his words.

"My King," Clarice asks, clutching her chest.

"Abbie, get changed in the room... Ivy, you will remain where you are," he says firmly, and my heart thumps erratically in my chest at his words.

Am I in trouble? I try to remember if I did something he might think is offensive or whether it was because I touched him. I thought maybe he had forgotten to hand down the punishment. I know I shouldn't have touched him, and now I will pay for that mistake.

The look on his face is unreadable, yet his gaze is intense. I don't remember doing anything else that would have provoked his attention, so it has to be the reason. But Abbie touched him too?

EIGHT

I VY

Clarice looks uncertain as she glances between the King and me before turning to face us. She gives me a sad smile. Abbie is still frozen beside me.

"Abbie, please get changed, dear," she says softly, motioning toward the changing room, and I swallow the bile that rises in my throat when she rushes off.

My cheeks heat under the intensity of his gaze, horrified that he expects me to strip before him.

"Forgive me, my King, but is there a reason you have requested her to change in front of you?" Clarice questions gently. I worry about her questioning him over me. However, she does not fear speaking out against him. Which I find odd.

"She lied to my Gamma," he answers her while I try to figure out what lie I spoke.

"Now change, Ivy. Remove your clothes," the King orders, and his aura hits me, causing goosebumps to form on my arms. "I'm not going to ask again."

I don't understand why I am being punished this way. It makes no sense. If he would just explain, I could apologize, yet I have no clue what I should apologize for other than touching him. His sudden anger makes no sense to me.

I glance at Clarice, and she nods, telling me to do what he asked and motioning for me to remove my clothes. The quiver of my lips can't be helped as it dawns on me that he is seriously going to watch me get changed. My fingers tremble as I try to undo the buttons. My hands tremble as I pop the first button on my blouse, my eyes filling with tears.

"Please, sir," I murmur, even though I know I shouldn't talk out of turn, but this is dehumanizing. If it were Clarice, it wouldn't bother me. She is a woman. But stripping off my clothes in front of a man, a King no less, makes me feel sick.

"Quiet. Remove them," he says, leaving no room for disagreement when a male servant walks in behind him.

"Out!" the King bellows at the man; he rushes off, and Clarice rushes over, shutting the door so no one else walks in. She stands in front of it like she is keeping guard and nods for me to proceed.

"Do I need to come over and undress you?" he asks, clearly running out of patience. Clarice glances at him nervously, then waves at me to hurry. I shake my head, quickly poking the buttons through the holes as I try to turn away from him to shield myself. My bra is so thin it is almost see-through, and my breathing is heavy as panic sets in.

"This is taking too long," the King snaps, storming over to me and appearing behind me. He grips my blouse and yanks it off me. I shriek in pain at the tearing fabric and also out of fear. I quickly cover myself with my hands when the King inhales a sharp breath. He growls low and deep in the back of his throat. The sound is menacing and threatening.

The deep, rough sound causes goosebumps across my entire body. My entire body sways under his aura, and Clarice looks like she is about to faint at the King's actions when he touches me. A filthy rogue. Or is she genuinely worried about me? Either way, she steps in quickly to distract the King, for which I am thankful.

"Sir, I can do that," I hear her say when I suddenly feel his fingers run down my back, over my scar-ravaged skin, and over the bandage wrapped around my torso and lower back where the newest wounds lie.

His fingers brush over the markings that the bandages can't cover entirely–they are too high up my back. Abbie wrapped them around my body as best she could. The bandages are so tight it is a little hard to breathe. Frozen with my fear, my face heats as blood rushes to it. I am mortified.

"Turn around," he says. His voice is suddenly softer. However, I shake my head, embarrassed by the situation I am in. I have never been naked in front of anyone except Abbie and Mrs. Daley. It wasn't enough to remove my blouse. Now he wants me to face him?

His hands fall on my shaking shoulders, and his breath sweeps across my neck. "Please turn around, Ivy," he whispers, turning me slowly. I clench my eyes shut, not wanting to see the disgust on his face when his hand cups my cheek, wiping a stray tear.

I'm used to people shuddering at the sight of a rogue, but for unknown reasons, I can't handle seeing that disgust on him. I curse myself for letting tears fall, knowing the punishment for such a transgression is usually the most horrific of them all.

Mrs. Daley could be unforgiving if we shed a tear— telling us tears wouldn't help us— she was right. They never did. They always made our punishments harsher when she would beat us for them.

"Put your arms down."

"Please, sir, my bra is see-through," I whisper, still refusing to open my eyes, hugging myself tighter. Suddenly, I feel his chest brush my hands. His hands slide up my arms, and my eyes fly open at his touch. He leans down, his stubble brushing my cheek.

"Use your hands; I just need your arms out of the way," he whispers, and I nod as his hands slide down my arms to grip my wrists, moving them so I cup my breasts with my hands.

I watch him fiddling with the bandages, his eyes moving to mine when he catches me watching him warily. "I won't hurt you," he murmurs, then unwraps them. My entire body trembles when I hear the door to the room Abbie was in open. Her gasp is clearly audible throughout the room.

My head turns at the noise, and she rushes forward, drops to her knees, and begs for me at his feet. "Please, she didn't mean it! She will be good! It startled her! I will take her punishment; just leave her be. Please, I beg you!" Abbie sobs.

The King stops, looking down at her like he thinks she is absurd.

"What are you talking about?" he asks her. When she doesn't answer, he looks at Clarice.

"Who is punishing whom?" he snaps at her, and she and the King look at me in unison.

His face is so close my breath lodges in my throat. My face heats as I stare at his silver eyes, framed by thick dark lashes, stubble creating shadows across his face, and full lips. He is gorgeous despite my fears.

"What is she talking about?" he demands, using his Alpha aura just enough not to cause me pain, yet I feel the tingle of his authority roll over me. I feel like bearing my neck to him so he doesn't think I am being deliberately defiant; I just don't know what he is asking or why.

"She said she would take the punishment, but it's fine, Abbie. You did nothing wrong," I tell her, and Abbie shakes her head.

"Why would I punish her?" he asks Abbie, looking genuinely confused.

"Because she cried out. She didn't mean it, I swear. We know not to make noise; she just didn't know the Beta would touch her back. Please," Abbie begs.

The King rubs his temples, looking frustrated and exhausted suddenly.

"Clarice, can you please explain what they are talking about?" he asks, pinching the bridge of his nose and squeezing his eyes shut tight.

"I think they are referring to being punished for reacting to pain?" Clarice says, looking at us, and Abbie nods to her.

He blinks like he is confused, and I look at Abbie, just as confused by his question. The King finally shakes his head and lets out a breath. Without saying a word, he peels off the bandages. When they fall away, he asks me to turn.

I do as he asks and brace myself for the lashings I know will come. Clarice gasps. Abbie whimpers, her fingers brushing my ankle as a reminder she is here with me.

"Who did this?" the King demands. I glance down at Abbie, who stares up at me from the floor with fear on her face.

"Rather than looking at each other, answer me—one of you now!" the King orders.

"Mrs. Daley," we both say in unison.

"She whipped you!" The tone of his voice is appalled and laced with anger.

"Yes," Abbie murmurs.

A person earns a day of solitude at the orphanage, sometimes for a week, for snitching or complaining. I learned early on when I told Mrs. Daley that Betty, Mrs. Daley's best friend, had broken the vase, not Taylor.

Taylor was another rogue we met when we first arrived. She was hated just as much as any other rogue in the orphanage. Mrs. Daley locked me in a closet for a week after defending her. Abbie snuck me water, and Taylor was sentenced to death for it when I got out.

"How many times?" King Kyson demands.

"I only got three; Ivy got twenty-four for our misconduct," Abbie answers.

"You must have done something terrible for this sort of punishment," the King states.

We both nod and drop our heads guiltily.

"So, what did you do?" he prompts.

"I forgot to dust three window sills, and Ivy took half my punishment. We shared the sweeping, but Ivy took all the blame. So she got two for each room. There was simply not enough time. We had to meet the Alpha, or we would have done it properly," Abbie explains in a rush.

"She whipped you over dust and un-swept floors?" he snarls. His reaction is so frightening we both jump, and I flinch away from the pure anger rushing off him as his aura erupts.

"Get some medicine and find some pain relief for me, Clarice," he says, his hands settling on my ribs; the warmth of them sends tingles across my skin. I don't move for fear of what will happen if I do. However, everything tells me a King should not touch a filthy rogue as low as me.

"Yes, sir," Clarice says, rushing out the door.

"Is your back like this?" he asks Abbie.

"No, sir, mine didn't break the skin," she whispers.

"Will you please get up? Why are you at my feet?" he asks her, and she quickly rises, placing her hands behind her back and standing with a straight posture.

"Go... sit over there," he tells her, waving her away. She hesitates but does as told.

Clarice comes back with fresh bandages, ointments, and a drink that smells strongly of herbs.

"Sir, I can do this; I am sure you don't need to tend to a servant," Clarice tells him.

"If I want help, I will ask for it; just hand me the ointment. Ivy, drink that; it will help with the pain," he says.

Clarice passes the ointment to him and the glass to me. I sip it, and despite its horrid smell, I can taste mint in it, like it is supposed to remove the awful taste. His fingers are warm as he rubs the ointment into the cuts. They sting, but his touch's tingling sensation is soothing, and I feel my back turning numb.

"Stay still for me," he says as he wraps the bandages around me quickly, his eyes looking me up and down. I feel like I'm on display, just like when I was back at the town square. He suddenly steps closer. I stare up at him with wide eyes as his chest presses against mine. His eyes flicker, turning a deep shade of black. His lips part, revealing sharp canines. I hold my breath when he grabs my hips. "My King?" Clarice speaks. He shakes his head and takes two steps away from me.

"Have either of you eaten?" he asks, and we both shake our heads. He nods, and Clarice speaks.

"I will organize their lunch. Where do you want to assign them, my King?" she asks while I quickly pull the maid's uniform on and start to button it. The King steps forward, and I flinch. He only helps button it up, his fingers replacing mine. Clarice watches, just as shocked as me that he would help a servant dress.

I remove my peasant skirt from under it when it is buttoned up and ball my clothes in my arms. Clarice comes over and takes them from me, tossing them in the bin.

"Ivy is to be my personal servant. She serves only me and remains in my quarters. Find somewhere for her friend Abbie that's close by. Maybe guard quarters?" he suggests. Clarice quickly nodded.

"Sir, what about your current servant?"

"Send her elsewhere; I want Ivy as my personal servant. If I find anyone else in my quarters besides Ivy, there will be hell to pay— only Ivy and no one else. As for Abbie, maybe see if Beta Damian needs a servant instead. Then she will be close if Ivy needs her, and the guards will watch over her. We should keep them both close while they settle in," he says, quickly turning on his heel and walking out.

We all stare after him. Clarice shakes her head a couple of times.

"That was the strangest interaction," she mutters to herself before turning to look at us.

CHAPTER

NINE

I VY
      Abbie and I are escorted to the area where we are supposed to work. The woman whose job I took does not look happy when Clarice opens the door to the King's quarters and gives her the news. She stands with her hand on her hip, her pouty lips pursed before her green eyes flick to me giving me a look of disgust. She flicks her long blonde hair over her shoulder, as she stomps off smacking my shoulder as she does. *Well, she seems pleasant,* I think.

I groan as I look back down at the stairs I just walked up. I will probably have to walk those stairs every day, toting cleaning supplies and laundry up and down constantly.

"Are you coming?" Clarice asks. I nod and chase after her down the long, wide corridor, where I can still hear echoes of the other woman whining about her lost job.

"Did he explain why? Did I do something wrong? I just don't understand why he moved me to the kitchen! I can't even cook!" shrieks the woman, Ester.

I think she's around the King's age. But come to think of it, I'm

53

not exactly sure how old the King is, since Lycans are immortal. He appears to be in his late twenties or early thirties, if I had to guess.

Despite her age, Ester's tantrums make her seem more like a toddler. She is clearly unhappy about being transferred to the kitchen and still refuses to leave, even after Clarice dismisses her multiple times. Ester is quite petite, with a small waist and curves in the right places. She has long, wavy blonde hair and bright green eyes glistening with anger. Her face is pinched up, her lips pursed in a thin line, and her posture is rigid and hostile. She is dressed in the maid's uniform, but it is too tight, showcasing her figure and ample cleavage more than it should.

"Come on Clarice this is bullshit and you know it!" she screeches in her high nasal voice as she complains. Clarice exhales loudly.

"Ester, it is out of my hands; the King specifically asked for Ivy to be placed in his quarters and you to be removed. Take it up with him if you don't like the decision," Clarice snaps at her.

"What the fuck does he see in her, anyway? What are you, like, twelve?" the Lycan woman shrieks before she shoves a broom at me which makes me take a step back. Her green eyes glare at me. She sneers, then tosses her blonde curly hair over her shoulder and looks at me with disgust.

"Ester, leave, or I will have you escorted out by the guards," Clarice warns her.

"This is bullcrap, and you know it," she snaps before turning her evil gaze back on me. She smiles and scoffs. "Oh well, the King will get bored with his new plaything anyway," she says, shoving past me and storming off down the corridor toward the stairs. Turning, I watch her leave, shocked by her tantrum and that that kind of behavior is tolerated around here.

"Never mind her. Ester has always been obsessed with the King. He let her in his bed once and now she thinks she owns him. She will get over it. The King has been looking for a replacement for a while now," Clarice says while ushering me along.

"Now, this entire floor needs to be kept clean at all times; the

King likes things a certain way, so pay attention to detail. Everything must be placed exactly where it was. So, if dusting, make sure you remember what and where you moved things. The King also likes to eat at certain times. If he is not here, you wait a bit and then return it to the kitchen if he does not arrive after twenty minutes." Clarice explains slowly so I understand everything clearly.

This entire floor is his quarters; there are at least five rooms that I can see off this corridor. It will be like cleaning the whole orphanage by myself. I peer, taking in the long and wide corridors with a sparkling marble floor and walls adorned with paintings and sculptures. In the middle of the corridor, on one wall a large set of double doors opened up to the King's chambers, guarded by two guards.

"Does the King spend much time in his quarters?" I ask nervously, wondering how much time he would be here.

"Not usually; he is usually tending to meetings or in his office downstairs. He is very particular about how he likes things to run and can be very impatient, so make sure you never leave him waiting and get everything done in a timely manner," she says as she wanders over to a door directly across from his bedroom.

"Now, this door– you must never go into this room, understand? The girl before Ester broke that rule, and she—-never mind what happened to her, but you must never go in unless he tells you to," she says.

Okay, one less room to clean, I think to myself. Clarice moves across to the guarded double doors.

"Now, this is the King's bedroom; everything must be kept in order and the linens changed daily," she explains as they open the doors for her.

"Each morning at sunrise, you are to open the drapes and let the light in. Usually, he wakes at seven. The bathroom is through there; make sure everything is stocked and fresh. The King has a love for reading, so make sure the books remain in order unless they are on the bedside table; if they are, do not touch them," she says, giving me a pointed look at the last part.

How am I supposed to know what order they should be in? I can't read. As rogues, Abbie and I weren't allowed that luxury and even when reading to the kids back home, we would just look at the pictures and interpret how we thought the story would unfold.

I nod, praying he puts his own books back because these bookshelves, I can tell, are going to be a nightmare. There are hundreds of books on them and nothing shows a specific order in which they should be placed.

There is a chair sitting beside the shelves next to a large lamp; I guess that's where he spends most of his time reading.

I look around the room. An enormous bed sits in the middle of the room along the wall. There is also a dresser with a mirror and two bedside tables. Huge, heavy maroon drapes cover the windows, which go from the floor to the ceiling, making the room darker. I turn to see another door leading to a bathroom off the side.

It appears the only personal touches are his books, except for one picture, which sits on the bedside table. I wander over and peer down at it. It depicts a woman and the King. His arms are wrapped around her shoulders and they're both laughing.

She has the same dark hair and glowing silver eyes as the King. However, her features are a little softer and she has a natural beauty that makes her glow. He looks younger in the photo, and I wonder where she is and who she is to him.

"Now, I will show you where the King has placed you if you'll follow me," Clarice says as she walks off.

I chase after her when she stops at the door directly across from the King's room and opens it up to a small room.

It has a single bed, a bedside table with a lamp, and a small wardrobe, but that is it. It will feel weird not sharing a bed with Abbie. Plus, the room's proximity to the King's room makes me nervous.

"He wants me to stay up here? I thought I could stay with Abbie?" I ask.

"The King asked for you to remain in his quarters; this is the only other room up here on this floor, so yes, you will stay here," Clarice answers, and I gulp.

"Can't I stay with the other maids and Abbie?" I plead.

Clarice smiles sadly and places her hand on my shoulder, gently squeezing it.

"I know you're scared, but he is a good King. Just stay out of his way and try to go unnoticed. Don't linger; he likes his privacy, and unless he speaks to you, remain quiet. Whatever you do, don't lie to him. As long as you stick to your work and keep your head down, you will be fine. You would have to do something terrible for him to punish you. Easy," Clarice advises, and my heart beats like a drum in my chest.

I nod and look at the room. The thought of being trapped with the King terrifies me and staying here means less time I will have with Abbie.

"Now, I need to return to work. All linens are kept in the laundry room. Ester has done most of his room already; you only have the study down there to do and bring him his dinner tonight at six pm, so don't be late. Try to come down just before as the cooks will have it waiting. You can place it on his table in his room. The maid's bathroom is downstairs for use. Make sure you bring your dress down every night to the King's laundry and grab a fresh one off the shelf. I will have some pajamas sent up for you and toiletries to keep in your room. You must always remain tidy and..." she glances down at my patched up flats and then looks up at me, pursing her lips. "I will have some new shoes sent up for you too," she adds, clicking her tongue.

"Make sure you sweep and mop the entire floor. You remember where to fill your buckets?"

I sigh but nod.

"One of the guards will send up some stuff for you to keep in your room. Once the King has finished dinner, come down to the kitchen with his plates so you can also eat. One of the guards or servants will bring you lunch today while you settle in. Breakfast is at six am, giving you plenty of time to wake the King at seven am," Clarice tells me. I try to remember everything she says by making a mental list and repeating it over and over.

Sighing nervously, I nod to the guards and turn around when she disappears. They remain still as statues not even acknowledging my presence. Shaking that thought off I set to work, praying I don't get punished on my first day.

A BBIE
       "Can't I stay with Ivy?" I ask, watching as Ivy walks in a different direction after retrieving a mop bucket from the closet on the bottom floor. She was in such a rush she didn't even notice me.

"No, the King asked for her specifically," Clarice explains.

"Why?" I blurt before I have a chance to stop myself. Clarice doesn't answer, so I sigh and drop my gaze, knowing better than to question my superiors. Clarice shows me to the other side of the castle. This place is huge, like a maze. One could easily get lost by taking a wrong turn, and I wonder how long it will take me to memorize the layout.

Most of this morning was spent in the kitchen while Clarice showed Ivy where she was being placed. Now I am being led to new quarters, though I instantly become nervous when I find out it's for the Beta.

I want to stay with the other female servants. Learning only the Beta and the King's private guard reside on this side of the castle made me nervous. I don't like the idea of being surrounded by so many men.

Clarice had explained to me that it was the closest quarters to Ivy, yet it feels further away than the servants' quarters. We climb the stairs to what appears to be some sort of loft area which actually opens up to a vast space.

"This is Beta Damian's room. You won't have to do much. Beta Damian is quite clean and hardly stays here, mostly changes and leaves," she tells me.

The room is quite nice, with a bathroom and wardrobe, yet the Beta doesn't seem to have much in the way of belongings besides his clothes. Everything is clean, and the bed looks like it hasn't been slept in. Heavy dark blue drapes hung from the windows, and a huge white rug lay on the floor, not a speck of dust in sight. Was I expected to keep it this clean, or is Clarice right that he hardly comes in here. The place doesn't look lived in; in fact, it looks empty.

Clarice leads me to a set of doors and stops, turning toward me, and finally his little library, which has been turned into a gym that all the men use," Clarice tells me. I peer inside to find heaps of gym equipment.

"Now, the floor below you will be in charge of cleaning too but stay out of everyone's rooms, especially the far two rooms," Clarice explains, leading me back downstairs and showing me around the quaint room that separates the two sides in the middle of the guard's quarters.

When she shows me around this floor. There are twelve doors lining the walls before a separate area with a small sitting room containing three armchairs, a TV, and some artwork. There are two more doors at the end.

"Now, the other rooms you can clean except these two." She points at them. I glance at them and then at her wondering why they're off-limits. "Don't enter into these two rooms unless asked to do so, and maybe stay away from that one completely. Liam can be somewhat unhinged at the best of times," she tells me, and I chew my lip.

"Liam?" I ask, nervously.

"Oh, you won't see much of him. The man is as silent as night, but this one," she points to the other door. "Gannon likes his privacy. You met him in the car earlier," Clarice says, and I nod. So his name is Gannon. I hadn't paid much attention to names other than Clarice's since she is in charge of us.

"Gannon is moody and temperamental, so steer clear and don't speak unless spoken to," Clarice says. Well, I had no intention of conversing with anyone of the opposite sex, so that was okay with me.

"So, how many people stay in these quarters?"

"Just the King's guard, so Beta Damian and the King's Gammas,"

"Shouldn't there only be one Gamma?" I ask her, trying to remember how the pack hierarchy worked.

"All the King's guards are Gammas, but they still have rank. Gannon is third in charge, while Dustin and Liam lead as fourth together. It depends on the trials; those I mentioned are the highest ranking in the royal guard. Trey is a bit touchy, so try to avoid him too, but the rest come and go depending on their shifts, but yes, they are all Gammas. You only need to worry about Beta Damian, Gannon, and Dustin. They will probably be the main ones you run into while staying here."

"So basically, I should avoid all of them," Clarice nods. Great, not only am I the only female, but all the men on this floor appear unapproachable and anti-social. Great!

"So everything is understood? I need to get back to the kitchen," Clarice asks, and I nod.

"Okay, well, dinner is at 6 pm for the servants, so make sure to head down then, and your room is this one," she says, wandering down the hall. She points to the door we didn't enter. Which I assume is a cleaning closet, so I have to clean this floor and share it with the men here. I would have preferred the bunked servants' quarters.

Clarice cups my cheek in her hand. "You'll do very well. They are a friendly bunch. Just stay out of their way," she says before turning.

61

Yeah, they sound super friendly after telling me not to go near pretty much all of them!

"Wait, when can I see Ivy?" I ask, and Clarice stops.

"When the King allows it," Clarice says, and my brows furrow. Wait, what is the King doing with her?

CHAPTER

ELEVEN

I VY

I spend most of the day cleaning. It's tedious work, but once it's done, I feel bored. I realize most of this work is just standing around, waiting for the King to need something. However, this isn't very often because he isn't anywhere in sight.

Clarice brings me new shoes, and I feel strange wearing shoes with actual soles. The brand-new shoes also give me blisters as I walk up and down stairs for hours on end.

Honestly, I don't understand why it's not possible to keep cleaning supplies up there. The stairs are a killer on my legs, and climbing the steps all day makes me exhausted, especially since I still haven't slept.

The majority of the time spent up here is wasted; I could have helped Clarice or Abbie with their chores. Instead, I sit on the bed, waiting for time to tick by while wishing I could see Abbie and check on her.

Just before 5:30 pm, I hear a crash in the corridor. When I open the door, I see Ester's silhouette walking away, her hips swaying as she leaves out the double doors. I glare at the mess she made; she knocked a potted plant over. When she reaches the stairs, she smirks at me over her shoulder. She saunters away. Cursing under my breath, I look at the mess she created. The soil has spilled all over the floor, and I groan when I see what she's done. However, at least it gives me something to do, so maybe I should thank her for saving me from boredom.

It's difficult for me to understand her instant dislike of me, almost as if she blames me for taking her job. I have done nothing to her. How could I have when I only met her today? Is she trying to get me in trouble so the King will punish me? In a panic, I rush down the steps to fetch a dustpan and broom.

Halfway down the steps, I turn onto the next staircase but don't notice her standing there until it's too late. Ester puts her foot out and trips me. A startled shriek leaves my lips as my body careens forward down the stairs. My stomach lurches as I tumble down the steps. Pain radiates through my body as I hit each step, and I can feel my skin scraping against the hard surface. The air is knocked out of my lungs, and my heart pounds in my chest. The thud of me hitting and rolling down the steps echoes in my ear that are ringing. Finally, I reach the bottom and come to a stop. With a hard thud, my face bounces off the corner of the stair, and I feel my eyebrow tear and split on impact. Sharp pain slivers up my spine as the lashes on my back reopen. In what feels like slow motion, I force myself to roll over onto my back. This causes shooting pain across my ribs, making my breath lodges in my throat. Ester strolls down the steps with a cunning smile on her lips. She stops beside me and looks pitifully down at me.

"Whoops, how clumsy of you; the King doesn't like things left in a mess," she says in a sickly-sweet voice, an evil glint in her eye.

How old is this woman? She's acting like a child, and I feel rage coursing through my veins at her childish actions. I am no different from her; perhaps only a rogue, but still a servant. Why would she want another servant punished?

I bite back tears, wondering what I did to deserve this sort of treatment from her. I never asked for it. All Abbie and I wanted was freedom. As for me, I had accepted my death; I'd come to terms with it. Now that we have a second shot, I want to be set free with Abbie, not become someone else's victim of abuse.

She smiles tauntingly as she walks around a corner and out of sight. I hiss as I stumble to get up, only to see a guard staring at me. His face shows no expression at all about what he just witnessed.

He appears to be guarding the double doors that lead outside. Is this sort of thing acceptable? Do people just abuse whoever they want in this castle? As a trickle of warm blood trickles down my face, I wipe it with the back of my hand.

My eyebrow is indeed split. *Great, another wound to tend to.* My back throbs as I clutch the banister and pull myself up.

Don't cry, don't cry, I tell myself probably for the millionth time in my life. *It's just a scratch; you are being a crybaby.* I try to remind myself that I have had more serious injuries and that I shouldn't let it get to me. But I ache all over, and I'm exhausted from the lack of sleep. I slowly make my way to the cleaning closet, my body aching with every step I take. I stumble towards the cleaning closet, keeping my head down and trying to ignore the pain as I walk, but it's nearly impossible not to wince as I take each step. Finally, I make it to the cleaning closet and collapse against the wall, relieved to be away from the guards.

I open the door and peer around at the shelves of cleaning supplies, finding a rag. I move toward the small sink that nestled in the corner next to the mops and buckets, wetting the rag and pressing it to my bleeding eyebrow. One thing I have realized over the years is that hand and face injuries bleed the worst but usually aren't as deep as they appear.

I take a deep breath and dig through the closet and grab the broom and dustpan. I shut the door with my hip which makes me drop the bucket. Pain slivers across my ribs. Bending down, I grip the handle and pick it up. With hesitant steps, I climb the staircase I am beginning to hate. Each step is agonizing and sends shooting pain all over. It hurts to breathe; it hurts to move. My heels and toes are blistered; my back is searing with pain, and I can feel the bruises already forming on my hip, back, and ribs.

My legs finally give out from under me, and I drop down next to the potted plant as my ass hits the ground hard. Trying to stifle my cry, I pocket the rag I used to stem my bleeding brow before fixing the pot. I put as much dirt as possible back in before cleaning up the remaining soil that had been spilled.

My entire body screams in protest. What a hellish day. I haven't slept since arriving here and was put straight to work. Time seems to be slipping away from me. We left our old pack in the afternoon and arrived at the castle in the morning.

Do Lycans not require sleep?

I pack everything up and head downstairs and outside, dumping the dirt in the garden beds outside the main entrance. Then, I put the equipment away. Once I have finished doing that, I head back upstairs before remembering it is nearly dinner. I look at the enormous grandfather clock next to the guard, who hasn't moved.

How can he stand so still? Then it dawns on me; it is 6 o'clock! I rush back down the few steps I had just walked up, though panic already has me moving quickly. Heading for the kitchen, I skid through the kitchen doors, my shoes screeching on the polished floors and slamming my hip against the countertop.

The moment I walk in, Clarice is waiting for me. She shoves the tray into my hands, clearly unhappy with my late arrival. She doesn't say anything, so I resist the urge to ask if I will be punished. Giving her a quick nod, I turn on my heels and race back upstairs while praying he isn't in his room yet.

I move as quickly as my body allows. With adrenaline coursing through my veins, it's actually pretty fast. As I burst into his room, I freeze immediately. He is already here, sitting in his chair by the bookshelf. The moment I enter, he drops his book onto the small table and he leans back in his chair watching me. I chew my lip nervously as his face twists into an expression of anger and annoyance. His brows furrow and his jaw clenches. He motions for me to do what I am here for. Yet when I move, his eyes narrow, and his lips press tightly together in a thin line. He is clearly displeased with my tardiness.

Hastily, I move quietly, trying not to draw attention to myself. I place the tray in front of him before taking a step back and bowing. He doesn't say a word, but he clearly isn't pleased that his routine was disrupted; that much is clear.

I escape the King's room and walk to mine. Exhausted, I sit on the bed. As I put my head in my hands, I remember the stupid cut eyebrow I have. The blood trickles down my face again, and I grab my damp rag and dab at the spot to stop it. I want Abbie, and I miss her terribly; we have only been separated for mere hours, and the ache to see her is already overwhelming. This is too hard without her by my side. We always get through everything together.

Sighing, I hold the rag against my brow, wincing at the slight sting. I try to lie down on my side and rest for a moment, trying to find a comfortable position. However, I give up and decide just to endure the pain. I will just close my eyes for a minute...

A knock at my door awakens me; Clarice steps into my small room. She sets her hands on her hips and gives me a disapproving look. Confused, I groan, sitting upright. Clarice's face is stern and her eyes narrow in disapproval. Her lips purse and her brows pinch as she glares at me. Great, another person is disappointed and frustrated with me.

"Are you mad? One day and you fall asleep on the job! The King has been waiting for you to clear his room for two hours!" she hisses at me. As Clarice scolds me, I feel a wave of fear and dread wash over me. My stomach drops as I realize the King has been waiting for me to clear the room for two hours. The thought alone makes me feel sick to my stomach, imagining the King's displeasure, and the consequences I'll have to face.

TWELVE

I<small>VY</small>
   My eyes flit to the small alarm clock on the small dresser.
"Two hours?" I shriek, and Clarice clicks her tongue. With a horrified
gasp, I jump to my feet in shock.

   "I'm sorry! I must have drifted off! I haven't slept! I will do it
now!" I tell Clarice while yanking my shoes on.

   "What do you mean you haven't slept?"

   "Abbie and I have been up since 3 am yesterday morning. Well,
Abbie fell asleep in the car here, but I couldn't sleep, and then we had
to work." I shrug, slipping my other shoe on.

   Clarice sighs and shakes her head. "Why didn't you tell me that
when you arrived? I didn't know, but you need to get your ass in
there. I tried to clean the King's room, but he said it's your job, so you
have to do it." I cringe at her words.

   "Is he mad? Am I in trouble?" I can't help but ask. I'm not sure I
can handle any more punishment at the moment.

   "Of course, he's mad; he's the King! You made him wait for a
rogue servant," she says, and tears brim in my eyes at her words,

making me notice what a silly question that was to even ask. I am the lowest of the low in society, the trash. Of course, he's mad at me. Clarice smiles sadly, yet her face is heavy with disappointment. She steps closer and pats my back in what is supposed to be a sympathetic gesture. However, I groan and jerk away from her touch as pain ripples up my back.

"Get it together, Ivy. You are the King's servant. I am trying to help, but I can only do so much," she snaps at me. Dropping my head, I give her a quick nod and she walks out, leaving me to slip out of the room after her.

Lying down had been the worst mistake. Now I feel stiff, which makes the pain even worse. I hesitate to knock on the door and nervously chew my lip. My heart races knowing I have no choice but to go in and face him. Lifting my hand--

"You can enter," he says before I have the chance to knock. I inhale a deep breath, forcing my legs to move. He is sitting on the chaise, reading under the lamp when I enter.

He wears blue pajama pants, his chest bare. I glance away, moving on to the task at hand. My hands tremble as I clean up the mess on his table. His aura tells me he is angry with me, and I fight the urge to cower under it. As I place everything back on the tray, I feel his gaze on me.

I bite my tongue to stop myself from crying out at standing upright. I am impressed with myself; not one noise escapes me, despite wanting to scream with each movement. Only when I look up, the King watches me still. I swallow, drop my head, and walk to the door.

"Come back and see me when you are done," he says, making me freeze. Glancing over my shoulder his gaze goes back to his book.

"Yes, sir," I answer as I turn and walk out. I make the horrendous trek once again down the steps, wondering what my punishment will be when I notice that guard again.

Maybe it is a statue? He hasn't moved. How is that possible? I wave my hand in front of his face. He looks real but nothing: no facial twitch, not even a blink. I shake my head as I move toward the kitchen.

"Dinner," Clarice says as she points to the plate on the bench when I enter through the doors.

"I can't. The King asked me to go back to see him," I explain.

"Very well, off you go then. Don't make him wait; you already did that," she says.

Turning, I leave with my stomach growling, but I ignore it. It is not the first time I have gone hungry, and it won't be the last–that I am sure of.

I use the banister to help force my legs up the stairs for the hundredth time today. This is a joke. Maybe after a while, if he doesn't kill me for messing up, he will let me keep some supplies in my room. This will save me from walking up the steps every time I need a cloth or a broom or something. I can only hope.

The King opens the door before I can knock. My stomach twists with dread; this is it. There's no doubt I'm about to be killed or hurt for my mistake.

He steps aside, and I keep my eyes on the floor when I move past him. I stand how Mrs. Daley taught us: hands behind my back, looking straight ahead. Everything burns and aches standing like this, yet I endure it. The King shuts the door and turns to me.

"Did Clarice give you your orders?" the King asks, walking around me. I briefly wonder if I will cop a cane or the whip.

"Yes, sir," I answer.

"So you chose to ignore chores and orders?" he asks.

I feel tears prick at the back of my eyes. I shake my head, and my lips part to explain, but quickly shut my mouth. I know it is my fault and I have no excuse good enough for not doing my tasks.

"You didn't answer," he states. I swallow. Am I allowed to argue back? "Well?" he demands. I chew my lip, and my fingers fiddle behind my back nervously.

"I fell asleep; it won't happen again," I stutter. King Kyson rubs his chin and jaw before he moves to his chaise and sits down. I watch as he places his elbows on his knees and leans forward.

"I have a strict schedule for a reason. My days are meticulously planned out. I can't have a servant who can't follow simple rules and stick to a simple timetable, do you understand?"

I nod. The King keeps staring at my face, which makes me nervous. I see his eyes narrow slightly at my split brow, but he says nothing. Why would he? I am a servant; he is the King. I should be grateful I am still standing and not thrown into a cell for my laziness.

"I understand," I tell him, chewing the inside of my lip when he sighs.

"You also forgot to clear the washing in the bathroom," he says, wiping a hand down his face.

I nod, about to set to the task, but he waves me off when I try to head for the bathroom.

"Forget it; I already had Ester grab everything while you slept," he says, and I look down, embarrassed.

I am already in trouble, and Ester got her wish to be his servant again. Well, she can have the job; I don't want it. I rather slave labor outdoors than feel like I'm walking on eggshells over every little thing while the King waits for me to slip up.

"You can leave," he says dismissively, and I quickly escape back to my room. I open my door to find a sandwich wrapped in cling wrap, as well as another maid's outfit and a small juice box.

Clarice must have snuck them to me. Relief floods me, and I sit on the bed peeling my new flats off. My heels are bleeding and I need to shower, but even that task feels impossible.

Giving myself a sniff, to my surprise, I smell clean, thanks to all the cleaning products. I settle on my bed, careful of my back, and pick up the sandwich and unwrap it. It feels like so much effort as I force myself to chew and swallow.

I feel exhausted but starving. Why did I have to be the king's servant? I know this will be the loneliest job in the castle, and what is up with his erratic behavior: so hot one moment and cold the next? One second, he almost seems kind, like he forgets he is speaking to a lowly rogue. The next moment, he looks at me like he wants to kill me.

CHAPTER
THIRTEEN

KYSON

I can't help but feel annoyed as I watch Ivy leave the room. What an idiot I am for tossing Ester to the curb when Ivy clearly doesn't know what she's doing. She might know how to clean, sure, but she doesn't understand what it takes to tend to an actual person. Ester was always on time, and she knew what I expected. Maybe I am being harsh. It is clear that the girl is terrified of me, and yes, I am aware that I can be an overbearing prick at times, so I should have known better than to throw her into a position she has never served in before. Maybe I should have asked Ester to train her...

But the thought of her being in someone else's chamber or with the male workers irks me. I am unsure why it bothers me so much. She's just a rogue girl, yet the pull I feel toward her has affected my choices and all day I have been distracted at work. My mind is constantly wandering back to her.

Even now my mind wanders back to her as I sit here reading – wondering if the deep lashings on her back were inflicted by that woman in the orphanage.

I can't believe Alpha Dean would allow such treatment of such a young girl, even a rogue. She is still his responsibility since she lives in his pack. Maybe that is why she couldn't perform her duties; perhaps she was in pain? Or perhaps I am insane for allowing a rogue girl I know nothing about to be my personal servant when she evidently has no experience.

I shake my head, trying to get my thoughts away from the girl sleeping in the room across from me. This is easier said than done. Everything in me screams for her to be close, my fingers itching to touch her. I want to feel her skin on mine, feel her curves against me, and to explore every inch of her body with my hands and my lips. I want to taste her. Feel her heart beating against mine. Listen to her moan with pleasure. I crave her in ways I shouldn't; ways that would be entirely inappropriate given our positions.

The urge to have her by my side dominates my mind. My body is here, yet my mind is with her, my thoughts utterly consumed by my rogue servant.

Could she be my mate? My other half and part of my soul, like Damian believes she is? Lycans rarely find their mates. We have immortal lifespans, so you would think that would make it easier to find our mates, but no.

Lycans are supposed to be mated to other Lycans. Apparently, our species is adapting these days, and now we are finding our mates in common werewolves–evolution at its finest. But for royalty to find a mate in a common werewolf is unheard of.

Unable to pull my attention away from her, I get up. As if my feet are making up my mind for me, I push the doors open and stride across to her room. Standing there for a few seconds, I try to conjure up a reason to have her come into my room. What am I thinking? I am the King. I can ask what I want of her! I don't need excuses. She'll do as she is told. Gathering enough courage, I push the door open slightly, peeking through the gap. Relief washes over me, and I let out a breath when I realize she has fallen asleep. She has half a sandwich in her hand but is clearly passed out, sitting upright on her bed.

Did it hurt too much to lay on her back? The urge to heal her is driving me insane because I don't understand the reasoning behind it. *I will have to change her dressings again,* I think to myself before realizing I shouldn't be doing that. *She's a servant,* I remind myself, realizing that people will eventually start to talk after observing this strange behavior.

I shake the thought away. It sounds ridiculous, a King tending to a servant. Someone else can tend to her, but why do I have the urge to do it myself? It overwhelms me–I want to be the one to look after her. I don't want anyone else touching her.

The possessiveness I feel over her is ridiculous. I am losing my damn mind. No one has ever had such an effect on me.

Doing my best to remain quiet, I slip further into the room, reaching down, taking the plate off her lap and the sandwich from her hand. I place it on the bedside table. Ivy doesn't even move. I go to pull her blanket up when I realize she is lying on it.

Looking around the small room, I don't see another one in here when I notice her feet. Blisters cover her heels, the skin red and angry; a few toes are even bleeding.

I look down at her shoes and sigh before walking into my room. I grab the spare comforter off the chair and a few pairs of my bed socks; they will be thicker than the thin ones she has been wearing. Walking back to her room, I drape the blanket over her, and she shifts in her sleep.

Her face twists in discomfort, and I freeze, hoping she doesn't wake up to me lurking in her room like some creep. I place the socks next to her shoes with her maid's outfit.

The urge to touch her consumes me. I want to run my fingers through her luscious, wavy locks. However, her hair is tied up, preventing me from doing such a thing. I turn to leave the room before hesitating when I notice the cut across her brow.

Stepping closer to her, I brush her cheek gently with the back of my hand. I then lick the pad of my thumb and trace it across the cut.

The wound closes quickly, leaving a small scar, but otherwise, it has healed her. Leaning down, I...

What the heck am I about to do? Quickly regaining my senses, I force myself out of her room before I do something stupid, like mate her!

I have already done more than I should, and I certainly shouldn't be in her room while she sleeps. It doesn't look very appropriate for a King to be in his maids' quarters, and I should have known better after Ester. I could have given Ivy the wrong idea as I did with Ester.

I need to find out more about this girl: who she is and where she came from because I should not feel the things I do toward her.

My Lycan side has me wanting to climb into bed with her and wrap my body around her petite one. It yearns to feel the warmth of her skin pressed against me. I want to shield her away from the world and keep her tucked tightly in my embrace, where I know she will be safe.

Lying back down in my bed, I hear a soft knock and lurch to my feet, wondering if it is her. Opening the door, I see Damian. I do my best to hide my disappointment.

"Expecting someone else?" he chuckles, and I step aside so he can enter.

"What is it?" I ask him while walking over to the bar and pouring us a drink. I hand him a glass of whiskey then pick up my own and sit on the edge of my bed.

"More bodies were washed up; one was a rogue child," Damian tells me.

Fuck. How many more before we catch the culprit? People are beginning to talk. It is one thing to find rogues–you expect them-but rogue children are supposed to be off-limits.

"There is more: this was found on one of the bodies. The guard said it was dropped off ten minutes ago by a messenger," Damian says, holding out a piece of fabric. I reach over and take it from him, unfolding the small piece of fabric. My blood instantly boils. Embla-zoned on the blue patch fabric is the hunter's insignia - a circular symbol with a black wolf silhouette in the center and a bloody sword running through the wolf's head.

"Hunter's insignia," I growl, and Damian nods.

We deal with human hunters, but this group isn't human. Their patches are red, and two swords are crossed over a shield. But in this one, the fabric is royal blue, meaning they are the hunters that specifically target the royal bloodlines.

Lycan bloodlines.

This patch belongs to the very people that have been hunting down Royal Lycan bloodlines for centuries. Four kingdoms have fallen, and four royal bloodlines have been snuffed out, leaving me the last remaining Lycan royal. They already killed my sister, her unborn child, and her husband.

They won't be happy until every royal is eradicated. I constantly have a target on my back.

"Kyson?" Damian asks gently as I glare down at the piece of fabric.

Lifting my head my eyes meet Damian's. "They're back..." I growl.

CHAPTER

FOURTEEN

KYSON

Damian opens his mouth, no doubt to tell me I need to keep my head but I cut him off, not wanting to hear it.

"Don't. I am fine," I tell him. I gulp down the last of my glass before trading my glass for the entire bottle. I haven't seen or heard a word of the rebels in years, yet I know they're out there. Why now? They are primarily werewolves, unhappy that Lycans still have control. There have been rumors that they've received help from human hunters over the years. This is one source of fear for Lycans, as they know the rebels have been gathering strength and resources, preparing to strike again. Plus, with the added support of humans and their technology, they have become a much bigger threat than before.

"Fourteen years since the fall of the Landeena Kingdom, and they have come back. So close to the anniversary too," I tell him angrily, swigging from the bottle.

"Yes, and it's been five years since the..." Damian doesn't finish.

I don't need the reminder that it's the fifth anniversary of my sister's death–of when they came for my Kingdom, the same day as the Landeenas fell, but five years after the fall of their kingdom. They took everything from me... they took her from me. We had already lost my parents, leaving only the two of us, but they robbed me of her too.

The Landeena kingdom was the closest to ours. King Garret and Queen Tatiana were aware of the threats and watched the other bloodlines get taken down. The other three Royal families were eradicated years before, leaving only the Landeenas and ours.

We were sure both our kingdoms would be attacked next. We believed it was an inside job, too. The King and Queen hadn't left their castle or been seen for four years before their murders. They thought keeping a low profile might stop them from being targeted. The only correspondence with them was by mail or phone until we got a call saying their kingdom had fallen.

The rebels constantly attacked on significant days, and it was the anniversary of the Landeenas' murder when they struck again. They had died almost exactly five years earlier. However, my sister insisted I leave, that we no longer had to worry because nothing had happened in the five years since their deaths.

That morning, I had a bad feeling, I knew something was amiss. But I ignored that stirring worry in my stomach and left to visit Dark Creek Pack about the rogue sightings. They'd been losing their supply trucks, so the meeting was over. That day has haunted me ever since. Just as it does now. The memory invades my mind vivid and as real as the day it happened.

"Why haven't you left?" Claire, my sister, had demanded when she came down to the kitchen wearing her floral robe. It was much too long for her. We were constantly scolding her for wearing it while pregnant, worried that she would trip over. It was my mother's and she favored that over everything else, but my mother was a good two feet taller than her.

"I will reschedule it," I told her, returning to my coffee and opening my newspaper.

"You've been putting it off the last three weeks, Kye," she scolded me. When I didn't answer, she walked over, snatching my newspaper. I growled at her, but she tossed it in the bin and walked back to fix her coffee. I often caught her down here in the early morning sneaking a mug.

"Have you forgotten what today is?" I asked her.

"No, I haven't, and I'll be fine. You worry too much," Claire told me. "Besides it's been five years, if they were planning to return they would have by now." She shrugged.

"We don't know that for sure," I told her.

"Well, no. But we can't keep putting our lives on hold, chasing ghosts, Kye. You are King, you have responsibilities, and they don't involve babysitting me. Now get up!" she snapped. I remained silent until she snatched the newspaper from the bin and hit me with it.

"Up now!" she commanded.

"Don't make me get your mate," I smirked at her, causing her to pout, a hint of my sister coming through.

"Does he know you're down here sneaking coffee?" I ask, and she glares at me when the maids wander into the kitchen to get ready for the day. She watches them move to the pantry, drumming her fingers on her mug, pursing her lips. Clarice wanders into the kitchen and pecks her cheek.

"Morning dear," Clarice told her. Claire smiled at her before wandering off to give the servants orders.

"Come with me then," I asked her. Claire shook her head.

"No, I have some things to take care of today. But go!" She gave me a pointed look as she walked toward where I sat. Sighing, I stood up. "Fine," I told her, pressing my lips to her forehead.

"Behave!" I mocked and she smiled.

"I will. I'm having my sneaky coffee, probably finish the last of yours off too," she laughed, eyeing my half-drunk mug.

"Then back to bed for a few hours."

"How can you drink coffee and be tired?" I shook my head at her.

"I was born tired," she mocked. I smiled before walking out the door and meeting my driver.

I shake the memory away before it sucks me in too deep. When the rebels made their move, she couldn't even fight back or shift to protect herself and her unborn child. Her husband was dead beside her.

I will never forgive myself for leaving that day.

One of our servants, a spy, waited for me to leave before plunging the silver dagger into my sister and her mate's chests while they slept. I found them the following day when I returned.

The servant, Marissa, turned rogue and vanished, never having to pay for what she had done. She had worked her way into the castle two years prior until she was conveniently placed in my sister's quarters. Then she murdered her in cold blood, nearly destroying me in the process.

"We will catch those responsible for your sister's death," Damian assures me.

The liquor reduces my searing anger to a simmer as it burns through my system. I try to forget; nothing good comes from dragging the past to the present.

"Now, how is your mate?" Damian asks, changing the subject.

"We don't know if she is," I tell him, and he raises an eyebrow at me. "Well, we don't know, not for sure anyway."

"Are you trying to convince yourself or me that she isn't your mate? You have never shown so much interest in any other woman. But her? I have seen how you look at her; I know she is your mate. And I have seen your reaction to her. Almost like you are about to jump out of your skin and mate with her on the spot," Damian states.

I roll my eyes at my Beta; the man is too observant for his own good.

"I know you, Kyson, so where is she?" he asks with a smirk plastered on his face, and I groan.

"In the room across from me," I tell him, my lips tugging up. Fuck. He's right. It is the only thing that explains the strange pull toward her.

"And you say she is not your mate, yet you have her sleeping in your quarters. Not even Ester could stay up here, hmm?"

"Fine, let's say she is. We don't have any info on her. She is a common werewolf and—"

"And you are the King. No one will say shit to you about her being a werewolf and not a Lycan. You could always change her anyway. If she is your mate, and I know she is, she is now in danger. The rebels are back, and if they find out she is your mate, Ivy will have a target on her back," Damian tells me.

"So, what are you saying? Spit it out," I tell him.

"I'm saying keep her close. She needs the training to protect herself. Ivy needs you near to help forge the bond quicker. She may not know who you are to her. But the more time you spend with her, the stronger the bond will solidify to ensure she survives you changing her. It will also strengthen you; Lycans aren't supposed to go without their mates once found. You know this, Kyson."

"Yeah, I know. She's across the hall, yet even that feels too far away," I tell him, and he laughs softly.

"Don't say it," I warn him, admitting what is right in front of me. Ivy is my mate. I just don't want to believe it. Knowing she will become my weakness and share the same knife hanging above my head, knowing it will now be above hers as well, frightens me. They will come for her to reach me if she is, in fact, my mate.

"I won't say a word. Gannon figured it out, but I told him to keep it to himself."

"Yes, keep it that way. I want her to find out on her own."

"Gannon and I have canceled all your appointments this week and next. You have the next two weeks off. None of us are comfortable knowing the rebels and hunters are back, and we want to ensure your - and potentially our queen's - safety. We don't advise you to leave the castle, my King."

"Keep my local appointments. They can visit the castle instead. I will go crazy not working; I always need a distraction this time of the year," I tell him.

"You have just the right distraction in the room across from you, but as you wish. We can't afford risks; early morning meetings and that is it, my King. Advisors agree, the risk is too high for you to be out and about."

"Yes, and I also don't want to leave her alone," I admit.

Damian smiles but adds nothing to my obsession with my mate. "I will have a guard stationed on this floor at all times and one on Ivy when you aren't with her," Damian explains, and I nod.

"I want her watched at all times. All times, Damian. I won't risk her getting hurt."

"As you wish, my King."

CHAPTER
FIFTEEN

ABBIE

Two days have passed, and I have hardly been able to talk to Ivy. I've only seen here in small intervals, here and there when we pass each other in the corridors. The King kept her ridiculously busy and spending so much time in these quarters by myself is incredibly boring. The men on this floor are hardly here, and I find myself wishing they were so that I would have something to clean. My days are becoming repetitive and blurring into one. Mopping floors that are never dirty or wiping non-existent dust from chandeliers and lamps. There is only so much one can tolerate and looking at the walls while listening to the emptiness of the place is beginning to bother me.

Filling my mop bucket, I drop in some cleaning chemicals and grab my mop. I struggle under the weight of the sloshing water as I make my way from the laundry, passing Clarice in the kitchens, who is busy making lunches, and out to the foyer. Water sloshes over the sides, spilling onto the floors. I curse as I set the bucket down and use the mop to clean up the mess I just made on the steps.

With a groan, I reach for the bucket, but only a hand grabs it for me; I have no idea where he came from and didn't even hear him sneak up the steps behind me. He grabs the bucket without a word and starts walking up the steps. He says nothing, and I glance at Gannon, who doesn't even look back and continues carrying the heavy bucket to his quarters. Once we step inside the guard quarters he sets it down on the top step and keeps walking.

"Thank you," I call after him, but he doesn't even acknowledge me, instead just keeps walking toward his bedroom. I watch him slip into his room and close the door. With a sigh, I start scrubbing the clean floors. I don't see him come back out of his room, and the floor is so quiet I am sure he must have slipped past at some point. Clarice eventually sends lunch up with Ester. She has blonde hair, and her servant's uniform is far too tight. Sometimes when she bends over, I can see her ass cheeks poking out from the bottom. I think it is a little inappropriate given how many men lurk around here, though they don't seem to mind her half-clad body and her boobs busting out her uniform.

She thrusts a plated sandwich at me. "Here, I haven't got all damn day. Some of us have real work to do," she snaps. *Well isn't she a joy to be around,* I think. I set my dust brush down and reach for the sandwich when she drops the plate. I don't understand what her problem is. It is clear she doesn't like Ivy and me. The entire castle heard about her ranting and raving about Ivy taking her job. Yet I have done nothing to her personally. The plate shatters on the ground, and she huffs, checking her nails. I shake my head and bend down to start cleaning it up when she speaks.

"Fucking clumsy half-breeds! Seriously get it together," she snaps, sashaying her hips as she walks off. I sigh, grabbing the dustpan and broom to clean up the broken glass, choosing to ignore her. It isn't worth the argument and even I know better than to speak back to authority. And her being a Lycan, she holds more status than I can ever dream of.

"Ester!" A booming voice growls behind me, making the woman stop. Her entire body tenses as she reaches the stairs.

Footsteps behind me make me peek over my shoulder to see who it is. So I am startled to see that Gannon is still up here. I for sure thought he had snuck out when I returned the mop bucket to the laundry. His footsteps stop, and I peer up at him to find his imposing body standing beside me. Instinctively, I shy away from his anger and swallow, dropping my gaze back to the task at hand.

"Yes, Gannon," Ester purrs in a sickly sweet voice. I roll my eyes, and it is clear that the woman is a power-hungry whiny brat. I pick up the ruined sandwich, dumping it in my little bucket before grabbing the dust broom when it is snatched from my hand, making me jump. He grabs my arm and hauls me upright and I look up to find him holding it.

"Clean it up," Gannon growls at her. The order rolling off his tongue makes my knees buckle, but his grip on my arm keeps me upright as my legs threaten to go out under his command. Gannon holds the dust broom out to Ester, and I gasp. Ester pins me with a glare that threatens to burn me before pursing her lips.

Yet even Ester doesn't appear stupid enough to challenge this man. Instead, she stalks forward and snatches it from him before bending down to clean up the broken glass. Her ass cheeks poke out from under her skirt, and Gannon growls menacingly, making me look at him to see him look away from her. His grip on my arm tightens as he pulls me away from her.

"And fucking find a longer dress. No one wants to see your ugly ass on display," Gannon snarls at Ester as he pulls me toward the stairs. I swallow, wondering if I am in trouble because he still hasn't let my arm go. Was he taking me to Clarice to tell her about my clumsiness? Or maybe about me and Ester not getting along? Unease pools in my stomach as he trudges down the steps.

"I'm sorry, I didn't mean to," I tell him when he stops abruptly on the steps. He looks at me and seems to realize he is still holding my arm.

"Sorry," he mutters, letting me go. I stand awkwardly while his eyes run the length of me before his gaze settles back on mine.

"You shouldn't let her speak to you like that. Ester can be a bitch, but she holds no more authority in this castle than any other servant, so don't put up with it, or she will walk all over you," he warns, and I glance back up the stairs. Did he not realize I am only a werewolf? She definitely holds more authority than me and could rip me to shreds. I am not stupid enough to cause confrontation, especially with a Lycan.

"Come on," he says, and my brows furrow, but I don't move. I am stationed to remain in the Beta's quarters.

"Now, Abbie," Gannon calls as he steps down a few steps.

"But I have to."

"I said now, come on," he says, stopping and looking at me expectantly. I chew my lip, wondering where he is taking me, but I know better than to refuse. I follow him, and he leads me to the kitchens. He gives me a nudge through the doors ahead of him, where Clarice looks up at me and smiles brightly.

"Finished already, dear," she smiles before her brows furrow when Gannon comes up behind me. Her eyes widen, and Clarice wipes her hands on the tea towel she is using.

"Gannon, Love. I am sure whatever she did," Clarice quickly defends me, but he says nothing. Instead, he steps past me and walks toward the pantry. Clarice rushes over to me. "You didn't go into any of the forbidden areas?" she whispers, and I shake my head when he returns with bread and condiments. He points to a stool beside him.

"Abbie, sit!" he says, and Clarice and I look at him and then at each other. She quickly nudges me to do what he asked. My hands shake as I use the bench to climb up onto the high stool. I sit there playing with my fingers.

"Is everything alright, son?" Clarice asks, touching his shoulder.

"Fine, ma," he says to her, pulling bread out of the bag when Ester comes in, dumping the dustpan and broom in the cleaning cupboard with an audible huff. Gannon growls at her and she glares at him.

"You can finish mopping the entire floor and take Abbie's duties for the day," Gannon says to her without looking up from making his sandwich. Ester growls, but he doesn't even glance at her.

"Either that or I will make you shovel shit with Peter in the stables, Ester, so choose," Gannon says, and she huffs but storms out. Clarice looks after her and glances between Gannon and me.

I shrug, unsure what to make of it when Gannon sets a BLT sandwich in front of me, cutting it in half and then cutting his own.

"Eat," he says, tapping the plate. I peek at Clarice and she nods to me telling me it is okay while Gannon takes the other stool beside me, eating his own sandwich.

CHAPTER

SIXTEEN

ABBIE

"Is Ester being troublesome?" Clarice asks, wandering back over to the sink. She grabs a dish towel and starts drying the dishes on the rack, and Gannon grunts in answer and Clarice sighs.

"Well, since you are free then, Abbie, you might as well come into town with me," Clarice says, and I stop mid-bite.

"Is that allowed?" I ask her, shocked that I can leave the castle grounds.

"Yes, why wouldn't it be? You're not a prisoner here," Clarice laughs, shaking her head while I stare at her in confusion. *Wait, I can leave the castle grounds?* It makes no sense that rogue servants can come and go as they please.

"I am off for a few hours. I will come with you," Gannon says with a shrug, and Clarice looks at him, her eyes narrowing slightly. She lifts a finger, pointing it at him accusingly.

"You want to grocery shop with us?" Clarice asks, raising an eyebrow at him.

"Or you can give me the list, and I will take her," Gannon says, finishing the last bite of his sandwich before taking his plate to the sink. Clarice watches him for a second, then shrugs. "Works for me. I wanted to send Ester, but seeing as she is now preoccupied and you're willing, you can go with Abbie."

I watch as she retrieves a pen and paper; she scribbles on it and hands it to me before handing me a keycard. I have seen one before but never used one. Mrs. Daley usually sent us with a list into town but never gave us money. The townspeople would just take the list and bill her at the end of the month.

"Just grab these things. They weren't on the delivery," Clarice says with a sigh. She holds the list out to me, and I take the list and glance at her cursive writing, and gulp. I chew my lip, wondering if I should tell her I can't read it, yet I don't want to embarrass myself either. So I remain quiet, and I figure I can just ask the clerk at the store. I put the list in my apron pocket as Gannon walks off toward the doors then stops, waiting for me.

"Are you sure I can leave?" I whisper to Clarice, not wanting to get into trouble with the King.

"Gannon is with you. And as I said, you're not a prisoner here, Abbie. If you want to go to town, you only have to ask," Clarice says, confusing me further. Ask? Is it possible for me to request to leave too?

"Abbie," Gannon says, and I hurry over to him, not wanting to anger him. Gannon leads me out of the castle, and I follow a few steps behind him so I don't get in his way.

"I'm not walking. Come on. I will drive us," he says, gripping my arm and leading me to some garages at the back of the stables. He rummages in a small cupboard full of keys, finding the ones he is after and shutting it.

I pause, watching as he moves toward a car. It makes me nervous about getting into the car with him. Not that he has given me any reason to fear him. He's just... powerful and imposing. And Clarice knows where I am and who I am with, yet unease creeps over me at the thought of being in a confined space with the intimidating man.

He opens the driver's side door before glancing at me. "Abbie?"

he says, and I chew my lip glancing at the doors we came through. He sighs, walking over to me.

"I don't bite," he says, grabbing my hand, but I pull away from him. His brows furrow. I know these sorts of niceties, and they always lead to some repayment or expectation.

I know that better than anyone. The butcher was kind at first, then he started stealing touches, then forcibly taking them. Until one day I refused to help him unload his truck. Mrs. Daley told me if I didn't assist him in the basement, she wouldn't let us eat. She promised us food if I just helped him. Panic courses through me. Is that why he is being nice? Clarice said to steer clear of him, so I find it odd that he is trying to be near me. What are his intentions?

"I won't hurt you, come on," he says, stepping away and toward his car. He walks around the other side and opens the passenger door.

"Abbie, please get in the car," he says, and I glance at the roller doors leading in. My mind wandered to what my chances of escape were. Yet even I knew it would be pointless. If I upset him, what if that got Ivy in trouble? So I reluctantly did as he asked.

Gannon shuts the door behind me, and I jump at the bang. He walks around the other side of the car and climbs in.

I glance around his car to notice duct tape, rope, and some other equipment that makes my heart race faster. *You idiot Abbie, I should have run.* My fingers tremble as I reach for the door handle as he starts the car. My movement does not go unmissed by the man, who quickly looks at me before following my gaze to the things on the floor. Gannon leans over, grabbing the crowbar from the footwell just as I click the door handle.

His hand falls on my knee, and my lip quivers as I look at him to find him staring at me.

"Sorry, I should have checked the car beforehand," he says, leaning down and snatching up the rest of the stuff in the footwell.

My hands tremble as he gathers the things in his arms before opening his door. "Just work equipment," he says, getting out and moving toward another car where he opens the back door. He tosses the stuff on the back floor while I try to calm my racing heart.

What kind of work did he do that requires duct tape, rope, and a bloody crowbar? Gannon climbs back into the car. Yet my hand is still on the door handle when he leans over, pulling my hand away that has a death grip on it. He sets my hand on my lap and quickly leans over closing my door properly.

"You spook easily," he mutters more to himself. I watch him as he clips in his seat belt and turns his attention back to the front. I fiddle with my fingers as he pulls out of the garage while playing with the radio.

"Do you like music?" he asks, and I nod, chewing on my fingernails. I know it is a terrible habit, but I find comfort in it while he finds a station he likes.

I stare out at the scenery as he drives. The drive to town is awkward and silent, and I hadn't noticed I had chewed one cuticle from my fingertip with my nervousness until Gannon stops the car and snatches the hand I am chewing on, which makes me jump. The man curses under his breath.

He growls, holding my hand up and examining it while I gasp at what I mindlessly have done, not realizing I had chewed it entirely down to the flesh beneath. He clicks his tongue and curses and reaches into the glove box, where he pulls out a tissue. Gannon wraps it around my fingertip, firmly pressing down on it.

"You didn't feel that you had bitten it off?" he asks. Disapproval is evident on his face. I don't answer. I hardly feel pain, especially mediocre pain like that. It is merely a flesh wound, and it will heal quick enough.

He checks my finger, and it has stopped bleeding. So he pockets the bloody tissue and shakes his head. I watch as he glares out the window and goes to speak but then climbs out of the car. We've pulled up at some kind of general store. I quickly climb out of the car just as Gannon reaches my door. I step away from him immediately, and put some space between us.

"Have you got your list?" he asks, and I nod, pulling the folded piece of paper from my apron. He nods, walking ahead and opening the glass shop door. A bell sounds as we enter, and I see aisles of stock lining the store and a friendly enough-looking woman behind the counter. The woman says hello to Gannon and quickly waves him over.

"Hey, Leisha," he says, nudging me toward the aisles and passing me a basket. I take it while he wanders off to speak with the friendly clerk he seems to know. She is an older woman about Clarice's age.

I open the note Clarice had given me, glancing between the paper and the things on the shelves. I try to match the cursive writing to what is written on the products. However, after a few minutes, I still haven't found a single thing that matches her handwriting when I feel a presence behind me. The warmth of his chest seeps into my back as he leans down behind me and peers over my shoulder at my empty basket.

"What are you doing?" he asks curiously. Heat floods my cheeks as I show him the list. He takes it, looks at it briefly, then peers down at me. My cheeks burn with humiliation, knowing I have to admit I can't read it. I avert my gaze to the back of the store.

"I... I can't read," I whisper to him.

"Pardon?" he questions as he leans closer. My entire body heats with embarrassment.

"I don't know how to read," I repeat, and Gannon seems taken aback as he stands.

"Why didn't you say so? I would have helped you," he whispers, taking my basket and grabbing my hand.

Gannon looks at the list before glancing around and dragging me to a different aisle. He reads each thing out, grabbing it from the shelf and placing it in the basket. He finds everything in a matter of minutes, and we are briskly walking back to the counter. The woman scans and bags everything and tells me the total.

I go to hand the woman the card when Gannon takes it from me and taps some small box on the counter. The woman behind the counter smiles, and Gannon hands me the card before using his own to buy smokes while I stand there awkwardly, not knowing what to do next.

"We just have to go to one more store, then I will take you back to the castle," Gannon tells me, and I nod, gathering up the bags, but he swiftly takes them from my hands. I wave to the woman, and she smiles softly, saying goodbye as we walk out to the car.

Gannon loads everything into the trunk and then grabs my hand, and drags me across the road to some candy store.

"Liam likes licorice, so I might as well grab it while I am here," he tells me, and I nod, following him inside the store. A man stands behind the counter with a huge smile on his face. It is clear he knows Gannon, and Gannon knows the store.

Gannon leaves me near the counter and walks off toward the back of the store after the man tells him what he's looking for is in the back.

"Are you one of the new servants at the castle?" the man asks. I nod, chewing my lips as I look at the color display of candies when he holds a jar out to me. "Try these. I made these last night," he says, but I shake my head.

Mrs. Daley would get so angry if she found out I accepted candy, I think to myself before remembering she isn't here. Still, I can't bring myself to accept the offer. Thankfully, Gannon returns. The man frowns when I refuse him.

"Kyle has won awards for his candies. Try one," Gannon tells me, and I chew my lip before taking one of the sponging red clouds from the jar. It's covered in sugar and smells delicious. After popping it into my mouth, my mouth salivates from the explosion of flavor.

"Is it good?" the man asks. He seems genuinely interested if I like his candy or not. I nod, licking my lips, and Gannon chuckles.

"Here," he offers me another one, but I shake my head.

"No, thank you, I shouldn't," I tell him. The man named Kyle seems disappointed when Gannon sets the licorice on the counter.

"And the clouds," Gannon tells him. The man nods, bagging

them in little paper bags while I wait. We leave the store and return to the car. I climb in while Gannon puts Liam's candy in the trunk. Only when he gets in the car, he drops the paper bag of candy clouds on my lap.

Before I have a chance to look at him, he speaks. "They're for you," he states, starting the car.

"No, you didn't have to," I tell him, trying to give them back, but he pushes the bag back toward me.

"I know I don't have to, Abbie. I wanted to. I can tell you liked them." His words confuse me. Did he expect something in return for them?

"No, I shouldn't," I tell him, and he looks at me confused.

"And why is that?" he asks, reversing out of his parking space. I don't answer. How can he ask that? His question is stupid. He knows why. Everyone knows why.

"You didn't answer," he says, navigating around the streets.

"Because I am a rogue!" I tell him.

"What has being a rogue got to do with candy?" he asks, his brows furrowing.

"Rogues don't deserve sweets. We should be grateful we're allowed to live," I find myself reciting Mrs. Daley's words before I can stop myself. Gannon growls, making me jump.

"Which twit told you that?" he demands. His anger startles me. I lift my hand when Gannon grabs it before I can chew on my thumbnail, not realizing I am about to do it.

"Eat the candy, Abbie," he says, then lets go of my hand. I offer him one.

"Will you try one?" I ask him, feeling odd eating them in front of him as he pulls into the castle grounds.

"Are they sour?" he asks, and I shake my head.

"You haven't tried them?"

"No, I mostly go for Liam's licorice," he answers as I dig one out of the bag for him and hold it out to him. Yet instead of taking it from me, he leans over, plucking it from my fingers with his lips. He sucks my fingers into his mouth with it before pulling back. I stare at him, shocked, when he laughs, sending me a wink. I chuckle, my face heating up as I laugh at his playfulness. He chews on it before swallowing it.

"It's very sugary," he says, licking the sugar from his lips. I offer him the bag, not wanting to lose my fingers, but he shakes his head. "No, you enjoy them," he says, pulling into the garage.

CHAPTER
SEVENTEEN

GANNON

I had just dropped Abbie back to the castle and left her with Clarice when Liam finds me. He is leaning against my door as I walk toward my room. Liam smiles when he spots me. He has cold and calculating eyes. "Looking for me?" I ask, and a smirk slips onto his face. His presence alone intimidates most people. You can tell there is something not quite right with Liam. He is unhinged. Despite his boyish good looks, nothing instills fear more than this man among the King's guard. Some call him the King's mad dog, and based on the things I've seen, it's an apt description.

"No, I figured I would just lean against your door because I am not waiting for you."

I grunt and shake my head. Danger emanates out of him. He has an air of superiority and seems to relish the power he has over others, just like he relishes cutting them into tiny pieces. The man is a psychopath, but then again, so am I. So his crazy compliments mine, which is why we are best friends.

"And where were you?" he drawls, and I roll my eyes at him. "I thought we were heading to the bar," he asks, pushing off my door frame, twisting the door handle, and waltzing into my room. I growl at him when he jumps onto my bed, making himself comfortable. He runs his fingers through his blonde hair and falls back on my bed.

"Something else came up," I tell him. Liam rolls over, pulling his knife from his pocket. He picks at my duvet with the tip before twirling his knife between his fingers and eyeing me suspiciously.

"Does it have anything to do with the pretty little redhead I saw you in town with earlier?" I look over my shoulder at him as I grab two beers from the mini fridge in the corner of my room. I chuck him one.

"If you already know where I was, why are you asking?"

He shrugs, popping the lid off with his knife and propping himself up with one elbow.

"The girl reminds me of," I growl warning him not to mention her name.

"Is that part of the allure you have toward her because she reminds you of your dead mate?" Liam questions, and I eye him, swigging from my bottle.

"She is nothing like her," I tell him, and Liam shrugs.

"That may be true, but you must admit they have an uncanny resemblance, don't you think?" he taunts, and my hand moves before I realize what I have done. My fingers find the blade I always keep strapped to my hip. It whizzes through the air, embedding itself in the bed head beside his head. Liam doesn't even flinch. He just lifts an eyebrow at me.

"Apparently, I'm right," he chuckles, yanking the blade from the headboard.

"I wonder if sweet little Abbie would enjoy your fetish for knives," he muses, examining it before moving so quickly I only just see the blade coming toward my face. I catch the blade before it hits me square between my eyes. The edges slice my palm and fingers as the knife slides between, cutting through my flesh, the point just nicking my skin between my eyes.

Liam chuckles, sipping his beer and leaning back against the headboard.

"Or are you envisioning carving her up like your mate, slicing that tender flesh and watching her bleed out the way you did her?"

"Fuck off, Liam, you know nothing," I tell him.

"Ah, but I do; I was there, remember? And I know you... and that girl is a timid little thing and so jumpy. Scared of her own shadow, she is."

"What are you getting at?" I snap, grabbing an old shirt to clean my bleeding hand. Liam shrugs.

"Just curious, Gan. I don't want you to break her. It would be a shame really, I don't mind watching her prance around in her little uniform." His words cut off when I launch myself at him, my hands locking around his throat, and he cackles his head off, laughing like a maniac.

"Seems I'm right. You like the girl," Liam laughs.

"I don't. I took her to town, and that is it. I took her for Clarice," I add.

"I can smell lies, but if you wish to tell yourself that, we can pretend," he says, sending me a wink, and I growl, shoving him back on the bed and climbing off him.

"I took her to town, Liam, nothing more," I tell him, wandering off into the bathroom. I wash my hands and remove my clothes, drop them in the hamper, and step into the shower, shutting the door. Liam leans on the doorframe, watching me.

"If that is so, why were you by her door last night and the night before, or better yet, what were you doing watching her from the old guard towers? You know, the ones? The ones that look directly into her bedroom window?"

"Explain to me why you are following me?" I retort, turning the water on and stepping under the water spray.

Turning, I look at him as his eyes wander the length of me. I know he is bisexual. His sexuality has never bothered me, and I am used to his comments and wandering gaze. However, he also knows I don't swing that way.

"Was curious about why you stood me up last night, for one. And then this morning you vanished and ever since she got here." He shrugs.

"Why, are you jealous Liam?" I laugh.

"Always. You know I am not good at sharing," he jokes, and I chuckle.

"Don't worry. You won't have to share me. I am not interested in the girl," I tell him.

"We'll see, though it wouldn't hurt if you were, as long as it isn't for nefarious reasons, Gannon," Liam says, and I swallow.

"Yes, she reminds me of my mate, but that isn't why." I shake my head. I am not interested in her. It's hard to imagine even having a conversation with her with how timid she is.

"I am leaving to run an errand for the King. Join me or don't," Liam states with a shrug, glancing out the bathroom window toward the forest surrounding the castle.

"She is a beauty, though," he mumbles, and I nod. Abbie is striking with her dark auburn hair and soft, sensual features. She is small and petite, and I like that about her. I like the way she stares curiously at everything around her. Like she is deciphering codes, genuinely curious about people yet soft-spoken. She is an observer. That much I have noticed. She exists without being seen and doesn't like the attention, but notices everyone else like she is waiting for something to jump out of the shadows at her.

"Hasn't she shifted yet? I could smell she has a wolf?" Liam asks curiously, still peering out the window. I lean around to see what he is looking at. Abbie is hanging out washing, yet stares vacantly toward the forest. My brows furrow, and I watch as she steps toward the trees, looking longingly at them, when I hear Clarice sing out to her. She pauses, glances over her shoulder, and rushes back to the clothesline as if she thinks she will get into trouble.

"To me, it seems she wants to go for a run," Liam says with a shrug, passing me a towel off the rack. His eyes are trained on the girl. I swallow because I had noticed she hasn't shifted once since being here. And I know she is of age. It makes me wonder what her wolf looks like.

"I'll cover for you if you wish," Liam offers, but I shake my head. No, I need to get away from here and slice some poor sucker who is dumb enough to capture the King's attention. It seems like the perfect excuse to leave.

"No need. I need to get out of here," I tell him.

"Out of here or away from her?" Liam asks. I growl, and he smirks.

"I'll meet you in the car, and I drive," he says, and I huff but let it slide. Liam is my best friend and the only one who truly knows me. We are alike in more ways than one.

CHAPTER
EIGHTEEN

ABBIE

I stare at the forest surrounding the castle, wishing I could shift and feel the air in my fur and the dirt beneath my paws. Though, I was actually never able to shift. Mrs. Daley forbade it. The only time I did was in our room back at the orphanage, and Ivy would keep a lookout. Not that Mrs. Daley came up to our room much, so I used to laze by the window where I could see the moon and feel its rays on my fur. I guess that is where the legend came from for humans about the moon and werewolves, etc. I've always felt drawn to the moon and night in general. I used to imagine what it would be like to roam freely and explore the woods, but instead, my paws only knew the floorboards of our tiny room, except for that one time.

Yet so close to the forest, the urge to run free is overwhelming. I take a step toward the forest, feeling my body tense with the urge to change and realign so I can take my werewolf form. There is nothing more freeing than the shift, yet it is also painful because I hardly did it.

"Abbie!" Clarice calls out to me, and I rush back to hang out the towels I was sent out to hang.

"Yes," I call back, looking toward the laundry door. Clarice emerges and peers over at me.

"Once done, come help me prepare for dinner."

I nod to her quickly and rush to finish hanging the washing out, wondering if maybe I could sneak out while everyone is asleep to shift. Clarice did say I could leave if I wanted. But I quickly dismiss the thought. The guards may stumble across me and think I am trespassing. It makes me shudder at the damage they could cause to my tiny wolf form.

After dinner and wandering back to my room, I find myself drawn to look out the window. So I give up avoiding it and sit on the windowsill looking at the castle grounds below. My skin itches with the need to shift. It is a clear night yet as I watch from the window I see the guards walking the forest edge and sigh.

Despite the promise of the forest, I realize that once again, my only place of solace with my wolf will be this room. So, I strip my clothes off, I get to my hands and knees, and a violent shudder ripples up my spine. I feel the first snap and clench my teeth as my bones start breaking and realigning into position.

My hands become paws and skin turns to fur and my nose and face elongate. I am careful not to let my claws scratch the floor as I stand on my hind legs and jump onto the sitting nook of the window ledge. I press my nose to the glass and lay down along the window, wishing I could run through the forest, wishing to know what it truly means to be a werewolf.

My mother used to tell me how freeing it was to run on four legs, zip through the trees, and feel the air and heat blow through her fur. I guess I will never know what that truly feels like. It is foolish to miss something I have never experienced, and probably won't ever experience again.

I end up falling asleep on the window ledge. It isn't until I hear a knock on the door that I wake up and crash to the ground with a thud. My entire body shakes when I hear the door handle twist, and I know I am going to be caught. Lowering my body to the ground, I try to fit under the bed, yet my furry body is much too big. Stupid Abbie, how could you fall asleep?

"Abbie?" Clarice's voice reaches my ears, and I peer around the edge of the bed. She gasps, and I quickly shift back, reaching for the sheet on my bed to tuck around me.

"I'm sorry, I promise I was careful and didn't scratch the floor." Tears burn my eyes and I peer down at the mess on the floor. "I promise I will clean up the fur," I quickly tell her, covering myself. Clarice stares at me, and my cheeks burn with embarrassment. I wonder how many lashes I will get for my selfishness.

"You're not in trouble, Abbie. I noticed you didn't come down for supper," she says, placing a food tray with a slice of pie on the bed.

"Sorry, I will get changed and come down," I tell her. She stares at me for a second before nodding and heading toward the door. She pauses just as Gannon and Dustin walk past my door.

"You know, Abbie, if you want to shift, you can go into the woods. Just let the guards know you're out there so they don't think you're a stranger." Clarice says, and I tug the blanket tighter when I notice Gannon has stopped and is staring past Clarice at me. I drop my gaze, unable to meet his gaze.

"It's okay, it won't happen again," I assure her.

"Abbie?" she speaks softly, and I lift my gaze to hers. Her brows furrow, and she looks at Gannon behind her.

"I'll take her for a run," Gannon offers, but I shake my head.

"No, it's fine. I think I will just take a shower and clean up the mess I made," I tell them. Gannon goes to say something but closes his mouth. With a swift nod, he walks off. I let out a breath and Clarice watches him leave. Clearly, my shifting inside has angered him.

"Try to get some rest, but if you want to shift, you can go to the woods to do so. I have told you, Abbie. You aren't a prisoner here," Clarice says kindly before leaving me. Yet she says that, but I cannot see Ivy, or even go to that floor. I don't much feel like tempting the Lycans by doing something, even if allowed.

Mrs. Daley used to like to play those games, get our hopes up and say we could have a break. The moment we did, she beat us bloody. Or like the time she said we could eat with the children at the dining table, only to humiliate us when we sat down with them. She tossed our food on the floor and made us eat like dogs. After that, when the children begged for us to sit with them, we never asked again. We were only twelve at the time.

We had finally given in to the children and thought for once we would ask; it sucked because the kids always asked. We only asked once because it was Mrs. Daley's birthday. We spent all day preparing the cake and making sure we had a delicious meal prepared for her. We thought if we worked extra hard and made her happy, she would let us join her and the other children. She had promised us that if we baked her favorite chocolate mud cake, and cooked a roast we could celebrate with her and try the cake we painstakingly created for her.

We were so excited, and when the other kids sat down, we served them food. Then we gathered our own plates. Usually, Mrs. Daley gave us whatever scraps the kids didn't eat or sometimes if she thought we were being lazy, she gave the scraps to the pigs and we went without. We were on our best behavior, she promised. Even Katrina was excited for us and helped us bake the cake. Yet as we plated our food and went to take our seats, she snapped at us.

"What are you doing?" she snarled, and we both froze and looked at Katrina who stared at her in confusion.

"They're going to join," Katrina says before she is interrupted by Mrs. Daley.

"Dogs don't sit at the table," she said, getting up.

"I said you could join us because I was feeling generous, but filthy rogues eat like filthy rogues," she said, snatching our plates. She emptied the plates onto the floor.

"Now sit and enjoy your meal," she ordered us. The humiliation and sadness at the broken promise nearly made me cry, but I held it back, knowing what tears earned us. With one last glance at Katrina, we saw her lips quiver, and she tossed her napkin before storming out.

I nudged Ivy as I went to sit on the floor. Ivy, I could tell, didn't want to eat it, though the floors were clean, we would know. We clean them daily. She had just glared at Mrs. Daley, and I had to nudge her, giving her a look to remind her we hadn't eaten in two days and she had fainted the day prior. Who cares if it was ruined? We still needed to eat, Ivy especially. She always got less than everyone. Mrs. Daley was exceptionally cruel to her. I would always sneak her food scraps when I could, knowing she wouldn't receive half of what I got or anything at all.

"Please," I whispered to her, nudging her with my elbow. Ivy looked at me and dropped her gaze to the floor. She then sank down beside me and scooped up a roasted potato from the floor and nibbled on it.

Looking at the slice of pie on the tray, makes me wonder if Ivy has eaten. Maybe I can sneak it over to her. Ivy is always too shy to ask for food. She has copped one too many beatings for it, so my conscience gnaws at me about how much I have eaten since being here, realizing she may not be eating at all. I quickly change, scoop up the plate and peer out the door, trying to sneak into the King's quarters. Yet it doesn't take long before Trey, one of the guards stationed there, spots me and sends me away.

CHAPTER
NINETEEN

I VY

The last three days have been a disaster. Ester keeps finding ways to sabotage me and get me in trouble. So far, I have been having trouble with Clarice, one of the cooks, and now I find myself staring down at the broken vase she deliberately shattered.

To top it off, I have a fever; my back seems to have an infection. I fight back the tears while retrieving my dustpan and broom and start to sweep the mess up. She isn't even supposed to be up here, yet I always catch her tampering with my work. She always waits to see my reaction, then darts off. This time, glass is scattered everywhere. It's a wonder it didn't cut me.

Gosh, I wonder how much it costs? It looks so expensive, so I know I'm in trouble. Hearing voices on the stairs, my breathing becomes erratic, and I start grabbing the big chunks and dropping them in the bin as quickly as possible. Yet this causes me to slice my fingertips, making me hiss. I'm so over the injuries. I'm over constantly aching. I just want to rest.

Being here is worse than being at the orphanage. I swear my ribs are broken on my left side. The bruising is now a deep dark purple with yellowing around the edges from Ester tripping me on the stairs.

My new shoes also give me hell, though someone keeps supplying me with thick socks for which I am grateful. In addition, someone gave me a blanket from the King's room. I had wondered if it was him since the first morning when I woke up with it draped over me. I cautiously place it back in his room, only to find it tossed over me again the following morning. I have kept it ever since.

I have noticed, though, that the King has been on edge and hasn't been working much or leaving his room much. I also saw him snap at a few guards.

Another thing I have noticed is that he is lately smelling heavily of liquor. The last few times I have brought him dinner I could tell he was drunk. His behavior has been strange. Sometimes I even notice him following me around, which is terrifying. I can't think with his intense staring, and I mess up constantly which ends up angering him even more.

Sweeping quickly, I hear the voices getting closer, and I can tell it's the King. A piece of glass scoots across the floor with the sweep of the broom before the guard's foot stops it. I blink, wondering if I imagined it. He bends down, picks it up, and tosses it in my bin before winking at me.

He used to guard the stairs and door on the below level, but he has been stationed up here for the last two days. This is the first time I have seen him move. At one point, I thought he was a statue, but now I have proof that he is a living, breathing being.

"Thank you," I whisper to him, and he nods before staring straight ahead again. I hiss, clutching my ribs as I bend to scoop up the last of the shattered glass into the dustpan. I am about to stand when King Kyson and Beta Damian turn into the corridor.

"Oh, for the love of God, what did you break this time?" King Kyson groans while shaking his head. I drop my eyes to the floor and swallow. That's it. I have done it now. I wonder how many lashings I will get for it.

"Sorry, sir," I tell him. It is better to take the blame than to have her come after me for snitching. I also don't want to risk his wrath by passing the blame onto someone else.

The King turns slightly and faces his Beta, who watches me get scolded by the king, making this entire ordeal more embarrassing.

"I will see you later, Damian," King Kyson tells him, walking into his bedroom.

"Ivy, come in here and shut the door behind you," the King yells out, and I pause at my task.

Oh no, please don't be too angry. *Shit!* I mouth to myself. Grabbing the bin and broom I set them next to the door. I gaze at the ceiling, blinking back tears as fear slivers along my veins. I clench my fists a few times, trying to build up the courage to walk in and face the King's wrath.

He has been in a terrible mood. I have seen so many sides of him in just a few days. I've witnessed his anger and noticed his stress as he paces his room, forgetting I am there while muttering to himself.

Clarice said some anniversary is coming up, but wouldn't tell me what the anniversary was—just that I should expect outbursts and try to steer clear of him. But it's challenging when he sometimes follows me to ensure I do my job correctly, always hovering and breathing down my neck.

"Ivy! Now!" King Kyson yells again, his tone of voice irritated. I step in, shutting the door to find him rummaging through a box while sitting on the edge of his bed. My stomach drops. What will he do to me?

"What took you so long? Come here," he says, pointing between his legs. I stare at the space where he wants me to stand then look at him, only to find him watching me again. "Do I need to drag you here? Now, Ivy. My patience is running low," he snaps, pointing to the space between his legs.

I force my feet to move and stand next to him. He growls and glares up at me, annoyed. Gripping my wrist, he yanks me to stand where he ordered, his knees touching my thighs.

Peering down, I realize he has medical supplies in the box and I step back, only for him to pull me back in place, pressing his knees on either side of my legs so I don't move away again.

"You haven't changed your bandages in days. Clarice said she sent you to the infirmary yesterday, but the nurse said she never saw you, and that you never came to see her. Why is that?" he questions.

He is correct; I knew my back was getting infected. But if the nurse sees the bruises and my ribs, she may put me off work, and if I can't work, what use am I? They would probably kill me if I didn't earn my keep. This isn't an orphanage, and I'm expected to work, and for the King of all people.

"It's all better now," I tell him, which does nothing but earn me a glare.

"Don't lie to me. I can smell it in your bloodstream. Don't forget what I am, Ivy; my senses are stronger than yours. Now remove the uniform and don't lie to me again," he says. Shaking my head I try to step back, but his legs hold me in place.

"Ivy, remove your uniform, or I will do it for you," he warns. His gaze holding mine dares me to disobey him. My lips quiver, and I grip the buttons, not wanting to take the dress off.

"I will ask to see the nurse now," I blurt out, and he growls at me, making me shake like a leaf.

He reaches for the buttons on my dress, and I slap his hand, trying to pull away from him when I realize what I just did. I freeze—nibbling on my bottom lip to stop it from quivering and suppressing a whimper at the look he gives me. I just slapped the King away! How could I be so stupid?

"Did you just slap...?" He doesn't finish; he shakes his head, reaching for my buttons again. My eyes burn with tears that threaten to spill over, yet I force myself not to react. Just block it out. I take a deep breath and try to focus on the wall behind him, willing myself to stay still.

"Will you stop shaking? Why do you smell of fear? Have I hurt you?" he snaps at me.

110

I shake my head as he stares at me.

"If I wanted to hurt you, I would have already. I could have punished you multiple times over the last two days for messing up and the vase you just broke, but I haven't. What is wrong with you and Abbie? So bloody skittish, it infuriates me," he growls.

"I'm sorry, sir. I will do better," I tell him while clutching the front of my dress.

"Kyson. My name is Kyson, and don't apologize. It's just annoying that you scare so easily when we have treated you with nothing but kindness," he says, reaching for my buttons again. He stops when he notices I am holding it, then reaches for my arms and growls. Grabbing my hands, he pries them away from my dress. He places my hands on his legs. When I move them off his thighs, he growls, making me return them.

"Ivy, I won't hurt you," he tells me while undoing the last button. Why is he insisting on doing this? I said I would see the nurse. He untucks the bandage's small clip, his eyes on the task as he fiddles with it.

"Now turn around," he says. His legs open to allow me to turn. I turn around, glad I don't have to see his face staring at my body. He pulls my dress down off my shoulders to bunch at my waist before moving further back onto the bed. Warm, firm hands move to my hips, and he pulls me to sit between his legs on the edge of his bed.

TWENTY

IVY The movement makes me cringe in pain as my ribs throb, and I clench my teeth to stop crying out. Quick movements always give me sharp pains and cause my breathing to become stifled.

"Sorry, did that hurt?" he asks. I shake my head. "Don't lie. Why do you lie about being in pain?" he asks while unraveling the bandages.

Unsure whether to answer, I remain quiet.

"I asked you a question?" he says, tapping the side of my leg and making me jump and blurt out an answer.

"Mrs. Daley would double our punishment if we made noise," I murmur, remembering the first time I cried out. I was eleven the first time she whipped me. Before that day, she would scold or smack us. But she never gave us the cane or whip until my refusal to sit on the butcher's lap which lost her the meat rations that week.

I had cried, begged, and cried some more, which turned three lashes into six. The next time the butcher visited, and I was ordered to sit on his lap, Abbie quickly took my spot. Had I known what it would cost her later, I would have taken the lashes; his vile touching only grew worse, just like Mrs. Daley's punishments. After a few times, we learned quickly not to make noise. It was always awful if we did.

"Is that why you have so many scars?" he asks.

"No, we learned to keep quiet. It just didn't matter how well we did our chores; Mrs. Daley always found something to punish us for."

I grit my teeth as the pressure supporting my broken ribs slips away when the bandages get down to the last layer. It feels like he's peeling my skin off from how soiled the bandages are.

"What happened to your ribs and back?" he questions, his fingers brushing my ribs.

I cringe away from his touch, gritting my teeth. A stifled whimper leaves my lips as he presses on the most painful one.

"You don't have to be quiet, Ivy. I won't punish you for being in pain. You would have to do something pretty extreme for me to punish you," he murmurs.

"Can you lift your arms above your head?" he asks, and I try to lift both arms; the left pulls at my side making my arms tremble.

"That's enough; this side looks like you have broken it. How did you do that?" he asks.

"I tripped down the stairs, sir," I tell him.

"When?"

"The day we arrived?"

"You have worked for days with broken ribs and said nothing?"

I choose to say nothing.

"You should have said something, Ivy. If you are in pain, you can't be expected to work in this condition."

"It's fine; I can still work," I tell him quickly.

"No, you will remain here with me, so I know you're resting."

"That's unnecessary; I can still work."

"It wasn't a choice. You'll remain with me," King Kyson says, grabbing a jar of ointment and rubbing it on the cuts.

I remain still while he cleans the markings that brand my skin. My face heats the longer he touches me. I feel dirty and embarrassed that he is touching me, his servant.

Yet the feel of his skin on mine feels oddly warming, my skin tingling everywhere he touches. He moves behind me, and the bed dips more.

"Stay there," he says, climbing off the bed and walking over to his dresser. He grabs a black shirt out of the drawer and climbs back onto the bed, then retakes his place behind me.

"I think you should leave the bandage off; let it get some air," he says when I feel his fingers pinch my bra, releasing the hooks. I shriek, covering myself before feeling his breath on my neck.

"Shh, Ivy, I can't see you," he whispers, and I stiffen at his closeness, feeling the heat radiating off his chest and seeping into my skin. His nose skims along my shoulder to the back of my ear; his hand on my stomach pulls me closer to him.

"I love your scent," he whispers, and tingles wash over me everywhere. He suddenly clears his throat, pulling his face away from me. "Sorry, I didn't mean to... you just smell nice," he states.

"It's fine, sir," I tell him, somewhat startled that he admitted to sniffing me and thinks I smell nice. Most rogues smell awful to pack wolves. Then again, he is a Lycan, so who knows?

"Kyson," he murmurs.

"Pardon me, sir?"

"My name. It is Kyson. I'd prefer you to use my name. Say it, Ivy," he whispers behind me. I shake my head at his words, looking toward the door.

"You can say my name, Ivy; I won't let anyone punish you for using my name," he whispers, sliding my bra straps down my arms and away from my body. He places it beside him.

"Say my name Ivy," he whispers once more, and I shiver when his breath skates across my neck. His fingers trail along my sides, but he avoids touching my saw ribs; instead, he grips my wrists and pulls my arms apart that cover me. He places my hands on his knees, and I breathe out shakily. "You don't need to fear me, Ivy." I peer at him over my shoulder to find his lips only a breath away.

He stares at me with fiery intensity, and I feel my heart pounding in my chest. I close my eyes, knowing I am powerless against him. His lips move closer to mine, and I quiver in anticipation of what he'll do. "If anyone needs to fear anyone around here, it is me that should fear you," he purrs, and my brows pinch in confusion. I open my eyes to see him press his lips on my shoulder.

He then pulls a shirt over my head.

It's the black shirt he retrieved from the dresser. His fingertips graze the sides of my breasts as I push my arms through the holes. The shirt falls to my hips. Yet his hands inside the shirt don't move. Instead, he brushes his thumbs across the sides of my breasts, making me shiver. I look down at it before pinching the front of the shirt and sniffing it, his scent making my mouth water.

"Do I smell alright?" he asks with a soft laugh, and his hands fall to my thighs.

"Yes, like vanilla and berries," I tell him before slapping a hand over my mouth for what I embarrassingly blurted out.

He laughs softly, his fingers fiddling with my ponytail. He gently removes my hair tie.

The King leans forward, his hand holding my hair aside as he inhales my scent, his breath skimming over my flesh as he speaks. "Don't be embarrassed, Ivy. You smell just as delicious to me, good enough to eat," he chuckles before sitting back and letting my hair fall. My hair falls to my waist, and he runs his fingers through it. I shiver at the feel of his fingers on my scalp.

"You still haven't said it yet," he says.

"Said what?" Having lost my train of thought, the only thing I can focus on is breathing as he uses his fingers to untangle my hair.

"My name," he says, and I shake my head. "I will get you to say it, eventually." He almost seems to be taunting me, his tone playful.

There is a knock on the door. I try to get up when he pulls me back down, his hand moving under his shirt, his thumb rubbing my belly.

"Come in, Damian," he says, and my heart beats erratically. Beta Damian walks in with a tray of food and a glass filled with ice cubes.

"Where do you want it, Kyson?" he asks.

"Just leave it there," the King says behind me, and my face heats up when King Kyson presses his face into my neck again. His Beta never looks in our direction, like he expected me to be half-undressed here and practically sitting on his King's lap.

How many servants has he found in this position, I wonder? Surely this isn't normal behavior, or maybe it is. Is this why Ester hates me?

"Anything else?" Beta Damian asks him.

"No, that is all. I will mindlink you if I need anything," the King says. I see his Beta nod; he walks out and shuts the door.

"Relax, Ivy," the King tells me, but I find that nearly impossible. I know if I anger him in some way, he can tell the guards to kill me, and they would without hesitation. How does he not see that being in his presence is intimidating? He climbs off the bed and retrieves the tray before pouring whiskey into a glass.

"Have you drank alcohol before?" he asks, and I shake my head.

He hands me the glass, and I sniff it. "I won't tell if you don't, but it will help with the pain," he says, pointing to my ribs. I sip it and nearly spit it back into the glass. He chuckles and pours the ice from the other cup into my glass.

"There, I watered it down a bit," he says, pouring himself a glass. I sniff it again and shake my head, trying to pass it back to him. But he adds more whiskey to the glass, half filling it.

"Drink it," he orders, and I am unable to help myself. I bring the glass to my lips. He watches me over the rim of his glass, and I cough when I finish drinking it all in one go.

"Sorry, I don't enjoy ordering you, but I knew you wouldn't drink it. You may feel woozy, but you won't hurt as badly."

116

Well, I definitely woozy alright. But I also feel warm and, after a few minutes, very heavy.

"Eat," he says, placing the tray between us. The tray is filled with small sandwiches cut into triangles and carrots, sticks, and dips. It also contains an assortment of cheeses and different crackers.

I stare at him confused. Despite being unfamiliar with a few things, it smells delicious. But a servant should not eat with a King. I shouldn't even be here.

"Ivy, eat. Or I will hand feed you," he warns. Still, I don't move. This is wrong. I shouldn't be here. That thought has me glancing at the door.

When I feel something press to my lips, making me pull away and look at the King.

"Do I need to feed you, Ivy?" I shake my head.

"No, My King," I answer, yet he insists, pressing the piece of cantaloupe against my lips. He isn't seriously still going to try? I briefly consider biting his fingertips for embarrassing me–instead, I open my mouth.

He pops the piece of cantaloupe into my mouth, and I chew it, the flavor coating my tongue. I have seen cantaloupe, though I've never tried it before. It tastes bitter but sweet, just the right combination.

Kyson rubs his thumb over my juice-covered lips, and I gape at him when he sucks the juice off his thumb.

Yet, before he can do it again, I pick up a cracker and nibble on it, not wanting to be hand fed. Gosh, how awkward! Although, he seems to enjoy watching me eat, pointing to different things, and telling me to try them. He only hand-feeds me fruit twice after that, both times just as awkward as the first. Yet he doesn't seem to notice the tension in me when he does. Almost as if he doesn't find it odd that he's feeding me.

I shake my head when he offers me a cantaloupe piece. He raises an eyebrow at me, pressing the fruit against my lips. Giving in to him, I open my mouth for him.

117

He smirks. "Good girl." I slowly chew and savor the taste, letting the sweet juices flood my mouth. He watches me, a satisfied smirk on his face.

CHAPTER
TWENTY-ONE

IVY

The day seems to drag on. There were a few times when I tried to sneak out of the room to do my chores, but every time I tried to do so, King Kyson would call me back into the room before pointing to his bed. "Rest," he would say before turning back to his work.

Eventually, I gave up trying. So I am relieved when he is finally called out of the room, which gives me a chance to breathe a little easier. He has been forcing me to eat, sit and watch him work all day.

I stick my head out the door to ensure he is gone. Then, I hurry down the corridor. He didn't say I couldn't leave the room before he left, and I know I am falling behind on my chores.

Retrieving my cleaning supplies from the downstairs cupboard, I quickly head back to the room, where I change the linens and clean the bathroom.

Each movement makes me cringe. However, I am glad to be doing something other than watching the King, who spends most of the day watching me over his laptop while he was supposed to be working. It made for some awkward stare-offs; the man could stare without blinking while I nervously stared around the room to avoid his gaze, which only seemed to amuse him.

Why does he insist on waiting around with his servant? He had hardly left the room all day. When I am done scrubbing the bathroom, I take my cleaning supplies back to the cupboard downstairs before making a quick dash to the servant's bathroom. I desperately need to pee. I have been holding my bladder all day.

Relieving myself quickly, I step out of the bathroom only to walk into the guard from upstairs.

"Sorry," I whisper, wondering why he is standing in front of the ladies bathroom. He says nothing, just remains in place, and stares at the door. The man is always silent! I make my way back to the cleaning cupboard only to notice him following me like an extra shadow. Is he ensuring I do my chores correctly?

I grab my dusting cloth and polish before heading back upstairs. My legs ache from working after spending most of the day sitting stiffly on the edge of the king's bed. Thankfully, the guard does not follow me into the room; instead, he waits by the door again.

I look at all the books on the King's enormous bookcase and gulp. My eyes scan over them, wondering if any are out of place. I also try to remember which book belongs where just in case I have to dust the books. What if I got them in the wrong order? The spines are all decorative and in impeccable order, not like the picture books in the orphanage that were falling apart and the pages were torn.

Maybe I shouldn't dust the shelf...

I can hardly read anything except my name, which my mother taught me before she died. Abbie is the same. We both struggle to read a simple sentence. There isn't much need to read when you are a rogue. Books are heavy and not easy to carry around.

I touch one, liking the fancy writing down the spine, when I hear his voice behind me, making me jump away from the shelf.

"You can read them," he says, leaning against the doorframe of his bedroom. He stares at me. How long has he been there before catching me?

"Sorry, My King," I tell him, dropping my gaze to the floor. Why did I touch it? I shouldn't have snooped. He walks over to his chair and sits on it while I try to avoid his gaze.

"Which one were you looking at?" he asks, and I glance at him. His eyes scan the bookcase, and I chew my lip nervously. His eyes dart to my lips, and I stop. Instead, I look down at my hands. Will he punish me for touching them? I was told to be careful around his books.

Mrs. Daley would have beaten me bloody if I touched anything of hers. Rogues were supposed to mind their place. Here, I sometimes forget that I'm nothing but a rogue on whom the King took pity. I still don't understand why he didn't cast us out or kill us.

"Pass it to me," he says, holding his hand out for the book. I look at the shelf and reach for the book but pause. What if it's a trick?

"Pass me the book, Ivy. You know I don't like repeating myself," he says softly, yet his voice is still firm. I nod and reach for the book with the golden letters, pulling it from the shelf and quickly handing it to him.

"Ah, *Treasure Island*," he says, reading the title. I wasn't sure what it said. I just liked the inscription on the side.

"Can you read?" he asks.

"No, sir," I answer honestly.

"Come here."

I look down at my hands, feeling nervous in his presence, though he has never hurt either of us. However, I know he can do it if he sees fit. He clicks his tongue, sitting up a bit more.

"Ivy, don't shy away from me now," he says, holding his hand out to me. Staring at his outstretched hand, I move hesitantly, walking toward him.

I always feel funny around this man. Being a rogue, I shouldn't even be in his presence, let alone allowed to talk to him. Touching him should be out of the question.

"Do you want me to command you?" he asks, and I look at his face to find him smiling. His smile is breathtaking, his silver eyes sparkling back at me.

Chewing my lip, I shake my head, walking over to him. When I am close enough, he reaches out and grabs my wrist. Then, he does something he definitely shouldn't... but then again, he has done plenty he shouldn't have done with his rogue servant already.

He pulls me onto his lap. I sit awkwardly and move, trying to climb off him. "My King," I exclaim when he holds me against him.

"Kyson. I hate that you keep calling me 'My King,'" he tells me.

"But you are, and I shouldn't be sitting on your lap," I tell him as I try to hop off, but his hand on my stomach pulls me back against him.

"That is enough, Ivy. You'll remain where you are. No one can see you. It is just you and me here."

"Yes, but, My King," I protest when he grabs my chin between his fingers and tilts my face toward his. Sparks rush over my skin, and I forget how to breathe, holding my breath at the sensation coursing through me.

"Kyson. You can call me, Kyson," he tells me again, his face so close that his breath fans my lips. I suddenly feel light-headed, and he brushes his thumb across my bottom lip, tugging it down slightly.

His eyes are mesmerizing, glowing brightly as they dart to my lips briefly before flicking back to mine. His scent is overwhelming and masculine, making me want to breathe in deeply to savor it. Yet somehow, I've forgotten how to breathe with his face so close to mine. His full lips move, and it takes me a second to register his words.

"Breathe, Ivy. I don't want you to pass out on me," he says, swallowing. His eyes are still on my lips. I let out a breath, and his lips tugged at the corners of his mouth before letting me go.

"Do you want me to read it to you?" he asks.

"No, I couldn't ask that. I am sure you are too busy," I say, straightening my spine.

"That's not what I asked Ivy. Calm down." He lifts his hand, placing it between my breasts. "Your heart is racing. How many times do I have to tell you I won't hurt you?" he asks, shaking his head. He abruptly moves, turns me on his lap, and pulls my legs up over his.

CHAPTER
TWENTY-TWO

IVY

The King pats his chest. This man was absurd to have his servant lying on him. He pats his chest again. He wasn't serious! Was he? If anyone walked in, I would be whipped for days if I was caught in this position.

"Ivy," he speaks one word, yet the warning in it makes me do as he wants, and I settle against him. He tugs my head down on his chest, and I can hear his heart's slow, steady rhythm beneath my ear. King Kyson grabs my hand, placing it in the center of his chest before he opens the book.

"Do you want me to read to you?" he asks again. I nod my head, looking at the book. "Good girl," he says, wrapping his arm around me to hold the book open with two hands.

He reads perfectly and never stutters as I used to when trying to read the books in the orphanage. I was forever trying to sound the words out when I read to the children.

The children at the orphanage are allowed in the classes that are taught; they aren't rogues. Rogues are not allowed the privilege of an education. They tried to help teach us, but they weren't the best teachers.

So, listening to the story as he reads it paints a picture in my head so vivid, I could listen to him speak all day; I finally understand his fascination with his books.

He stops when I start yawning, gently placing the book down and rubbing my thigh.

"We can read more tomorrow. You are tired," he states, and I nod against his shoulder before climbing off his lap. I walk toward his door, heading for my room.

I miss Abbie. I haven't seen even a glimpse of her today. She must be worried about me; she always used to worry.

"Ivy, where are you going?" he asks, and I freeze, puzzled by his question, before cursing under my breath. I turn away, realizing he hadn't dismissed me.

"I'm sorry, I thought you meant..." I didn't know what he meant; I was too tired and walked off without permission. Did he ask me to do something? My thoughts are plagued with how Abbie is doing that I'm hardly paying attention to my surroundings.

The King watches me for a second, turning his head to the side, looking me up and down.

"You may go. I will see you at breakfast."

I bow slightly before taking my leave. I rush back to my tiny room, relieved that I am now on my own and don't have to worry about being watched.

Only when I lay down did I realize something– the King's blanket is gone, the one I always found placed in my room whenever I tried to return it. At least, I had assumed it was his. It saddens me. I had grown attached to it for some reason, and the King's lingering scent comforted me.

I sigh and lay down, trying to find a comfortable position when the door opens, and I sit upright. The King walks in with the blanket, and I stand up immediately.

"Remain where you are," he says. What is he doing here? "I had it washed for you," he says, placing the blanket over me. My brows furrow as the floral scent of the soap wafts to my nose. I sniff the blanket and instantly realize it smells different. I shouldn't find that disappointing, but I do.

"You seem upset," he states while observing me, making me realize I forgot he was in the room.

"No, My King. It just smells different—the soap."

He chuckles as if what I said had amused him.

"Different, how?" he asks, stepping further into my tiny room.

"Just different," I lie, not wanting to admit that it doesn't smell like him.

"Hmm, and that is all?" He smiles. I feel my face heat with embarrassment when he suddenly walks out before returning with a pillow.

"I will swap you," he says, making my brows furrow, confused by what he means. He points to the pillow behind me.

"Pardon, sir?"

"Hand me your pillow, Ivy."

Oh gosh, what was he up to now? He could be so bizarre sometimes.

"Ivy?"

I glance at my pillow before grabbing it and holding it to me. I sniff it. Surely, he doesn't want to swap pillows? Mine will stink with the scent of a rogue. I know my smell repulses most wolves. It is what helps separate us, to help identify pack wolves from rogues.

However, for me, everyone just has their own unique scent. I can't differentiate between rogue and pack wolf; to me, everyone just smells different. Abbie always said something was wrong with me because everyone smelled the same to her back at the orphanage, while we were the odd ones that didn't have a pack scent.

"May I?" the King asks before reaching for my pillow tucked in my arms. He takes it before handing me his.

I sniff it involuntarily, only stopping when I hear him laugh softly, and the blood runs to my face at what I did in front of him.

"Don't be embarrassed, Ivy. You have been sleeping with my scent all week," he says as he tugs the corner of my blanket—well, his blanket.

"You knew?" I ask him, confused.

"Who else would keep putting it in your room when you kept returning it?" he says.

I know the thought of him being in here while I slept should have creeped me out, but it didn't, funnily enough. I guess I was getting used to his presence.

"It's called nesting. You are used to my scent. After a while, scents become comforting, familiar; it will get stronger when I..." he pauses.

When he what? What was he going to do to me? Panic fills me, and my heart rate quickens at the possibilities.

"Do you know what nesting is?" he asks. The only thing that comes to mind is a bird nesting its eggs, so his words make no sense. I shake my head.

"They didn't teach you in the orphanage school?"

"We weren't allowed to attend, we had chores, and rogues aren't-" I stop, having spoken too much. The King growls, and my eyes darted to his.

"You should know the basics, at least of Lycan and werewolves, Ivy," the King says. "I will explain later. For now, get some sleep." He moves to the door before he pauses and looks back at me again.

"If my scent fades, just grab another pillow off my bed or help yourself to my shirts, Ivy. You know where everything in my room is."

Huh, what does he mean? Why is he so strange sometimes?

"If it helps you sleep. Or you could always sleep..." he pauses again. Why is he having so much trouble with his words? He never fumbled over his words this much before.

"Never mind, I will see you in the morning," he says quickly, leaving the room. I can vaguely hear him talking to the guard outside through the closed door. I rearrange my bed and place the pillow down. The moment my head hits the pillow, my entire body relaxes as I become cocooned in his scent.

CHAPTER
TWENTY-THREE

I VY

The sound of banging and crashing wakes me up. As soon as I hear the sound, my body is immediately on high alert. My heart races as I turn my head to peer over at the door. The shadows of movement flicker in from the gap beneath the door. The next thing I hear is running in the corridor. The banging and crashing noises are loud and abrupt, echoing through the hallway and making my heart pound. I can hear the shuffling of feet and the clattering of objects being smashed into the walls. The noise becomes increasingly louder, making me sit up, wondering if we are under attack. Rising to my feet, I rush to the door and peer out through the gap as I open it.

It takes me two seconds to realize the noise is coming from the King's room. Guards rush into his room only to be tossed back out, and my heart races when I see one thrown into the wall next to my door as the King bellows furiously at them.

"Get the fuck out!" he screams, and I flinch when I hear the sound of glass breaking. The guards rush out, and I hear one of them scream and say to get his Beta.

The smashing sounds and growls continue, and my heart rate

increases as I'm frantically trying to figure out what's going on and what has angered the king. While one guard rushes off, the rest are standing guard in the hall. The man on the ground shakes himself off, and another grabs his arm hauling him to his feet. Yet as he turns, I see the deep claw marks slashed down his chest, having ripped through his clothes. I gasp at the sight. Did the King do that to him? I glance at the clock, which tells me it's a little after 2 am.

"What is going on?" Beta Damian asks as he stalks down the corridor in just his boxer shorts. The guards stiffen, and one steps forward.

"The King appears to be drunk, and he's destroying his room," I overhear a guard explain.

The Beta growls and looks up at the ceiling. "I knew it wouldn't last." Beta Damian growls again as he runs his hands down his face.

"You know what date we are approaching, and you also know what we found a few hours ago, so why didn't someone inform me he was drinking heavily?" he snaps. The men look away guiltily.

"Leave all of you. I will deal with it. Dustin, you remain on guard - he is used to your scent in this state."

I wonder which one is Dustin?

"And one of you, get me his servant before you leave." Beta Damian looks at my door, where I stand frozen, watching. I have been caught.

"Ivy, I need your help to clean up," he says, and my hands tremble as I glance at the King's bedroom door. Surely he doesn't want me to go in there while he is angry.

"Ivy!" Beta Damian snaps, yanking me from my thoughts.

"You'll help me clean up!"

"Yes, sir." I gulp down my fear.

I look down at my clothes before nodding, knowing I have no choice. Turning around to grab my shoes, I spot the blanket that was covering me. Picking it up, I sniff it; it's drenched in the King's scent. It is the one from his bed. The other one from my bed is missing. Did he replace it with a new one while I was asleep again so that I could have his scent?

"Ivy, now please," Beta Damian says more urgently, and I spin around to see him standing in my doorway.

Hearing another crash from the room, Beta Damian growls and rushes out. I quickly follow, grabbing my shoes as I move to the door. He pushes the door open, and I gasp at the sight. The walls are marked with deep claw marks, furniture is overturned and smashed to pieces, and all the decorations and paintings have been ripped down and thrown across the room. Shards of broken glass and ceramics from broken tall vases and other items litter the ground, and the curtains have been torn and slashed. The King's bed is the only thing that seems to have been left untouched, but even it is in disarray, with the sheets and blankets haphazardly thrown around. Stepping inside, I see most of his precious books have survived his wrath, but even some of those have been destroyed too.

As I venture further into the room, my heart races as my eyes scan the room to find the King is sitting in a corner with his head in his hands. Beta Damian murmurs to him as he calms him down. The drapes are torn with claw marks down them, and a mirror is smashed; I can't do much about the drapes, so I decide to pick up the broken mirror while also stacking his precious books that have been tossed around carelessly.

However, once I have finished picking up the bigger chunks of broken mirror, I realize I stepped into the room without any supplies. I quietly walk backward toward the door.

I quickly rush out and down the stairs. Clarice is already in the cleaning cupboard with a basket full of supplies and a broom.

"Go, take this, give this to Beta Damian or Gannon. They are the only ones that can get close to him when he is behaving like this. Just leave it at the door and knock," she says, stuffing everything into my arms. My brows pinch because I was just in his room, yet having said that, he was distracted by Beta Damian. However, I am relieved I don't have to go back in there after seeing what he did to the guard.

"Does he get like this a lot?" I ask.

"Only when it's nearing the anniversary. The rebels making an appearance seem to have set him off. I thought this might be the year he didn't break. Unfortunately, I was wrong." Clarice sighs heavily. "Keep those supplies up there. You will need them," Clarice tells me.

Excellent, I'm going to be awoken every night because of some anniversary that triggers him, and no one will even tell me the significance of it. I can't help but wonder what anniversary affects him this way.

Walking up the steps, I hear Beta Damian talking and someone growling. The sound is menacing, and I freeze on the steps. "Fuck, where did she go?" Beta Damian snaps at someone when I am nearly at the top of the steps. "Kyson, you need to calm down. I will find her." Damian assures him.

Find who? I wonder.

I quickly rush up the last couple of steps and stop outside the door, listening to things being tossed around. Beta Damian opens the door when I knock. Clarice said he would take them from me, and I needed to stay away from the King. What I am not expecting is for him to grab me by the front of my shirt and jerk me inside the room!

Taking in the room, I observe the King is pacing like a caged animal, and I can't tear my eyes away from him. Fur is sprouting along his arms, his claws are slipping out, and he rubs a hand down his face before he stops in place.

A deep, menacing growl leaves him when he suddenly shifts, his bones cracking. It is a terrifying sight to watch him shift into a tall and powerful Lycan. His body contorts and expands, and his height rises. Thick fur grows across his entire body, his bones crack and change shape, and his claws extend out of his fingertips. He towers over me when he is done, his eyes glowing with a feral intensity. His muscles ripple beneath the thick layer of fur, and his sharp teeth glint in the dim light. Within seconds, he has gone from man to beast. Fur covers every inch of him, and his teeth have elongated to sharp points. He is terrifying to look at, and a gasp escapes me, making his gaze flicker to mine. I stagger back when he turns on me, bumping into his Beta.

A scream bubbles up my throat and leaves me when he stalks me. I have never seen a shifted Lycan before. I know they stand on two feet and have heard the stories, but it's one thing hearing the tales and quite another witnessing them. Beta Damian grips my arms. "Don't you dare run!" he snaps at me. My feet become rooted to the spot. My fear paralyzes me.

"Kyson! It's just Ivy, your servant!" Damian tells him. Yet the beast he has become doesn't seem to register his words. Instead, his cold, calculating eyes are fixated on me.

"It is Ivy! Kyson. It's not an intruder. Can't you smell her?" Beta Damian shouts as he launches himself in front of me and into the King's path, just as the King barrels towards me.

My heart beats like a drum in my chest as I clutch the broom in my shaky hands.

He shoves past his Beta and sniffs the air. And I turn to run when Damian moves to hold up his hand.

"Ivy, hold still!" Damian snaps and my eyes dart to him. Is he mad? Does he not see the monster on the verge of killing me? However, my feet stop, doing as he has asked. The King stops in front of me. His canines protrude; his face has lengthened into a Lycan, revealing his sharp teeth.

He is at least three feet taller than before, and I only come up to his stomach. He would need to duck to fit through the door! It's obvious his claws are deadly- they're so long and sharp looking. The evidence is around us with the deep gashes in the walls. His breathing is harsh, and his fur is so black it has a blue hue under the dim lights.

Despite knowing I should run from this monster, I cannot move. His gaze is inhuman, calculating, menacing, and curious all in one. I can't help but feel a strange sense of wonder for the creature in front of me. I am terrified, yet strangely mesmerized. Is he going to eat me?

Or rip me to pieces? He leans down and sniffs my face. I am shaking and worried I might wet myself! My legs tremble so badly that I think they might give out at any second.

The King moves closer. My feet finally seem to work, yet it does me no good because he backs me into the wall. My eyes widen as he stalks me. I can feel his breath on my neck. It's hot, and I can feel the hairs on my body standing on end. He pauses.

With the wall behind my back, I close my eyes, waiting for death. I feel a soft breeze in my hair as he sniffs at me. His nose trails down the side of my face to my neck. His breath brushes my skin when he puffs softly and licks my cheek. His furry rough hands grip my arms, his claws sliding gently around my arms when he presses closer.

"Ivy!" his voice rumbles, and I shiver. Beta Damian lets out a breath that makes my eyes open. I turn my face away from the King's sharp teeth as he dips his face lower and continues to sniff me.

"Yes, Kyson. Ivy. Your servant girl, remember her?" Beta Damian comes and takes the broom from my hands; my hands lock around it, not wanting him to take it.

"He won't hurt you. He has trouble recognizing people in this form; his anger sometimes blinds him to everyone. Just remember not to touch him or approach him from behind; he is more animal than a man in this state."

I blink at him. I have no intention of touching him at all; he's the one touching me. I don't even want to be in here right now, especially while he's like this! He looks terrifying. Gosh, what chaos my life has turned into so suddenly.

Beta Damian pulls him away, and I let out a breath. Slowly, I reach down, grabbing a trash bag, refusing to take my eyes off the King in case he attacks me.

Beta Damian helps me clean up while the King watches, following me around the room. Damian a few times reminds him of who I am, yet the King still stalks me, he seems almost fascinated with everything I am doing when I hiss. Picking up a piece of cloth, I don't notice the broken glass, and slice my fingers. I jerk my hand back only to have it snatched away and caught in his grip. He growls holding my hand before his face when the door opens. The King moves with impossible speed and grabs me. I shriek. He shoves me behind him like he is protecting me from whoever just entered his quarters.

A feral growl leaves him as he turns to face the intruder. I peer around him and recognize the person who has just stepped into the room: it's the man from the car, Gannon.

"It is Gannon, My King," he addresses him, barring his neck, yet he isn't afraid of the King at all as he enters, moving to help Damian.

"Sorry, Gannon," the King says, and the man nods, walking over and grabbing a bag. I am still trapped behind the King between the bed and the wall, and he blocks my way.

Would it be rude if I walked over the top of his bed to get past him? I push that thought away. It would definitely be rude.

I clear my throat awkwardly, but he doesn't hear me over the low growling emanating coming from him. I look at the other two men for help. Is his Beta laughing at me, trying to squeeze past him?

No matter what I do, I will brush up against him, so I hesitantly reach up and tap his shoulder with my index finger. His reflexes are so quick I don't even see him move. I trip over my own feet, stepping away from him when he suddenly has my hand that taps him in his grip. He is suddenly facing me.

He blinks, cocking his head to the side and staring at me strangely like he is trying to remember who I am. His silver eyes reflect back at me. I swallow, bumping into his bedside table when I step back.

"I, um, can I get past?" I squeak out, trying to maneuver around him. But everywhere I step, he steps in my path until I step into him. He growls when his eyes dart to my fingers, and his tongue sneaks out and licks them. I gasp at the tingling sensation when his tongue laps up the blood that runs down my arm. He's going to eat me!

I jerk my hand from his grip, finding my fingers healed when he tilts his head to the side, watching me. Feeling his dark gaze on me, I try to step around him, but he blocks my path and keeps doing so. He growls, the sound becoming annoyed. His furry hands grip my arms and lift me. My feet leave the ground and dangle in the air when he brings me face-to-face with him.

"What are you doing?" he asks, his voice sounding much deeper and rougher in this form. I didn't expect him to be able to talk so well in this form. Werewolves can mindlink but not speak with their mouths in wolf form. And also did before when he spoke my name so seeing it is quite shocking. My feet dangle as he brings me to eye level with him.

I blink at him, stunned at how close his face is to mine, before hyperventilating. I think I'm having a panic attack. My clammy hands grip his huge furry shoulders, his head dropping to look at them touching him when he growls, his eyes snapping back to mine. He tilts his head to the side, watching me closely when I notice his tongue roll across his razor sharp pointed teeth. It suddenly becomes extremely hard to breathe as my panic sets in. My heart is racing so fast I can hear it in my ears.

He is going to kill me.

He is going to eat me.

His teeth look sharp. I'm about to be a Lycan snack.

"Please don't eat me," I blurt out, fisting the fur on his shoulders, trying to push away from him. He laughs, his eyes twinkling with amusement. The sound is odd, rough, and echoey. My breathing becomes harsher, and I feel dizzy as I push away from him, yet his grip does not waiver. He pulls me to him, crushing me against his chest, his tongue running up the column of my neck and I gasp at the feel while one arm moves to wrap my legs around his waist. My hands gripping his thick fur loosen as my body turns languid in his strong arm. I need air.

I can't breathe...

I'm aware of the sensation of falling as I tumble back in his arms, the room spinning around me as I choke for breath. His hand moves quickly to catch me, his claws scraping the sides of my neck.

"Ivy?" he purrs, sniffing me, then he growls, the sound thunderous.

My eyes roll into the back of my head, and darkness swallows me.

He can kill me now; at least I won't feel it.

CHAPTER
TWENTY-FOUR

I VY
I wake up, not knowing how much time has passed. I don't recognize where I am, so I look up at the ceiling only to see the King's bed canopy above me. Blinking, I vaguely hear people talking when something beside me moves which makes the bed dip. I glance around, seeing Beta Damian and Gannon at the end of the bed. Turning my head, I see the King sitting beside me. I am in his bed!

"Sleeping beauty awakens," Beta Damian announces. I jerk upright, only for a hand to land on my shoulder and push me down again. My back protests at being lain on.

"Lie back down. I gave you quite the scare. I didn't mean to, but you will stay in here with me tonight," the King says calmly, and I shake my head, trying to get back up.

"You will stay with me tonight," he repeats, leaving no room for argument.

Frantically, I look to his Beta and Gamma, who say nothing in my defense. Are they really planning to leave me in here with him? He was a beast a few seconds ago. What about Clarice's words? She said not to come near him in this form and stay out of his way. I can't do that if he forces me to remain here with him.

"I'm sorry to get you all out of bed. Leave the rest. I will have it fixed tomorrow," King Kyson tells them.

"You sure you can handle the mess?" his Beta asks.

"I am sure I can manage," the King tells them, and both men's eyes dart to me for a second before they both bare their necks and walk out, leaving me alone with a man that could become a savage beast at any moment. Only minutes ago, I thought I would die.

The door clicks shut softly and my breathing picks up. Despite the room's vast size, I suddenly feel claustrophobic and caged in like a mouse trapped in a lion's den.

Overwhelmed, I pray that I will pass out again. Terror fills me, and I am suddenly too frightened to move.

"I won't hurt you, Ivy. I didn't mean to lose control like that," he says, his voice calm and composed, as if nothing had happened. "You can speak freely. It's just us, not that Damian or Gannon would ever speak against you," he says.

I am already very aware of that fact. Because they just left me alone and trapped me in here with a man that looked more like a terrifying creature than a person mere moments ago. I swing my legs over the side of the bed, wanting to go back to the safety of my room.

"Lie back down now," he orders, and my body falls back on the bed under the command, unable to fight it as it washes over me like a tidal wave of pure Alpha dominance.

His blankets are soft under my hands, but my back shouts in protest and I can't help the whimper that escapes my lips. "You don't leave me!" he growls and tears prick my eyes.

"What's wrong? Answer me," he asks, leaning over me.

"My back... Please, I can't lay on it," I tell him, and his eyes widen and he pulls away.

"Sorry, I forgot. You may roll on your side," he says, turning me to face him. His skin is clear – no longer covered in fur – except for the shadowing of stubble on his face. His dark eyes watch me curiously.

"I am a man, not a beast now. Don't be frightened," he says, grabbing my hand and placing it on his chest. He holds it there, and my eyes look at my hand, his skin warm beneath my palm.

All I can do is blink at the man that is becoming stranger by the second—and why does he keep touching me? Does he have a rogue fetish?

I have heard of such things mentioned by the adults at the orphanage. Abbie and I once overheard one of the gardeners speaking to Mrs. Daley about having a rogue fetish.

He said that he liked being a 'puppet master' and that he hoped we would be auctioned off when we came of age so he could buy one of us to use for his fantasies.

For some reason, that day is forever ingrained in my memory. I clench my eyes shut, trying to shove the memory away. Yet, no matter how hard I try to shake the thoughts off, they eventually consume me and force me back there to relive them. Our past is always lurking in the shadows of our minds, haunting us like ghosts.

On that terrible day, the gardener had leaned against his shovel, having just dug up the vegetable patch as he talked to the butcher who had just dropped off the meat rations. He was a middle-aged man with a thick build and sun-weathered skin. He had a gruff, stern demeanor, and his dark eyes hinted at something sinister. He had a thick beard, and his clothes were dirty and tattered from his garden work.

Abbie and I picked up the last of the carrots he dug up and dropped them into our baskets.

"Mrs. Daley," the gardener had said as Mrs. Daley set some lemonade down on the steps

"Hmm?" she hummed.

"How much?" he had asked, making me glance over at him to find his dark eyes on us. I peered down at the carrots in the basket.

"I'd like to buy one of them. I'm sure they'd make a good servant or even a pet." He chuckled, and Mrs. Daley huffed.

"Servant, yes, that is about all they're good for!"

"Well, I can think of a few other ways," the butcher laughed. Mrs. Daley purses her lips, and I watch her through the veil of my hair as I continue to rummage for carrots in the upturned soil.

"Are they obedient?" the gardener questioned. Mrs. Daley whistled, and we both looked up.

"Get up!" she snapped. Abbie and I both immediately stand, wiping our hands on our aprons.

The gardener laughed. "Perfect, nothing I love more than playing puppet master." Abbie and I looked at each other.

"Are the rogue girls at the brothel not doing it for you no more?" the butcher inquired.

"Don't pretend you don't have a rogue fetish, Martin. I have seen how you order them around." The butcher laughed.

"I never denied it, but they aren't as obedient as these two," the gardener stated, nodding toward us.

"Back to work!" Mrs. Daley snapped at us, and we dropped back to the ground, gathering the carrots.

"Hands off the redhead. I've got that one well-trained. You can have the other," the butcher replied.

"That is if the Alpha lets them live!" Mrs. Daley huffed, causing the gardener to groan.

"Why did you have to say that? Ruin my fantasy... Charlene," the gardener said. Abbie and I glanced at one another. That was the first time we heard someone use her first name. The gardener stomped off to his gardening.

"Such a shame that the chances they live are so slim... Such a waste," the butcher exclaimed.

The butcher gave her the bill, and Mrs. Daley opened her purse to pay.

"Maybe one day we could find another arrangement?" asked the butcher. Mrs. Daley looked at him strangely.

"We can discuss it another time, Doyle. When Katrina is not around. You know she is fond of the mutts."

The Butcher, too, was just as sick, if not worse, because he eventually acted on his sick amusements.

Back then, we didn't know what he meant when we heard the term. We were only twelve, and it wasn't until we grew older that we learned what they truly meant by those words and the intentions behind them – it meant becoming his sex slave, to be dominated by some sicko. Abbie swore she would kill herself if he or the butcher bought her and I vowed the same.

"I know you're scared, but please don't fear me. I don't want you to be scared of me," the King says, tearing me from the invading memory. I blink and turn my attention to the King.

"And just for the record, Lycans don't eat people," he says with a soft laugh.

Was this the same man as before? I briefly entertain the idea that he had a lobotomy while I was passed out. He seems so carefree now, just an ordinary person with how he speaks so casually. I could almost lose sight of the fact that he was a King.

"Where did you just go?" he asks, leaning down and sniffing at me. I freeze as he leans over me, pressing his nose into my neck. He pulls away, giving me a strange look. "Surely, I didn't make your fear this potent?" he asks.

"Nowhere, my King," I answer, not wanting to anger him.

"Not physically, Ivy. Your mind, where did it take you? You seem confused," he states, and I nod, sucking my bottom lip into my mouth. Yet he still holds my hand.

"You are the only person, other than Gannon and Damian, that has gotten near me in that state and not been hurt or killed. In my Lycan form, I recognized you even after I lost control," he says, and my brows pinch. Was that supposed to make me feel better about the situation–that he didn't kill me?

"You speak very little. You're so quiet all the time," he states, looking at me inquisitively. What am I supposed to say? *I'm a filthy rogue that you ordered to lie in your bed with you for some reason, and you are rubbing my hand encased in your huge one like I am some pet you are trying to decide whether to put out of its misery?*

He tilts his head to the side, watching me for a second as he holds my gaze. I can't pull mine away. He shakes his head in amusement, releasing the hold he has over me. The King then yawns, covering his mouth and rolling onto his back. Yet he doesn't let go of my hand, still clasping it in his.

I want to tug it away from him, but I also like the feel of his big hand covering mine – the tingles make my body relax, and I yawn, too, wondering what time it is.

The King eventually falls asleep, soft snores filling the room, and I think I lie there frozen for about an hour before I gain the courage to reclaim my hand and carefully sit up.

With slow movements, I try to move toward the edge of the bed. I'm careful not to move the bed too much.

I stand up and take a step, and the floorboard creaks under my foot. I freeze. My heartbeat thumps in my ears frantically. I glance over at him before taking another when he speaks.

"I will give you three seconds to get back in the bed with me, or you may find yourself tied to it and unable ever to leave it, Ivy. The choice is yours," King Kyson states with a mischievous smile on his face. I gulp, my heart pounding in my chest at his words while I consider my options.

CHAPTER
TWENTY-FIVE

I VY

I peek over at him. He hasn't moved, and his eyes remain closed, which makes me wonder if I imagined his words. I am exhausted after all. I take another step toward the door, wondering if he's sleep-talking.

"I do not advise you to move another step, Ivy," he says, and my entire body turns rigid. So he is definitely awake, then. I don't move, and I wait for him to continue speaking, but he doesn't. I feel a chill down my spine. I swallow hard, my heart racing as I turn to face him.

"Can I... just go back...?" I try to ask, but he cuts me off.

"One," he purrs. Frantically, I turn to look at the door. It's just there. A few meters away...

"But..." and I suck in a deep breath glancing at him.

"Two," he says, opening one eye to peep at me. He smirks before closing his eyes again and yawning.

"My King, I don't think..."

Suddenly, he moves too quickly for my eyes to track, and the air is knocked from my lungs. A shriek of fear escapes me, and the next second, I am pinned beneath him on the bed. My brain suddenly forgets how to breathe, forgets a natural bodily function as fear steals my capacity to function.

"Three..."

The King smiles down at me. He purrs, the noise making his chest vibrate against mine. When he moves, I become very aware of the fact that he is pressed between my legs, and his entire body covers me. I gulp, seeing his face so close to mine, and he smirks. His eyes flash as he stares back for a second.

He drops his face closer to mine, running his nose along my cheek.

The purring emanating from him grows louder before he presses his nose in my neck and inhales deeply. This sends my heart rate leaping and spluttering in my chest.

I try to remind myself that Lycans don't eat people – he said they don't eat people – yet he sniffs me like he's about to devour his favorite meal and is savoring its scent before consuming it.

"I could devour you, and it would never be enough," he growls as if to corroborate my thoughts, and goosebumps rise on my arms at the sound of his voice.

"But Lycans don't eat people," I squeak, praying he wasn't lying. He runs his nose back up my neck and across my cheek, stopping at my lips. The King laughs, his stubble tickling my face while I stare wide-eyed at his erratic behavior.

"Not that sort of devouring," he laughs, shaking his head. "So pure," he mumbles, rubbing my lips with his thumb, his eyes trained on them. I silently pray Damian and Gannon will return. I don't even care about the position they find me in as long as they can get me out of here.

"No, I am a rogue," I blurt, confused. Does he not see that I am the least pure there is? Rogues have no pack, nothing. We are the mutts of society.

Kyson pulls away from me, sitting up on his elbows and looking down at me. Although his position never changes, his weight no longer crushes the air from my lungs.

"How old were you when you were brought to the orphanage again?" he asks curiously.

"Ten, My King," I answer.

"And you had no schooling at all? Not even before that?"

"No," I tell him. Kyson clicks his tongue and looks away. He appears annoyed by my answer. Did I say something wrong?

Wiggling, I shuffle beneath him, trying to get out from underneath him. However, when his eyes move back to mine, they make me freeze and shrink back into the bed.

"You know nothing about Lycans or werewolves or anything at all?" he questions.

"I know how to clean. I can cook a bit, too," I say, not understanding why he questions my ability. What purpose would knowledge serve me when I am a rogue?

"Do you know what sex is?"

My jaw drops, and my face heats up. That word, I do know. I nod, shrinking away from him.

"But yet you're a virgin...pure," he emphasizes the last word, and my face heats further at my idiocy of what he meant before.

The lack of oxygen must have muddled my brain or stunned it. I must have sounded like an idiot. No wonder he questions me. He must have thought something was with me... mentally. I mean I can't read, and from the way I'm talking, it sounds like I don't know anything about the world. Embarrassment floods through me when his words finally register.

Wait.... Did he want me to become his sex slave? The thought horrifies me. Tears suddenly burn the backs of my eyes, and I squeeze them shut, trying to will myself to calm down and not make noise.

He is the King; he can do what he wants with me. I am a rogue; he could kill me, and no one would care even to ask why.

"Is that why I am here? Are you going...?" I ask before stopping, like not knowing would somehow lessen the horror of it.

"Ivy, I am not going to have sex with you. I was just asking a question," he says, brushing my cheek with his hand. I open my eyes and peek up at him. He almost seems sad before his eyes flicker black for a second. He sighs heavily and drops his head on my chest.

"I hate how skittish you are; it makes me want to kill your head-mistress," he growls. I don't know what to say.

"I don't want you to be scared. I don't know how many more times I can say that before you believe it. Even Abbie spilled stew all over Damian earlier, and she begged at his feet for her life. It's madness," Kyson growls.

His words make my mind wander to Abbie, and I wonder if she is alright. I haven't seen her in what feels like forever. I miss her terribly.

"I won't hurt you, Ivy. Not ever. Do you understand?" I nod, and he growls.

"No, say it," the King growls.

"I understand," I whisper.

"No, say it. Say, I won't hurt you."

"You won't hurt me," I sputter out, turning my face away from his angry gaze. Only his fingers on my chin turn my face back to his.

"I won't hurt you. I don't want to hurt you. Therefore, I won't," the King tells me. He may not want to hurt me right now, but that can change. It always changes.

He studies me for a second. His hand moves back to my face. His thumb brushes over my lips again before he tugs the bottom one down.

"Um, sir...?"

He smiles as if my awkwardness amuses him in some way.

"Kyson," he murmurs. His eyes flick to mine for a second, yet his thumb keeps playing with my bottom lip. He settles his weight back on top of me, and my breath lodges in my throat like a ball threatening to choke me to death.

"I have to leave the castle tomorrow. I need to go to a nearby kingdom. Damian and Gannon will remain here with you unless you want to come with me," the King says.

Are there more kingdoms nearby here? I wonder.

"I thought you were the last Lycan Royal?" I ask without thinking. He smiles back at me.

"There is that voice. You can ask me anything, Ivy. I like your questions, and I like hearing your voice." I swallow. The King laughs softly, his chest rumbling against mine.

"It reminds me that you are still breathing," he laughs again. Wow, even the King is aware of my brain cells that randomly die in his presence.

"And yes, I am the Last Lycan Royal. Damian and Gannon don't want me to leave the castle since the rebellion has risen from the shadows again. However, we need to go back to the old crime scene. The castle I will be visiting used to belong to the last fallen King and Queen."

A memory tinkers in the back of my mind, pulling me back to a time I try not to remember... A time I wish I'd forgotten. Before I know it, the room fades as the memory surges back in.

)◉(

We were camped out by a stream. The night was warm and still. The air was heavy with humidity, and the stars twinkled in the dark night sky. The sound of the stream rushing down toward the waterfall drowned out the sound of the crickets. I remember that night so vividly, from the breeze in my hair to the smell of damp earth and wildflowers that filled the air. The moon shone bright, casting a gentle glow over the area and illuminating the trees and grass. Abbie and I, just two young girls, had been lying on the grass under an old oak tree, our feet on the trunk. My mother and Abbie's mother, Lina, sat around the fire, talking softly when Abbie suggested we dip our feet in the water. Abbie and I both got up to wade our feet through the water. I hummed to a tune. I have no memory of where I heard it, but it always brought comfort to me for some reason.

"Girls, not too close to the water. It is deeper than it looks," my mother scolded.

I peered over my shoulder to my mother who was suddenly on her feet, alert. She always panicked when either of us came too close to the river. Neither of us could swim a stroke to save our lives. I nearly drowned once when we were on the run; I sank straight to the bottom like a stone. My father pulled me out, but it has made me wary of water since. We turned back and moved closer to the edge when a sound startled me.

I looked back to the river when a noise sounded among the trees, and her startled expression went to both of us. My father burst through the trees looking terrified. I had never seen him so scared. He was typically the stoic one.

His eyes scanned the area frantically, looking pale as though he'd seen a ghost. His hair was wet, and he was sweating when the cloying scent of wolfsbane reached my nose. He was drenched in blood, and he had an arrow sticking out of his shoulder. Seeing his pain-stricken face was like something out of a nightmare. Every alarm bell in my brain sounded. My mother rushed over to him, her face contorted with worry.

"What happened?" she demanded to know as she quickly broke the arrow, leaving the point in his shoulder. She tried to pull it out, but my father stopped her, telling her we didn't have time.

"We need to run." His eyes scanned all of us when the sound of shouting in the distance drew closer.

"Dad?" Abbie questioned, and I looked for him. Where was he?

"Run!" he bellowed as he ran straight toward me. My mother grabbed Lina, Abbie's mother's hand, and yanked her up.

"It's the King's guard! They have found us! They have come for..."

"For what?" I had asked as my father gripped me around the waist and jumped into the water, swimming to the other side. Lina had Abbie, who was screaming for her father, but Lina said nothing as she swam across;.

149

"Why are they chasing us?" I asked, scared when something burst from the trees with savage snarls.

"Because of King Garret and Queen Tatiana. Now run! Don't stop, don't look back, run!" my father growled.

"Go, girls, hurry!" Lina snapped at us.

"Wait, where is dad?" Abbie demanded. Lina shakes her head.

"You need to run!"

"Not without dad." Lina grabbed her face in her hands.

"They took him."

"Who?"

"The King's guard," Lina shouted, half crying.

"We don't have time for this!" my mother snarled at her while my father's eyes scanned the trees.

"I don't understand..." I looked at my father for answers, but it was my mother who answered.

"That wannabe Queen bitch... Landeena...Now the Valkyrie's," she snarled furiously. I still don't know what she meant to this day. Something sounded across the river, and my father snarled.

My mother spun, glancing across the river, then she turned on us. "Run!" The panic on her face set us moving.

Abbie gripped my hand, and we both took off running through the darkened forest until we could run no more, not knowing our lives would be forever changed.

)❀(

That was how we came across Alpha Dean and his cruel son's pack; we were driven right into their clutches after running for days. Our families were originally headed in the other direction.

CHAPTER
TWENTY-SIX

I VY "Queen Tatiana and King Garret?" I ask. I don't know why I said those names, but I vaguely remember overhearing my mother mention those names before she was killed. In fact, she screamed it. Screamed it with so much hatred that it must have stuck with me.

"I am surprised you know those names. You would have only been a small child during their power," the King says, his eyes studying me.

"I remember hearing the names. Is that where you are...?" I ask before shutting my mouth and mentally cursing myself. *Quiet Ivy, you don't question the King*, I remind myself, yet he said I could ask questions. But old habits make me question every little thing; is it a trick; is he using it to find something to punish me for?

"Why do you do that? You're going to say something, then stop?" he asks before rolling and tugging me with him. My stomach lurches when he pulls me to straddle his lap as he sits up and leans against the headboard of the bed.

This new position is even more awkward than the last, and I

become rigid. My hands awkwardly clutch my thighs as I sit up, wanting to climb off him. It's impossible to relax in a position like this.

The King grabs my hands. I try to pull out of his grip when he places both of them on his naked chest. I stare at my hands touching him, my eyes roaming over him. His chest was broad and hard, with defined muscles and lightly tanned skin. There is a light dusting of dark hair across his chest, yet his skin is soft despite the hardness of muscle beneath his skin.

His skin is hot under my palms, and I can feel his heart beating steadily in his chest while mine sputters, threatening to rip free of my body.

"You never answered?" the King says, making me try to remember his question. "Why do you stop when you want to know something? Knowledge is the key. You should ask questions. How else would you learn the answers? I like it when you speak. I want to know everything about you. I find you fascinating."

Me? Fascinating? How? The only thing he could learn from me was how to change his bedsheets and fold his towels the way he likes them. There is absolutely nothing remarkable about me that he could want to know.

"And to answer your question, yes, I am going there tomorrow, but I would like it if you came with me. Would you like to come?"

"Is it okay for me to leave the castle?" I ask.

"Under guard, but yes, you can leave."

Why would I need a guard? I wonder, but the thought of leaving excites me.

"Can Abbie come?"

"She can, but I would rather it be just us. I want to spend time with you. Although, if you would be more comfortable with her coming, I can arrange it," he says.

"Why?" I blurt like an idiot. It makes no sense as to why he would want to spend time with his servant. It is odd. The King smiles. I don't think I have seen him smile as much as I have tonight. Yet I find that I like it when he does.

"So you can speak your mind... and you now you ask the right questions," he chuckles, his hands landing on my thighs.

He runs his hands up to the apex of my legs, and it hits me–I glance down at my naked legs. Shame washes over me. Where did my pants go? I tug, trying to get my oversized shirt down, when I realize it is one of his.

"My King?" I ask, tugging at the neckline of the shirt I am wearing.

"Mmm?" he asks, his eyes on his hands as he pushes the hemline of his shirt higher, revealing my cotton panties beneath it. "I changed your clothes; I prefer it when you smell like me," he tells me, answering the question I needed to know but couldn't bring myself to ask. His words make me swallow.

"They didn't see you; I made them turn around," he murmurs, yet his eyes still watch his hands as they slide up to my hips. His thumbs brush over my panties, and he inhales deeply.

"I don't want you sleeping in that room anymore. You will remain with me. I will have your things brought in here tomorrow when we are gone."

My brain buzzes, yet I am still stuck on the question of why.

His eyes dart to mine. "You want to know why? It must be confusing."

I nod my head.

"I have never wanted someone the way I have wanted you, and I won't get much sleep with you so far away. I want you close," he says, looking up at me.

"But sir, I am your slave," I speak slowly, hoping my words will sink in and make him see reason, or at least clarify what he wants with me.

"And I am the King. No one would dare question my intentions, Ivy."

"What are your intentions?" I whisper.

"What do you think they are?" he asks in return.

Well, if I knew, I wouldn't be asking, I think dryly.

"Speak freely, Ivy. You are safe with me."

I briefly wonder if I should say it, yet he keeps telling me I can ask, and the burning desire to know is bothering me. What's the worst he could do, kill me? At least I would die knowing.

"Do you have a rogue fetish?" I ask. His eyebrows raise and he appears to be shocked by my words.

His lips tug up into a grin before he laughs. His whole body moves beneath me like he can't contain his laughter at what I asked.

"No, I don't have a rogue fetish, Ivy. I also don't eat people; I am not trying to have sex with you, though I wouldn't say no if you wanted to, and I don't want you to be my slave anymore. Does that clear up any of your odd questions, or are there more?" he chuckles again. The blood rushes to my face when he speaks again.

"And what is a rogue fetish? Where did you hear that?" he asks, his eyes narrowing in a playful way. My face heats up more at his question. I didn't think I would have to explain it to him. Shouldn't he know?

"Um, at the orphanage..."

"At the orphanage? By whom?" he asks, his facial expression suddenly turning serious.

"The gardener... Abbie and I overheard him saying he had a fetish for rogues. He liked that he could do what he wanted to them, and no one would care. He hoped we would be sold so he could buy us and said we were more obedient than other girls."

"He said that in front of you both?"

"No, we weren't supposed to be listening." I scratch my neck and try to climb off him, but his hands move to my thighs, holding me in place.

"When? Just before I saw you?" he asks.

I shake my head. "No, when I was twelve. We didn't understand what he meant... not until Abbie asked Katrina."

The King growls angrily and his eyes flicker.

"Children are off-limits! I hate how they treat the rogues," he snarls, making me jump slightly at his tone, though his words confuse me; wasn't he the one that made the laws?

CHAPTER
TWENTY-SEVEN

I VY

"I am not angry at you, Ivy," he clarifies.

"If you hate the way they treat rogues, why do you let them?" I realize instantly the mistake I had made. I just questioned the King's ability to rule fairly, insinuating he is unfit. His eyes lift to mine instantly, and I gasp.

"I... I didn't mean... You are a good King," I blurt out in a panic. His features don't change, though I am shocked by his response.

"I am working on it. Adults know their crimes and are responsible for them. We stopped the killing of rogue children, and most packs agreed to take them in or cast them out once they were of age. Some, however, did not agree with the laws, and then some packs started systematically killing them again. Eventually, that also stopped, but rogue children have started showing up dead again recently; that is why I came to your pack that day. We were investigating your Alpha."

"You want to help the rogues?" I ask, incredulous.

"Yes, they are still part of my rule. Just because some are problematic doesn't mean all are, Ivy. I never agreed with them killing rogue children. Children are salvageable, innocent. And I tried to prevent it. But I will try harder," he says.

"Why my Alpha, though?" I question.

"Because his pack is the only pack that still kills rogues when they come of age. Also, I found it odd that only two girls were listed in the orphanage as rogues."

I nod. "Yes, we had a few come and go, but once the new Alpha took over, no one lived. He killed them all," I reply.

"All of them?" he asked.

"Yes. Eventually, we were the only ones left. I overheard Mrs. Daley speaking of the rogue attacks – that she expected new children to come – but they never did," I answer him. His brows crease together, and he nods.

"I will have to go back there then."

"So, you don't have a fetish?"

"No, more like an obsession. But only with one rogue," he says, cutting me off. I blink down at him before realizing where my hands have fallen.

"Sorry," I mutter, moving them off his muscular abs. The King places them back.

"I like it when you touch me, Ivy, so don't be afraid to," he whispers, making my eyes dart to his.

He moves my hands over his abs, pecs, and chest to his shoulders, forcing me closer to him. My palms tingle violently, and I pull my hand back, looking at it.

My brows pinch, wondering why it tingles the way it does. Turning my face back to him, I find I am half lying on him, and his face is barely an inch from mine. His scent is overwhelmingly strong, so close to his neck, and I inhale and before I can stop myself, I press my face to the side of his neck. I only realize what I have done when his fingers run through my hair, and I jump.

"What do your instincts tell you to do, Ivy?" the King asks.

But I can't answer that; my instincts are all over the place. I want to touch him, caress him, smell him, lick him. My mind falters at the last one. I shouldn't want to lick him. What a weird thing to have the urge to do!

"What if I told you my instincts are the same as yours; you're just better at suppressing them right now?" he whispers, and I turn my face to look at him.

"Pardon, my King?" I ask.

"What if I want to touch you, smell you, have you close, share my bed with you, Ivy?"

"Sir?" I ask and try to pull away, but he grips my neck and pulls me back close, forcing me to lean against his chest.

"What if I wanted you to do the same? What if I wanted to kiss you?" he asks, his fingers massaging the back of my neck. His eyes flicker black, and he smiles as he moves his face closer.

Did he want to kiss me?

Does he want to kiss his rogue servant? Yet, with that thought – as crazy as it sounds – I can't help but wonder what his lips would feel like against mine. Would the same tingling sensation burn them?

"Would you stop me, Ivy?" he asks, his lips brushing against mine as he speaks. I gulp. Could I stop him? Was I allowed? Did I want to? Why was everything so confusing? I shake my head, and he purrs, the sound slowing my heart rate like a low thrumming, calling me to him when I feel his lips press against mine. A strangled noise escapes my lips that turns to a gasp as he pulls me closer.

His tongue brushes over my bottom lip before I feel his thumb press on my chin, forcing my mouth to open slightly. My lips burn and tingle, and I don't think the sensation can get stronger when his tongue suddenly slips between them, brushing against mine. I have never kissed anyone in my life before; never even come close.

He groans, crushing me against his chest, and his grip tightens on my hair. His tongue brushes mine again, and a moan escapes me at the taste of him before I kiss him back, loving the taste and the feel of him holding me. The King deepens the kiss, his tongue leaving no part of my mouth untouched.

Eventually, I pull back from him, feeling lightheaded and needing air, and he lets me, pecking my lips softly. He doesn't let me pull away though; instead, he pulls me down and presses my head against his shoulder.

I inhale his scent, feeling confused while breathing the smell of him in. He turns his face toward mine and kisses me below my eye.

"So, will you come with me tomorrow, or should I organize Abbie? But I promise I have no ill intentions with you, Ivy."

"Yes, My King," I answer, feeling weird that I just kissed a man. No, not a man... the Lycan King!

"For God's sake, woman, call me Kyson! Just say it once, please," he says, pulling away to look at me. I peek at his waiting face. "Say my name, Ivy," he demands.

I chew my lip, and his eyes dart to them before he brushes my face with his nose and purrs. Closing my eyes, I suck in a shaky breath.

"Kyson," I whisper.

"Say it again," he murmurs, and I shake my head against his shoulder, and he growls. A squeak escapes my lips as he moves, trapping me beneath him again. My heart beats frantically, and he purrs loudly, rubbing his chest against mine and burying his face in my neck. I feel his tongue run over my exposed skin before his lips press below my ear.

"Say it again."

My voice shakes as I stammer his name out like I have any right to mutter it. "Kyson."

He growls, but the noise is more playful when he presses his lips against mine again, only harder while his hand moves to my hair, tilting my head up. He once again steals my breath, kissing me deeply. His hands tug at the strands, sending shivers down my spine when he breaks it, pulls away, and peers down at me.

"Good girl," he purrs. "My girl," he murmurs then smiles as he leans in softly pecking them again.

"You call me Kyson. Not King, not Sir, not Lord, or any other term you can conjure up – only my name from now on."

"But-"

"I don't care where we are. You are to call me Kyson. Am I clear?"

I nod, staring at his neck.

He kisses my forehead. "We should sleep. We must be up in a couple of hours," he says, rolling off me.

He tugs the blanket back and climbs under them before patting the spot beside him. When I don't move, he rolls his eyes, grabs my legs, hauls me over to him, and tugs the blanket up.

The King then slides his arm under my pillow, bringing my back flush against his chest. He places his other arm around me before kissing my shoulder.

"Sleep, Ivy," he whispers, and I sigh but close my eyes, wondering how long this behavior of his will last before he realizes what a mistake he's making and kicks me out. But for now, I will sleep.

CHAPTER
TWENTY-EIGHT

IVY

Gentle hands move across my skin; tingles rush over me, and the warmth of the King's chest spreads across my back. Opening my eyes, I can see light filtering into the room, but not much. It must be early morning. The sun is just rising and chasing the shadows in the room away.

His wandering hand is now beneath the shirt I'm wearing as he caresses my skin. The King's touch reminds me of last night, and I feel the blood rush to my face at the memory.

His purr is deep, resonating from the center of his chest and vibrating against my back as his light touch moves higher. Kyson moves behind me, and I roll onto my back beside him to find him propped up on one elbow, staring down at me.

He smiles that breathtaking smile, leaning his face toward mine as he speaks. "Morning," he growls before I can reply. His lips are capturing mine.

His tongue traces over the seam of my lips, his hand trails higher underneath my shirt and he cups my breast in his large hand. The pad of his thumb flicks over my hardened nipple as he toys with it.

I gasp and pull away – unsure what to do with his touch – and he chuckles, nipping at my chin and jaw up to my ear. Yet, his hand remains inside my shirt making my skin burn with sensations I've never felt before.

"My King," I murmur. My voice sounds breathy even to my own ears. What is this insane man doing now? The King ignores my words; his only answer is in a low growl that makes me jump as his hand squeezes and plays with my breast.

My entire body feels warm from his touch as his lips move back to mine, swallowing any words I may have wanted to say. My body feels foreign, and his touch brings strange sensations.

The King presses his knee between my legs as he presses me into the soft thick mattress. His leg pushes between my thighs, and an unfamiliar sensation moves through my abdomen, between my legs; a pulse I have never encountered before. Slightly uncomfortable, I jerk away, breaking the kiss. The space between my thighs feels wet and has developed a pulse. His touch sends shockwaves through my body, awakening a part of me I did not know existed. The heat radiates from my core, and the desire to be close to him is overwhelming.

"Ky- son," I stutter out, feeling flustered as his hand trails across my lower stomach.

His hand stops and he pulls back to look down at me. His eyes scan me up and down as he lets out a soft growl, making my pulse quicken. My legs try to snap shut, but his knee prevents them from closing.

The King smirks as he looks down at my trembling legs before his eyes move back to mine. His hand travels across my stomach, then his fingertips sneak beneath the waistband. My hand instinctively moves and I quickly grab his wrist.

"Am I making you flustered? Do you feel warmer?" he chuckles, leaning closer, brushing his nose across my cheek, and inhaling my scent. He purrs, making my grip tighten on his wrist as the throbbing between my legs worsens.

"You smell good enough to eat," he growls, pressing his face into my neck; his tongue tastes my skin before sucking on the same spot. A purr - a noiseI've never made before – escapes my lips. My face turns away, offering him more of my neck like it was suddenly commanded to.

"That's it, Ivy. Let your body tell you what it wants," he purrs.

But that was the thing; it doesn't feel like my body; it feels foreign. I can't explain any of the things he's making me feel as he keeps nipping and licking my skin–only that I want more, but I also don't because I know it's wrong for him to be touching me like this.

This is wrong.

He is a King, and I am nothing but his servant; I shouldn't even be in his room. The difference in our titles, what we are doing, and the trouble I will be in all fills me with anxiety. It goes against everything I have ever known.

"My King," I stutter as a violent rippling shiver rushes up my spine when he sucks at the spot where my neck meets my shoulder.

He growled. However, the noise sounds annoyed, and the shiver turns to a frigid chill as his aura rushes over me, crushing the air from my lungs.

"What did I say about calling me that? I let the first time slide, Ivy. Once more, and you will be punished." I stare at him horrified. "Is that what it will take to get you to use my name? Do I have to punish you?" he growls.

"I'm sorry, I didn't mean to upset you," I blubber. The mere thought of punishment from a King causes my heart to race. My blood turns to ice in my veins as my stomach drops deep inside me, forming a deep pit of dread. I swallow, and he growls again, but this time I'm unsure why he's angry now. He suddenly sits up and turns away from me.

My fear becomes more intense when I watch the muscles in his back flex and tense. His spine ripples. Is he fighting the urge to shift? I don't understand how calling him by his title could anger him so much.

"I have told you not to call me that, and you still continue to." His words come out slowly, and the firmness behind them makes my hands tremble when he growls. The noise sends a tremor through my entire body.

Images flash behind my eyelids with each blink: *the times I have been punished; the darkness in the cupboards that Mrs. Daley would lock me in; the feel of the whip on my back; the countless times I received the strap across the back of my knees; the weakness that would come from hunger when she would punish us by depriving us of anything to eat. Then the sound of the sword across the stone where it should have ended.*

I squeeze my eyes shut as they burn with tears that want to fall.

"I have asked little of you, but if I ask for one thing, it is for you to use my damn name," the King snarls. I can hear the anger in his voice, and feel his aura pressing down on me, threatening, promising the violence of his wrath. "Are you listening?" he snaps, and the whimper I tried to suppress breaks past my lips. I feel the sudden motion of the bed as he moves.

Don't make noise. Don't let them hear your pain.

The mantra we lived by for years echoes through my head.

'Tears won't help you, so why waste them? Tears help nobody, they only make you look uglier," Mrs. Daley's voice booms in my head.

"Ivy?"

My entire body trembles and tenses as I try to fight the urge to tuck tail and run as he scolds me. I feel his hands run up my arms.

"Shhh, Shhh."

A yelp slips past my lips when I am ripped across the bed. My eyes fly open at the motion, expecting to be tossed like garbage, but I don't hit the floor. I don't feel any pain. Instead, I find myself on his lap.

CHAPTER
TWENTY-NINE

I VY "I won't hurt you; I would never hurt you, Ivy. I didn't mean..." the King whispers next to my ear. He sighs heavily, dropping his face in my neck as he tucks me against him. Yet, I am rigid in his arms. My entire body screams at me to run and I start to itch. My fingers ache to claw at my skin to stop the tremors rattling my nerves.

"You're not in trouble, my love," the King whispers before he starts purring, the sound vibrating against my side. I feel my heart rate begin to slow. I find it odd his purr has that effect on me, like an instant muscle relaxant. My entire body relaxes as I melt against him, the thrum lulling away my shakes.

"That's it, Ivy. I need to remember to watch what I say," he murmurs. "I forget where you come from. You never have to fear me, Ivy."

I try to listen to his words, but my eyes are growing heavy. I blink, trying to fight the urge to let them close. Each blink makes it harder to open my eyes. I feel funny, like the time he gave me whiskey. The jostling of my body as he stands and his purring stop-

JESSICA HALL

ping make my eyes open. I try to lift my head when it starts again, the sound makes me feel heavy and my head foggy as it falls back on his shoulder.

Vaguely, I can hear running water and feel his hands on my body, caressing and touching, becoming lost in the sensation when hot water laps at my skin. He moves behind me; the deep, resonating purr has quieted to a soft whisper. The water swishes around my waist and my eyes no longer feel glued shut.

Instead, I open them as the King turns me on his lap. Blinking, I look around to find I am in the bath, the King sitting behind me with his legs on either side of mine.

"Lift your arms, Ivy," he says, but I was trying to figure out when he ran a bath and how I got in it.

His hands grip the hem of my shirt before lifting it. My arms rise above my head at the soft command as he tugs it off, my waking mind trying to figure out what is going on.

"I feel strange," I murmur to myself.

"It's the calling, something Lycans can do; you were upset."

I try to process his words, but nothing comes to mind at what he said.

Maybe I heard wrong. The water moves as he grabs my hands, placing them on his thighs, and I look down to see he has no pants on before looking at my naked chest.

"My..."

"Kyson," he cuts me off.

"How... Why... I um... I have no shirt," I blurt, confused at the change in the situation. My mind is excessively cloudy, like a fog has shrouded my waking thoughts as I try to process everything.

"You're about to have no panties, too," he whispers before I see his claws slip from his fingertips under the water. I go to grab his hands when he purrs again, making my hands drop back on his legs as if he had made a command.

He presses his lips firmly against my shoulder. Suddenly, my underwear is reduced to tatters before hearing a wet slap as he

166

tosses them from the bath onto the tile floor. He pulls me against him before moving my hair over my other shoulder.

"I didn't mean to frighten you, Ivy. That was never my intention," he whispers against my skin as his lips travel up my neck to my jaw.

Wet fingers graze my chin as he turns my face up and toward his. His mouth covers mine as he licks my lips before sucking the bottom one into his mouth. He groans in pleasure, the sound making my legs tremble.

I try to pull away, but his hand on my neck and thumb on my jaw keep my face where he wants. His legs move underneath mine; he bends his knees, pulling my legs up and over his and spreading them apart.

His other hand is on my stomach, and he drags me closer while deepening the kiss, his tongue tangling with mine. His hand moves higher, palming my breast before plucking at my nipple. It's at this point I can feel his erection digging into my lower back.

His hand moves lower, caressing over my skin and finding its way between my thighs. My legs tremble as I try to shut them, but he presses them against the walls of the bathtub, trapping them. He purrs against my lips before nipping them. When his hand cups my pussy, he growls. The aching pulse returns with a vengeance, and I am sure he can feel it against his fingertips.

My mind screams at me, telling me he shouldn't be touching me there, yet my body demands his touch. He squeezes – more firmly this time – as his fingers rub my tender flesh, and I pull my lips from his. At this, his purr grows louder, his silver eyes watching my face. My cheeks heat under his watchful gaze as he tilts his head.

The strange sensation is all-consuming. My skin feels hot, every part of me threatening to overheat when one of his fingers slides between the seam of my lower lips before brushing against my clit. The sensation causes my hips to jerk, and he smiles. The points of his canines poke out between his lips, and his eyes flash to black at the movement, like he enjoyed the reaction he provoked from me.

His finger moves lower, rubbing around my entrance as his thumb brushes over the same spot, earning the same reaction. I moan, my eyes flutter, and I become lost in bliss.

He growls softly again before his lips crash passionately against mine in hunger. In obedience, I answer his kiss eagerly, my body aching for his touch despite my head telling me it's wrong. My legs tremble as he continues brushing the same spot with his thumb while his finger presses against my entrance.

As he does this, the water moves, lapping at my skin as his other hand grips my breast and squeezes hard, making an audible little whine escape me.

I have no idea why I am allowing him to touch me this way, not that I have much choice – he's the King. Yet, the feeling building in my stomach and the heat ravaging through me makes me feel like putty in his hands. He can do as he wishes as long as he doesn't stop. My eyes drift shut, my lips pulling from his as my head falls back on his shoulder. My hips rock against his playful fingers... and play me, they do, like a well-tuned musical instrument.

His thumb brushes my clit, rubbing and flicking, when I feel his finger force its way inside me. My eyes squeeze tighter at the intrusion, and my hips jerk back when I feel his hardness dig into my back. My heart rate spikes once more at the realization, and my eyes fly open.

"Shh, Ivy, it's like that because I am touching you. It doesn't mean I will do anything with it," the King says, pressing his lips to my shoulder. He forces his finger in deeper, and I squirm as I feel my walls try to stretch, clamping tightly around him. Open-mouth kisses trail over my shoulder and neck as he withdraws it before pushing back in.

CHAPTER
THIRTY

I VY
I squirm on his lap when he purrs softly. The sound makes my mind foggy, and he stops. "Do you want me to stop?" he purrs, and my head falls heavily on his shoulder, my eyes fluttering.

"I feel strange," I admit.

"It's my calling. It won't hurt you," he whispers, his lips trailing along the column of my neck. I know I should question what he means, but the haze that is sweeping through me makes it difficult to generate a cognitive thought. My hips move against his hand, chasing the building sensation he is creating.

"Is that a no?"

"No..." I breathe out.

"So a yes?" he purrs.

"No... I... you shouldn't," I try to tell him it's wrong, but my thoughts and words become jumbled.

"But you want to?" he asks, then runs his tongue up my neck before flicking my ear. A moan escapes me, and my hips move against his hand.

"Ivy, tell me to stop because I won't unless you do," he whispers before brushing his thumb against my clit.

He slips his finger out, pushing it back in. My walls flutter as he slowly withdraws it and presses it back in. I moan, and my hips begin to move in time with his thrusts. "That's it," Kyson purrs, the sound growing louder and deeper, and I turn languid in his arms. His erection twitches against my lower back when I wiggle my hips, wanting more.

"Do you want more?" Kyson purrs, the sound vibrating through my body. His fingers move faster when he drags me higher up his body. He groans when his cock slides against my ass.

He then slips his finger out, teasing my clit between his fingers, and my hips rock against his hand. When I feel two fingers prod at my entrance, I tense, and when he pushes them in, there is more resistance than before, my body trying to accommodate them, and my entire body tenses more. I squirm, my legs shaking and trying to close. Kyson traps them against the sides of the tub but raises his knees more, spreading me wider. "Shh, I won't hurt you," he purrs, the sound lulling me deeper into the haze, forcing me to relax.

"Good girl," he says, forcing both fingers inside me as deep as they can go. "Fuck you feel good," he growls while his thumb rubs my clit. "I can't wait to feel how tight your pussy is around my cock," he whispers, his breath hot on my neck. I moan, and my hips rock against his hand.

"That's it," Kyson purrs. His fingers move faster, harder. My body arches as pleasure radiates through every nerve, my hips moving in rhythm with his fingers. He turns his face, and his lips meet mine, and I'm lost in the sensations he is creating.

"Don't stop," I breathe against his lips.

His deep, resounding purr forces my body to relax, and I melt against him. My legs are no longer shaking. Instead, they fall heavily over his legs. He works his fingers in and out of me, his thumb rubbing on my clit, making me moan as I give in to the building sensation.

My stomach tenses, and heat burns through me when he pulls his wet fingers from my pulsating heat before adding another, making me cry out. His lips swallow the sound that escapes me as he works three fingers into me, pushing in deeper. At the same time, his other hand falls to my stomach, holding me still.

"Relax," he instructs, and I do under his gentle command, and his purring grows louder, more intense.

He presses on my lower abdomen, his fingers curling upward and stroking against a sensitive spot that makes me gasp as he nibbles on my lip.

Unable to help it, my hips move against his fingers. My head rolls back against his shoulder as he moves his fingers faster, rougher, stretching me around them as he curls them. My walls flutter, clamping down on his fingers.

My moans echo off the tiled walls, louder than I intend, as his thumb presses down on my swollen clit, the friction building and climbing until I feel like I will combust from the heat, making my skin flush.

Suddenly, my mind goes blank. My eyes flutter, and his name spills from my lips. With a gasp, my walls squeeze and pulse wildly.

Pleasure ripples through me, making me cry out in pure ecstasy, stealing my breath from me as wave after wave courses through me. My entire body feels heavy as I sag against him. The King nips at my neck and chin as I recover, and I feel him gently pull his fingers from me.

In a daze, I blink up at the ceiling when he reaches for the loofah and soap, his purr lulling me quiet. I feel ridiculously relaxed – as if my whole body has turned to jelly – probably more relaxed than I have ever been in my life. I feel him chuckle and hear him talking, but my brain is mushy with the after-effects of what he did. He kisses my cheek, running the loofa over my skin when there's a knock on the door.

"Get out," the King says firmly, his tone leaving no room for argument as I hear the person walking away.

"Just one of the guards. We should have left an hour ago," he says as he washes me, gently running the loofa over my heated skin. Goosebumps rise on my arms as the warmth that filled me slowly leaves, and I shiver against his warm skin.

"Do you still want to come to the castle with me?"

"I want to sleep," I mumble, suppressing a yawn. He hums, brushing his nose across my shoulder.

"I loved your scent before, but I love the smell of your arousal better," he says, nipping at my neck and then sucking that one spot he seems to graze with his teeth constantly.

"How far is it?" I yawn sleepily. He chuckles, running the loofa over my breasts.

"A couple of days' drive. We will stop on the way, but you need to promise not to leave my side," he whispers.

I nod. I think I probably would have agreed to anything he said right now.

"That's my girl." He grabs a small jug and dips it in the water before tipping it over my chest and shoulders to remove the soap.

The King then pulls the plug out of the bath, letting the water drain out. Gripping his knees for support, I stand, completely forgetting I'm naked and no longer covered by foamy water.

As soon as I realize it, I try to cover myself by keeping my back to him when I feel a towel draped over my shoulders. I pull it closed before turning around and facing him. He has a towel wrapped around his waist. My eyes trail over his muscular body.

His abs look hand-carved to perfection and ripple with each movement he makes. His tanned skin glistens under water the droplets, and I step closer and then stop, shaking my head as the need to touch him almost overwhelms me. He laughs softly, closing the distance and wrapping his arms around me. My nose presses against his chest, and I breathe in deeply as his scent invades my senses.

"We should get dressed if you still want to leave today," he whispers.

"I don't think I should be going with you. What would people think?" I ask, worried.

"I won't be leaving if you stay here," the King says, with finality in his tone. "I won't leave you here by yourself."

My brows pinch, and I chew my bottom lip. I can't help but wonder how long this will last, how long before the King tosses me aside when he realizes he is fooling around with his servant... someone unworthy of royalty.

What if we go, and he gets sick of me and casts me out? At least here I have Abbie; I would have no one out there. The thought of leaving her sickens me, and so does the thought of being without her.

The King leads me back to his bedroom. "Get dressed," he says, pointing to a neat pile of clothes at the end of the bed.

I walk over to inspect the clothes. They're not my servant's uniform. Surely, he doesn't want me to wear regular clothes? Who even brought these up here? As I turn to look at the king, I see him rummaging through his wardrobe before pulling out jeans and a T-shirt.

"My uniform?"

"You won't be wearing it anymore," he says, coming back over to me. I shake my head when he grips my chin between his fingers. "I don't want you to be my servant anymore."

"But I am, My..." His eyes harden to steel at my words, and I swallow.

"But I am, Kyson," I murmur, swallowing down the urge to use his title.

"No, you are so much more than that, Ivy."

I shake my head in disbelief, and he kisses the side of my mouth.

"Put the clothes on, Ivy," he whispers, letting me go. I glance at them, scratching my arm nervously. "Do I need to dress you?"

I shake my head.

"Get dressed, or I will dress you," he warns.

"But servants wear dresses, tunics..."

"I just told you that I don't want you as my servant," he says, his voice growing more frustrated.

But what else was I supposed to be? That's all I know. Rogues are always slaves or servants, which is all they can and should be. We aren't supposed to be pampered and treated nicely. We aren't good enough to be seen as people. His treatment of Abbie and me is absurd, and I know everyone will think the same.

Same as I know he will realize his mistake, eventually.

"Kyson..." My lips quiver. How does he not see this is wrong?

Kyson turns around slowly, his eyes going to me, then the clothes sitting on the bed, and his jaw clenches. "1..."

"I'll go, but can I wear my uniform?" I plead.

"2..." he says, buttoning up his shirt. When I don't move, he slowly walks toward me, buttoning up his shirt as he does.

"Don't make me say it, Ivy."

"But..." his eyes lift to mine, and the anger I see in his gaze makes me flinch.

"But what? Because you want to remain a servant?" he asks, moving closer, and I step back. "Because you're worried I am using you for your body, as a sex slave?" he snaps at me. Another few steps which I match, stepping back only for my knees to hit the back of the bed.

"Because you're a rogue, and I am King?" he growls, and I fall back when he towers over me. Kyson leans over my body, forcing me on my back with his hands on either side of my face.

"Any more excuses?" he asks, and I shake my head, my hands trembling against his chest.

"Your King said to get dressed, so you get dressed and put the clothes on."

I gulp and quickly nod... When his eyes go to my hands, clutching his shirt in my shaky grip.

"No more excuses. Put the clothes on," he says softly, pressing his lips to mine briefly before pushing off the bed and allowing me to get up. I snatch the clothes and start slipping them on.

For now, there is nothing I can do but play his strange game and accept it, so I nod and reach for them with a sigh.

CHAPTER
THIRTY-ONE

K YSON
Her awkwardness is adorable, though also slightly annoying when it persists. I can tell how uncomfortable she is doing everyday, mundane things that should be normal to anybody. It shows me just how damaged her life has been.

Ivy always stands like she's waiting for orders or waiting for me to ask her to do something. Unless I force her to sit, she'll remain standing. Simple things no one would even question doing; she has to be told to do. It's irritating and infuriating to me. At least she put the clothes on, but now she's standing at the door with her eyes straight ahead, hands behind her back.

We just bathed together, yet she is still trying to be my servant. She acts like it's uncomfortable for her to be herself, or maybe she just isn't used to being herself—only used to the version of what everyone wants her to be. It's like watching someone who is institutionalized. She can't function outside of the routine she is used to, the script others wrote for her, or her brain will short-circuit.

When another knock raps on the door, I know the car is ready. I watch her move to open it before standing back in her corner as if she can blend into the bookcase. I growl and shake my head. She shifts her weight from one foot to the other as my Beta walks in, noticing her and looking her over.

He knows she is my mate. He also knows my struggle with her to be a person and not a damn slave that answers my every whim. I so much as mutter about something, and she is going to clean it or fix it! I rub my temples feeling a headache building. I want to scream and break something. She is driving me crazy and I feel like I am walking on eggshells trying not to scare her.

As soon Ivy got dressed, she raced around cleaning up the mess I had made the night before, even after I told her not to. She muttered about it being her job to clean. When I tried to help, she would get to it before I could. It got to the point where I was trying to race her. I managed a few things – being quicker on my feet than her – yet I could see it bothered her that I was doing tasks that had originally been assigned to her. It's almost as though she thought she would get in trouble if someone walked in on me cleaning my own room. Eventually, I just shake my head and let her continue whatever she was doing.

"Morning, Ivy," Damian says to her, and she bows respectfully, showing her neck to him.

"Morning, Beta," she answers politely.

Damian scratches his neck awkwardly while looking at me as I try to suppress a growl. I know it also irritates him that she uses his title, especially since she will outrank him once she figures out that I am her mate. Shit, she will probably outrank me! I don't think I could deny her anything. However, the chances of her actually ever asking for anything, I am realizing, are very slim.

Damian drops his backpack on the ground by the door, and Ivy moves to pick it up. In response, I growl, and she jumps, not expecting it. "Leave it!" I tell her, my words coming off harsher than intended. I don't want her picking up after me, let alone anyone else. Her eyes immediately fell to the floor. I click my tongue and purse my lips before Damian's voice flits through my head as he mind-links me.

"*I thought you two were on the same page?*" he says.

"*So did I, but she still insists on being my servant. She has been standing there for ten minutes now.*"

"*But I could have sworn you were in the bath with her this morning.*"

"*I was,*" I answer flatly, and his brows furrow.

"*Did you have a fight?*"

"*What? No, I think it's just how she is,*" I tell him.

I grab my phone and wallet and toss them to Damian, who catches them and puts them in his pocket.

"*Maybe she thinks she is your sex slave or something,*" Damian suggests, still using the link.

"*She does. Only, we didn't have sex,*" I answer.

"Ivy, come. We are leaving," I tell her, and she nods, following a few steps behind us down the hall. Damian stops to wait for her to fall in line with me, but she also stops.

"Ivy," I snap at her. She looks at me, and I motion her toward me before grabbing her hand. She glances at my fingers linked through hers. Her entire body tenses as she looks at the guards who pay no attention whatsoever, just like they are trained to do.

"My..."

She begins to address me, and I growl at her. I know she is going to protest me touching her in public, as she keeps glancing at the guards, who are well aware of who she is to me. I'm pretty sure the entire castle knows, except Ivy and Abbie.

How they haven't figured it out yet is beyond me. So I notice instantly when she tries to pull her hand from mine gently, but I don't allow it.

"They won't hurt you. You are doing nothing wrong," I try to reassure her, but she is still frozen in place like she's waiting for someone to scream 'Off with her head' for merely being near me.

I try to remain calm, but I am fuming at how timid she is. Damian has complained all week about Abbie being the same. He said it's like she is mute. She even managed to scare him a couple of times with how quiet she is. Meanwhile, Ivy tries to tug her hand from mine again, and I tighten my grip.

Ivy's heart races when I yank her to me, crushing her petite frame against my chest. I press my lips against hers quickly, and she pulls away from me. She looks around nervously before I use the calling on her, forcing her to submit to me.

There are many perks to being a Lycan man—the calling for one. I have used it on her a few times, and she still hasn't realized what it is and why it calms her. However, it only works on our mates.

I used to laugh when my sister would get all worked up and be a blubbering mess or a screaming banshee from pregnancy hormones – until her mate would start purring. I think he could sway her to do anything when he used it.

It was odd to me whenever I witnessed it. I couldn't figure out how it worked. When I was younger, I had asked about why Lycan men used it on their mates. I hadn't understood the need to use it, but now, with Ivy, I can understand it and why it is called a calling; I found I did it without even thinking about it with Ivy. Like some extra sense picking up on her distress.

The calling is like a sedative of sorts that only a mate could use to subdue their other half. I am sure it was used in more barbaric situations initially, like with my mother.

My father was an excellent King and father, although I know my mother wasn't his fated mate. It was an arranged marriage, and she refused him when they married... declining to be marked by him.

Neither wanted to marry, but once he marked her, the rest was history. I often watched growing up how she always seemed calm around him. It wasn't until after they passed, and I saw my sister and her mate, that I understood why my father always purred when my mother was near.

Ivy hadn't been marked, though. And when I first did it, without her being of age, I couldn't exactly be a hundred percent positive she was my mate, until I realized the calling sedated her.

It could only be used on mates or those marked and taken as mates.

So, I knew without a doubt – like Damian had been suspecting – that she was, in fact, my mate, or it wouldn't have worked without me marking her.

Ivy presses closer, seeking me out, her body turning languid in my arms as I pull her to me. Gripping her chin, I tilt her face up and kiss her. She tries to fight the haze washing over her, I pull her closer, my chest vibrating against her hands, and I deepen the kiss. Her tongue plays with mine, and I smile against her lips before letting her go, but not her hand.

Her face flushes pink, and as she glances around, Damian nods and smiles at her. The guards stare straight ahead. She turns, looking toward the stairs, when she suddenly steps back, bumping into me. I follow her gaze to see Ester at the end of the corridor watching us. Ivy tenses and shifts her weight awkwardly, trying to move behind me. I pull back in front of me, wrapping my arm around her waist, my fingers pressing into her in warning not to move. The look on Ester's face shows her jealousy, while Ivy's shows fear. Now, why is my mate scared of this servant?

"Ester, what are you doing here? You don't work on my floor anymore," I tell her. I don't like the way she glares at Ivy. When her gaze turns to me, her entire demeanor changes swiftly.

"My King, Clarice wanted to know if you were ready to leave. She packed some lunch for your drive," Ester says in a sugary-sweet voice. I nod to her, yet Ivy won't even look in her direction, her fingers gripping the back of my jacket so tightly her knuckles are pressing under her skin, turning them white. My hand covers hers, prying it off, and I lift it, pressing my lips to her knuckles. "What is it?" I whisper to her and she glances at Ester briefly.

"Nothing, my King," she whispers. I want to yell at her for using my title, but I can see she is scared.

'Is Ester not her friend?' I ask Damian through the mindlink.

'I haven't seen them together,' he answers simply.

I nod and tug on Ivy's hand. Her heart pounds in her chest, and I glance down at where she stands slightly behind me, staring vacantly at the wall.

"You may leave, Ester," I say without looking at her, not taking my eyes off my mate. Maybe she feels awkward because Ester is a servant like she used to be, or I hope she used to be. I don't want her waiting on me anymore, but getting that habit to stop is becoming a challenge.

"The King dismissed you, Ester; on your way," Damian snaps, and I hear her footsteps as she rushes off down the stairs.

"You don't like Ester?" I ask Ivy, and she looks at me before shaking her head.

"No, she is fine. I just don't know her very well," Ivy answers when the guard clears his throat. I glance at him. So does Ivy, and he nods to her. Clearly, something is going on I'm unaware of.

I will have to find out when we get back, but something tells me she is lying. And that doesn't sit well with me, and if she keeps it up, she will learn, one way or another, not to do it again.

"Ivy..."

She looks up at me. My jaw clenches, and I take a deep breath. I can feel my temper rising. "Do I need to do something about Ester?" I ask her, and she gasps.

Her eyes widen, and she shakes her head. "No, no. She's done nothing wrong," she blurts out, but I hear the way her heart sputters at my question. My eyes go to the guard over her shoulder, and he clenches his jaw.

I don't like being lied to, and it's a trait that I won't tolerate. She'll learn dishonesty has consequences if she keeps it up.

CHAPTER
THIRTY-TWO

I VY
The King leads me downstairs, and I fight the urge to run so I can race to the servant's area to pee; I have been busting all morning. As we step down the last step, Clarice waits with an insulated bag in her hands.

"Good morning, King Kyson," she exclaims cheerfully. She smiles at me, and Damian takes the bags from her.

"I can carry them," I tell him. Beta Damian shakes his head. My brows furrow. I don't know what to do with myself as the King speaks to the guard that was waiting with Clarice.

I notice the upstairs guard standing behind me when I hear chattering and look up the hall.

Abbie walks out of the billiard room down the corridor, and my eyes light up. I try to run to her when I realize the King has a hold of my hand. Abbie's eyes also brighten as she suppresses her urge to do the same.

I remain still, however, when the King feels a tug on his hand. He glances down at me before bringing my hand to his lips. My eyes widen, and I look away when Clarice smiles at me.

Shouldn't she be scolding me? She scolded Ester for the way she carried on around the King. Here I am, the lowest of the servants, and she smiles and says nothing?

The guards don't even bat an eyelash at his outrageous affections.

"What is it?" the King asks, and I shake my head; only he grips my chin, tilting my face up toward his.

I am pretty sure all the blood runs from my face when he brushes his lips on mine briefly, and dread fills my stomach. There are around twenty guards stationed along the walls! Yet, none move to kill me.

"What is it?" he repeats.

"It's Abbie, my King," Clarice answers for me, and he lets my chin go and looks over my shoulder. He nods to her and lets go of my hand.

"Go see her if you want to before we leave," he answers, and I bounce on my feet. I look at Clarice, who nods to me, letting me know it's alright.

I must look like a child in a candy store with my excitement as I rush toward her. A sob bursts from Abbie's lips when I crash against her, smothering her with my hug. She squeezes tight like she can't bear to let me go, and I never want her to.

Her hands fussily wipe my tears and mine hers. "I was so worried when I didn't see you for a few days. I thought they got rid of you," she says, holding me at arm's length. I grip her arms when she looks me up and down.

"Where is your uniform?" she questions.

"I have to go with the King somewhere. He told me to wear this."

"You're leaving the castle?"

I nod to her, feeling nervous seeing her nervousness. She also knows it isn't normal for a rogue to be taken places.

"But you're coming back, right?" she says, and I watch the blood drain from her face. She glances down at my clothes again.

"Yes, I will bring her back, Abbie," the King tells her, and she instantly straightens, letting me go. She bows to him, glancing between us and I feel his chest press against my back while his hand brushes my side.

"It's time to leave," he says, placing his hand on my hip. Abbie's eyes dart to his hand before her gaze meets mine. The King pulls me away from her.

"I love you," Abbie blurts, and the King stops when I look back at her. I escape his grip and quickly hug her. She squeezes me tighter when I kiss her cheek.

"I love you too," I whisper to her. I don't care if I get scolded for it or even whipped. I need that last hug if it turns out to be my last one from her.

"More than my life," Abbie whispers in my ear, her voice breaking.

"More than my life," I whisper back before letting her go. The King's brows furrow as I approach him. He resumes his grip on my hand, tugging me toward where Damian and Clarice are waiting. Glancing back at Abbie, I see Gannon approaching her. King Kyson stops talking to a guard while I turn to see what Gannon wants from Abbie, hoping she isn't in trouble. However, he cups her cheek. She seems quite comfortable in his presence, which is shocking because Abbie is wary of men in general.

Eavesdropping, I hear him tell her he left a present in his room on his bed for her. Abbie blushes, glancing around, and I drop my gaze to see a servant drop a suitcase beside the King and wander off.

Leaning down, I attempt to grab it when the guard usually stationed upstairs does. He nods to me, and I look at the King, but he just continues walking out the double-arched doors pulling me with him.

I really hope the drive isn't long, or maybe there's a gas station on the way; I really need to pee. He stops beside the limousine, and the driver opens the door. I look back at the castle while he speaks with the driver and two men, one from each of the black cars parked nearby.

I see Ester walk around the side of the castle with a basket of apples. *Oh no,* I think. That particular side of the castle is full of fruit trees; the trees run along the fence line alongside the castle. She pauses, also noticing me, and glares in my direction.

I don't understand her issue; I have done nothing to her, yet she is always nasty. She stalks inside quickly, and I look back at the King only to see this Beta watching me. He glances at Ester's retreating form before looking back at me again. I drop my gaze.

Pressing my legs together, I berate myself. Why didn't I ask to use the bathroom when speaking with Abbie? I know I will have to ask. I just hope I don't anger the king. Or maybe he will leave without me; then I could stay with Abbie, though that thought upsets me for some reason, too.

I go to address him before settling for tapping on his arm. I know if I use his title, he will become angry, yet I also can't bring myself to say his name with so many people listening. The King stops, and I move from one foot to the other. I am about to burst or wet myself—either one.

"One second, love," he says, and I chew my lip.

Beta Damian steps closer and leans down. "What's wrong?" he asks, and my face heats as the King lets my hand go to look at some maps the two men are going over on the hood of the Limo.

"Ivy?" Beta Damian asks, stepping closer to me.

"I need to pee," I whisper.

"Why didn't you use the bathroom?" he asks with a heavy sigh.

"Go on," he says, and I dart back into the castle. I run to the servant's bathroom. I must have looked like a mad woman running through the halls.

Racing into the stall, I rip my pants down, cursing them. Not only were they giving me a wedgie, but I nearly peed myself while trying to get them off.

When I finish, I flush the toilet, feeling lighter now. My bladder isn't screaming at me, and I no longer feel like I will explode. I unlock the door and step out to wash my hands, only to find Ester leaning against the sink, looking evil as usual. I try to step out of the stall when she shoves me so hard that I slam into the wall. I grunt, rubbing my arm.

Choosing to ignore, I move for the sink.

CHAPTER
THIRTY-THREE

I VY

The cruel sneer on her face tells me she's here to cause trouble. Ester grabs my hair, and I cry out, clutching her wrist. "Fucking whore... I knew you were lying on your back for him, or is it on your knees where he likes you?" she growls at me. She shoves me into the sink. However, before she can open her mouth to say anything more, her words are cut off when the guard suddenly walks in.

He stands there looking between us, and I quickly wash my hands, using him as my escape. When I walk toward him, Ester snorts a laugh, making me stop.

"You think the guard cares about some rogue slut?" Ester spits at me. She walks toward me and I move slightly worried she'll hurt me.

"Ester, I don't know what your problem is. We are the same; I am a servant, just like you," I tell her when I feel the guard's hand grip my hip, pushing me behind him slightly.

"The King's quarters is my station, you fucking bitch," she spits before raising her hand to slap me.

I see her hand come straight toward my face, and my eyes widen. The guard moves effortlessly and grips her wrist. It's the first time I have seen him interfere before or follow me into a bathroom, for that matter. I assumed he wasn't allowed. But then again, she had never gone to hit me, either. Maybe they can stop violence because it causes a disturbance. Ester cries out and the guard's grip tightens making her knees buckle and I hear the sickening crack of her wrist. My eyes widen when she screams out and then chokes on her pain. My entire body trembles at what he just did.

"Ma'am, the King is waiting for you," the guard speaks gently.

"Unhand me! How dare you touch me?" Ester snarls, but I don't wait around. Instead, I escape into the hall only to run directly into the Beta. I bounce off his chest, not seeing him, and he grips my arms to steady me.

"Where is your guard?" he asks, confusing me. Did he mean the guard in the bathroom? I glance at the door when Ester suddenly rushes out, cradling her wrist with her face streaked with tears. The guard steps out behind her before nodding at the Beta. Beta Damian, however, watches Ester rush down the corridor.

"Do we need to have a chat?" he asks the guard behind me, who nods once.

"I take full responsibility. I should have said something earlier," the guard replies, and my brows furrow, wondering what is going on with him and what he is talking about.

He always follows me, but he never says anything. He occasionally smiles, and he has moved a couple of times: once to pick up a broken piece of glass and another to point me in the right direction. Other than that, he followed me like a shadow, watching me as I worked. However, this is the first time I have heard his voice.

"Is that so?" Beta Damian questions, and the guard nods, showing no emotion at all as he stands staring straight ahead. Damian growls and grabs my arm.

"This way, Ivy," he tells me, his hand moving to my back and pushing me back the way I came in from outside. The guard follows, and when I walk out, I see the King still standing there, looking extremely angry, his arms folded across his chest. When I approach him, he opens the back door.

He motions for me to get in without saying a word. I slide into the car and he shuts the door and remains outside, talking to his Beta.

"Find out," I hear him say when he opens the door and climbs in beside me. The driver shuts the door, and I watch the guard follow Beta Damian to the black car in front before they both climb in.

My attention is pulled back to the King as he leans over me, plugging my seatbelt in, and making me look at him. His jaw is tense, and he looks angry as he stares out his window. I shouldn't have made him wait. I want to apologize, but I don't want to get scolded either, so I hold my tongue.

The drive is awkward for the first twenty minutes as we sit in silence. The King looks like he is thinking hard about something when he suddenly removes his seatbelt and moves to the other side of the Limo.

After rummaging through the small cooler, he grabs two glasses and moves back toward me. He presses a button, and a small tray pops out between our seats.

"Have you drank wine before?"

I shake my head.

"You can speak, Ivy. Your silence is driving me a bit crazy."

I watch as he fills a wine glass with dark red liquid before handing it to me. I sniff the wine; it smells fruity and sweet. He pours whiskey into his own glass.

"Drink," he says, nodding at the glass clutched in my hand.

The command washes over me gently, yet even though he barely uses it, I can't fight it. I hate that, being a rogue, I am commanded so easily. Although I am glad the servants have never commanded Abbie and me.

Clarice had, but it was almost a motherly nudge coming from her instead of an outright command. Yet the King has done it a few times, but he never made me do anything other than eat or drink.

The King orders me to finish the glass and then pours another, but I feel woozy and so hot. The King watches me. He nods to the glass in my hand, and I shake my head.

It kind of snuck up on me. It tastes sweet, but its effects creep up slowly before hitting me.

"Drink it," he repeats.

Why is he so intent on me drinking? I want to puke from the car's motion and the heavy feeling in my stomach.

"No thank you," I murmur trying to set the glass down.

"I said drink," the King orders. I glance at him, my hand trembling as I try to fight it. Yet, I can't help myself; my hand shakes while I bring the glass to my lips. "All of it," he adds and I drink the entire glass in three huge mouthfuls.

When I am done he pours more into the glass and tears burn my eyes. Why is he doing this?

I think I drank four entire glasses, each a little fuller than the last. When I empty the glass again, he goes to pour more!

"Please, My... Kyson, no more. I feel sick," I tell him, and he raises an eyebrow at me. My belly feels extremely heavy, and my face feels hot. My eyelids don't seem to want to stay open.

Why do so many people enjoy feeling like this? I feel like shit. He places the bottle down in the holder. I lost count of how many whiskeys he had. They seem to have little or no effect on him, yet my words slur as they leave my lips. The door beside me is pretty much holding me up as I lean heavily against it, and my vision blurs.

"You won't lie to me again," he states.

My brows pinch together, and I rest my head against the cool window glass. His words confuse me. And why is it so hot in this car? I'm sweating profusely.

"I don't like punishing you, so don't make me," the King tells me. My lips feel like rubber when he hands me another glass. My mouth feels dry from the wine, and I shake my head.

"Will you lie to me again?" he questions.

"I don't know what you mean. I didn't lie," I try to tell him, but my words are garbled. He growls, and I undo my seatbelt, the pressure on my stomach making me feel worse.

"Drink it," the King says.

A whimper escapes me, and tears roll down my cheeks. "Please, Kyson," I beg, and he clenches his jaw.

"Now!" he commands before tapping on the driver's window.

I feel the car slow as I swallow down the sickly-sweet wine. My stomach lurches, and I try to keep the wine down as it rises up my throat. I cover my mouth when he reaches for another bottle.

I shake my head, snatching it from him, yet the motion sends me falling forward. Before I can hit the ground though, his hands grab me, and he hauls me into his lap. He pries the bottle from my grip, and I whimper, not wanting to drink anymore. My hands slap his hand away when I see him pop the cork off and bring the bottle toward me.

"You'll drink it," he growls, but I twist in his tight grip, turning on his lap and pressing my face into his neck so he can't force the bottle to my lips.

"Ivy..." he growls. I shake my head, inhaling his scent when he sighs. I hear him set the bottle down, and one hand moves to my hair while the other moves to my backside. He squeezes my ass, hauling me higher and forcing me to straddle his waist. I don't care what he does; I know if I move right now, I'm going to puke.

"You lied to me..."

I shake my head, and he growls.

"Twice you've lied today." My brows pinch. I haven't lied to him. Why does he believe I lied to him?

CHAPTER
THIRTY-FOUR

IVY

I gag right as the limo stops. The door opens, and I rush toward it, stumbling out of the car and nearly tripping headfirst into the dirt before the King grabs my arm. Retching, I try to pull out of his grip, knowing I'm going to throw up, but it is too late, and I puke all over the ground, narrowly missing our feet. My entire body feels hot by the time I am done. Kyson's grip on my arm is growing increasingly painful, his body shaking as he holds onto me as if he believes I might run at any moment. Catching my breath and gripping my knees, I glance around, my surroundings spinning slightly.

"You won't lie to me again, will you, Ivy?" the King asks. My brows furrow as I peer up at him over my shoulder. His jaw clenches tight as he looks straight ahead.

Why does he keep asking me that and saying it that way? I hear car doors open and I stand up straight when the King passes me a handkerchief. Looking up, I see my surroundings spin. I wipe my mouth, feeling somewhat better but very unsteady on my feet.

My vision is terrible, and my head is pounding to its own beat, pulsing in my ears loudly. The only things I can make out are that I am on the side of the road, the scent of damp earth, and the King standing beside me. Peering around, the forest is a blur of green along both sides of the road.

The King's Beta comes over to me with a bottle of water. He cracks the lid, handing it to me. Shakily, I take it.

"Get her toiletries bag, please. I would say she wants to rid the taste from her mouth," the King states. His tone of voice is cold and sends a shiver up my spine.

Damian nods once and walks off. I chug the water down before the Beta comes over with a cloth and toiletries bag.

"I don't feel too good," I mumble just as one of the guards brings another bottle of water over, and I lean heavily on the king, unable to hold myself up. His arm slips around my waist while the Beta grabs my arm to help keep me upright. I wonder briefly if this is what it feels like to walk on the moon because gravity and I are not mixing very well. My limbs feel so heavy, and everything sways with the breeze—or maybe I am swaying. I'm not sure.

My entire body feels heavy and hot.

"Hold her for a second," Kyson tells his Beta. I feel like a rag doll as Damian pulls me to him, taking most of my weight. His scent prickles my nose and I try to pull away from him, wanting the King's familiar smell. Not that Damian smells bad, but his scent is nauseating compared to the King's. The King has a masculine yet sweet scent, and while Damian definitely smells similar, there's a sour taint to it that burns my nose. I push off his chest while the King fiddles with the toiletries bag.

"Ivy!" King Kyson scolds me when I stumble backward over my own feet.

Damian's hand snakes out, his long fingers wrapping around my arm before I fall on my butt.

"He smells wrong," I groan as Damian pulls me back to him.

"Wrong," Damian says blandly. "Well, I feel kind of insulted, yet also relieved," Damian chuckles. "Might have had a few issues if I smelled right to you, Ivy," he adds, which confuses my already muddled thoughts as I try to push him away.

"Definitely would have caused issues," Kyson growls. I feel the comforting, familiar tingles rush up my arm when Kyson pulls my pliable body back to him. I face-plant into his chest. Why anyone would like this feeling is beyond me. Wine should be banned; it doesn't feel safe. Actually, I don't feel much of anything, which is the problem. I can't feel my limbs or get them to cooperate properly.

The King wets a cloth before wiping my face, and I feel fingers graze the back of my neck as Damian lifts my hair. The King dampens the cloth again, the chill water cooling me down so I no longer feel like I'm boiling from the inside out.

"Tilt her head back for me," Kyson grumbles, yet the motion of my head moving makes me gag, as the world tilts around me. Kyson pours some water from the bottle into my hair, and I shiver at the icy feeling. I sigh at the coolness of it against my heated skin before he washes my face again like I am some toddler. I'm too wobbly to care or be embarrassed, though. I am pretty much a rag doll as he pulls me around. "Get her something to eat."

"I have some protein bars," Damian tells him, wandering off.

"Are you feeling better now? Or am I sticking my fingers down your throat to make you sick again?" Kyson asks, and I shake my head. I would die from humiliation if he did that.

"I think she learned her lesson, my king," the Beta chuckles when he returns. He opens a protein bar and forces it into my hand.

Yet I am trying to wrap my mind around what the King just said, staring at him in disbelief.

"I had to improvise. I don't think she'd appreciate going over my knee," the King says, confusing me more.

"Maybe not yet," Damian chuckles darkly.

"I don't understand," I slur.

"You lied to me," the King repeats simply, lifting my hand and stuffing the protein bar in my mouth.

I shake my head at his words.

"I have another bottle. Would you like to drink that too?" the King asks me. I stop mid chew and nearly choke on my protein bar when I virtually inhale it.

Huh, is that why he kept making me drink? As some sort of sick punishment? But for what? I haven't lied. At least, I don't think I have. I quickly shake my head.

My legs wobble under my weight, and Beta Damian's grip tightens on my arm. I try to look around again and find all the men out of their cars, looking at the forest and road. Oh my gosh, all these people just watched me puke.

"Do you want to rinse your mouth?" the King asks me.

I nod, though the task seems like it will be too much; but I need to get this taste out of my mouth along with this protein bar that is so chewy it is hurting my jaw.

"I spewed," I slur, my words not coming out right. I know what I want to say, but they don't come out correctly.

"Yes, you did," the King says, pulling me back to the car and placing me on the seat.

I don't want to get back into the stuffy car – the cool outside air feels good on my skin. The Beta hands me the toiletries bag, placing it on my lap.

"Eat!" Kyson orders, and I groan when he lifts my hand to my mouth. I try to bite the stupid bar but instead bite him.

He hisses, jerking his hand back. "You bit me," he states.

"Don't stick your finger in my mouth," I slur.

"If you don't hurry up, I will stick something else in your mouth, and it won't be my finger," he tells me.

"You're daring considering she just bit you," Damian laughs.

It takes my sluggish brain a few seconds to catch up to what he said, and I scrunch my face. "I bite," I blab.

Kyson grips my chin between two fingers. "So do I, now eat," Kyson purrs.

"You eat it," I tell him, not meaning for so much sass to come out of my mouth, yet my brain-to-mouth filter feels out of tune. Oddly enough, I don't even care. I'm more focused on how odd my tongue feels in my mouth.

"And an attitude! Anyone would think she forgot you're a King," Damian laughs.

"One could fucking hope. Maybe she'll stop being my damn slave if she does," Kyson states.

"Rogues..." my words trail off, forgetting what I was going to say and what they were talking about.

"Eat!" he orders when I don't move to put the protein bar in my mouth.

His command rolls over me, jolting me. However, the power of it works, and I finish it in two more huge bites. I lean against the door frame while my fingers fumble as I try to open it.

The King takes it from me and pulls out some mouthwash. He unscrews the cap before handing it to me.

"You can brush your teeth when we get to the hotel. For now, just rinse your mouth," he tells me.

"You're very bossy," I snap at him when he pours some mouthwash into the cap. I hear his Beta chuckle.

"Rinse your mouth."

I can't fight his command and snatch the cap – spilling some as I do – and Kyson sighs, muttering under his breath when I obey. I glare at him before spitting the mouthwash into the tiny cup he hands me.

"She is feisty when drunk," Beta Damian states.

"It appears so," the King chuckles, taking the cup from my hands. One of the guards takes it from him, and the King motions for me to hop in. I shake my head.

"No?" he asks.

"It's too hot," I tell him, although I don't think the words came out like that, but he doesn't seem to have trouble understanding what I mean.

"I know; I had the driver put the heater on," he laughs.

I blink at him, wondering why he would do that when it's stifling hot already.

"In the car, Ivy," the King says. I shake my head again.

"Ivy!"

"Kyson!" I slur before covering my mouth, having blurted that out in front of his Beta and his guards that I know are close enough to have overheard. My heart beats in my chest faster and my eyes burn.

"And she is one of those drunks: first whiny, then feisty, now the waterworks," Damian chuckles.

"I'm not drunk!" I growl at him, startling myself with the noise that leaves me.

Kyson smirks, and my eyes widen at what I did. "I...I'm sor–"

He peels my hands away. "You can growl at him, Ivy. I growl at him sometimes, too."

"Most of the time," Damian states.

"You are not helping."

Damian shrugs.

"I didn't mean it."

"Growl all you want, my Q.... Ivy. I promise I don't scare easy," Damian says.

"Now, in the car. I will get the driver to put the air conditioning on," Kyson tells me.

I briefly wonder if the King is coming down with something for him to be cold. Do Lycans get the flu like werewolves? I shake the thought away and lift my legs in, turning on the seat before shuffling heavily over to my side of the car.

I lean against the other door when Kyson climbs in, turning on the air conditioning and a little fan. After his Beta climbs in the car beside me, Kyson taps on the glass and speaks to the driver.

His Beta hands me another water bottle, and I drink it thirstily, gulping it down just like the rest.

"Fuck, it is hot in here," the Beta says, and I gasp at his language in front of the King. My shock must have been evident because the King also laughs, tugging his shirt off over his head.

"Nope, I can't sit in here with this heat," Beta Damian whines.

"I turned the air conditioner on," the King tells him. His Beta shakes his head and hops back out, not even waiting for the King to dismiss him.

"He just got out, and he swore, but you didn't punish him?" I slur angrily.

The King laughs, reaching for me. My eyes open wide as his hands grab me, making me realize I spoke out of turn once again.

Instead of punishing me for snapping at him, he pulls me on his chest directly under the air conditioning. I feel the limo start moving and I groan, not liking the movement, pressing my face into his neck to steal his addictive scent.

"Damian is my best friend; he can do what he likes. Same you, Ivy."

I shake my head.

"You lied," I tell him.

"I am the liar, am I?"

I nod, turning my face where I am draped over him, enjoying the icy cold air conditioning blasting me. The King tugs my shirt off, but I am too limp to stop him and feel too terrible to care.

"When did I lie?" the King asks.

"You said I could do what I want. I didn't want to drink. You made me," I tell him, and before I can stop it, a growl slips past my lips. I startle myself again, jumping slightly, yet the King just laughs.

"First Damian and now you just growled at me," he chuckles softly, and I feel my pulse slow when he doesn't become angry.

"I'm sorry," I murmur.

"Don't be. You are coming of age to shift soon; you will make noises when showing emotion."

I nod, wondering how much shifting will hurt. I heard it is terribly painful for werewolves during their first shift, and witnessing Abbie's, I am positive it is. Her first shift was horrifying, though she tried to remain quiet.

"And, technically, I didn't lie; that was a punishment. I would have preferred using other means, which would not be appropriate until after you shift, or spanking you..." he chuckles, "but somehow I think that would have traumatized you more."

I must have heard that wrong. I shake my head at his outrageous words.

"But I didn't lie." I needed to stop talking. I must be sounding whiny. Plus, I am already pushing my luck after nearly puking on him.

"You did. I asked you earlier if you liked Ester, and you never told me she had been giving you trouble," he says.

I shake my head, but this time he growls, wrapping his arms around me, holding me in place when I try to get up.

"So you like Ester, then?" he questions, and I pause to think. I didn't hate her, and I wasn't one to hold grudges.

"I don't think she likes me," I answer.

"That wasn't what I asked; I asked if you liked her," the King says.

"Well, I don't dislike her; I don't know her," I tell him.

He nods, pressing his nose to my cheek as he pulls me higher against him. I nuzzle my face into his neck, enjoying his scent when he starts to purr. I love the sounds he makes, except when he growls.

I love his smell, too. But it also makes me wonder how much it will hurt when he tosses me aside, as everyone else has. Can I go without smelling his scent everywhere? Feeling his touch?

"I like it when he does that," I think to myself, and he chuckles.

"Is there someone else I should know about? Some competition I am unknowingly competing against?" the King asks.

"Did I say that out loud?" I ask, mortified.

"Yes, so it better be me you are speaking of. If I find anyone else purring at you, I will remove their vocal cords and lungs," the King laughs, kissing the side of my mouth.

"Why are you..." I mumble, my words becoming harder to form the more he purrs.

"Sleep, Ivy. I will wake you when we get to the hotel," he says, and I feel myself sucked under as sleep and his command takes me.

CHAPTER
THIRTY-FIVE

K YSON
I didn't want to punish her, but she lied to me once again, and I had no choice. I knew something was up with her and Ester, and Ester would pay for whatever she has done. However, I should be able to count on my mate to tell me the truth. Damian said he would tell me later when we got back to the castle, so whatever it was, he found out from Dustin, one of my guards. He was afraid of speaking about it in front of Ivy in case I lost control again.

Her breathing evens out as I hold her. My skin tingles where hers touches mine and drives me crazy with desire, my cock hardening beneath her. I unclip her bra, letting it open, and she sighs as I pull it off and out from under her. Her pink, hardened nipples graze my chest.

I must admit, I like her drunk. She has loosened up significantly, forgetting my title and her own. Yet I can't keep her constantly intoxicated, even though seeing her like this has its appeal.

I trace my fingers down her back, and a growl escapes me as I trace the scars that litter it. The lash marks that cover her back are deep and jagged, with a purplish-red hue. They criss cross each other in patterns. Her skin is rough under my fingertips. Some are still healing, while others have faded. She whimpers and stirs, but I turn the calling back on her again. I love how she melts against me, pressing closer and turning her face into my neck.

The car begins to slow as we pull over for gas. When we do, Damian climbs in the back with me and slides onto the seat across from me. Gannon climbs in behind him a few seconds later and closes the door.

Both of them notice her state of undress and avert their gazes to the windows while Damian rummages through the storage under his seat and pulls out a thin throw blanket. He hands it to me, and I quickly drape it over her to cover her bare back.

"You can turn," I tell them, and they both face me.

"We may need to take an alternate route. I don't like the Black Forest; there are too many hiding places for an ambush," Damian tells me.

"It will be an extra half a day's drive," I tell him.

"I'm sorry, Kyson, but it is not a risk I am willing to take," he says.

I peek down at Ivy in my arms, and I notice out of the corner of my eye that he does too.

"You're right, whatever is safer," I tell him, and Damian nods, releasing a breath of relief. I won't risk her life over half a day. I know that is why both of them came in to tell me such news –they worried I would argue with them over this, but when it involves Ivy's safety, I won't take unnecessary risks.

"Did you find out more about her history, her last name, anything about her?" I ask, turning my attention to Gannon.

"No, but I reached out to the old Alpha. He said he would dig her files out, and I could come to collect them next week."

"I will come with you," I tell him, and he nods.

"He was curious as to why we wanted to know about her, though," Gannon says.

"What did you say?"

"Nothing, of course. I told him I wanted Abbie's files too – told him that we wanted to know if they could be trusted amongst the other servants."

I nod at his words. He's always a quick thinker when put on the spot, which is why he's my third in command.

My fingertips trace down her back under the blanket, feeling the ridges of her spine and her scars. She's underweight, which bothers me just as much as the scars lining her back, and I suddenly feel guilty for making her sick. I would have to make it up to her.

"He said she was young when she came, and her parents put up a fight. Apparently, her father killed the orphanage headmistress's mate," Gannon tells me.

"Would explain why she was punished so brutally. Why would he let her remain with the headmistress, knowing that?" I growl.

Gannon growls while shaking his head.

"Did he say why there were only two rogue children in the orphanage?" I ask.

"No, but he became very nervous when I asked. I think he was covering up for his son."

"Makes sense. I got the same vibe when I spoke to him," Damian tells me, and I tilt my head to look at him. He looks away guiltily.

"You weren't assigned to look into it. Gannon was, so why did you speak to him?"

"Same reason: I was curious about her. I needed to know she wasn't a threat to you. It is my job as your Beta."

I nod, looking down at Ivy.

"Well, is she?" I ask him with a chuckle, knowing full well she is no threat to me. No one was, but unfortunately, not everyone fights fair, and Lycans have always been hunted, even by the werewolves.

"She is," Damian says with a smirk, and I raise an eyebrow at him.

"Don't tell me it wouldn't break you if she suddenly left," Damian challenges, and I growl at his words. She is never leaving me; I won't allow it. I will chain her to me if needed.

"My point is proven. Physically, being a werewolf, she is no match, but that doesn't mean she can't break you in other ways," Damian laughs.

"She won't. I won't allow it," I snap.

"But she could," he says, and I nod once, tugging her closer and burying my face in her neck. Damian chuckles, and Gannon snorts, trying to hold his laugh in.

"Shut up, the both of you," I snap at them. I know they find my obsession with the girl amusing, yet they will understand when they find their mates one day.

"Don't get your panties in a knot now that you realize she holds all the power," Damian laughs.

"I am still a King," I tell him.

"And she is your Queen." Gannon nods at her, and I smile.

Yes, she will one day be my Queen if she will have me, I think before stopping myself, realizing my line of thought—if she will have me.

If!

I look at Damian, who has a knowing look on his face. He can read me too well sometimes.

"I'm still the King," I tell them, and Damian smirks.

"So you keep saying," he laughs.

"My word is law."

"For now," Gannon teases.

"I could always keep her as my servant," I tell them, and Damian folds his arms across his chest with an incredulous look on his face.

"I didn't say I would," I tell him.

"I know you won't," Damian says.

"Unless, obviously, she did something bad," Gannon adds, and Damian and I both glare at him.

"Now, why would you say that? What bad bone does the girl have in her body?" Damian asks.

"I'm just saying," Gannon says with a shrug.

"It would have to be something horrendous. Even then, I am not sure," I admit. I think nothing would stop me from loving Ivy or wanting her. She could try to kill me, and I would probably ask her to forgive me for angering her. I chuckle at the thought.

"Something funny, my King?" Gannon asks.

"No, Gannon. I just can't wait until her birthday, and she realizes I am her mate," I tell them while leaning my head back and closing my eyes.

It is well into the night when we arrive at the grand hotel. The place is enormous, modern, and all sleek design, exactly what is expected in this modern era. I arranged for us to leave no later than 6 am.. I can't wait for Ivy to see the castle, but I also can't wait to be alone with her either.

I cover her with the blanket and carry her inside the huge hotel. My men surround me, obscuring her from the view of any other people as I make my way to our suite.

Damian steps ahead of me and searches the room before allowing me to enter. When I hear the door click shut as he leaves, I place her on the bed before climbing on it myself. She stirs now that I have dropped the calling, allowing her to wake. Her beautiful eyes flutter open dazedly, and my lips devour hers before she has a chance to speak.

Her skin heats beneath my palm as I grip her breast, rubbing my thumb over her nipple. My lips travel down her neck, and I desperately feel the urge to mark her.

"My King," she blurts, and the growl that leaves me makes her tremble beneath me. Anger courses through me, and I stifle it, reminding myself she just woke up and isn't clear-headed enough to remember. Her hands shake against my chest, and I can feel her breath on my neck.

"I didn't mean to startle you. Are you hungry?" I ask her.

She shakes her head, but her stomach betrays her.

"I will give you one chance to correct that answer, Ivy," I tell her, pulling back to look down at her. She averts her gaze to my chest, and I sigh, brushing her cheek gently with my hand.

"You don't need to fear me. I haven't hurt you, and I won't hurt you."

She licks her lips, and my attention diverts briefly to them. They look dry and cracked.

"Are you hungry?"

She nods, and I peck her lips, then roll off her, grabbing the phone to order room service. I feel Ivy move on the bed behind me. While I wait for them to answer, I move toward the small fridge and retrieve a bottle of water before making my way back to her. She squirms on the spot where she sits but takes the water, placing it beside her.

THIRTY-SIX

I VY

There is no memory of the rest of the journey, coming to the hotel, or being placed in this bed at all. As the King speaks on the phone, I watch him. But I am on the verge of bursting and need to pee.

I wonder where the servant's bathroom is when the King walks to the bar fridge before coming over and handing me a cold bottle of water. I place it beside me, its coldness making the urge to pee ten times worse.

He watches me for a second and speaks to someone on the phone, then hangs up and places it on the bedside table.

"What is wrong?" he asks as he turns back to face me.

"Is there a servant's bathroom? I really need to pee."

His eyebrows raise, and he points to the bathroom behind him.

"Bathroom is right there. Why would you use a servant's bathroom?"

"Because Clarice said that's what the servants use." Why do I feel like I am answering questions about rules he probably set?

"Ivy, you are not my servant."

I squirm. I'm about to pee on this bed if he keeps talking, especially knowing the bathroom is right there. What is it with bathrooms when you need to pee? The moment you notice one, the urge grows worse.

"Go; I will bring you some towels so you can shower. We can talk about it later," he says, motioning to the bathroom with his hand.

I hurry off, shutting the door behind me. After washing my hands, I'm about to walk out when the door opens, and King Kyson steps into the bathroom, blocking me from exiting.

"Where are you going?" he asks while looking down at me. He has towels in his hands.

"Out so you can shower," I tell him as I try to step around him. He blocks my path.

"Do you want to shower with me?" he asks, stepping so close I have to crane my neck to look up at him. He stares back at me. "You don't have to, but you can if you want to."

"Do you want me to?" I ask him, looking over my shoulder at the gigantic shower.

"Or we could have a bath?" he chuckles, making my face heat as I remember the last time I bathed with him.

"Shower is fine," I blurt, and his brows furrow. Crap, I upset him. "I didn't mean to upset you," I blurt foolishly. He cocks an eyebrow at me.

"Why would you think you upset me?"

Why does he ask so many questions?

"Are you upset?" I ask, and he laughs. My eyes widen. Did I say something funny? I don't get why he is laughing; what did I miss? I need to go back to sleep, hopefully, wake up with a functioning brain because mine is mush right now.

"No, I am not upset. You don't have to do anything you don't want to, Ivy. That is why I asked. You don't have to shower with me unless you want to. The choice is yours," the King says.

Huh, what choices? Since when do rogues have choices? He waits expectantly to see what I will say, but I want to see how many options I truly have.

"I will have one after," I tell him before swallowing down my fear after saying no to him. I wait for his wrath, my skin prickling, preparing for it to come, but he just shrugs.

"That's fine. I will shower quickly, then. Dinner will be here soon," he tells me, and I nod while he steps aside, allowing me to pass him.

I rush out, expecting him to shut the door, but he leaves it open. The shower starts, and I find myself looking around the room. With nothing to do, I decide to get his clothes ready for him and lay out the two suitcases on the floor. Only when I open the first one, I find it is filled with women's clothes. I look back at the door, shaking my head, closing it, and opening the other one. I pull his pajama pants out and place them on his bed before finding him some socks.

When I am done, I zip up the bag and sit on the edge of the bed. Bored, I stare around the room before glancing at the bathroom door. He really gave me a choice.

I expected him to command me to hop in there with him, but he didn't. Yet, the ache to go to him remains, and I'm not sure if it's nerves because I am waiting for him to come out and snap at me or if I actually want to shower with him.

Steam wafts out of the bathroom, along with his heady, exotic scent. I only understand how potent it is when I find myself standing next to the bathroom door. My mouth waters, and I clutch the door-frame to refrain from stepping inside. Everything about this man calls to me, thrills me, excites me, yet also terrifies me at the same time.

It's unnatural for someone like me to be affected and become almost obsessed with their master. Regardless, the ache to be near him remains, no matter how much the thought terrifies me. One question lingers, though: is he my master? He gave me a choice, yet denying him only makes me needier.

I hadn't realized with the anxiety of him ordering me around how much I longed for him to do so, just so I could be within his presence; it makes no sense.

"Ivy, are you okay?" the King asks, and my head snaps up only to find my body led me into the bathroom, completely ignoring the rational part of me – if that is even rational any more. Whenever I think of anything to do with the king, my body reacts like it knows before I do what it wants.

I nod, but my eyes seem to have a mind of their own as they trail over his hard, muscular body, perfectly sculpted in all the right places, his aura alluring. I step toward him.

I kind of wish he would do that calling thingy he does. At least then, I could explain away the weird feelings this man stirs within me.

CHAPTER

THIRTY-SEVEN

I VY

I glance at the bathroom door, wondering if I should walk out.

"Ivy," Kyson murmurs, and I can feel the King watching me. He pushes the shower screen door open, and I look at it before looking up at him. "What do you want to do?"

I can't seem to answer the question because I am confused. This is wrong, yet I keep doing things wrong.

"Why are you in here?" he asks, tilting his head to the side as he watches me, but I have a feeling he already knows what I want because he turns back to the shower to rinse the soap off, yet he leaves the shower screen open.

"Don't think, Ivy, just do what you want."

I growl at his words. What I want is confusing the hell out of me. My brain tells me to run, while the rest of me wants to rub myself on him and smother myself in his scent. I shake my head; where the heck did that come from?

"Do you know what you want?" the King asks, turning to face me.

I shake my head but then nod before looking down. I feel like ripping my hair out in frustration. At the same time, I can't seem to force myself to leave the bathroom.

"Does what you want scare you?" Kyson asks.

I don't answer, my eyes too busy taking in the sight of him. I should not have looked down. My eyes widen as I stare at his manhood. I gulp. The thing is huge. As I stare, the King clears his throat, making my eyes snap to his.

"My eyes are up here," he laughs, and my face heats under the intensity of his gaze.

"You want to shower with me?" he asks, but it sounds more like a statement than an actual question.

I chew my lip. "Yes, but I don't know why," I admit.

"Why do you think you do?" he asks, reaching his hand out and gripping the front of my shirt. He pulls me toward him, and I squeak as he pulls me closer and into the shower with him, drenching me.

"You didn't answer me," he says, peeling my shirt off and unclipping my bra with one hand. He tosses them out of the shower before undoing the button on my jeans, then stops and looks at me.

"I'm going to take these off you, or would you prefer they remain on?"

"Why do you keep asking questions?" I respond.

"Because I want you to understand you have a choice, Ivy. I don't want you as my slave or servant. I just want you, and every time I think you understand that you revert back to being my servant."

"If you don't want me as a servant, then what do you want me for?" I find myself asking.

Panic bubbles in me, and I remember the look Abbie gave me as I left, the fear that filled her eyes before she told me she loved me.

"I just want you, and I want you to want me, too," he says as he kneels and peels down my now-soaked pants that are sticking to my skin.

I step out of them, and he tosses them out the door. I grip his shoulder, nearly losing my balance when he looks up at me. My heart skips a beat when he grips my underwear, his eyes not leaving mine. He kisses my thigh as he removes my underwear. Those, too, are thrown from the shower to join the rest of our clothes lying in disarray on the floor.

"Would you like to be mine, Ivy?" the King asks, looking up at me.

I swallow, waiting for him to stand, but he doesn't as I watch him lean closer and kiss my thigh just above my knee. He nips at my skin, gripping my ankle gently, then rubs his thumb over my skin while his hand glides up my leg to my knee.

"Would you like me to be yours?" he asks as his hand trails higher.

I shiver under his scorching hot touch, my skin alight with that tingling sensation. I moan softly, unable to stop the noise from escaping me. His touch is gentle as he pushes me slightly back so I'm leaning against the tiled wall.

"Would you like that, Ivy?" he repeats as his fingers brush between the apex of my legs.

"I need an answer, Ivy. Your own answer – not what you think I want to hear. I want to know if you want the same," he asks, looking up at me. He leans closer, kissing my stomach, and it flutters spastically as he nips at me with his teeth.

Only the goddess knows how much I want these things, but he is a King and I am his slave. But, just this once, I will answer because, just this once, I want something, and that is him. No matter how wrong and foolish it is, I want him, and I am sick of denying it. Even if he tosses me aside tomorrow, I can say for once I got what I wanted.

"Yes, I would like that," I answer honestly, and the King smiles up at me. Boldly, my hand reaches toward his face, wanting to touch him. I cup his cheek, and he doesn't pull away; instead, he leans into my touch.

His stubble brushes the inside of my palm as he turns his face into my hand and kisses it. My entire body buzzes when I feel his hand move between my legs. His thumb strokes the seam of my lips, and my stomach tightens. Between my legs, I feel an almost violent throb as he glides his thumb between my slick folds before pressing down on my clit.

My hips jerk when the King presses his lips to my hip before nipping lower. His hot mouth on my flesh makes my legs tremble. He bites and licks at my thighs, his hand traveling down my leg to the back of my knee.

Then he growls and grips my knee, lifting my leg slightly before he looks up at me.

"Can I taste you, Ivy?" he asks, looking up at me, his silver eyes sparkling and his breathing harsher, fanning over my skin.

I have no idea what he wants to do, but I know I want to find out, so I nod. He pushes my leg open, and I gasp as he lifts one leg over his shoulder, pressing his face between my legs.

His hands grip my ass, tilting my hips forward before his hot mouth covers me completely. His tongue runs between my wet folds, and he groans before his grip tightens, the sound vibrating through me.

CHAPTER
THIRTY-EIGHT

I VY

Kyson's tongue runs between my lips to my clit, making my hips jerk when he sucks it into his mouth. I exhale, pressing back heavily against the wall while he licks and nips at it. I rock against his face, earning me a growl as he sucks it deeper.

His hand moves to my leg over his shoulder and he grips my thigh, pulling my leg wider and giving him more access as he licks and sucks on my flesh.

Moans spill from my lips, and I grip his hair and tug on it. His tongue is relentless when he plunges it inside me, tasting my arousal as it gushes from me. His mouth moves, tasting every inch of me before returning to my clit, teasing and circling as he sucks hard, making me cry out.

Automatically, I move against his mouth as my skin prickles at the sensation he is inducing. My entire body tenses and heats as he devours me, my hips moving gently towards him as I climb to the precipice, then spill over violently.

His hands gripping me are the only thing that are holding me upright as I cum on his tongue. My walls flutter, and my pussy pulsates as my orgasm ripples through me. Without thinking, I grip his hair, moving my hips against his mouth as I ride it out. His tongue laps up my juices when my grip on him turns slack, and I am left trying to catch my breath.

Tenderly, he runs his tongue between my folds again, then sucks and nips at my thigh before letting my shaking leg down, but not letting me go, for which I am thankful, because I feel severely at risk of having my legs go out from under me.

Finally, he rises, keeping me pressed against the tiled wall. With his huge hand gripping the back of my neck, he tilts my face up and kisses me, forcing me to taste myself on his tongue as it invades my mouth. I moan at the taste of myself mingled with him, and my hands trail up his side to his chest.

When I feel the vibration of his calling rumble through his chest, I pull away from him before kissing his chest. His hand slips into my hair, and as he tugs my head back, his lips cover mine again.

The King presses his erection against me and I pull him closer, my hand moving to his hip. I want to touch and taste him, but am unsure if he will let me.

"What are you thinking?" he mumbles against my lips. His mouth moves and he nips at my chin.

"I want to touch you," I tell him. My hand reaches between our bodies, and I trail my fingertips over his aroused flesh. It twitches when I touch it. He steps back, allowing me to watch as I touch him, exploring his body like the novelty it is.

I have never touched a man before, so am unsure of what to do with it; he groans when I wrap my fingers around his cock. I peek up at him to find him watching me, bracing his hands on the wall behind me.

I run my hand up the length of him, and he purrs, the sound making his chest vibrate. His eyes close, and his lips part. I have no idea what I am doing, however, I like watching his face as I touch him. I'm not sure if I am doing it right, but he doesn't stop me or pull away. Standing on my toes, I press my lips to his, and his eyes fly open.

Only, I am staring at the eyes of the beast he can become, his dark demonic eyes peering back at me. I pull away, and he watches my face with a predatory gleam in his eyes.

Should I stop? Before I can act on that thought, his canines slip out when his hand moves. He grips the back of my neck and his lips smash against mine almost violently. His kiss is soul-devouring and bruising until he pulls away.

"Don't be scared. I won't hurt you," he murmurs against my lips.

I let out a breath, and the hammering of my heart against my ribcage slows slightly before he thrusts into my hand as he presses closer to me.

His tongue licks across my lips, causing mine to part. I feel his canines graze them as he nibbles on my bottom lip before moving to my chin, teeth grazing as he leaves open mouth kisses down my neck.

He stops, buries his face in my neck, and a throaty growl leaves him as he nicks my skin. The points of his teeth are like needles as they break the skin, but not deep enough to mark me, just enough to cause slight discomfort.

"Kyson," I hiss, and he pauses, pulling back.

His eyes move to my shoulder where his teeth bit into me, and I expect him to freak out at what he did, but he doesn't. He just leans forward and runs his tongue over it. The spot tingles and throbs, aching like it wants his teeth embedded in my flesh.

"Sorry, did I hurt you?" he asks. My blood is smeared across his lips.

Shaking my head, I touch the spot he bit me, only to find it has healed. I pull my fingers back but find no blood staining them, yet somehow his lips are tainted with my blood.

"It healed," I murmur.

"Lycan saliva, Ivy. I think you sometimes forget what I am," he chuckles.

"But I don't understand?" I'm puzzled. I have heard of people healing each other when they are mates, but can Lycans do it all the time? Now, that is a handy gift to have. I wonder if he can heal himself?

"I have been wanting to heal you for ages but didn't want you to freak out."

I think about my blisters and how they had healed overnight, which I thought was odd at the time.

"You want to heal me?" I ask, a little shocked he would want to.

The King nods, and his hand moves from my shoulder and trails down my back. "It would still scar, but I can close them if you let me, or I could give you my blood, but it won't be as effective, not as quick."

"Does it hurt you when you do it?"

He shakes his head.

"So, will you let me?" he asks, pressing his lips to the corner of my mouth. The thought of him licking my back kind of weirds me out a little.

"And you just have to lick me?"

He chuckles and nods. "Yes, but it would be easier in my other form. My saliva is more potent. This form, it would take longer," he says, and my brows furrow. Fear, I know, is etched into my face.

"I won't hurt you. My Lycan side recognizes his own. I recognize you, Ivy. I promise you I won't harm you; you just need to trust me."

I swallow when a knock sounds on the door. The King looks toward the door, instantly pulling me behind him.

"Just me, your highness," Gannon calls out, making the King exhale.

"Just leave it. We will be out in a minute," he answers, and I listen to Gannon leave, the door shutting behind him. The King shuts off the water and reaches out the door, then passes me a towel. I wrap it around myself, and the King steps out of the shower, turning to face me.

"Is that a yes?" he asks expectantly.

"You won't hurt me when you are like that?" I ask, pulling my towel a little tighter when he suddenly presses me against the sink basin, his eyes flickering dangerously as he smiles, his sharp teeth on display, and his voice deepens, turning gravelly.

"Never," he purrs, and I exhale, chewing my lip.

Well, if he kills me, it would be quick, so I nod.

"There are so many things I want to do to you, but hurting you isn't one of them," he growls, nipping at my neck.

THIRTY-NINE

I VY

I follow him into the room, and as I do, I notice Gannon has placed a food tray on the bed. King Kyson doesn't even bother to get dressed, and I feel a little strange just standing around in a towel. He motions for me to come over to him before flicking the TV on and moving the tray to the bedside table while I stand awkwardly at the edge of the bed.

"Ivy, come," he tells me, and I chew my lip. He shakes his head and reaches over, gripping my wrist and yanking me on top of him. The motion makes an audible squeak leave my lips as I collide with his chest, and he chuckles at my awkwardness.

I scramble upright, placing my hands on his chest. Just as I push off him, he grips my thighs, tugging me back down on him and forcing me to sit.

My towel has risen precariously, and my face heats as he looks between my legs. I try to close them, but his hands tighten, preventing such action.

"I just had my mouth down there, yet you are embarrassed over me seeing you," he says, and my face heats even more at his words.

Does he have to say it out loud? Why does he have to say such vulgar things? Is he trying to embarrass me?

His hands trail higher underneath the towel, exposing me even more to wandering eyes. Before I can tug it down, he grips my hips and places me directly over where his hard cock is.

"Kyson!" I hiss, feeling his hardened length through the thin towel between us. He sighs and lets me move to wiggle higher, but pulls me back down when I try to climb off to sit beside him.

"Your birthday is soon," the King says, and I frown slightly. Is it a question or just a statement? I don't understand what he's getting at. He can be quite bizarre sometimes, and I don't know if his question warrants an actual answer.

"Are you nervous about shifting?"

"Kind of. Not really. I try not to think about it. Why?" I ask. I am slightly petrified after witnessing Abbie's shift though. That night will forever haunt me, but I know it wasn't supposed to be that way.

"Because when a werewolf comes of age, they find their mate," he says.

"Isn't it supposed to be rare to actually find them, though? Werewolves hardly travel away from the pack, so unless their mates are in it, most don't find theirs."

"Well, I will be returning to your old pack next week," the King tells me.

"What for?"

"To speak with the old Alpha, find out a few things. But that is not why I asked about your birthday." He squeezes my thighs gently while his thumbs rub against the inside of my thighs.

"What do you know of Lycans?" he asks while looking up at me.

"That they are different from werewolves, superior species, immortal, and what you have told me," I answer.

The King nods and seems to think for a second.

"Anything else?"

I shrug, not getting his point or where he is going with this conversation.

"Is there a reason you're asking? Because I don't know much. Abbie and I weren't allowed to attend classes, so I am not sure what you are asking or if you even are asking something?" I chew my lip.

"I am asking something, but it needs to wait until after your first shift," he says, tugging at the towel knot between my cleavage. I grip his hand and he raises an eyebrow at me. I let his wrist go.

He undoes it, letting it fall away so I am sitting on him completely naked. The King moves underneath me, pulling me with him until he is leaning against the headboard with me straddling his lap.

"For Lycans, it is harder to find their mates," he explains.

"Because they are a dying species," I nod, and so does he. "Yet, how are you a dying species if you are immortal?" I blurt out. That was one question that always puzzled me.

King Kyson laughs like he thinks what I said is funny, but I am genuinely curious about how so few exist.

"Immortal means our life span has no end. That doesn't mean we aren't killable. We can still die the same as everyone else if mortally injured. We are just more durable," he tells me.

"So if I shot you, you would die?"

"Depends on what sort of bullet and how close it got to my heart. Why? Are you planning on killing me? Because if you are, I may have to reconsider my next question," he laughs.

"No. And I don't even know how to use a gun, much less find one," I answer, thinking about it.

"How about you promise not to kill me, and I promise not to kill you?"

I raise an eyebrow at him.

"What?" he smirks.

"Somehow, I don't think it would be possible for me to kill you."

"It's possible in more ways than you know," he says with a strange glint reflecting in his silver eyes.

"What do you mean?" I ask.

"That doesn't matter, for now. What matters is my next question.

I just want to make sure you are making a choice because you want to, not because you shifted first."

"Why? Do you think I would change my mind at whatever your question is?" I say, genuinely curious. No one has ever prepared me for what would be different after shifting.

"Yes, I believe you would, but I want your answer now, not after."

"You are making no sense, my King." Kyson tilts his head to the side, watching me. I drop my gaze. "Sorry," I mutter.

He exhales, his hand moving over my hip and up to my ribs, his thumb caressing the side of my breast.

"You will understand that power is everything to wolves, especially she-wolves. Even those with mates always seek out dominant males. So yes, I believe after you shift, it would sway you to agree to what I want to ask. You would be more inclined to say yes."

"Unless you're a rogue. We are bound to no one. We have no status, so I fail to see what you're getting at?"

"I am hoping that will change. I want to change your title, Ivy."

"I thought only Lycans were part of the King's pack?"

He nods his head.

"I am a werewolf. I am not like you, and I don't think your Lycan pack would take too kindly to a werewolf amongst them. Besides, what about Abbie?" I smile at the thought of her. I miss her already and it has only been half a day since I last saw her.

CHAPTER
FORTY

I VY

"What if I changed you, made you into a Lycan?" the King asks, and my eyes lock onto his. I shake my head, horrified.

I don't want to be an immortal, and I don't want to watch Abbie grow old and die without me; we made a pact that we would go out together. What is he asking? But another thought suddenly occurs to me. Why? Why would he want to change me?

"Why?" I blurt out.

"Because I want to change your title, as I said," he answers.

"By making me a Lycan? That doesn't automatically change my title. And what about Abbie? And what would people think? No, that is a terrible idea, Kyson. They would kill me," I ramble in a panic.

"Who would kill you?" he asks with a menacing growl.

"The other Lycans, everyone who knew what I was before. And it wouldn't automatically change my status just because I would be immortal. I am still rogue, I would still be a servant, and I don't want to be an enslaved person for eternity!"

What just happened? I can't process anything. My mind feels blank, and I must have continued rambling and blubbering because,

223

finally, he presses a finger to my lips to silence me. The King drops his head against my collarbone.

"Don't you get it, Ivy? You are not understanding. I have been saying it for days. I even told you in the shower; I don't want you as my servant. I want you," he breathes.

"I only know how to be a servant, Kyson—a rogue or slave. That is what I am destined to be," I growl before covering my mouth. "Sorry, I didn't mean to growl at you. I keep doing it. I'm sorry."

"You're coming of age. That's why you keep growling, and your emotions are heightened. Growl at me all you want," he laughs.

I exhale, embarrassed at my outburst. Though, I remember how moody Abbie got before she first shifted. What a traumatizing experience that was. We were forever getting the cane that week, then her shift...

I try not to think about it too often.

Mrs. Daley wouldn't let her go outside under the moon. She explained that the first shift is easier if it is a full moon and you can feel its light. It induces our animalistic side to come forward faster. I have heard horror stories of no moon for days and some werewolves being stuck in a semi-shifted state.

Mrs. Daley forbade Abbie from going outside and locked us in our tiny room without even a window because she had ordered the handyman to board it up to make her shift more painful.

Abbie screamed for hours, and every time she got too loud, Mrs. Daley would come up and whip her. It got to the point where I ended up muffling her sounds with my hands because I couldn't handle watching her be beaten in that state when she cried out too loudly.

I come back to the present when the King clicks his fingers in front of my face. "Ivy, where did you just go?" he asks, waving his hand in front of me.

"Sorry, I was just thinking."

"Of what? You looked like you were stuck in a nightmare."

"Of Abbie's first shift," I answer, trying to erase her horrid screams from my mind.

"Ah, yes. It isn't pleasant, the first one."

"No, especially when it is a full moon, but you are locked in a room with no windows." I shake the sounds of her screams away; I can remember it as if it was yesterday.

"What?"

"Mrs. Daley, she wouldn't let Abbie go outside, and it was a full moon. One of the cooks, Katrina, was nice when Mrs. Daley wasn't around. She told Abbie to go outside, told her that the transition would be faster if she did. But Mrs. Daley wouldn't let her. She locked us in the room."

"She locked you in the room with a transitioning werewolf?" Kyson asks.

"Yeah, well, we shared a room," I shrug.

"I don't know what I am more horrified at, the fact she locked her away from the moon or the fact she locked her in there with you," the King says, his eyes darkening.

"What do you mean? I'm pretty sure sharing a room with her was the least of her worries; I have seen her naked plenty of times," I tell him.

"No, I mean Abbie could have killed you. Transitioning were-wolves are dangerous on their first shift; they can lash out. They struggle to control their wolves in the shift, their baser instincts come out."

My eyes widen in horror. I had no idea. Although Abbie turned a little angrier and snapped at me a few times, I just thought she was in pain. She then lay down on her tummy and I brushed her fur all night, waiting for her to shift back.

"Your headmistress has a lot to answer for regarding yours and Abbie's treatment," the King growls, shaking his head.

"Your shift won't be like that, I promise. I will remain with you."

"But you just said—"

"I will remain with you. A few werewolf bites won't hurt me," he says, cutting me off.

He cups my face with his hand, and the scent of his skin so close to my nose makes me inhale before I lick his wrist. My eyes widen at what I did, and I clamp my lips together, horrified that I just licked him!

However, he snickers and lifts his knees behind me, forcing me closer. He smells heavenly, and I can't help myself; I inhale and sniff him like some deranged freak.

He turns his head up with a smile on his lips as he offers his neck to me, tilting it to the side so I have better access, and some foreign urge comes over me at the sight of it.

I sniff him, running my nose up his throat and down again before stopping in the crook of his neck. His hand slips into my hair, and I try to stop myself. Yet, the urge is too intense... verging on pain. Much to my horror, I lick his neck.

He shivers, pressing me closer when I suddenly bite into him – and I don't mean gently either – like a damn savage animal. It's like I lose all control and the urge just takes over completely. He groans, and I swear I feel his cock twitch beneath me. His blood rushes into my mouth like a slap of clarity in the face.

FORTY-ONE

IVY

The shock of what I did makes me gasp, letting him go, but he pulls me closer.

"You can bite me, Ivy," the King purrs, but I am mortified at my vile actions.

I shake my head. "I made you bleed!" I shriek, trying to get off him. He will surely whip me now. Shit, his guards will, the moment they notice what I did.

I try frantically to get off him, but he grips my arms, holding me in place.

"Shhh, breathe. Do I sound mad?" he asks, running his hands up my arms. His fingers move across the back of my neck, pulling my head down to the crook of his neck. Then he holds my face and my lips press against his warm skin.

I clamp my teeth together as the urge returns.

"It's okay, love. If you want to bite me, bite me. I am yours to do what you want with," Kyson murmurs next to my ear. I try to pull away from him, but his grip holds strong.

"A servant—"

"Call yourself that again and see what happens. I don't know how much clearer I can be; I have told you I don't want you as my servant, that I want to change you," he sighs, his grip loosening slightly, but not enough for me to escape it.

"I want you to be mine, and I want to be yours. I want to make you my Queen. Do you understand that? I want to mark you after you shift, Ivy. I want to change you, and I want you to be my Luna Queen."

I jerk in his hold. He growls but lets me sit up, although he refuses to let me get off his lap, his fingers pressing into my thighs.

"You want to mark me?" I ask, and he nods.

Is he insane? This man has truly lost his marbles. How he can perceive a slave as a potential Queen is beyond me.

"Yes, I want to mark and mate you. I also want to change you," he says, running his finger down the side of my neck, making me shiver.

"But I am a rogue, a servant."

"Not to me, you're not. I don't care about your status, and neither will my pack. I want you, but I want you to want me too."

"Wait, you don't want me to be a sex slave?" Is this why he's being nice? Because he wants something else?

"What?" he says, his face twisting in outrage at my words. "Is that what you thought all this was?" he snaps at me. All calmness has gone from his face. His eyes darken and his face twists in anger.

I swallow, but nod. What else was I supposed to think? I know what happens to the rogues – the same thing that always happens. We're either slaves to our owners, sex slaves, or dead. We are never given any other options. We are the mutts of society, the vermin.

He is the one with unrealistic expectations of what I am to him, delusional. I, however, know exactly my status that he seems to keep forgetting. It has hung over mine and Abbie's heads for years, since we were kids. Rogues are unworthy, dirty, and unwanted. Mrs. Daley made sure we didn't forget our place; she even branded it into our skin so we wouldn't forget.

We aren't people; we're objects, free labor, someone to kick when they feel particularly shitty about their lives – a quick power boost because we have no power of our own.

Rogues don't deserve power.

"I figured you would throw me away when you got bored, which is fine. You don't have to promise things or do things. I know how this works. I won't fight you. It's okay. It is what it is," I answer. Even though the thought petrifies me, I can't abandon Abbie. If he wants a sex slave, I can learn to deal with it. I can do that for Abbie. It's his right. It's just sex, right? It's what's expected of me... Like an extra chore.

Kyson growls, and the sound vibrates against my chest, making my heart beat erratically. "If I wanted to fuck you, I would have ordered you on your back, Ivy. I certainly wouldn't be explaining myself to you for it, either. So let me make one thing clear. I do not want a sex slave; I want a mate, and I want you to let me be yours, equals. And I certainly don't want you as a piece of property to own... I want you; not for you to do things because you believe it's what I want or because you feel obligated to because I am the King."

His anger is terrifying as I watch his eyes flicker to the beast within him.

"Equals, Ivy. I won't pull rank over you unless it has to do with your safety or something I feel strongly about, and I sure as hell would never force myself on you or anyone. If I make you uncomfortable, you tell me. I won't get mad, and I won't punish you for how you feel. Equals: if you want something, tell me; if you don't, tell me. And I will do the same for you. Is that understood?" he asks, glaring at me.

Words fail me. Most would dream of being with a Lycan King. However, my wishes aren't like anyone else's – I wish for freedom, a voice, because mine has been squashed for so long.

Sometimes I wonder if I even have one left; I certainly never use it, so I find words hard, except with Abbie. Speaking back earns punishment, a pain I know very well... I am not about to start asking for more of it – especially for something as silly as not thinking something is fair or because something I don't like is asked of me. I take orders. I know the consequences of speaking back. It's written across my back...

A voice? I almost scoff. I can't just unlearn silence. At this point, its reflex, muscle memory; remain quiet and hope to go unnoticed.

Who would want a Queen that was submissive to life because she never had one? Abbie and I always spoke to each other of what we would do with our freedom, but honestly, they were just dreams; something we knew would never come to fruition.

If given a chance at freedom, we would probably fall back into the same place, not knowing anything else. Comfortably familiar in our misery.

"Ivy?"

"I don't think I can be what you want," I tell him, and he sighs.

"We still have time, but one thing remains clear: you are not my servant. You are just Ivy. And I don't want to hear you bring up being my servant again."

His words confuse me, not because I don't understand what he said, but because I don't know who I am. Who I thought I would become was always just a dream to me; one so out of reach it faded away, long forgotten; trampled into dust and floating off into the wind. This is reality, and in reality, I am no one; just a rogue. Insignificant, unimportant, and unwanted. I am an imposter of who I once was, a reflection of what they made me to be. Now I am 'you', the name they gave us because ours wasn't worth speaking.

"What are you thinking?" Kyson asks me, and I sniffle. Words are not my thing, so I find it odd that he always requests them.

"I don't know who I am if I am not a slave or servant, Kyson. I am either a slave, forced to work, or a true rogue, running constantly but never free."

"I know exactly who you are," he whispers, pecking my lips softly. He nibbles on the bottom one. His warm palms caress my ribs up to the sides of my breasts while his lips trail down my jawline.

"You are the woman I want, the woman I will love and cherish.

You are mine just as I am yours," he murmurs as he trails open mouth kisses down my neck, making me purr.

He pauses and chuckles at the sound I make before he presses his lips in a spot similar to where I accidentally bit him.

"And when you realize that," he whispers, then sucks the same spot, "I will place my mark right here, so everyone knows I am yours, and you are my queen," he says, breaking the skin with his teeth. I jump at the sting, but his tongue is already lapping over it.

Heat rushes through me, and my skin tingles and vibrates, my nerves buzzing at his touch. He pulls his face from my neck, and I touch the spot with my fingertips.

"I didn't mark you, Ivy. I won't until you shift, but I must say I do like the look of my teeth on your skin."

My eyes go to the mark I left on him. It's healed already but is scarred, which I find odd. I touch it again and he shivers.

"They're called promise bites. You haven't got canines yet, but once you shift, you will be able to mark me," he tells me. His hands cup my face and his thumbs go to my upper lip, pushing it up. His brows pinch in the middle before he does the same to my bottom lip.

"What is it?" I ask him.

"Nothing, just you already have canines. It sometimes happens with werewolves, and they won't extend fully until you shift, but are you sure your birthday is a couple of weeks away?"

"I think so," I tell him.

"Strange, though not unheard of. Just, usually they come down a couple of days before a shift, not weeks before, unless you're Lycan. Mine were always longer than werewolves' or human teeth," he shrugs.

"Something is wrong with my teeth?" I ask, touching them with my finger. They feel the same as always, no different, and surely, I would notice. Wouldn't my speech change?

"No, nothing is wrong with them. They just look a little more extended than normal. That's why I asked about your birthday."

I shrug, unsure. Mom said it was on that day, and she would have known.

"Want to hear something funny?" he asks. I raise an eyebrow at him but nod.

"Lycans are born with their canines. My baby photos look pretty funny," he chuckles. I laugh; that would look funny.

"We should eat. Our food is probably cold, and we have to be up early to get to the castle by lunchtime."

"Did you know the King and Queen well?" I ask, changing the subject.

"Kind of. They kept to themselves mostly. My parents were close to them. When I was a child, my parents had an arrangement with theirs," he answers.

"What sort of arrangement?" I ask.

"A marriage one. If they had a daughter, she was to be promised to me when she came of age, to help keep the royal bloodlines strong. But that went down the drain, obviously."

"Were you upset?"

He shrugs. "No, not really. I didn't know her. They kept her a secret, paranoid about the hunters finding out about her. Plus, I would have had to wait years anyway, but I am not sure I would have gone through with it if she said no."

"Why's that?"

"Because my parents had an arranged marriage. My mother disagreed at first," he tells me.

"Your parents didn't like each other?"

"No, they loved each other, but at first, no – not until my father marked her. I just wanted to try to find my mate first."

"What happened to the girl?" I ask.

"They killed her. We found her blood-stained clothes and some of her hair. Since half the kingdom was slaughtered along with them, we couldn't exactly be sure which child she was, and also not knowing exactly how old she was didn't help us. We only had the clothes to go off for approximate size, and so many kids turned up in the river." He shakes his head at the memory, which obviously stayed with him all these years because I can see it haunts him still.

" And if she lived?" I ask curiously.

"I probably would have given her to my sister to raise. It would be awkward raising my future mate, don't you think?" he laughs.

"Yes, that would certainly be different," I chuckle.

CHAPTER
FORTY-TWO

K YSON

Ivy's scent perfumes the room and calms my nerves, which is the only thing keeping me sane right now. Tomorrow is my sister's murder anniversary, so I am on edge. Ivy is unaware that I am watching her.

No matter how much I try to pry my eyes from her sleeping form tangled in the sheets, my eyes always drift back to her or I find myself standing over her, fighting the urge to touch her, caress her.

My senses are all over the place with her. The desire to mark her grows stronger with the bond as it forges. I can tell Ivy is just as affected by the way her arousal will fill my nose, her instincts pulling her closer while they wage war with her mind telling her to stay away.

I must admit, that is one thing I love about she-wolves. Their ability to become lost to their baser instincts makes them compliant. Although I don't want that from Ivy—I want her to challenge me, maybe because she is the only one that could get away with it.

However, looking at her, I doubt she ever will. Lycans are worse tempered, and sometimes I forget she's an ordinary werewolf. I should be gentler. Ivy isn't as durable as a Lycan. Despite how much she sometimes reminds me of a Lycan, instincts so similar, yet so far apart at the same time. I need to remember she isn't because I worry I will push her too far, or scare her beyond repair.

I wonder briefly what her wolf will be like, what color fur she will have. She has the most abnormal eyes for a werewolf. Every time I look at her, I get this bizarre feeling something is off about her.

Her deep, cerulean-blue eyes remind me of someone. I can't figure out why or who. Even a few guards and Damian have commented on how odd her eye coloring is.

Blue is an odd color for werewolves—Lycans not so much. It isn't unheard of, but it is rare for werewolves to have those deep blue eyes. Sometimes genetic mutations or super strong bloodlines cause it in werewolves.

We'll find out soon enough. Maybe her father was human. That would explain why I can't sense her wolf side as much. Perhaps she doesn't have one.

No, that can't be it, because she can growl and purr. My thoughts run rampant as I watch her until I am pulled from them when I feel the mindlink open up.

"Are you awake, my King?" Gannon asks. I stare at the glass of whiskey in my hand before downing it.

"You know I am, or you wouldn't be asking," I reply as I get out of bed and wander over to the bar. I pour another glass, and the door to my room opens.

Damian and Gannon step in, averting their gazes from Ivy and looking at me. Damian walks over to the armchair and takes a seat in one of the armchairs while Gannon wanders toward her on the bed. I raise an eyebrow at him, but he only tosses the throw blanket over her back to cover her before taking a seat across from Damian. I hand them both a glass before retrieving my own.

"What is it?" I ask them, wanting to know why they suddenly decided on a midnight visit.

"I thought you were going to heal her?" Gannon asks, looking over at her sleeping.

"She fell asleep while eating," I answer. Anger courses through me at the thought of why she needs healing, though they're no longer gaping wounds across her back. Still, I hate seeing the angry red lines that litter her skin.

"Why did that stop you?" he asks.

"I would rather do it while she's awake. She needs to know not to fear me in that form."

Gannon nods in understanding, turning his attention back to me.

"So why the middle of the night invasion of my room?" I ask.

"Couldn't sleep," Damian answers.

"Me, neither," I tell him, and he chuckles.

"How many of those have you had?" he asks, pointing to my glass.

"A few too many," I shrug and his brows furrow with worry – a look I have seen plenty of times on his face.

"Are you sure that is wise with her around?" Damian questions.

"She isn't going anywhere, and I won't hurt her," I growl.

"I'm not worried about you hurting her, my King. I'm worried about you spooking her," Damian answers.

"I am fine," I answer while moving across the room to sit on the edge of the bed facing them.

"I assume you came to see me for a reason other than insomnia?"

"Yes, my King. We know we agreed to 6 am, but the men are antsy. This place is unfamiliar and too hard to keep watch over the entire perimeter," Gannon answers.

"You want to leave earlier?"

They both nod their heads, looking at Ivy on the bed behind me.

"You doubt my ability to keep her safe?" I ask them.

"Never, my King. We just worry about our King and future Queen's safety in this hotel... too many people and too many hiding spots; and with the anniversary tomorrow, we want to keep moving," Damian answers.

"The driver?" I ask.

"Also ready to go," he replies and I nod.

"Give me an hour," I answer, glancing at the clock. It's a little after 2 am. My head turns back to them; they're both getting to their feet.

"I want to heal her first; at least then she may sleep in the car."

"Do you want me to stay?" Damian asks. I glance at Ivy before looking back at him.

"Won't be necessary," I tell him. He nods and both of them take their leave. Placing the glass down, I strip off my shorts before shifting. I twist and crack my neck as my bones readjust and snap swiftly with my shift. My vision and sense of smell adjust, my senses intensifying as I walk toward the bed and climb onto it.

Ivy's back is rising and falling as she breathes in and out, and I gently tug the blankets off her. My claws slice through the thin sheets as I peel them away.

Ivy moves in her sleep, and goosebumps rise on her delicate skin, now exposed to the night air. I sniff the back of her neck while my clawed hand trails up her side, and she stirs. I don't want her to wake startled, so I move slowly as I bury my face in her neck, inhaling her scent.

She continues to stir, and I can feel the orgasmic tingling sensation that contact with her skin causes to rush over my hands. Something stirs within me as I watch her—some desire to claim what belongs to me—and before I can stop myself, I nip her.

She jumps in her sleep, then tenses, freezing. Her senses warn her a predator is near, something more dangerous than her. I hear her heart thumping in her chest like a hummingbird's wings. So I run my tongue over my bite, licking up the blood that trails down her shoulder blade.

"Kyson?" Her voice is barely a whisper, and I press my nose against her cheek. She trembles beneath me as I push my chest to her back and start purring. Her tremors stop, and she sighs as I press my weight against her.

"You're safe with me, always," I purr, releasing her from my calling. She remains still, and I can tell she is scared, but it shows she trusts me enough not to hurt her when she doesn't try to escape me.

I sniff her neck, and when she turns her face slightly, I press my nose against hers. Her giggle makes me chuckle, then lick her lips.

"That was gross, like a dog's tongue," she chuckles.

"Well then, I guess I am your pet," I snicker. I lift my weight slightly off her and she rolls beneath me, looking up at me curiously, warily.

Her hands move shakily to my face before her thumb runs over one of my teeth. She jerks her hand away when it slices the pad of her thumb and she sucks on it.

"What did you expect? For them not to be sharp?" I chuckle.

She pulls her thumb from her mouth and examines the slice. I quickly lick it, letting her watch it heal. She seems in awe as she studies the now-non-existent cut.

"How?" she mutters. I don't answer, not wanting to tell her it's because I am her mate. I want that to be a surprise for her to find out on her own.

"Roll over," I whisper to her, and her eyes dart to mine. She sucks in a breath, and I nudge her.

CHAPTER

FORTY-THREE

I VY

     Kyson hovers above me. Despite staring right into the eyes of the true Lycan King, despite his weight pressing down on me and his scary exterior, I somehow know he would never harm me.

His hands are gentle, and his tone of voice is calm, though also sounds rougher; it reassures everything in me that made me fear him. My life could end at any time, but I don't fear death from the man-turned-beast above me.

No, I can't see myself ever fearing him; I know it's because he doesn't want me to. He allows me to have that trust in him because he could ideally end me.

Some instinctual part of me calls out to him, to ruin or to love, yet the tenderness of his touch assures me it is just that: tenderness and love. It seems impossible to feel so much for someone after such a short time, or maybe I am naïve in thinking it is love and I'm not merely an object to him.

Yet he calms my anxiety, and the content feeling of finally being home when around him made me roll onto my stomach when he asked.

King Kyson is home. In whatever way I could have him, I want him. Whether it's at his feet or by his side, I would take it. Home is something I had never felt. Even with my parents, it never existed.

A sense of safety and belonging was never felt with them, either. I am a stranger to my own existence and place in this world.

I always thought Abbie was my home, my safe place, and she is. However, now I wonder, if only for a while, if home could be with my King.

As I am lost in the sleepy thought, the King moves above me and his chest rumbles against my back. I loved the noises he made, loved what he calls the calling. It feels familiar and like it is mine alone.

Kyson presses his face into my neck and sniffs at me. His whiskers and fur tickle, a rough contrast against my skin, and I tuck my chin, feeling his tongue lick a line across my shoulder blade.

His tongue traces the lines that mar my flesh. A tingling sensation and warmth spread across it, and I feel the tissue closing. The jagged edges sewing together again. It's like the last remnants of my old life are closing, the hole over my heart that I thought would never close, filling in.

After all this time, a spot left gaping from abuse and rejection, of neglect and hopelessness, didn't ache like it used to.

The pain fades away with the memory of the countless times my skin was branded while my stomach twists with my desire to dream of better things.

What if I loved and lost it?

Though how do you love when you've never known it? Sure, my parents loved me and cuddled me, but for so long, all I've felt is pain. Warm hugs turned to whips and chains that restrained my life. Could I break the mold they forced me into, break the chains that held me back? Take back a life that was beaten out of me and suppressed for so long?

I am not sure, but I am determined to find out, even if it is only brief and ends badly, I can own those moments. I'll never know until I try.

For once, I will trust the words spoken, the intention behind them. For once, I will let myself feel free, even if only fleetingly. So I remain still, except when his tongue traces down my ribs, his whiskers and fur tickling.

Only then do I squirm and cringe away. The pain fades quickly, turning to desire. Despite my mind being structured to believe the worst, my heart is set, and my body is willing to be his, and his only.

His tongue feels hot and wet as it glides across my ribs once more. The moment he finishes, I know by the sound of his bones realigning before I feel his bare skin press against mine; the rise and fall of his chest as his breathing falls in time with mine.

The King presses himself against me, his thighs pressing against mine, and his erection digs into my lower back. He purrs, the sound bringing forth my own as his nose trails across my cheek. He kisses the side of my mouth before nipping at my ear, and I feel the slickness between my thighs.

The foreign feeling of desire that only he can bring forth, a desire I anticipated and feared because despite my body craving something it has no idea how to explain. It feels right. How had I not noticed it before, the complete feeling he induces, like a half to another, making me feel whole, as the pieces of the puzzle aligned in perfect synchronization.

He groans, and I shiver at the sound. Goosebumps emerge on my flesh as he flicks my ear with his tongue.

"As much as I want to remain here and ravage your body, we have to leave," he whispers, flicking my ear again. Despite my brain trying to override the sound from escaping past my lips, my whine is audible.

The King chuckles. "I promise later, Ivy. When we get back home, you can have me all to yourself, but we must leave," he whispers, pecking my cheek.

His weight lifts off me and the chill of the room drifts over my skin with him gone. I roll onto my side and sit up while the King retrieves his boxers off the floor.

"How much further is it?" I ask him.

"Couple of hours, you can sleep in the car," he says while placing a suitcase beside me. He opens it before grabbing the other, which he got his pants out of.

"Are you going to get dressed?" he asks, and I look in the suitcase. All the clothes are brand new, and I look at him, wondering when he had time to get them.

CHAPTER
FORTY-FOUR

I VY

"Where did you get all these?" I ask him before pulling out an oversized off-shoulder sweater and some jeans. I've never seen this many clothes in my life.

"Are these alright?" I ask him, holding them up to show him. I wasn't used to picking my own clothes and worried I will pick the wrong thing. I've only ever worn rags or a uniform.

"Wear what you want. I prefer you naked, but since we have to leave, I suppose you will have to wear something," he laughs.

"Or I could walk around naked, my King, if you prefer," I challenge, and his eyes flicker.

"Very well, all their deaths will be on your hands, though," he retorts.

"Whose deaths?" I ask in confusion.

"Those who look at what's mine," he says, stepping closer and pressing his lips to my forehead. I quickly slip the clothes on.

"Wise choice," he teases, closing the suitcases and placing them by the door.

"If you want to go shopping with Clarice and Beta Damian when we get back, you can, if you don't like what she chose for you," Kyson says.

"Clarice went and got these for me?"

"Yes, I have already informed her you are no longer my servant, and those important already know who you are to me."

I glance down at my hands, feeling guilty and worrying what they will think if they thought I wasn't one of them anymore, I don't want them to treat me any differently.

Kyson's fingertips graze my chin and tilt my face upward. "Why do you look upset?" he asks.

"I wonder what Abbie will think," I admit.

"You don't think she would be happy for you?" he asks.

"She is like my sister, my family, and if I let you change me, what would become of her, of us?"

He pauses to think for a second. "Is that why you said no, because of Abbie?" he asks.

"No, well, kind of. I don't want to watch her grow old and die without me."

"And is that your only worry, that you will lose her?" he asks.

"I don't think I can meet the expectations you want. Everyone will think I'm weak," I tell him honestly.

"The only expectation I have of you is that you remain by my side, Ivy. The rest will come, but no one would dare call my Queen weak," the King growls.

I went to protest, but the firm look he gives me makes me remain quiet.

"Would you accept if I had Abbie changed too?" he asks. "If she wanted to, of course, I won't force her, but if she agrees, I am sure Gannon won't mind changing her."

"You won't do it?" I ask.

"No, but Gannon has a crush on Abbie. He has been harassing Damian to give her to him as his maid," he chuckles.

"Pardon?" I ask, incredulous.

"He likes Abbie, Gannon has no mate, and for me to change her I could accidentally bond her to me, not like a mate bond, but those lines can become blurred, especially for the person changed, make them compliant to my demands. Not that I will ever push you to do something you don't want," Kyson explains.

"What if she says no?"

"Then that is her choice, but then that will also mean you have to make one, Ivy," he tells me. "I can't change for you, but I would if I could."

"You would give up being a Lycan, an immortal?" I ask, wondering why anyone would do that.

"Yes, when you have lived as long as I have, time no longer holds meaning, not if it is wasted. Without you, it wouldn't be worth keeping track of," he says simply.

"Wait, how old are you?" I ask.

He shrugs. "I like to think I am still young. I don't feel old. Why do I look it?" he laughs, and his lips tug into a sly smile as he waits for my answer. I shake my head yet am still intrigued to know. Maybe it is morbid curiosity.

"How old?" I ask.

"As old as the castle in which we live."

I gasp. I have no idea how old it is, but it is clear it isn't from this century, and looks like something from medieval times.

"Still want to know my age, or would you prefer the age I stopped aging?"

"Yes, the age you stopped aging, or I may have to call you grandpa," I snicker. He raises an eyebrow at me.

"I stopped aging just shy of 30. Most men stop aging around the age of 30, women a little different, between the ages of 23 and 30," he says, motioning me with his hand to the door.

"But Clarice?"

"Certain things can age us, but given her age, she looks young still."

My brows pinch together, but he doesn't elaborate.

I get up just when we hear a knock at the door. Kyson's hand drops to my hip as he tugs me against him. At least he looks around the age that I thought, and I couldn't imagine living for that long. It sounds lonely.

"I may be old, but with age comes experience and some things I have perfected," he says, dipping his face in my neck.

He runs his tongue across my neck, and his hand move, pressing flat against my stomach as he pulls me against him. He pulls his face from my neck before tugging my head back by my hair gently with his other hand.

His tongue invades my mouth in a way that should be illegal. It is lewd and teasing. I moan into his mouth as his tongue plays with mine, and his hand on my stomach slips between my legs to my core. He squeezes, enticing a moan from my lips.

He bites my lip as he pulls away, leaving me breathless as the door opens. Gannon steps in and past us, retrieving our bags, then walks back out while my face heats.

No doubt Gannon can smell my arousal in the room, making the situation even more embarrassing. Between my legs developed its own heartbeat at his obscene kiss. If he keeps this up, I'll run out of panties long before we get home, I think, feeling the slickness between my legs. Kyson presses his lips to mine and growls softly.

"You will want to calm that desire, my love, or I just may eat you," Kyson growls.

My face heats at his words, knowing that he, too, can smell the scent of my arousal. It makes it all the more awkward when I step into the hall to notice Damian smirking at us as he leans against the wall.

"Ready, my King?"

Kyson nods to him before draping his arm across my shoulders and tucking me closer. He leans down and kisses my temple, then whispers. "You think home is grand? Wait until you see the Landeena Kingdom. It was the biggest Kingdom of all."

CHAPTER
FORTY-FIVE

I VY

The drive to the castle is long, and the roads are bendy, making my stomach roll. We've had to stop at the side of the road multiple times while my stomach heaved violently. Kyson kept having to ask the driver to pull over so I could throw up.

I wipe my mouth on the tissues Beta Damian has ready, and the King passes me a water bottle, toothpaste, and toothbrush. As I remove the foul taste from my mouth, I welcome the minty freshness. I knew I shouldn't have eaten that egg and bacon muffin; I am now paying dearly for it.

Reaching for the bottled water, I swish it through my mouth. I feel hot and clammy. The entourage of cars circled around us, and the King's guards have their backs to us, for which I am thankful.

My stomach is becoming embarrassing, and it is definitely not ladylike to be tossing my stomach.

What made it all the more humiliating was how the King has witnessed my stomach's upheaval multiple times since I met him.

Mrs. Daley would have whipped me good. Thank God the King didn't seem fazed, more concerned if anything, and I had to keep pushing him away when he kept trying to hold my hair because I was worried I would puke on his shiny shoes.

"Not much further, I promise," Kyson eventually says while I rinse my mouth one last time before climbing back into the car.

I crawl across the seat and lay down directly under the air-conditioning vent, feeling hot. Kyson climbs back in, and the cars pull off the curb and continue.

"Ivy, your seat belt," Kyson says. I ignore him, turning my face into the seat.

"Ivy!" His tone is warning me, and I huff, closing my eyes.

I am too sick to care right now. My mind solely focused on the sickly feeling in my stomach. *Meh, I had a good run. Nearly 18 years is a good length of time,* I think.

"I will give you two seconds, Ivy, to place your seatbelt on." I groan and turn my head to look at him before turning back to face the rear of the seat and curling into a ball on my side.

I am not putting it on. It digs into my belly, making the sloshing worse, and I feel uncomfortable with it on.

"One."

I roll my eyes and growl before snickering at the fact I did growl at him.

It is becoming more frequent and as embarrassing as it is hearing the strange noises I now make. I also like that I can growl back at him.

It is strange, like when boys hit puberty and their voices change. Instead, I am hitting the werewolf phase and now making animal noises. How ridiculous.

"You did not just growl at me," he says disapprovingly. I snicker and shake my head.

"One and a half, Ivy!" Kyson growls, and I growl back at him, though his growl is more controlled, louder. Since I forced it that time, it came out more of a purring meow. The King clicks his tongue.

"Are you seriously being disobedient over a seatbelt? You do not want me to get to three?" I roll my eyes, but thankfully he doesn't see. "Ivy!"

"Two," I count for him, not caring about his counting. I am not putting that seatbelt on. I don't care if I sound like a stubborn child. He isn't the one with his belly churning because the damn road there is like a roller-coaster. Not that I have been on one, but I don't think I would go near one after being on this road that seems to have no end.

"Well, aren't you in quite the mood? If I didn't know it was your werewolf side slowly coming forward, I would have spanked you by now?" Kyson growls. I scrunch my face up at his words. He wouldn't, would he?

"Last chance, Ivy. Put your seatbelt on."

I am near tempted to tell him to make me, but I know he will, so I keep my mouth shut, hoping he will give up and let it slide. He growls. The noise causes goosebumps to rise on my arms, and I roll over.

"No, it makes it worse," I whine, turning my head to face him. He raises an eyebrow at me and purses his lips. I huff and glare when I realize he doesn't have his seatbelt on, yet he is complaining about me not wearing one.

"Why do I have to wear one when you don't?" I snap at him, and both of his eyebrows raise at my tone. Geez, my words sound a little snarky even to me that time. My mind feels like mush, and I react before thinking and spewing the word vomit.

"Maybe because I am more durable than you. Now put the seat-belt on, Ivy."

"Put yours on then," I retort. The King growls once more. He seems to enjoy doing that, so I growl back at him, unable to stop myself. He presses his lips in a line, and his eyes flicker.

"Sorry," I blurt out.

"You are lucky I am patient. If you were anyone else, Ivy, I would not put up with the attitude. Hormones and werewolf instincts coming in or not," he snaps, clicking his tongue.

He leans forward, and his hand grips the front of my pants. In one swift yank, he pulls me across. I think I will hit the floor between the seats when he grabs me.

A yelp escapes me, and I suddenly find myself on his lap. I pull my pants from my ass crack from the wedgie he gave me when he grabbed my pants. The King chuckles, watching me try to fix my pants while he holds me in place.

The King then stretches his legs out and rearranges me so my back is against his chest and my legs rested over his. He places his feet on the seat across from us. He clips the seatbelt across us both.

"I have my seatbelt on, happy?" I tell him and he purrs, and I tug on the strap around my waist when he pulls on it. He then places his hand on my stomach where my shirt had risen, exposing my mid-drift.

"Now try to sleep," he says, pulling my head against his chest. He starts purring, and the sound lulls me as I blink, trying to remain awake. Kyson moves and then chuckles before pushing my eyelids down with his fingers.

"I said sleep or my guards may kill us both if I have to ask them to pull over again," he laughs. His calling grows stronger until I can no longer fight it, and I am forced to sleep.

FORTY-SIX

I VY

"Ivy, wake up. We are here."

I groan, turning my face into his chest before feeling my cheek and lips become wet. I sit up, startled, and look at him before looking at his shirt, which is covered in drool. My eyes widen and my face heats with embarrassment. The warm sunlight filters through the car window, casting a golden glow on his features.

"Yes, I may have gone somewhat overboard with the calling, but you kept complaining your stomach hurts," he says, unclipping the seat belt.

He leans forward, tugs his shirt off, and reaches for a hand towel to wipe his chest. I blink before finding my fingers brushing through the hair on his chest. The King stops, glancing at me, yet my eyes are on his chest.

"Ivy?" he murmurs, gripping my chin and tilting my face up to his. He tilts his head to the side, watching me for a second, his eyes crinkling with worry. He pries open my upper lip, only to hiss when his thumb catches on teeth that feel much too sharp suddenly. Yet the taste of his blood washing over my tongue awakens something. I bite into one of his pecs and then his collarbone. I shake my head, I don't even remember moving; I just did it.

The King hisses when my teeth break his skin, and I don't know what comes over me. Some possessive urge to claim him takes over, making me turn into a savage. Blood runs down his chest, and the car door opens. The cool mountain air breezes through the open door, mingling with wildflowers and pine scents.

"Close it." His tone is commanding and powerful, sending a shiver down my spine while I blubber out an apology.

"It's fine, my love," he says, gripping my face. His touch is tender and reassuring despite the circumstances. He looks down at his chest before prying my lips apart, examining my teeth, and I bite down on his finger. He groans and presses his lips together while I try to unlatch my jaw. What is wrong with me? He probably thinks I'm some freak.

His blood runs across my tongue, a feral growl escapes me. My teeth let his finger go, but before I can stop myself or even think about it, my teeth sink into his shoulder. The door opens again, and the King growls menacingly.

"Next one to open that fucking door will lose a hand. Close it."

Tears burn my vision as instincts I'm not used to take over. I have no control over my actions, and it's humiliating. The salty taste of my tears mixes with the coppery tang of his blood, and I bite my own tongue to stop from attacking him, but it does not work.

The door shuts quickly, the sound making my senses kick in. I am mortified. By the time I finish attacking the King, I think he has probably 20 bite marks across his chest and shoulders. He just let me do it – just took it, which horrifies me even more.

"Shh, stop crying, Ivy. It's fine. It's not your fault; it's mine." Is he nuts? He didn't ask me to do it.

"As I said before, I went overboard with the calling. It can make you react oddly, possessively, because it strengthens the... It strengthens your instincts. It's fine. You didn't hurt me," he says, wiping away my tears. My face is scorching with shame.

"Stop; I'm okay. You haven't hurt me," Kyson repeats soothingly. Leaning forward, he retrieves the hand towel, cleaning up the blood. I take the towel from him, wiping it off. The indents of my teeth that litter his chest. I won't be surprised if he muzzles me after this. I would deserve it.

"I didn't mean to," I cry, and he clutches my face in his hands. His thumbs pry my eyelids open.

"We need to get your files from the orphanage. Your pupils are over-dilated," he says, looking at me with deep concern. His piercing gaze searches mine.

"Huh?"

"Your eyes are changing, and your teeth have come through more. I think you're wrong about your birthday. Your pupils usually dilate days before your shift, not weeks," Kyson explains.

How could I have my birthday wrong? How could my mother?

"We should get this over with. I want to get you back home," he says while tossing the bloody hand towel onto the seat.

"Come on, let's go see the castle," he says, sliding me off his lap beside him and sliding across the seat. I grab his hand as he reaches for the door handle.

"They will see." I cringe at the thought of them seeing what I did to him. The King sits back in his seat and sighs and I watch his eyes glaze over. Someone taps on the window a few moments later, and I jump.

"It's just Damian," he whispers, and the door opens. The King takes the shirt from him. Damian closes the door while Kyson pulls it on. Even with the shirt, I can still see some of the marks I left on him.

Once he has his shirt on, the King reaches for me and kisses me before nibbling on my lips. "This place is amazing. I can't wait for you to see it," the King says while pushing the door open.

He steps out onto a quartz-covered driveway. I follow and find we are deep within the tall, peaking mountains. The breathtaking view of the snow-capped peaks, and the verdant valley below instills awe in me. Tall sandstone walls surround the place, with blooming rose vines climbing them. The castle is easily two times the size of the Ling's palace, it even has watchtowers. The stone it is made of is covered in flowering vines and moss, and it looks like a castle from some magical fairytale.

A massive Lycan statue stands in the center of the driveway. It has a crown on its head, and the gates leading to the place are huge. I can just see the small town outside its gates. Though it is a ghost town, everything is well-maintained and picturesque.

Yet I swear I have dreamed of this place, maybe even seen it before. I can't explain the feeling this place churns within me, but it is like a sense of déjà vu has washed over me. I shake the feeling off.

"Sir, we will go to the quarters and recheck the old murder scene. Some scouts are also heading to the river to secure it," Damian says, and Kyson nods. *Murder scene? Why would it still be the same?* I think.

The King shows me around the outside of the castle before taking me inside. Inside everything is made of marble, even the stairs. Huge crystal chandeliers hang from the roof, sparkling like stars in the dimly lit hallway. Their reflections dance on the polished marble floors, making the floor glitter. The walls are adorned with intricate tapestries and paintings, each telling a story of its own.

The place becomes even more exquisite as we walk around, yet that nagging feeling returns. I can't help but marvel at the attention to detail and the beauty of it all. It feels like stepping into a dream, one that I can't quite remember but this place feels familiar. I shake the ridiculous thought out of my head.

"So, how old do you think the Queen's daughter would have been?" I ask, my voice echoing slightly in the vast halls.

"Probably around your age, maybe a little older or younger. We couldn't determine her age. The King and Queen went to extensive lengths to keep her hidden," Kyson answers. "Though some of the Landeena guards that survived estimated her to be four at the time of the attack, so if true, she would be nearly 18."

"If she was hidden, how do you know the baby was a girl?"

"All the baby items we found were pink, and so was the crib, plus her name was etched into her bed. As I said, a few guards...," I stop in the foyer when I notice some of his men waiting to speak to him. Their expressions are serious and somber, a stark contrast to the extravagance surrounding us.

The men exchange a few words with the King, their voices low and hushed. Kyson's face remains expressionless, but I can sense tension radiating off him. Something about whatever they're talking about has him on edge, and I can't help but feel a creeping sense of unease as well.

As we continue to explore the castle, I find myself constantly looking over my shoulder, expecting something to jump out of the shadows, but the only thing behind us is the guards trailing us.

We eventually reach a set of large, ornate double doors, which Kyson pushes open to reveal a breathtaking library. Towering shelves filled with books and scrolls line the walls, and a beautiful stained-glass window casts a rainbow of colors onto the polished floor.

"This was the Queen's favorite room," Kyson explains. "She spent most of her time here studying and reading."

"Did you know the Queen well?" I ask. Kyson shakes his head.

"No, I was familiar with her from the trials between kingdoms, but do you really know anybody? Let alone a Queen in a rival king-dom?" he asks. He has a point.

"So, how do you know she spent most of her time here?"

"Cedric, he was one of her guards and now lives in my Kingdom. A few of her personal guards lived, although a lot of the time, I get this bizarre sense they wished they had died when Landeena fell," he tells me, and my brows furrow.

As we make our way back through the castle, the sense of déjà vu becomes even more pronounced. It's as if I'm walking through a memory, one that I can't quite grasp but feel inexplicably drawn to. The castle's beauty and mystery captivate me when I see guards stop in our path.

CHAPTER
FORTY-SEVEN

IVY

He motions for them to wait, and they stop their approach as I ask my next question. "What was her name?"

"Azalea," he replies, just as the men step closer to speak to him.

The King stops to talk to one man, and I wander around before stopping at the door. A song I used to love pops into my mind, probably because it is the only one that ever stuck with me, and I whisper the tune as I enter the room.

In this charade, a dance of hate,
A broken alliance, we still create.
The throne may bind us, but I stand tall,
A Queen unbowed, refusing to fall.
Through the fire, I'll rise above,
My spirit strong, my heart full of love.
You'll never break me, I'll never bend,
My voice will echo until the very end.
You have my hand, but not my heart,
A mere possession torn apart.
Bound by duty, a kingdom's will,

In a loveless union, my heart lies still.

It was the King and Queen's bedroom, and I knew I stumbled into the old murder scene by the old flaking forensic tape. It was like this place was untouched, left in the exact state of how it was in this room. Though no evidence was left behind, I could tell by the disarray it had been combed through but not put back exactly the way it was.

"Where did you hear that song?" the King asks, spooking me and making me jump; his footsteps were silent as he came up behind me.

The King enters beside me, and I look at him. "I don't know, I just know it," I tell him, and he watches me curiously.

"Do you know it?" I ask, and he nods.

"Yes, only the version I know is slightly different," he tells me, watching me. His gaze makes me uncomfortable, scrutinizing almost.

"What version do you know?" I ask curiously. I don't even know where I heard it.

"It's the same, but has an extra verse the Kingdom people added on to the end. Hang on." The King looks around and calls out to one of his guards.

"Trey!" he calls out, and a man wanders over. He is wearing all black, and the Valkyrie Kingdom emblem is emblazoned on his chest, showing he is one of the king's guards but not as high up as Damian or Gannon. I've seen it on the other guards, like the guard that the King usually has following me around while in the castle.

The man looks me over curiously. "Yes, my King?"

"Do you remember the Landeena Anthem? The part added on to Tatiana's wedding song?"

"Of course, as if I could forget," he says before swallowing, and looking away.

"Well?" Kyson asks him, and Trey's brows furrow.

"Why?"

"I was telling Ivy about how the anthem came about."

Trey clenches his jaw and nods once. However, he doesn't sing it, he recites it like a poem, yet as he does, he looks on the verge of becoming emotional. Yet when he gets past the part, I know the song changes significantly from what I know.

"So sing this anthem, a testament bold,
Of love and loss and courage untold.
In the anguish, we'll find our grace,
A warrior's spirit, as fears we face.
From the ashes, we rise, our voices clear,
A warrior's heart conquers all fear.
Our voices echo far and wide.
A spirit unbroken, we'll never hide.
In the midst of pain, we find our might,
To stand our ground and embrace the fight.
Fueled by anger, a force untamed,
A burning ember, a heart inflamed."

"Is that all, my King?" Trey asks, and Kyson nods once, and he quickly wanders off.

"He seemed upset," I tell Kyson.

"Yes, it was Queen Tatiana and King Garrett's wedding song. It then became the castle anthem, which was the song the Queen sang at their wedding. Trey came from the Landeena Kingdom," he tells me, and my brows furrow.

"Doesn't sound like a wedding song," I tell him.

"Because it was an arranged marriage, she didn't want to marry him. But the kingdom's people thought it was an anthem. Somehow it turned into the Landeena anthem."

"So they hated each other?"

"Maybe at the start, but I don't think so, kinda like my mother and father. Arranged marriages are common among royals to strengthen alliances. They stayed together and had a baby, so she couldn't have hated him that much in the end," Kyson shrugs.

"So, did many survive from the Landeena Kingdom, and how many other kingdoms remain?" I ask, curious.

"Around fifty or so. They reside in the Valkyrie Kingdom. And no other kingdom remains but mine. They were taken out by the hunters. There are a few survivors from each kingdom still. Why your sudden curiosity about the kingdoms?"

I shrug; I just find it interesting.

He eyes me suspiciously, which I find strange, before he starts looking around the room. He stops by the bed; the old sheets are gone, but the mattress is still covered in blood. Old stains and stab marks litter the mattress.

"Come, you shouldn't be in here," he says, showing me back out. The King leads me away, but he seems distant and deep in thought.

"Your parents' names. What were they?" he asks.

"My father's name was Jordan, and my mother Della. I was ten when they were killed," I answer.

"Do you know their last names?" I shake my head, unsure. "Why?"

"No reason. It's just odd that you know that song. It was only sung by the Queen and townsfolk; it was a ceremonial song and an anthem, as I said," he says, and I notice Gannon and Damian have come over to listen to our conversation.

"My King, I know we were planning on staying the night, but the men are nervous. Security is hard to keep here, and they found tire tracks through the forest close to here," Beta Damian says when the King waves him off.

"No, it is fine; I want to get Ivy home, anyway. You also need to call that Alpha; I need her paperwork. I believe she is closer to shifting than we believe." They both look at me, and I blush. I know they didn't miss the two bite marks on him that his shirt didn't cover.

The moment I climb into the limo, Kyson is pulling me onto his lap. He has been tense since we left the King and Queen's quarters, but even more so now. I try to scramble off his lap into my seat, but he pulls me back.

"What about my seatbelt?" I mumble as I feel the same senses that awoke on the drive here, reawaken, only now with a vengeance since he barely touched me while here. He quickly clips the surrounding seatbelt, effectively trapping me against him.

"Go to sleep. We will be driving through the night," he informs me, and I sigh. His touch is like fire as his hands graze beneath my shirt. His skin is hot, his hands are scorching, and the moment he touches me, my senses go wild.

Kyson's purr is primal and animalistic as it vibrates against my chest. The rumble reverberates through my body, forcing me to relax against him.

"Please don't force me to sleep," I groan, fighting it with all my might. He chuckles, gripping my chin and forcing me to meet his gaze.

His eyes meet mine, and I can see the flames of desire dancing in them. His hair is as dark as the night, and his lips are mere inches from mine when he turns my face away.

He kisses the side of my neck, his teeth brush against my skin, and a shiver slivers up my spine. "You should sleep," he murmurs against my skin.

"I'm not tired," I whisper, my voice barely audible as sparks rush across my skin at his touch.

"I can help with that," he promises darkly when his lips graze mine. The taste of him is like the sweetest honey, warm and inviting.

I let out a shaky breath as his lips move over mine, our tongues tangling as he deepens the kiss, and I can't help but moan into his mouth as he pulls me closer. His hands run up and down my back, causing shivers to run through my body.

Kyson moves his hands to my shirt, pulling it up and off in one swift motion. The cool air from the AC in the limo caresses my skin, making me shiver as his hands trace up my sides, teasing me as he goes. He unclips the seatbelt.

"God, you're beautiful," he murmurs against my skin as he runs his hands over my breasts, his thumbs circling my hardened nipples.

My senses go wild, his scent becoming all-consuming. Unable to take it anymore, I tangle my fingers in his hair and pull him towards me for another kiss. This time it's wilder, fiercer than before as we both struggle to catch our breath.

"Kyson," I moan out his name as he moves down to leave kisses on my neck and collarbone. "Please..."

He pauses, looking up at me. "Please what?" he smiles mischievously.

"You know what..." I groan, rocking my hips against him, when suddenly his shirt is torn to pieces, and my teeth sink into his chest.

"Hmm, maybe... maybe I want you to say it, though," he purrs as my fingers fumble for his belt. Only he seizes my hands, making me growl.

"So impatient," he purrs, nipping at my lips; he moves my hands to his chest and releases my wrists. My hands instantly move to seek what I want, but he growls.

"Place them back," he orders, and my hands move back to his chest. He undoes the buttons on my jeans while his lips trail down my neck so slowly that my hands shake with my desire to touch him.

His hands grip the waistband of my pants, and he tugs them down before slamming me down on the spacious leather seat; he tugs them all the way off, and before I can sit up, his mouth is on me, his hot tongue swiping between my folds to my clit.

His hands skim over my thighs, teasing me more and more with each stroke of his tongue. The flicks of his tongue become harder and faster until I can no longer contain the pleasure radiating through me.

The fabric of the leather seats, the friction of stubble against my thighs, and his fiery tongue have my senses in overdrive when I feel the warmth spread through me, stealing my breath as waves of ecstasy ripple through me, so powerful that it makes everything else disappear but him.

I gasp for breath, pushing my fingers through his hair as he looks up at me with a sly grin on his face while setting off such a blissful calm throughout my entire being. My body turns languid, and I would be content never to move again with how relaxed I feel. He pulls me back on his lap, and I am a rag doll, limp in his arms as he tucks the blanket around my naked form.

"Now try to sleep," he purrs, nibbling on my lip when I yawn, fighting sleep.

The King hardly speaks on the way home, and we only stop for fuel, driving through the night. We reach home the following day, and Abbie is waiting out the front for the luggage. I bounce in my seat excitedly, wanting to go see her as we pull up.

The King rolls his eyes when I reach for the seatbelt.

"Go on, I have a few things to do, anyway," the King says, and I rush to open the door.

"Ah, Ivy..." he speaks, and I glance back at him. His eyes trail the length of me.

"You're still naked," he chuckles, and I glance down. My eyes widen, and I rush to snatch my clothes off the floor while the King puts his ruined shirt on, and groans. "Your senses are growing stronger. At this rate, I will run out of clothes," he tells me, and I slip my shirt on. I giggle, watching as he climbs out of the car. A few seconds later, I step out after him.

"Remain with Ivy," I hear him tell the guard that usually followed me everywhere before he walks off, clearly distracted by something. He nods, and I rush to Abbie's side. She embraces me and helps me carry the luggage to the laundry room. As we enter, I spot Clarice.

Clarice smiles warmly at me, while Abbie gushes excitedly after telling her the King wanted to claim me once I shifted on my birthday. Seeing her excitement put me more at ease. I reach for a tunic on the shelf when Clarice clears her throat.

"Ivy, the King has told me you are no longer his servant."

"But I want to help Abbie with her chores," I tell her. Clarice looks at my guard, who also doesn't know what to say and only frowns.

"I'm sorry, Ivy, but unless the King allows it, I can't let you put on that uniform. Those here would treat you like a servant in that uniform, and I don't want any staff killed for that mistake," Clarice explains. I look at Abbie, and my shoulders sag.

"It's fine; I can just wear this, I guess; I will speak with the King later," I tell her. Clarice glances at my guard, who shrugs, and Clarice sighs.

"Very well, but you make sure you tell the King you wanted to help. I don't want to be scolded for making you work," Clarice states.

"But what else is there to do if not work?" I ask her.

"Live," Clarice answers, squeezing my shoulder gently.

For hours, I follow and help Abbie. However, once evening comes, the guard steps away from the wall where he stood watching us.

"Ivy, the King, is looking for you; he wants you back to your chambers," he says. I press my lips together, wanting to spend time with Abbie, but she shoos me away.

CHAPTER
FORTY-EIGHT

A BBIE
For two days, Ivy was gone, and when Clarice finally tells me she's on her way back, I remain by the front door for over an hour. I need to make sure she's okay. I am excitedly bursting at the seams when I see the limo pull in. The King says something to Ivy before she rushes over and hugs me. I squeeze her tight, relieved she is okay.

Grabbing their luggage, Ivy helps me haul it to the laundry room. "Abbie, I have something to tell you," Ivy says, nudging me as we walk down the corridor. She has a guard following closely behind her.

As Ivy and I walk down the corridor, I can't help but notice the delicate patterns on the wallpaper. The intricate designs lend an air of sophistication and elegance to our surroundings. The sound of our footsteps is softened by the plush carpet beneath us, and the warm glow of the sconces on the walls casts a welcoming light.

"What?" I ask, glancing nervously at her. The excitement in her eyes is contagious. Her cheeks are flushed with a rosy hue. I see her lips tug up in the corners slightly before she leans into me. "The King wants me to be his mate," she whispers, and I stop dead in my tracks.

I take a moment to absorb the news, my heart pounding in my chest like a wild animal, desperate to break free. "Mate, as in his mate, he wants to make you his Queen?" I ask, my voice trembling with emotion. I blink back tears that threaten to spill over, a mixture of joy and disbelief clouding my vision.

"Means we will be free, we won't have to go back, Abbie, we can stay here for good," she tells me, her voice full of hope. As Ivy whispers the news of the King's proposal, a myriad of emotions wash over me. Surprise, joy, and an overwhelming sense of relief mingle together, creating a tidal wave that threatens to engulf me. The tears that brim in my eyes seem to shimmer in the warm, golden light that bathes the hallway, casting long, dancing shadows on the walls.

"We can stay?" I ask, the words sounding like a dream as they leave my lips. She grabs my arm, tugging me along as the scent of fresh flowers wafts through the air. She smiles and nods, leaning her head on my shoulder as we walk through the kitchens. The kitchen we pass through is a whirlwind of activity. The aroma of freshly baked bread and savory spices fills the air, tickling my nostrils and making my stomach rumble in response. Cooks and kitchen staff bustle about, their faces flushed with heat and exertion as they prepare the evening meal.

When we reach the laundry room, the hum of the washing machines fills the space, providing a soothing rhythm to our exchange. The scent of detergent is sharp and clean, a sensory reminder of the new beginning that lies before us.

As we talk about Gannon, my cheeks grow warm, and Ivy notices my reaction. "What's wrong?" she asks, her brow furrowing with concern.

"Nothing, but are you sure Gannon will want to change me?" I ask, trying to keep my voice steady. When Ivy mentions Gannon, I can't help but feel a warmth blossoming in my chest, accompanied by a flutter of butterflies in my stomach. I struggle to tamp down the rising tide of emotions. However, the thought of him wanting to change me and caring enough to ask fills me with a giddy sense of hope and wonder. I couldn't believe our luck. Just a couple weeks ago we thought we were as good as dead.

Ivy shrugs, her eyes sparkling with determination. "If not, once the King changes me, I will ask him how to change you and do it myself, but I think Gannon will change you," she tells me, her confidence in her words bolstering my own.

As we move to load the clothes into the washer, Ivy leans in next to me, her voice barely more than a whisper. "I think Gannon likes you," she giggles, her laughter like music to my ears. As we load the clothes into the washers, the comforting hum of the machines fills the laundry room. The scent of detergent fills the air. Its clean, sharp fragrance cuts through the lingering traces of our earlier excitement. Ivy's giggle is a bright, melodious sound that echoes through the space, and I can't help but join her laughter. The idea of Gannon liking me is both thrilling and terrifying, making my pulse race and my cheeks flush with heat.

"What makes you say that?" I laugh, my heart skipping a beat at the thought.

Ivy grins, her eyes gleaming with mischief. "Just something the King said. He mentioned that Gannon has never shown interest in anyone. He also asked Damian and him if he could have you as his personal servant. Gannon doesn't want you working as a servant," she explains, her excitement for me evident in her voice.

We stand there for a moment, the implications of her words sinking in. "We would be safe here, Abbie. I think the King is a good man, don't you think?" Ivy asks, her expression earnest. I nibble my lip, considering her question. The King had been nothing but kind to us, even though his presence is always intimidating.

"I do," I agree. The words feel like a weight lifted from my chest. "He's done nothing to harm us, and if he can offer us a real home, a life of safety and happiness, then maybe we should take it, especially if it means we can remain together."

Clarice's entrance brings new energy to our conversation. Her presence is a calming, grounding force. Her warm smile and gentle demeanor bring a sense of order and stability to our whirlwind of emotions.

She smiles warmly at us, and we eagerly share our good news. As we speak, I notice the way the light catches in her eyes, her genuine happiness for us shining through.

I can't help my excitement that I could stay with Ivy and that she would become the King's mate. This was the best news we had received in eight years, and it was like all our missed Christmases came at once.

"You have your chores, Abbie," Clarice tells me, and I almost forget with my excitement, and I rush to grab my cleaning supplies, and Ivy comes to help me.

"Ivy, the King, has told me you are no longer his servant," Clarice says, making us stop.

"But I want to help Abbie with her chores," Ivy tells her. Clarice looks at Ivy's guard, who also doesn't know what to say. He only frowns. Ivy had introduced him as Dustin, and he had remained silent. I already know who he is; I had seen him sneak into Liam's room and Liam into his a few times.

"I'm sorry, Ivy, but I can't let you wear that uniform unless the King allows it. Those here would treat you like a servant in that uniform, and I don't want any staff killed for that mistake," Clarice explains. Ivy looks at me, and her shoulders sag.

"It's fine; I can just wear this, I guess; I will speak with the King later," Ivy tells her. Clarice glances at the guard nervously, thinking she will get into trouble. Dustin shrugs, and Clarice sighs, wiping a hand down her face.

"Very well, but you make sure you tell the King you wanted to help. I don't want to be scolded for making you work." Clarice tells her, and Ivy rocks on her back heels excitedly. My heart gives a flutter of excitement, knowing I could spend the day with her.

"But what else is there to do except work?" Ivy asks, and she is right. It would be bloody boring sitting in my room all day. I would rather work, and I knew Ivy would feel the same.

"Live," Clarice answers, squeezing her shoulder gently and walking off.

Later, when Ivy's guard tells her that the King is looking for her, I can see the reluctance in her eyes, and her desire to stay and help me. But I shoo her away, reassuring her that I'll be fine on my own.

"Ivy, the King, is looking for you; we really must go; he wants you back to your chambers," he says. Ivy's shoulders drop, and she presses her lips together, wanting to stay, but I shoo her away.

"Go, maybe the King will let you hang out with me while I work tomorrow," I tell her, and she sighs.

"I will ask. Hopefully, he will say yes."

"He did say he had to go away tomorrow, so I don't see the harm in it," she says, a glimmer of hope in her eyes as she looks at her guard, Dustin.

As Ivy leaves, I feel a pang of sadness, but it's quickly overshadowed by the anticipation of what she told me. I turn back to my chores, determined to finish them quickly.

I'm nearly done when Gannon appears, sticking his head into the sitting room where I'm dusting.

"Abbie?" he says, his voice deep and rough. I turn to face him, my heart racing as I wonder what he wants. He waggles his finger at me to come to him, and I wander over, my stomach fluttering with nerves, wondering if I did something wrong or if he wanted me to clean something.

As I approach him, I notice the way the light from the room casts a soft glow on his features, highlighting the strong lines on his face and the intensity in his eyes. He reaches out, gently taking my hand in his.

FORTY-NINE

ABBIE

"You didn't take your presents," he states, his voice gentle yet firm as he walks me to his room. The air between us is heavy with anticipation, and I can't help but chew my lip nervously. I glance up at him, and I'm met with his piercing gaze. He sighs, his breath warm against my skin as he pushes his door open, revealing the gifts he bought me, still sitting untouched in the center of his bed.

"Did you not like them? Are they the wrong ones?" he asks me, his eyes filled with concern. I'm struck by the earnestness in his voice, and I quickly shake my head.

"I can change them," he offers, his tone gentle and reassuring.

"No, no, it's not that, I just...you shouldn't," I suck in a breath when Liam waltzes into the room, his footsteps light and graceful as he falls onto Gannon's bed. He props his arm behind his head and smiles slyly, an impish glint in his eyes. Gannon shakes his head at him but turns back to face me.

"What is it, Abbie?" Gannon asks, his eyes searching mine for the answer. I tear my gaze from Liam, my heart racing as I try to find the words.

"You shouldn't buy gifts for a servant, Gamma," I tell him, using his title since Liam was around.

"Gannon, not Gamma. You don't address me by title. We have been over this. And why can't I, Abbie?"

"Because it is wrong," I tell him, feeling the weight of their stares on me. He looks at me as if I am absurd, his brow furrowing in confusion.

"Wrong, how?" he asks, his voice soft and patient. I feel Liam's eyes on the side of my face, his presence adding to the tension in the room and making me even more nervous as he watches us.

"It's just a gift," Liam chimes in, his voice light and teasing.

"Yes, but servants don't get gifts, not for free," I tell him, my voice wavering slightly.

"What do you mean? That is what a gift is, or have I been doing gifts wrong all this time? Gannon? I don't understand this one; I bought Dustin some boxers with my face on them the other day. Maybe I should have asked for something in return," he chuckles, his laughter filling the room like a warm embrace.

"Liam, give me a moment, geez, go annoy Dustin," Gannon says, his voice firm but not unkind.

"Gladly, I might be able to con him to suck my dick," Liam says, sending me a wink. I cringe at his vulgar words, feeling a blush creep up my cheeks. Liam gets up and pats Gannon on the back as he passes.

"Don't forget you leave early tomorrow," Liam reminds him.

"And yes, I can cover your shift if you want to spend time with Abbie," he calls over his shoulder as he walks out, leaving Gannon and me alone in the room.

Gannon turns his attention back to the presents he bought, sitting on the edge of the bed. The soft rustling of the bags seems to fill the room, and I can't help but watch him, his every movement deliberate and graceful. He reaches over and grips my hand, his touch warm and comforting. "Dustin told me earlier that Ivy told you the King wants to change her and make her his mate?" Gannon says, his voice low and serious. I nod, my stomach twisting with a mixture of fear and excitement at the thought.

"What if I said I wanted to do the same with you?" I can't help but chuckle at his question, my laughter tinged with nervous energy.

"You barely know me," I respond, attempting to hide the uncertainty in my voice.

"And the King barely knows Ivy, Abbie. It is no different, not really anyway," Gannon counters, his tone soft and persuasive.

"But what if you find your mate?"

"I won't and it wouldn't matter even if I did."

"Why would you want me, though?" I ask, my heart pounding in my chest at the unexpected revelation. He scratches the back of his neck nervously, his eyes locked on mine.

"Because I like you. Why else?" he says, a hint of vulnerability creeping into his voice.

"Liking someone and loving them are two different things."

"We could learn to love each other, Abbie. We would have all the time in the world," he says, reaching forward and tugging me between his legs. He wraps his arms around my waist and looks at me intently. Even sitting face to face, his height is imposing.

"Will you think about it?" he asks, his voice a gentle whisper. I chew my lip, my mind racing. Ivy did tell me Gannon would change me and I did like him, but the thought of taking such a leap is daunting.

"But what if I find my mate?" I ask him, my voice barely audible. He sighs, a hint of sadness in his eyes.

"Well, I am hoping you don't, but if you did, and you wanted to be with them, I would let you go if that is what you wanted." I nod, my heart aching at the thought of leaving Gannon behind. He lets me go, turning back to the bags filled with presents.

"Please take your gifts, Abbie. I got them for you, and I expect nothing in return. I just wanted to see you smile," he says, his voice warm and sincere. I can't help but smile at his words, my cheeks heating when he reaches up, brushing my cheek with his hand.

"There it is," he says, a gentle smile playing on his lips before cupping my face in his hand.

"I have to go with the King tomorrow to your old pack," he says, switching the subject.

"You're going back?" I ask him, my voice thick with emotion. He nods, his eyes filled with determination.

"I have a bit of a strange request to ask, and you can say no if you like," he says, his voice tentative. My brows furrow, curiosity piqued.

"What is it?"

"Can I count how many lashes are on your back? The King wanted to know. He counted Ivy's while she slept, but he wants to punish Mrs. Daley, and he needs to know what charges to bring against her," Gannon tells me, his voice laced with anger.

"He wants to punish Mrs. Daley?" I ask, shock registering in my voice. She has always been this figure who I believed could never be punished.

"You and Ivy never should have been treated like that. I have counted the ones on the back of your legs," he says, looking away as if he did something wrong.

"But can I count the ones on your back, as I said you can say no?"

I swallow hard. It's not like he hasn't seen my back before or my butt. I chew my lip, considering his request.

"You just want to count them, that's it?" I ask, my voice wavering yet trusting Gannon.

"That is all, Abbie," he says, sincerity shining in his eyes. The thought of Mrs. Daley being held accountable for her actions is thrilling, and despite my reservations, I nod my head.

Gannon taps my thighs, gets up, closes the door, and returns to sit on the bed. Turning around, I unbutton my dress before pulling my arms out and only leaving my waist covered. Gannon pulls me to sit between my legs, and I feel his fingers tracing my skin gently. His touch sends shivers down my spine, and my face flushes when I feel his lips press tenderly against my shoulder.

"Thank you, Abbie," he whispers, and I turn my face to look at him. He helps me pull my arms back into my dress before turning me as I stand to help me with the buttons. When I do up the last one, his hand bunches my dress on my hip as he tugs me closer.

"I promise she will be punished," he whispers, and I nod. Any punishment was good enough for me. She needed to know the error of her ways, and I wished death upon her. What she let the butcher do would forever haunt me; bruises and lashes heal, yet what he did scarred my mind, and she allowed it. Tainted my dreams and haunted my soul.

"Can you check on the kids?"

"I can try if the King allows it. We will be in a time crunch. The King wants to get back so he can change Ivy and take her as his mate," he tells me, and I sigh. I would love to know how my Tyson is, but if the King was genuinely going to punish her, maybe that would make her change her ways.

"What's wrong?" Gannon asks, genuine concern in his voice.

"Nothing, I just worry about the children, especially the younger ones," I admit. Gannon brushes his knuckles across my cheek, his touch gentle and reassuring.

"Maybe one day I can take you back to see them," he says, and I smile, hope kindling in my heart.

"Really?" I ask before my smile fades. What if I run into the butcher? Panic begins to rise within me. I can't go back. What if he takes me, keeps me like he always said he would?

"If that is what you want," Gannon says, his voice steady and supportive. My skin itches at the thought of the butcher, and I scratch the back of my neck, only for Gannon to capture my hand.

"One day, you will tell me what makes you so nervous," he says, his eyes searching mine as he kisses my fingers.

"Maybe one day," I tell him, a soft smile playing on my lips as he tilts his head to the side, observing me. I observe him back when he leans in, and I hold my breath, wondering what he will do when his lips brush mine softly. I gasp at the sensation, and he tugs me closer, yet he doesn't deepen the kiss or press for more. When he goes to pull away, I gather my courage. *It's just a kiss*, I tell myself, trying to remind myself that I like Gannon.

So I kiss him back. I feel him smile against my lips before feeling his tongue sweep across my bottom lip, not forcibly. He is seeing if I would invite him in, and I do. My lips part when his hand moves to the nape of my neck. His fingers massage the back of my neck before tangling in my hair. His tongue brushes mine, and his taste overwhelms me as I kiss him back.

When I eventually pull away from him, he sucks on my bottom lip but allows me space, and my face flames at what I let him do. Yet I like kissing him, and he appears to like it too because he smiles at me before pecking my cheek.

"I have work to do, but can I come to see you later?" he asks, and I nod, my heart pounding in my chest as I wonder if more kissing would be involved. I turn to walk out when he grabs my hand and tugs me back. He nods to my presents.

"Draw me something," he says, his voice gentle and expectant. I chew the inside of my lip, feeling a mix of excitement and nervousness. I nod, accepting the gift before rushing out, and I hear him chuckle as I close the door. I race back to my room and shut the door, hearing him leave a few moments later.

As I settle down in my room, I open the gifts Gannon had given me. The art supplies he had chosen were of excellent quality, making me appreciate his thoughtfulness even more. I let my fingers glide over the smooth, cold surface of the sketchpad, feeling the potential of the empty pages, waiting to be filled with my thoughts and emotions.

I take a deep breath and start drawing, something I haven't done in ages. The world around me fades away, leaving only the scratching sound of the pencil on paper. My hand moves with a life of its own, guided by my heart and memories, and I find myself pouring all of my feelings and experiences onto the paper.

Time seems to stand still as I work on the drawing, completely immersed in the process. It wasn't until I put the finishing touches on the piece that I realize how much time had passed. I take a step back to look at one of my creations, a mix of nervousness and vulnerability fills my chest.

The drawing depicts Gannon and me standing under a tree, our fingers intertwined. The sun filters through the leaves, casting a warm golden light over us. Our expressions convey happiness, and I can't help but feel a twinge of longing for the future we might have together. But that nagging voice reminds me. I am a rogue; he will see that, turn me away, and toss me aside. Rogues don't deserve kindness. I was about to tear the paper up when I hear footsteps approaching my door; I quickly hide the drawing in my sketchpad and turn to face the door. Gannon walks in, his eyes sparkling with anticipation. "Did you draw something?" he asks, his voice filled with curiosity and excitement. I chew my lip, and he tilts his head to the side. His eyes go to my fingers and the pastels that cover them.

"Will you show me?" he asks.

I hesitate for a moment, feeling vulnerable as I hand him the sketchpad. He flips through the pages until he finds the drawing I just completed. His eyes widen as he takes in the image before him, and I watch as a slow smile spreads across his face.

"This is beautiful, Abbie," he says softly, his voice filled with emotion.

"Thank you." He carefully closes the sketchpad and hands it back to me, his eyes never leaving mine.

As we stand there, our hands touching, I can't help but feel hope and warmth in my heart.

FIFTY

I VY

    The guard led me to the other side of the castle, his footsteps echoing softly on the stone floor. The guard is tall and muscular, with a chiseled jawline and short black hair. He wears a black uniform that is perfectly tailored to fit his body, the same uniform most of the guards wear, complete with polished black boots and a silver and gold emblem on his chest, indicating he is one of the king's main guards. His eyes are a deep blue-gray, and they seem to be able to look right through me whenever he glances my way.

    Sighing, I turn my attention back to where we are going, and I can't help but notice the way the sunlight filters through the tall, narrow windows, casting intricate patterns on the walls. "What is your name?" I ask him, curious about the silent figure who is always by my side or standing in the halls wherever I go. He glances at me, his eyes guarded, but says nothing.

    "Come on, you follow me everywhere. I feel weird not knowing it," I admit, trying to put him at ease with a small smile. There was something about his presence that felt comforting, even though he remained so stoic.

"Dustin, my Queen," he says finally, his voice deep and steady. I scrunch up my face at his words, feeling the weight of the title pressing down on me.

"Please don't call me that. It sounds wrong, given I am a rogue," I protest, the idea of being Queen, still feeling so foreign and strange.

"But you will be," he reminds me, his expression unreadable.

"Even then, I don't think I want to be called that," I admit.

"It cannot be helped; it will be your title," he says simply, his gaze never wavering from the path ahead.

I yawn as I climb the stairs, my legs feeling heavy from exhaustion. The castle is a maze of corridors, with seemingly endless rooms hidden behind intricately carved wooden doors. I stop halfway down the corridor when I notice the forbidden door slightly ajar. Stepping closer, curiosity getting the better of me, I peer inside and see that it appears to be a baby's room. The soft colors and the gently rocking crib evoke a feeling of innocence and warmth, making me wonder about the story behind the room and why it is in the King's quarters.

"Miss Ivy, I don't think you should go in there," Dustin whispers, his voice filled with concern. I went to step away, heeding his warning, just as the King turns the corner into the hall. The King's face is a mask of fury, his eyes blazing, and his lips pressed into a thin line. His body is tense, and his hands are clenched into fists. He is clearly angry, and his presence is intimidating. His eyes, sharp, immediately dart to the door as I step back from it, my heart pounding in my chest.

"What do you think you're doing?" he snaps, his voice like a whip, becoming enraged.

"Nothing, I was..." I stutter, my words failing me under the weight of his anger.

He strides over, his face a storm of emotions, and he shuts the door with so much force it makes me jump. Then he points at me angrily, his eyes blazing, making me step back from him. "You do not go in there, ever," he snarls, and I shrink away from his abrupt anger, feeling like a scolded child, the King goes to grab my arm when

Dustin grips his wrist and steps between us. Kyson bumps into him, and my heart sputters in my chest that he just grabbed the King. Kyson tilts his head to the side, his eyes flicker sadistically at his guard interfering, and I am just as shocked to see the guard step between me and his King, I find the notion odd that he would defend me against his King.

"My King, she was merely closing the door. The wind must have blown it open," Dustin interjects, his voice calm and steady. The King looks at him, his anger momentarily halted, and Dustin lets his wrist go.

"I should have closed the door, my King. MY *Queen* is not to be blamed," Dustin states, emphasizing the word Queen oddly like to him; it meant something else entirely.

The guard nods toward an open window I hadn't noticed, its curtains billowing gently in the breeze. Kyson's eyes flick to me and then to Dustin, who still stands between us. "Very well," Kyson states. Dustin nods once. King Kyson looks at me, his expression softening ever so slightly, and I quickly nod, going along with Dustin's story, thankful he saved me. I wasn't going to go in there; I just peeked inside.

"You may stand down, Dustin," Kyson tells him, making my brows furrow in confusion. Dustin swiftly steps aside, and I glance between them, but Dustin gives nothing away, his eyes straight ahead, staring at the wall.

The King sighs, the anger dissipating from his face, replaced by a weariness that made him seem more human.

"I apologize, Ivy. That room is just off-limits. I shouldn't have snapped at you," he says, scrubbing a hand down his face as if trying to erase the stress of the moment. Kyson places his hand on my lower back, the warmth of his touch seeping through my clothes, and leads me to the bedroom. I glance over my shoulder at the guard, who nods to me in understanding.

CHAPTER
FIFTY-ONE

K YSON

The guilt I feel for snapping at her is horrendous, gnawing at the pit of my stomach like a ravenous beast. I hated myself for it; the way she shrank back made it all the more terrible. I couldn't erase the fear on her face from my outburst from my mind, like a haunting image that threatened to stay with me forever.

My instincts were all over the place, a whirlwind of emotions I struggled to contain. The anniversary of my sister's death loomed heavily over me, casting a dark shadow on my thoughts. Then Ivy's birthday was obviously looming, and her attitude, as well as fighting, and my own instincts were becoming too much to bear. Although it's not her fault, she's temperamental these days. I can't blame her, though; I am too even at the best of times. She doesn't understand what is happening, whereas I do, since I have shifted and seen many werewolves shift over the decades.

The closer she gets, the more animalistic she will become before finally shifting. With me being so close, it only enhances those instincts and makes her urges so much more intense as her body and brain try to process that I am her mate. The air between us is thick with tension, and I can feel the magnetic pull of our connection growing stronger each day.

I run my hand down her spine. She shivers as she sleeps on my chest. The scent of her hair, a mixture of wildflowers and the faintest hint of vanilla fills my senses as I breathe her in. Ivy had whined and growled earlier, complaining that I kept putting her to sleep. But the more she sleeps, the better her transition will be when she shifts.

Our bond is strong, and I can tell that it's almost forged. I knew when she shifts that she will recognize me as her mate instantly, maybe even beforehand. The thought of our bond becoming complete fills me with an anticipation that is both thrilling and terrifying.

A knock at the door pulls me from my thoughts. I had enjoyed the quiet and reveled in the feel of her body pressed against mine, her soft skin a balm to my frayed nerves. So the knock annoyed me, an unwelcome intrusion into our peaceful cocoon. The door cracks open, and Damian walks in before sitting down in the armchair. His tall, muscular frame is draped in casual clothes, his dark hair disheveled as if he'd been running his fingers through it.

"Turn away for a second," I tell him, my voice firm. He obliges, turning his gaze to my bookshelf. Its rows of leather-bound tomes cast in the warm glow of the room's soft lighting. I roll Ivy onto her back before covering her naked body with the blanket, tucking it under her chin. She whimpers, so I jam my pillow next to her face. I watch as she buries her nose in it while Damian chuckles softly, his deep voice like a comforting hum in the air.

"I see the bond has formed. I think she will wake up and recognize you soon enough," he observes, his eyes flickering between Ivy and me.

"Yes," I tell him, emerging from the bed. Damian looks at my arms and chest that are covered in her bite marks. She even bit me three times while she was asleep. This marks shows our growing connection, a reminder of the fire that burns between us.

"Definitely almost forged," he laughs as I sit down across from him, his eyes twinkling with amusement.

"Why the drop-in? It's nearly 1 am," I inquire, my brows furrowing in curiosity.

"Have you slept?" he asks, eyeing me with a mix of concern and skepticism.

"What do you think?" I retort, feeling the weight of exhaustion bearing down on me.

He shakes his head. "Kyson, you have to sleep."

"You don't think I've tried," I say, scrubbing a hand down my face, feeling the rough stubble that has grown since my last shave.

"It can wait until you do," he says, hopping up from his seat.

"No, tell me. It must be important," I insist, my voice tinged with impatience as I look back at him.

He glances at Ivy on the bed before clearing his throat awkwardly. My brows furrow, and he nods toward her, keeping his gaze on me. I look over to find she had kicked the blankets off. I get up and quickly recover her before returning, only for her to kick them off again. The rhythmic sound of her breathing fills the room, a soothing lullaby that threatens to lull me into slumber as well.

Damian turns his seat to face the wall, hearing the ruffle of blankets as she overheats. "You have a thing for her being naked," he laughs, the corners of his eyes crinkling with amusement.

"I like the feel of her skin. It keeps my Lycan side calm," I explain, my voice taking on a defensive edge.

"So, you haven't shifted?" Damian asks, his tone serious now. Usually around the anniversary, I am almost permanently stuck in my Lycan form, ruled by emotion.

"Not because of the anniversary, though I lost my temper earlier. I thought she went into..." I stop, the words catching in my throat. I can't even bring myself to admit what the room was for.

"Dustin told me," Damian says, his voice gentle as he tries to offer comfort. I nod my head and swallow guiltily.

"Well, as long as you're in control, I suppose I will tell you," he says, brushing his fingers through his hair, a nervous habit he's had since we were children.

"We spoke to Alpha Dean. His son, Brock, wasn't very helpful. Anyway, Alpha Dean is still trying to find the rest of the information from the night Ivy and Abbie were brought in, and you were right about her being ready for her shift. Her birthday is in two days," he reveals, his voice steady and informative.

I nod. That made more sense. "So why is that an issue? If anything, that is good news," I tell him, glad I didn't have to wait weeks.

"Alpha Dean asked for us to come to see him. He wants to be sure and has asked for some files to be sent over. He wants to know if we can come to visit him today."

"What for?" I ask, concern creeping into my voice.

"He wouldn't say, just said it was important, and it is to do with Ivy," Damian answers, his eyes searching mine for a reaction.

I glance over at her sleepy, peaceful form. "When are we leaving?"

"At noon, the men need sleep before we move out."

I nod and rub my chin, wondering what Alpha Dean could have to say that he wouldn't say it over the phone.

"I am not sure Ivy will want to go back there just yet," I admit, glancing at her. "And I don't want her to fall back into old habits," I tell my Beta, concern etched into my features.

"Gannon can stay, or I will. I will assign extra guards to her."

"I would rather you remain with her," I decide, trusting Damian more than anyone else.

"Very well, I will. Try to get some sleep, Kyson," Damian says before getting up and leaving the room. The door closes with a soft click, leaving me alone with my thoughts and the steady rhythm of Ivy's breathing.

Worry gnaws at me as I get to my feet and walk over to my bar. Grabbing the bottle of whiskey off the shelf, I go to pour a glass before deciding to drink straight from the bottle when I see only a quarter of the bottle is left. The liquid warmth spreads through my chest, dulling the edges of my anxiety for a moment.

Ivy moves on the bed, tossing the blanket off and bunching it between her legs. I can't help but think about how I can't wait until she starts nesting and destroying the sheets. Nesting she-wolves become territorial, and I'm not even sure she'll allow Damian and Gannon in here when that time comes.

Judging by the way she's bunching the sheets now, it won't be too far off. She'll make this her haven, and once I make her a Lycan, she will kill anyone who enters her den. The memory of my sister accidentally killing her handmaiden when she started nesting surfaces in my mind, a painful reminder of the dangers that come with this stage. She felt terrible, but I would ensure that didn't happen with Ivy.

I bring the bottle to my lips and take another swig, enjoying the smooth, sweet taste while my eyes trail over Ivy. Her pink, bare form is on full display as she lies on her stomach with her leg bent. My cock twitches, and I can't wait to bury it in her, but I will wait and let her decide. So until she asks, I will endure it.

Walking over to the bed, I place my whiskey bottle on the bedside table. My hand skims up the inside of her leg from her ankle, brushing between the apex of her legs. A smile splits onto my face as she moans softly, pushing back against my hand. Leaning over the bed, I plant a gentle kiss on her naked shoulder, but before nipping at her jaw, she groans.

The sound sends a shiver down my spine, and I can't help but be entranced by her every movement. The room is bathed in the soft glow of moonlight streaming through the window, casting delicate shadows across her skin. The scent of her arousal fills the air, a heady mix of sweet and musky that threatens to overwhelm my senses.

Despite the urgency of our impending visit to Alpha Dean and the lingering sense of guilt from earlier, I can't tear my eyes away from Ivy. As I watch her sleep, a fierce protectiveness wells up within me as I move toward her.

FIFTY-TWO

K YSON
       Her arousal causes my nostrils to flare, and my eyes flicker as I inhale her intoxicating scent. The fragrant aroma of her desire mingles with the soft scent of lavender from the bed linens, weaving a spell around me that tightens with every breath. I wanted to fuck her, sheath myself in her tight confines. Moving behind her, I cup her pussy with my hand as I crawl on the bed and press my chest to her back. Her skin feels like silk beneath my fingertips, warm and supple, sending shivers down my spine.

Her reaction is instant, proving how powerful the bond is becoming. She moans again, and I can tell she is waking at my touch. My nose runs across her shoulder, and I nip her skin. The taste of her was a heady mixture of salt and sweetness, a flavor that seemed to echo her very essence. Wanting her to wake up, I squeeze between her legs and she rocks her hips against my hand.

I run my finger through her wet folds, and she whines, pushing against my finger as I tease her by circling it around her entrance, coating it in her arousal. The wet sounds of her desire fill my ears, making my cock throb in anticipation. "Ivy, wake up," I whisper, and she moans, pushing against my finger. I refuse to shove in her. I laugh softly as she becomes annoyed.

"Kyson!" she growls a whine.

"Hmm," I hum as she growls at me. I circle her clit, and she jolts, before moving back to her tight hole and shoving my finger deep inside her. Her walls clamp around it, and I slowly withdraw it before working it back into her warm, wet entrance. Ivy moans, and I groan at the sound she makes before sitting up and using my other hand, I pull her cheeks apart so I can watch my finger fuck her.

I add another, watching as her pussy stretches and clenches around them. She lifts her hips slightly, letting them slide in deeper as I pick up my pace, enjoying the way she shudders and spasms around them. The delicate arch of her back, the curve of her hips, and the way her legs tensed and flexed, all paint a picture of a woman lost in her pleasure.

I am captivated by her, loving the way my name rolls off her tongue and spills out her lips as her pleasure grows. "Fuck, you're so wet," I groan as her tight walls clenched my fingers hard, her arousal spilling onto the mattress and between her milky thighs. I can feel the heat of her body against my hands, a living flame that seems to promise endless passion and pleasure if I could only stoke it to greater heights.

I pull my fingers from her, wanting to taste her sweet nectar. Ivy cries at the loss of my fingers when I grip her hips. She shrieks as I pull her hips into the air. I pull her to the edge of the bed before dropping to my knees on the floor.

"Kyson!" she shrieks, and I know she was feeling exposed in this position. She tries to pull away when I squeeze her ass before my mouth covers her completely, sucking her sweet lips into my mouth.

The top half of her body sinks into the mattress at the feel of my tongue sliding between her folds. I chuckle as she melts against the bed. Her legs tremble as she pushes back against my mouth as I devour her. The muffled sounds of her pleasure, combined with the gentle rustle of sheets beneath her, creates a symphony that makes my heart race and my blood sign with desire.

Her desire overrules her embarrassment that her ass is in my face, and I push her legs further apart before tilting my face. Ivy shivers when my stubble brushes her clit as I jam my tongue inside her. The sensation of her velvety flesh against my tongue is intoxicating, and I couldn't get enough of her taste.

Her sweet taste on my tongue makes me groan, and my cock ached painfully, wanting to be buried deep inside her. My hands squeeze her thighs as I open her up wider, sucking and licking every crease and fold before trailing my tongue between her cheeks and running it over her tight hole. The air around us is heavy with the scent of our lust, making every breath a reminder of our shared passion.

She jerks, feeling my tongue poke and prod around her back passage, but I grip her thighs, not allowing her to escape as my tongue travels back to her pink, swollen pussy. I slip my fingers in her quickly, coating them in her juices, then trace them up to her ass crack.

I rasp when my finger meets the tight resistance of her asshole as I shove my finger in. She bucked, but I sucked on her clit harder as I worked my finger inside her, her body relaxing and her muscles easing as I fuck her ass with my finger.

Ivy moans and writhes as I tasted every part of her before working another finger into her. Stretching her tight hole while lapping at the juices as they spilled out of her. She pushes against my face, rocking her hips in ecstasy against my mouth and fingers before she screams and exploding on my tongue.

I lick up her juices, gently sliding my fingers from her as she moans, my tongue slowing as she rides out her orgasm. Her sweet nectar coats my lips and tongue when she collapses on her stomach on the bed. I chuckle, grabbing her ass after I stand up.

Her face is flushed, and her eyes heavy. I lean over the top of her and kiss her shoulder. The touch of my lips to her skin sends a shiver down her spine, and I can feel her body gradually relaxing beneath me. Standing up, I step into the bathroom and wash my hands. The sound of water running echoes through the room, a soothing counterpoint to the intensity of our passion.

When I come out, she has fallen back asleep, and I sit on the bed, tucking her body against mine, and finally, I too am able to settle down enough to fall asleep for the first time in two days. As I lay there, her soft breaths against my chest and the gentle rise and fall of her body lulling me into slumber, I realize we have forged a connection that could never be broken.

FIFTY-THREE

I VY

The sunlight filters through the cracks in the heavy drapes, casting a golden glow on the ornate ceiling above us. The scent of Kyson's aftershave still lingers in the air, a mix of cedar and sandalwood that has become a comforting reminder of his presence. The sheets beneath us are soft, a gentle caress against my skin. I can hear the faint rustling of leaves outside the window and the morning birds.

As Kyson begins to stir, the muscles in his arms flex beneath my fingers. The hardness of his body is evident even at rest. Seeing his muscular body brings a feeling of security and warmth, and I can't help but snuggle closer to him. He inhales deeply, his chest rising and falling with each breath, and I can feel the steady rhythm of his heartbeat beneath my ear.

Relief floods me seeing him sleeping for the first time in days. This is the first time I've woken up to him asleep. I was beginning to wonder if not sleeping was a Lycan thing or a Kyson thing.

My body feels heavy with his leg draped over my hip and mine tucked between his legs. I run my fingers through his chest hair.

I trace one of my bite marks on his chest before pressing my lips together. My teeth ache, and my gums tingle with the need to bite him, claim him, and I try to stamp it down, though it is making me twitchy.

I hope it settles down because I don't think I can live with the crazy urges I keep having. Kyson explained that it was the hormones, but it only happened near him. I hadn't bitten anyone else, only him.

Clarice said she-wolves tended to bite those they felt safest with, those with stronger auras. Which, in turn, makes sense. We are primal, possessive creatures; biting is a form of marking, but I don't get that urge around Beta Damian, despite his relatively strong aura.

Lost in my thoughts, I am entirely unaware I am even licking him until he chuckles, pulling me from the mind bubble I locked myself in. Oh no, I woke him. That wasn't my intention. Sitting up slightly, I place two fingers on his opening eyes and try to close them, making him laugh when he grabs my hand and kisses it before putting it on his chest.

"Morning," he mumbles, tugging me closer. I clench my jaw, unable to reply now that I have stopped licking him. I want to climb on him, soak up his scent, and bite him.

The urges are driving me insane, and I try to roll away when he removes his leg from over my waist and grips my thigh, hauling me on top of him.

"I have told you you aren't hurting me, so stop fighting it."

I shake my head, unable to trust, opening my mouth in case I bite him like a damn cannibal.

"Maybe I should hold off," Kyson murmurs to himself, and I look at him. I want to ask what he means, but I can't right now, as I'm fighting a battle with my mind and body. The King grips the back of my head, pressing my face into his neck. I try to push him away, earning a growl from him.

"I am supposed to leave today for the night. I will be back tomorrow, but now I worry I shouldn't leave you while you're like this, especially when you're fighting it. I'm worried you will fret," he says.

I try to process his words, and when I'm unable to control myself any longer, I sink my teeth into his chest once more. He groans, and tears burn my eyes as his blood floods into my mouth. I hate this, hate it, hate the damn urges overriding every part of me.

"You're not hurting me, love. I promise," he whispers, kissing my face as I try to stop myself. I shake my head.

The King grips my hips, dragging me down his body as I sink my teeth in once again. My nails dig into his skin as I grab him when he rolls my hips against him, and I stop and moan before biting his arm. His cock twitches against my pussy, and I freeze. He turns his face toward my ear.

"See, you're not hurting me, just making me aroused," he whispers, rolling my hips against him again. His cock slides between my wet folds, and I moan at the friction he is creating.

My teeth leave his skin, but only briefly as I kiss him. My tongue invades his mouth, and he chuckles as I maul him before kissing me back.

He lets me touch and claw at him until the urges dissipate. The King then rolls, forcing me onto my back and climbing between my legs. His hard length presses against my slit, and I move my hips against him, coating his length with my desire. The King groans and presses his hips against mine.

My walls clench, wanting to feel him buried deep within my confines, wanting to feel him move inside me. The King clenches his jaw, and I kiss him. Tugging his face down to mine, he grabs my thigh, hoisting it up and wrapping it around his waist; I grind my hips against him, uncaring, just wanting him closer.

"Ivy?" he groans, and my name leaving his lips like that makes my walls clench. I tug on his hip, and he pushes up on his arms, looking down at me.

He knows what I want, but he also wants me to ask or probably beg. I growl at him and bite his bicep, tugging him back down to me.

"You want this?" he purrs, and a whine escapes my lips as he thrust his cock between my slick folds.

"Words, Ivy, I need you to say it, or I will stop," he says, nipping at my chin. I gulp and nod, and his nose skims across my cheek before he bites my lips.

"Yes?" he purrs, and I clench my eyes shut, embarrassed he is going to make me say it. My thoughts and urges alone are vulgar enough without me speaking them aloud.

"Ivy, I don't speak, nods, or moans, so words or," he pulls away, and I grip his arms. He settles between my legs again, kissing me, when suddenly a knock is heard on the door.

"My King, the car is ready. We have to leave," I hear Gannon's voice through the door. The King glances at the clock on the bedside table. "Ah, I can stay. I am worried about leaving you on your own anyway," he tells me.

"You're leaving?" I ask.

"Yes, I have to visit your old pack, or do you want to come?" As Kyson speaks, his voice is low and gravelly, sending a shiver down my spine. I can hear his concern in his tone and how he worries about me despite his own exhaustion and schedule. When he mentions visiting my old pack, the memories of that place come flooding back, a tidal wave of emotions that I struggle to keep at bay. I shake my head. I never wanted to go back there again. "Then I will tell them another day," he sighs.

"No, it's fine. I will just help Abbie," I answer, and he stares at me.

"What do you mean you will help Abbie, Ivy? You are not a servant," he demands.

"I enjoy helping her; I get to spend time with her, and I really don't mind... It gives me something to do," I tell him, and he sighs.

He grips my face, tilting my head and kissing my jaw. "You are to be my Queen, not the housekeeper." He growls against my skin.

"Please," I beg. The King growls and pulls back, looking down at me.

"I don't like this, Ivy," he says in exasperation.

"It's the only way I can spend time with her. Besides, working with Abbie isn't working for me; it's fun," I tell him.

"Fine, but only until I return, and you are not to work in a uniform. I will not have people treating you like the help."

I nod excitedly, and he pecks my lips, sitting up. "Beta Damian will stay, and I will be back tomorrow. Are you sure you don't want me to stay with you?" he says, pecking my lips once again. I shake my head. I did not want to be the reason he is kept from his work.

I watch Kyson dress quickly and gracefully despite his large size. His dark hair is tousled. He pulls on his shirt, the fabric clinging to his chiseled chest and highlighting the curve of his biceps. I can't help but admire the man he is, both in strength and for the kindness he has shown me and Abbie. For the first time in my life, I feel like I really am safe here.

As he slips on his shoes, he glances back at me. The intensity of his gaze is almost palpable, and I feel a renewed surge of desire coursing through me. Thankfully, he turns away, or I may beg him to stay.

Instead, I focus on the sounds of the room, the creaking floorboards, and the distant hum of voices echoing through the halls. I shuffle through my new clothes, trying to find the plainest outfit I can; something that feels more like me and less like the regal attire befitting a future Queen. I don't want it to draw too much attention to me. I hate the idea of Abbie feeling less than me because I am not in uniform.

CHAPTER
FIFTY-FOUR

KYSON
    A nauseating feeling washes over me as I contemplate leaving Ivy. However, seeing her excitement at the prospect of meeting up with Abbie eases my tension ever so slightly.

Together, Ivy and I make our way to the kitchen, where Clarice instructs several servants with a firm yet kind voice. She looks up as we enter, her eyes narrowing in disapproval as they land on Ivy.

"Ivy, dear, this is no place for our future Queen," she says with a hint of concern.

I can see Ivy's shoulders tense at the title, and it doesn't escape my notice. "The King said..."

I interrupt her with a low growl, irritated by the formal title she uses for me.

"Want to rephrase that, Ivy?" I ask. My voice is firm but gentle. Her eyes widen in surprise, and she stammers for a moment before I approach her. The heat of my chest brushes against her back, and I feel the tension in her body dissipate.

"Kyson said I could help Abbie until he returns," she says with newfound confidence. I reward her with a soft kiss on the cheek and a nod, confirming her statement. Clarice lets out a resigned sigh.

"Very well. Abbie is in Beta Damian's quarters," she says, her tone relenting. Ivy turns to leave but then hesitates, caught in indecision between continuing to Abbie or returning to me.

"Ivy, are you okay?" I ask, concern lacing my voice. I'm close to changing my mind about leaving her today, but she nods. Quickly, she rushes back to me and wraps her arms around me in a tight embrace. I lift her up, allowing her to bury her face in the crook of my neck and inhale my scent, finding the comfort she seeks. When I set her back down on her feet, she seems torn about leaving, but ultimately, she hurries off to join Abbie.

With a heavy sigh, I turn my attention to Clarice, who has been watching Ivy with a worried expression. She offers me a warm, sympathetic smile, and I beckon her closer.

Clarice steps forward, and I guide her to a more secluded corner of the room. "I need to leave, but I won't be back until late tomorrow. I wondered if you could organize a cake and dinner for Ivy's 18th birthday tomorrow," I request in a hushed tone.

"I thought her birthday wasn't for a couple more weeks," Clarice says, a questioning look in her eyes.

"Damian spoke with the Alpha from her old pack. Ivy had her dates wrong. Her birthday is tomorrow, and I want to celebrate when I get back," I explain, hoping to make the day special for her.

"Of course, my King. I would be honored. Am I right in assuming you want this to be a surprise?" she asks, anticipating my answer. I nod in agreement, grateful for her knowing me so well.

"I will organize something special for her then," she says, her eyes twinkling enthusiastically. I place my hand on her arm and squeeze it gently. Then, I turn on my heel and exit the kitchen, my footsteps echoing down the castle's corridors as I walk to the front entrance.

As soon as I step outside, the cool air greets me, and my instincts urge me to find Ivy to ensure her safety and comfort. Gannon, a trusted ally, waits patiently by the car, and Damian approaches us, his steady gaze meeting mine.

"She will be fine, and I will call you if anything happens," Damian assures me, his words carrying the weight of years of unwavering loyalty. I glance back at the castle one last time before nodding and climbing into the car. I trust Damian with my life; I know he will protect Ivy with the same devotion he has shown me repeatedly.

The drive is long and boring, and I can't help but feel a gnawing anxiety about leaving Ivy behind. At the same time, curiosity stirs within me about what Alpha Dean might have discovered regarding my little mate's lineage and her life before the orphanage. I hope that this meeting will provide some much-needed answers.

A dark thought crosses my mind – I must visit Mrs. Daley, the headmistress who had abused Ivy. By the time I'm through with her, her back will bear the same marks she inflicted on my mate. If I'm in a merciful mood, I might even let her keep her miserable life and not kill her. But I can't make any promises; the horrific stories I've heard and the whispers from the castle guards enrage me beyond measure. Just seeing the jumpiness and fear that bitch has conditioned into Ivy and Abbie is enough to make me see red.

I also need to deal with Ester, I think to myself. I realize I long for the ability to communicate with Ivy through a mindlink. That way, I could hear her voice whenever I desire. Damian's presence interrupts my thoughts as our connection opens.

'Yes, Damian?' I ask, sensing his aura through the link.

'Just checking in,' he replies, his voice steady and reassuring.

'How is my mate?' I inquire, concern evident in my voice.

'She is okay, helping rake leaves in the garden.'

I can't help but growl at the thought of her working. Ivy has spent her entire life doing constant labor, and now, given the chance to do as she pleases, she reverts to performing household tasks. It's infuriating. She could be enjoying her freedom, painting, anything but cleaning and acting a slave.

'*Make sure she is in bed by eight. She needs to sleep before tomorrow night,*' I instruct him, my tone firm.

'*Yes, I was going to tell her to come in soon, anyway. It is getting quite overcast. How far out are you now?*' he asks, genuine concern in his voice.

'*Why are you worried about me, Damian?*'

'*Always, Kyson. It is my job to worry. I understand why you left me with Ivy, but that doesn't mean I have stopped worrying about you,*' he answers sincerely.

'*An hour out, not much longer,*' I inform him, trying to put his mind at ease.

'*Good. Tell Gannon to check in when you get there and keep in touch.*'

I sever the mindlink, and Gannon nods at me as if he already knows to check in with his Beta.

"Do you know what Alpha Dean wants to see me for?" I ask him, my curiosity piqued. Gannon shakes his head.

"No idea, Kyson. I called him this morning, and he only said it was about her parents, that he thinks he found something alarming." I nod, pondering what could be so secretive.

"Anything on the children yet?"

"No, but I believe it has something to do with that no-good son of his," Gannon replies, his tone darkening.

"Just remain alert. I want to get back to my mate as soon as possible, in and out. Shit, I also need to deal with the headmistress."

"I called ahead. I figured you would want a word with her. So the Alpha has had her strung up in the town square waiting for you," Gannon smirks, his eyes flickering with anticipation. I can't help but feel a spark of satisfaction at the thought of exacting vengeance on the woman. She will pay for what she has done to my mate, and she will pay dearly.

CHAPTER
FIFTY-FIVE

K YSON

The sun dips low in the sky, casting long, golden rays across the landscape as we near the sleepy little town where I first discovered my mate. The once bustling center of life now appears to be a shadow of its former self, the streets littered with broken signs and crumbling buildings. The scent of decay and neglect hangs heavily in the air, starkly contrasting the vibrant, bustling town it once was. *I hate this place,* I think, feeling like I'll be happy to never set foot here again.

As we pull into the town square, true to the Alpha's word, Mrs. Daley stands with her bony wrists tied above her head, shivering against the wind that whips at her ragged clothing. The once proud headmistress now looks half livid, half terrified. Her eyes dart around wildly, seeking an escape from her impending punishment. Seeing her struggle, I feel a deep sense of satisfaction.

Alpha Dean and Alpha Brock stand nearby, waiting to greet us. Alpha Dean steps forward first to shake my hand while his son Brock keeps his head hung. The older Alpha is dressed in a suit with his jacket undone, his shirt wrinkled as though he had been working all day. He looks tired, his once strong frame now slightly hunched, and his hair peppered with streaks of gray. In contrast, his son, Brock, appears careless in his attire, dressed in shorts and a tank top. His bare feet are covered in dirt, and I sneer at his lack of respect for my arrival.

Brock bares his neck to me, a smart move considering my growing impatience and need to return to Ivy's side. The air around us feels tense, and I can practically taste his fear.

"Tied and waiting, sir, as you asked. May I ask what she did wrong?" Alpha Dean inquires, his voice steady but edged with concern. Mrs. Daley whimpers at his words, her eyes wide with terror.

"I think the question is what she did right because there is no reasoning that could explain why you would leave a cruel, spiteful woman in charge of raising innocent children," I tell the Alpha, my tone icy and unyielding.

"Right, right. I um. I can see that she is punished if I know what I am punishing her for?" Alpha Dean stammers, casting a wary glance at his son. Clearly, he wasn't aware of the treatment, but the palpable fear emanating from Brock suggests he knew all too well.

"Punishment is already decided, Alpha. I wanted to do it myself, but Gannon has volunteered so that we could get this over with quickly. He even brought his own whip." I smile coldly at Mrs. Daley, whose face pales further.

"How many lashings did we count on the girls' backs?" I ask Gannon, turning to look at him.

"Damian and I believe around 70 on Abbie's," Gannon states, his voice devoid of emotion.

"And from what I could count, roughly 135 on Ivy's, though I know that number is a lot higher because it's hard to count when the skin is terribly marred," I growl, my fury boiling just beneath the surface.

"My King, 200 lashes, she won't be able to stand. She couldn't possibly heal fast enough," Alpha Dean interjects, his voice laced with unease. Mrs. Daley's pleading eyes meet mine as she begs for mercy, but I remain unmoved. It's not like Abbie and Ivy were ever able to heal.

"Quite right, we can't have that," I muse.

The Alpha lets out a breath, seemingly relieved. I turn to Gannon, my voice cold and firm.

"Double it; I don't want her standing at all."

The woman screams and thrashes against her restraints, her desperate cries echoing through the run-down town square. The two Alphas look at me in horror, but I don't waver. They must understand the gravity of the situation and the severity of her actions.

"Shall we get this meeting over with?" I motion toward the pack house. Both Alphas hurry ahead, their shoulders tense and their steps quick. As we make our way to the house, I can't help but glance back at Gannon as he prepares to unleash his fury on Mrs. Daley. His eyes gleam with a twisted sense of revenge, reflecting the darkness within us all.

"Gannon?" I call out to him.

"Yes, my King?" he responds, looking up at me with an unsettling eagerness.

"Make sure you swap arms. I wouldn't want you to get a cramp or tire out."

"Of course, my King," he nods before stalking towards the cowering headmistress. Her blood-curdling scream follows the sharp swish of the whip slicing through the air as it comes down on her back. The chilling sound resonates through the town square, a stark reminder of the consequences of cruelty.

I climb the steps into the pack house, where both Alphas stand, staring out at the headmistress with a mixture of horror and disbelief. Ironically, they have no problem killing children, yet witnessing Mrs. Daley's much-deserved punishment unsettles them.

The only thing better would be to do it myself, but my eagerness to return home to Ivy prevents me from indulging in that pleasure. When Gannon offered, I took him up on it without hesitation.

"My King, would you like coffee, water, maybe tea?" Alpha Dean asks, his voice unsteady, clearly shaken.

"Have you got whiskey?" I inquire, needing something more potent to calm my nerves.

"Yes, of course. Go fetch some Brock. We will be in the basement," Alpha Dean orders his son, who looks humiliated by the command. I raise an eyebrow at him, and he scampers off.

Two of my guards follow me, and the other stalks ahead of Alpha Dean, pointing to a door. Alpha Dean nods, and we wait until he goes down and calls clear before descending into the dimly lit basement. The damp, musty air clings to our skin as we navigate the cluttered space filled with boxes upon boxes of files. A table and lamp sit in the middle of the room, surrounded by pictures and various documents.

"What is all this?" I inquire, peering down at the table.

"Her parents, my King. I have some distressing news about little Ivy. I have no idea how I didn't put the pieces together before," Alpha Dean admits, looking ashamed. He hands me a picture of a dead woman, her throat torn out and her guts spilled open on the autopsy table. Her face is barely recognizable as female, if not for her long, mangled hair.

"What is this?" I demand, my heart pounding in my chest.

"Ivy's mother. She went by the name Della Hunley, and this is her father, or so he claimed," Alpha Dean explains, handing me another gruesome autopsy photograph of a man. Their faces are riddled with teeth and claw marks, unrecognizable even if I had known them.

"Okay?" I shake my head, irritated by the apparent waste of time. Alpha Dean then retrieves a clear bag from a box filled with dirty, blood-stained clothes. My eyes are immediately drawn to the hunter's insignia patch as he tips the bag, letting it fall onto the table. I pick it up, my grip tightening around it.

"Where did you get this?" I demand my voice tight with anger.

"Both her mother and father had matching ones," Alpha Dean reveals, his expression grave.

"Abbie's parents?" I ask, still confused about who owned the insignia.

"No, Ivy's. Abbie's parents were indeed who they said they were and posed no threat. They fell in with bad people," Alpha Dean clarifies.

"What do you mean?" I question, my eyes scanning the documents and photographs on the table. My stomach churns, and I struggle to suppress the urge to vomit.

Alpha Dean rummages through the paperwork before producing two photographs. As he hands them to me, my blood runs cold. I snarl, recognizing the woman instantly. I've been hunting her since she killed my sister and her family.

"I take it you recognize her," Alpha Dean says grimly.

"Marissa Talbot wanted for murder in the highest degree," I growl through clenched teeth.

"Yes, that is why I asked you here. You see, Della Hunley is Marissa Talbot. We have yet to identify her father; he has no records, but fingerprints for the mother match everything else. Ivy's parents are part of the hunter's organization. They are also responsible for not only your sister and her unborn child's death but also King Garret and Queen Tatiana and their murdered baby. You have a traitor living in your castle, my King," Alpha Dean warns me.

Fury and betrayal washes over me as I process the information. The air in the basement feels heavier, suffocating me as I try to wrap my head around the fact that Ivy, my mate, is the child of the very people who took so much from me.

"Thank you for bringing this to my attention, Alpha Dean," I say, my voice steady despite the storm raging inside me. "We will deal with this situation accordingly."

CHAPTER
FIFTY-SIX

GANNON

I count every strike against the old hag's back, watching as she hangs limp in the restraints. My eyes wander to the pack house from which the King has yet to emerge. My brows furrow, and I glance around at the guards. I am so preoccupied with dealing with Mrs. Daley that I don't realize the King is still inside the pack house.

I wipe my hands on my jeans, which are drenched in blood from the back spray from off the whip. "Is he still in there?" I ask one of the men standing guard by the doors. He nods his head.

"Yes, Gamma, we tried to go in, but he told us not to disturb him," the man speaks, and I raise an eyebrow at him as I climb the steps before shoving the rickety old door in. Alpha Dean and Alpha Brock are sitting on the steps in the hallway.

"Where is the King?" I ask before Alpha Dean lifts a shaking finger and points toward the basement door.

"He told us to get out and wait up here," Alpha Dean says, and by how pale he is, something has scared the life out of the old man. As I open the door, I can hear the King muttering, and I curse at myself for leaving him on his own.

Walking down the steps, I can tell he isn't in the right state of mind because of his aura, which makes my knees shake and goose-bumps raise every hair on my body. That is proven more by the moment my feet touch the concrete floor, and I peer over at him where he stands by a table in the center of the dusty old room. The place is floor-to-ceiling high in boxes and files.

His entire body tenses as he senses the incoming intruder. Everyone is petrified of this side of the King. The monster that lurks beneath the skin of this man. In this form, he is a predator, the biggest predator, a lethal beast, and he shows it within seconds of me spotting him.

One minute, he is standing by the table under the hanging light. The next, his hands grip my shirt's front, and I am airborne as he tosses me. The air fizzles in my lungs as I hit a stack of boxes.

"Kyson!" I choke as his fist connects with my head. I growl before it's cut off by his hands around my throat. I grip his wrists, only for him to lift and slam me onto the table that he was standing over when I came down here.

Damian usually deals with him when he is in fits of rage, and usually, the King keeps this part of him locked up tight until it explodes as it has now.

"Kyson!" I choke out as his grip tightens; his eyes are black and plagued with the horrors of his past, where he couldn't protect his sister, a past full of bloodshed and unimaginable horrors. A place he is currently trapped in, like the nightmares that plague him, and I have yet to figure out what has triggered him.

I tilt my head to the side just as his fist comes down on the table before punching him in the ribs. His grip never wavers as he hits me again, and I hear the wood crack as my head smashes back against the table. He will forgive me because I'm not taking a pounding from him, and he wants to burn off some anger.

From what I will figure out after, as he raises his clawed fist again, I shift under his grip, his tight grip making the transition painful as my neck elongates and the bones in my face break and move, my jaws lock around his fist catching it, and I jam my claws in his ribs.

He grunts, stunned by the sudden pain he feels, that momentary distraction making his grip on my throat lessen, and my claws slip free of him as he staggers back, allowing me to roll off the table. Only this time, I am ready and prepared for his attack.

By the time he comes back to his senses, I don't think an inch of either of us isn't torn, scratched, or bruised. His anger diminishes as his eyes settle on me, the King returning, and, damn, next time, Damian is going with him – every part of me aches and stings.

The King gasps, blinking. His eyes return to normal as he sits up from where I tossed him off. The basement is destroyed, and I take comfort in knowing I won't be cleaning it.

"Gannon?"

"My King," I reply, baring my neck to him, hoping not to set him off again. We both breathe heavily, and I feel every bit of the 411 years I have spent on this earth.

"You want to tell me what that was about?" I ask him, trying to catch my breath as he shifts back. He leans back against the bench and crooked shelf, bracing his arms on his knees. I still don't shift back, not yet. He is unpredictable at the best of times, an emotional, ticking time bomb running off pure instinct.

He clutches his hair in his fists, and I leave the question instead of getting up and upturning what is left of the table, the papers scattered across the floor. I am nearly tempted to drag Alpha Dean down here when he doesn't answer when I spot some photographs. One of the women I barely recognize because she is ripped apart, but the two orphanage photos of the two little girls I recognize instantly.

"This has something to do with Ivy?"

"She belongs to that monster," Kyson breathes, and I glance over my shoulder to find him resting his head back on the shelf and staring at the swinging light. I turn back to the paperwork, picking up scattered pieces and trying to figure out his words when I spot a photo of a woman I recognize to be Marrissa Talbot, the woman responsible for killing his sister.

It doesn't take long before I realize what he means: Marrissa is Ivy's mother.

"Fuck!" I curse, knowing full well what that woman's crimes were.

"I can't be with her, not after knowing who mothered her."

"We don't know for certain," I mutter, picking up more files only to stumble across Abbie's. I stack the documents in a pile.

"I am certain that she isn't her mother, Kyson. How you could even entertain the idea of them being the same is beyond me. Besides, that girl was a child and not part of her mother's crimes if she is, in fact, her daughter," I tell him.

"And if she is, what do I do with her?" Kyson asks me.

"Does it matter? She is your mate!" I tell him while gathering all the documents.

"I won't have a monster for a mate!"

"Ivy is not her mother? You can't blame her for the crimes of her mother. She was just a child then."

"I can't punish her mother for her crimes, yet she left behind a daughter that I can!" he growls before storming out of the basement.

"Fuck!" I curse, gathering everything and moving after him. *This is not going to end well,* I think, feeling my ability to handle this situation slowly slipping away.

The dingy basement is destroyed, as if someone had set off a bomb downstairs. Shaking my head at the mess, I follow after the King. I hear him barking orders at his men, demanding to leave. I turn to Alpha Dean as he rises from where he still sits on the steps. "Couldn't you have told us this over the phone or faxed this crap?" I ask, shaking it in the jerk's face. He says nothing, and I look at his pathetic son.

"You'll need to retrieve a broom," I tell him. If it were me, I would lock the door and declare the basement no longer exists, as there's probably no fixing this place. Kyson is still arguing with his men about hurrying and securing the place. *I better get up there,* I think, knowing that members of his guard may not be as prepared to deal with him in this state. He is impatient and wants to leave, but we have protocols to follow before that is possible.

I snap my fingers at the driver, who jumps into the front seat. Glancing around at the men, I say, "Forget it. Mark, go ahead of us. We leave now unless you want him tearing this pack apart." The man runs to one of the cars. The King isn't going to wait, and I sure as hell don't feel like chasing him on foot if he decides to run out his anger.

Climbing into the car, I slide across the seat and shut the door. The car takes off immediately, and the King looks for clothes. After dropping the documents on the seat, I lean forward and lift the bench seat with the storage underneath. I toss him some clothes, taking a pair of shorts and a tank top out for myself.

I pull them on, jerking sideways as the limo goes around corners before tugging the shirt over my head.

The King's aura is suffocating in the small space, and Damian will kill me when he finds out, but he isn't the one sitting with him. So, I reach into the fridge and pull out a liquor bottle. I try to hand him a glass, but he twists the cap off and puts the bottle to his lips before I can. Liquor dribbles down his chin, and he pulls the bottle from his lips, wiping his face on the back of his hand, and sighs.

We all know he is an alcoholic. He has been since his sister died, and right now, I'm not helping the issue, but I can handle him drunk; it takes the edge of. I don't feel like going round two with him right now, and it sure as hell won't be the first or the last time I watch him find himself at the bottom of a bottle or two.

Halfway through the third bottle, he passes out drunk. It is a long drive back, and I am relieved to watch his eyes grow heavier before his head slumps forward. Sighing, I take the bottle from his grip and sit beside the two empty ones. I tap on the screen between the driver and me, causing the driver to roll down the window.

"He's passed out?" the driver asks, sounding as relieved as I feel.

Towards the end, his aura made me queasy, so I know he feels the same. "Thank God!" he answers when I see his eyes dart to the mirror.

We chat a bit, and he pulls over briefly, allowing the cars behind us to catch up and drive ahead while I hop out for a smoke. I retrieve a blanket from the trunk, and the driver goes in, tucking the King in like a child. Usually, that is done by Damian, but today, I tasked the driver, Bill, with it. He always feels regret the days after or embarrassment, but I have a feeling this won't be the last of his anger. I briefly wonder if I should mindlink Damian to warn him of the storm that's coming their way. I shudder to think what's going to happen next.

The driver hops back in just as three cars pull up behind us, and three have gone ahead of us now.

I toss the last of my smoke, climbing back in with the King. Retrieving the files, I decide to go over them to find out more about Marrissa and take a peek at Abbie's files.

Not much is said about Marrissa because, by the looks of it, Alpha Dean isn't even aware of who his pack has killed.

Shaking my head, I set that file aside before pulling out Abbie's. I open it to the orphanage photo, which must have been taken that night they were found. She looks petrified as she stares at the camera, her childlike eyes wide with fear and blood drenching her clothes. Turning the page, I nearly drop the files when I find her parent's ID.

More importantly, when I find her mother's. *That's impossible... I watched her die.* I knew she was dead because I killed her myself.

I blink down at the picture; her face is exactly how I remember it, similar to Abbie's. The resemblance is uncanny, yet when I look at the name, it is wrong except for the last name.

This woman looks exactly like my mate. Identical, and now I figure out the allure I had to her. Liam is right. I can no longer deny it, and now I know why they share such a resemblance. I have a feeling the woman I am staring at in the photo is my mate's twin.

CHAPTER
FIFTY-SEVEN

GANNON

It takes a while for the King to wake up from his drunken stupor, and the moment he does, he reaches for the bottle. I snatch it, needing him to come to his senses, needing his word that he won't hurt her. Which, in turn, would hurt Abbie. He loves Ivy. Everyone in the castle is aware of his affection for the girl, and for once, the castle and everyone in it can finally breathe.

We have all lived through his depression, his anger, and relentless torment. I've watched him destroy himself more times than I can count. None of us want to see him return to that dark place, and I also worry that he will lose his Kingdom if he can't see past who her parents were. This would no doubt divide people.

Kyson reaches forward to snatch the bottle, but I pull it away. "I'll give it to you. First, we need to talk," I tell him. He's far too drunk to cause me any real damage, his eyes bloodshot, and he reeks of liquor.

We still have a couple more hours left before we reach home, and he needs to either get his frustration and anger out now or talk it out. Either one I'm okay with. Everyone back home has prayed for the miracle that the King would find his mate, find someone to help tame him, and bring him back to us, and Ivy is doing that without even knowing it.

"Gannon!" Kyson growls, but I fold the bottle in my arms as I cross them over my chest. He sighs. "Fine, I'll talk, but give me the damn bottle."

I raise an eyebrow at him.

"No, talk first, then, depending on how I feel about your mood afterward; I will decide whether I will return it," I tell him. He presses his lips in a line. He could command me, but I know some piece of him knows he needs me to prevent him from letting the monster inside him out; his father would command anyone and everyone. I don't remember you holding a normal conversation with that man; it was best to steer clear of him and avoid his inevitable wrath.

Even though Kyson respected and loved his father, we all know that's why he hated commanding his men. However, he seems to get a kick from using that and his calling on Ivy. At first, it shocked Damian and me. We both put it down to it being a mate thing and his Alpha instincts to keep her under his control and safe.

One thing I like about him being King is he will give you a chance to answer, only using his command when needed or if you genuinely piss him off. Rarely will you see him use it. He doesn't need to use his aura most of the time because he earned the respect of his people, and they answer truthfully, though sometimes I wonder if he's a little too trusting.

He strives to be a better man than his father, who was a right prick, not that anyone told Kyson that. We dance the line when it comes to mentioning his father. Kyson had always looked up to him, despite him putting so much pressure on his son when he was alive that it almost killed him.

Growing up, he endured his father for his sister's sake so she didn't have to. Once she was gone, I've lost count of the number of times Damian, Liam, and I have had to pull him back from the brink of madness and stop him from ending it, and oh, how he has tried. His sister was his to protect, and he believes he failed her because of Marrissa Talbot, and now he has a constant reminder in his mate.

If I had known this was what Alpha Dean wanted to speak to him about, Damian and I would have covered it up so he never found out. This piece of information isn't needed and will only cause harm. Looking at Kyson, I can tell he wants to hurt Marrissa in the only way he can now, and that is through Ivy. It would've been better for everyone if he never learned of this.

"She isn't her mother," I tell him, and the low growl that leaves him makes me clench my jaw, feeling his aura wash over me.

"Alpha Dean could be lying," I continue when he says nothing.

"What reason would he have to lie?"

"Kyson, you know the pact you had us all make. It may have been years ago, but it hasn't changed. We can't allow you to kill her. We will put you down if you try."

"I'm not stupid, Gannon, I know that. I wouldn't kill her, anyway."

I let out a breath of relief that is very short-lived.

"Because if I did, I would only be killing myself, and that means that bitch won in eradicating the royal families."

I groan. That's not the answer I wanted to hear.

"Let me double-check with Ivy. I don't want you near her until we are sure, and you need to speak to Damian about this. Her safety depends on it," I tell him. His eyes flicker, turning black as coal. His canines slipped out.

"You won't hurt her," I tell him.

"Then what? I can't keep her either; I don't fucking want to look at Marrissa's spawn every damn second."

"Well, you can't keep her locked up in the fucking dungeons; I won't allow it."

"It isn't your choice, she is my mate, and I am fucking King!" he bellows.

"Right now, the only thing you are is a fucking idiot. Now, you need to pull yourself together. You need to see past who her mother was!" I snap at him when he growls, leaning forward on his seat.

His claws slip out, cutting into the leather upholstery, and I curse, knowing what he wants. He wants to forget, wants to drown himself with the bottle, and clearly, I'm not getting anywhere and need to hope Damian gets through to him because I can't.

"Promise me you won't do anything stupid. Promise you won't destroy your bond."

"I can't promise that," he says, and I grit my teeth.

"At least promise to speak with Damian before you do anything you will regret, Kyson. You're upset, and if you break the little trust you have built with her, you will regret it. You don't want to harm her!" I don't finish. He knows what will happen if he tries to kill her. We all took the same pact—a pact he made us take after losing his sister.

A pact that ensures his Queen's safety, no matter the circumstance. If his future mate's life is in danger, we are to choose her over him, every time, no matter what. If it comes to her and him, we take a bullet for her and let him die. We chose to take that pact, and he begged us to take it. That goes for him, too. He tries to kill her, and we will be forced to put him down to save her. He can order us to stand down. Technically, until he marks her, the pact won't be in full swing, not until his mark lies on her neck. Yet we will still honor it, knowing who she is to him.

"I promise I will speak to Damian first," Kyson tells me, and I suck in a breath of relief.

"You go straight to Damian. I want your word. You won't sneak off to your office. You won't look for her. Give me your word, Kyson, that you will go to him." He's furious, but he also knows I'm right. Damian is his calm place.

Those two are more like brothers who have some strange understanding. Kyson is like my brother, but those two are synced oddly. They are an extension of each other, being raised like brothers, enduring the same torment at the hands of Kyson's father. Damian is also the only one who, if I can't talk him down, Damian usually can.

"Fine, just give me the drink."

"I want to hear you say it."

"I will go straight to Damian, okay."

I sigh before I relent and pass him the bottle. He takes it, and I don't miss the tremble of his hands as he twists off the cap. Usually, that only happens the few times we try to get him sober. It never lasts long before we give up. His tremors are always terrible, and we hate seeing him like that. The King is an alcoholic, and everyone knows it, yet with Ivy, we see hope because it is apparent he tries not to drink himself into a stupor while with her.

CHAPTER
FIFTY-EIGHT

I VY

All day, I work with Abbie around the castle. The place seems to be buzzing with excitement; it has me second-glancing at servants as they pass and whisper excitedly about something. Clarice is in an exceptional mood; we even caught her singing in the kitchen and dancing with the other cooks before she noticed me and ushered me out of the kitchen. Clarice even let Abbie choose her chores halfway through the day, so we spent it outside while throwing the leaves at each other, which led to more raking.

It's the most fun we have had in ages. Both Dustin and Damian follow me like my shadow, but even Dustin and Beta Damian join when we have our leaf fight. It's great spending the day with Abbie, but when Damian finishes mindlinking the King, he calls me over to him. I wander over, pulling leaves from my hair.

"My Queen, it is time to go in. I think a storm is coming, and you should come inside before it rains," he states, turning all business-like again.

"Just a while longer, please?"

"I'm sorry, my Queen, I must insist. The King wants you in bed by 8 pm.," he tells me.

"Fine, but stop calling me your queen," I say, noticing his lips tug up in the corners.

"As you wish."

I say goodbye to Abbie, feeling a little sad I must go. That sadness grows worse once back in the room. The King's scent is everywhere, flooding my senses, and before I can stop myself, I dash to the bed, jump on it, and roll all over it. I roll myself up in the blanket, soaking up his scent, breathing it in. However, pain twinges in my chest that he isn't here with me.

I'm still squirming and rolling across the bed like a madwoman when Beta Damian walks in with my dinner. I freeze, then growl at him, the noise threatening. It startles me and cuts off abruptly when I realize what I did.

"Sorry, Beta Damian," I apologize quickly.

"You can call me Damian, Ivy, and don't be. Kyson was worried you may fret without him. It must be hard to be away from him." He places a food tray on the coffee table, yet I'm not hungry.

"If you get too uncomfortable without him, call out. I will be in the hall all night, but maybe put some of his clothes on. It will help," he says before bowing and leaving the room.

Once showered, I get out and put on one of Kyson's shirts. I pick at my food, not tasting it, and my hunger is gone.

All night, I toss and turn, my stomach cramping and pain I can't explain ravages through me. The pain is almost crippling as it writhes through me.

My mind races; I feel manic and delirious, snapping and snarling, pacing the room as I struggle to sit still. I don't know what's wrong with me, but everything is telling me to leave, to go and look for him. Burrowed beneath the blankets, I must have started crying again because the door burst open.

My growl is thunderous, and I tear off the bed, about to attack, only stopping when Beta Damian grabs my arms.

315

"Ivy, it's me, your Beta."

It takes me a second to recognize his scent. Damian's grip on my arms is tight when I sniff the air while blinking away the savage haze. He remains still as I sniff him, my nose crinkling. "See, just me, Ivy. I'm no threat to you," he whispers, letting me go.

I shake my head and clutch at my chest. Embarrassment washes over me, but it's nothing compared to the pain I feel. The distress and anguish in my chest hurt the most. It burns like a hot poker is stabbed through it.

"What is wrong with me?" I cry, collapsing on the ground.

"You're fretting. It's natural. I will call the King. Maybe speaking to him will help ease the discomfort." I am not sure of this fretting thing; the notion seems odd. But I have no other way to explain this crippling pain.

I nod.

Beta Damian pulls his phone from his pocket and dials the King. I listen to it ring before he steps closer to the bookshelf. They speak for a bit. I can't quite hear what is said, but the King sounds angry.

"Kyson, she is right here; I will put her on."

The King says something back to him. "What do you mean?" Damian asks, confusion etched on his face, and I could have sworn I heard him say he doesn't want to speak to me.

"Can you at least tell me what is wrong?" he asks cautiously. "But my King, she's fretting. Could you please maybe just talk to her on the phone until she falls asleep?"

"My King?" Damian looks at his phone; then I see his eyes glaze over.

A few minutes later, Dustin steps into the room slowly and watches me warily. By now, I have calmed down and want to know what happened to Kyson. Is he ok?

CHAPTER
FIFTY-NINE

I VY

After the strange fiasco this morning, once I step out of the room, the strange fogginess and the territorial behavior diminish, and I'm fine. I walk the castle grounds with Abbie by my side most of the day.

It's peaceful, yet I feel different. Everything feels more enhanced, even my sight, sense of taste, and touch. It feels more intense and foreign. Even the colors have changed a little. Everything appears different, brighter, yet also the same.

Abbie looks at me strangely when I try to explain it to her. She appears worried as if she's expecting me to return to the mess I was in last night. I know I must have scared her. It scared me, too. The last couple of days have been bizarre.

I try to remain away from the bedroom all day, only going up there if it's vital. Dustin doesn't seem to mind following me around and appears to enjoy the sunset as we head back toward the castle from the rear gardens.

King Kyson still hasn't returned, and no one has heard from him. Beta Damian has been on edge all day because he can't get a hold of him or any of the King's guards. He left to contact the old Alpha to see if he was gone.

As I approach the stairs leading back to the castle, I hear car tires on the gravel and the shouts of men. My heart speeds up as I listen to the doors closing in the distance, and I know he's back.

"That would be your King, Miss Ivy," Dustin says, and I feel giddy knowing I am about to see him. I've missed him so much; one night away felt like a lifetime.

"Go on. I know you want to see your future husband," Abbie giggles. I slap her arm, and she returns it with a hug. "I have to go help Clarice with the upcoming celebrations," Abbie tells me.

"What celebrations?" I ask her. She shrugs and smiles.

"Oh, nothing you need to worry about. Now go see the King. I bet he missed you just as much as you missed him," she says as we approach the front of the castle.

Abbie goes toward the kitchens, and I move toward the stairs. I race up them, taking them two at a time. Though I become puffed out by the time I reach the top, Dustin chuckles as he walks ahead before taking his usual spot outside our door.

My world stands still when I enter the corridor and spot the King at the other end. A gasp escapes me, and the same giddy feeling I have had all day whenever I went into his room returns, only a million times more potent. My chest constricts, and my heart swells with love as I stare at him.

Every particle of me wants to race toward him, my soul yearning for him, for my mate. The King is my mate. *THE KING IS MY MATE!*

I feel my lips tug up as excitement bubbles within me.

Dreams can come true, and I couldn't ask for a better mate. I loved him before I even knew he was my mate. So this is just the topping on the cake. He is truly mine, and my eyes light up when I realize. Dustin, I notice, smiles at my excitement at seeing him, and I am all but bouncing on my feet.

My feet move before I can contain my excitement, my footsteps loud on the floors. My King, my mate, is standing talking to his Beta. They seem deep in conversation as I get closer.

"Kyson!" I shriek excitedly and rush toward him. I have never been so happy. It explains so much. Did he know? He had to have known, and he kept it to himself. Did he want me to figure it out on my own? I have so many questions. My heart leaps in my chest as I race toward him. My stomach feels like it is filled with butterflies; I'm that excited.

His entire body tenses, his posture straightens, and he steals the air from my lungs when he turns around to face me, and I see his handsome face.

"Mate," I whisper, trying to contain my joy as I rush toward him when suddenly my entire body seizes mid-stride. It's like I hit a brick wall. Every part of me locks up painfully; my muscles seize and cramp. Then pain slivers through my veins, and I feel like I've been punched in the stomach.

"Halt," comes one word, one full-blown command. I never would've believed it came from Kyson if I hadn't seen his lips move.

My entire body becomes immobile as his aura rushes over me like the weight of a car crushing me. It feels so heavy I find it difficult to breathe, crushing the air from my lungs. Like a stone tossed in a lake, my stomach sinks painfully, yet the sinking feeling has no end, like a bottomless pit. Only then do I finally take in his expression.

A murderous glare pins me to the spot, his aura making my knees shake. Sweat coats my skin, and my entire body burns. It feels like he has set me alight and is watching me burn. Hotter than the sun, his gaze sears me.

The look he is giving me makes my chest hurt, like a needle piercing it. Something is very wrong. Pain ripples through me as I try to move; only my limbs feel paralyzed.

What did I do? Did I interrupt? I don't understand. Kyson was all happy and cuddly when he left yesterday. *Did I do something wrong?*

CHAPTER
SIXTY

IVY Kyson growls at me, and the sound makes goosebumps rise all over my body. My hair stands on end as a shiver rushes up my spine. Dustin looks at me in stunned horror before his eyes go to Kyson. His mouth opens and closes like he is trying to figure out what is happening. Damian grips the King's shoulder. Kyson glances at him, then turns his back on me, walking off toward his room.

Finally, his command drops, which releases me and allows me to breathe and move. However, the way it abruptly dropped has me staggering, and I barely remain upright, having to use my hand to catch myself on the wall. My eyes dart to Dustin, but he is back to doing the seeing-without-seeing thing he does. His eyes are straight ahead, staring blankly at the wall, yet I see him swallow, his hands clenched at his sides. Beta Damian stares after the King in what appears to be shock as I hesitantly approach the King again. If he tells me what I did wrong, I will apologize. Maybe he is upset because he saw the mess I made in his closet. I will clean it.

"Kyson?" I call, and he stops. His entire body tenses again and ripples like he is about to shift. The King spins around to face me. He

320

snarls, baring his teeth at me as they elongate. The look on his face and his intense gaze make me take a step back from him.

"You dare address me so casually," he growls at me, and I stagger back when he stalks me while pointing his finger at me. My lip quivers as I look at Damian for an answer—some explanation.

"But.... You said I have to call you..." I stutter. But I stop myself from repeating the same mistake. "Sorry, my King," I whisper.

He takes another step forward before stopping, and I catch the movement of his Beta behind him when he pauses, and his hands clench into fists at his sides. Kyson turns and addresses Beta Damian, and my heart nearly stops at his following words.

"Get her out of my face, put her in the stables. She is no longer welcome in the castle. I don't want to see it again," The King snaps, turning toward his bedroom door.

"Kyson?" Damian murmurs.

The King growls furiously. "Remember your place, Beta. I said, put her in the fucking stables."

"But she's your mate!" Dustin speaks out abruptly.

"Does my mark lay on her skin?" Kyson growls. Dustin presses his lips in a line. Wait, did they all know all along? Dustin quickly shakes his head.

"Then you have no issue doing as you're told. Now put the fucking rogue in the stables before I order her to be placed in the fucking dungeons!" Kyson bellows. Beta Damian's eyes flick to me, then back to the King, who walks away.

"Yes, my King," Beta Damian answers, his voice stammering as the King pushes his bedroom door open without glancing back at me. My legs move like they have a mind of their own, and I race to the door, gripping the frame.

"Please." I cry out. Why is he being like this? "Wait, did I do something wrong?" I ask. Tears burn my eyes, and my vision blurs when he slams the door in my face and locks it. I can't understand what I have done. I stare at the closed door separating me from my mate.

It takes a few seconds before the pain in my chest becomes distinguishable from that of the pain in my hand. Blinking, I look at my hand clutching the frame, wondering why my hand looks funny. I take a few seconds to notice that the now-sealed door is crushing it. The moment I lay eyes on my hand, pain flies up my arm, and I jerk my hand and nearly choke on my sob when it doesn't budge.

I try again to pull it free in disbelief, but it only causes me more pain. I can feel every groove of my now bent fingers that are trapped. Blood seeps down the crevice of the door and my wrist and arm, dripping onto the floor. My blood fills the air with the tangy, coppery scent.

Out of the corner of my eye, I see his Beta take a step toward me, and I swallow down the scream threatening to leave me. My eyes focus on the engravings on the door, and I clear my throat while forcing the tears to hold back. *Tears won't help you.*

My lips quiver, and nothing I do would have held back the choked whimper that escapes me when I lift my other hand.

Don't cry, don't cry. You have had worse. I remind myself as I knock on the door.

I can hear movement on the other side of the door, and then I feel the lock mechanism slide out of my palm. The door swings open, revealing the furious King.

"What!" the King bellows, his canines peeking out from between his parted lips; his eyes are as black as charcoal, and his entire body trembles with rage. I pull my hand free and clutch my broken, bleeding hand to my chest while fighting back the urge to cry out in pain.

"Nothing, my King. Sorry to disturb you," I whisper, unable to meet his gaze. Quickly, I turn on my heel and walk away.

I walk away from my mate.

The sound of the door slamming again is loud as I walk off and seems to echo off the walls, but I don't look back. When I am halfway down the steps, movement catches my eye, and I see Clarice and

Abbie walking out of the kitchens, chatting excitedly. They both look up at me, their smiles slipping from their faces.

"Oh my gosh, Ivy, what happened to your hand?" Abbie shrieks, rushing over to me. Words fail me, and I can only stare as she fusses over me. Unsure what hurts more, my hand or my heart, which feels like the King just tore from my chest.

"I will get the first aid," Clarice panics, hurriedly rushing back toward the kitchen when two guards walk over and stop beside me and Abbie. My eyes dart to the tallest one. Trey.

"Miss Ivy, you need to come with me," one of them says, yet I am not paying enough attention to see who it is. I look at them and nod.

"Just a second. Just let me wrap Ivy's hand first. How did you do it, Ivy?" Clarice asks as she rushes back out with a box in her hands.

"I'm sorry, but I have been asked to escort her out of the castle immediately," the guard answers, and my heart sinks somewhere deep inside me, forming a pit.

"What, why? Do you have any idea who this girl is? The King would pitch a fit," Clarice argues with him.

"I am aware she is the King's mate. The King was the one who gave the orders. Now, Ivy, if you would follow me, please," the guard says, turning on his heel.

"Excuse me?" Clarice says, looking baffled.

"Wait, where are you taking her?" Abbie asks, holding my arm, starting to panic.

"Just let me fix her hand. She is bleeding everywhere," Clarice begs, but the guard seizes my arm and yanks me away.

"I'm sorry, I have orders," Trey states.

Clarice tries to hand me the bandages when the other guard steps forward, and only then do I notice it's Dustin.

"I will take them; I will wrap her hand," he tells Clarice, then giving me a sympathetic look. The other guard, Trey, glares at Dustin but says nothing as he drags me toward the doors.

"Can you at least tell me where you are taking her so I know where to go when I am sent to come to find her?" Clarice asks.

"The stables. She isn't allowed to come inside the castle. The King said she is no longer welcome." Trey replies.

Abbie and Clarice gasp, and I look back at them. Both appear shocked, just as shocked as me. What did I do? The guard tugs me out the door, and I stare ahead.

I knew it was too good to be true, that I would be nothing more than a rogue. Only now, I'm the rogue whose mate is the King. He's come to his senses and realized what a mistake he made by choosing me. Now, fate has tied us, but not even that is enough to stop him from getting rid of me.

ABOUT THE AUTHOR

Join my Facebook group to connect with me
    https://www.facebook.com/jessicahall91

Enjoy all of my series
    https://www.amazon.com/Jessica-Hall/e/B09TSM8RZ7

FB: Jessica Hall Author Page
Website: jessicahallauthor.com
Insta: Jessica.hall.author
Goodreads: Jessica_Hall

ALSO BY JESSICA HALL

Authors I Recommend

Jane Knight

Want books with an immersive story that sucks you in until you're left wanting more? Queen of spice, Jane Knight has got you covered with her mix of paranormal and contemporary romance stories. She's a master of heat, but not all of her characters are nice. They're dark and controlling and not afraid to take their mates over their knees for a good spanking that will leave you just as shaken as the leading ladies. Or if you'd prefer the daddy-do type, she writes those too just so they can tell you that you are a good girl before growling in you ear. Her writing is dark and erotic. Her reverse-harems will leave you craving more and the kinks will have you wondering if you'll call the safe word or keep going for that happily every after.]

Follow her on facebook.com/janeknightwrites

Check out her books on https://www.amazon.com/stores/Jane-Knight/author/B08B1M8WD8

Moonlight Muse

Looking for a storyline that will have you on the edge of your seat? The spice levels are high with a plot that will keep you flipping to the next page and ready for more. You won't be disappointed with Moonlight Muse.

Her women as sassy and her men are possessive alpha-holes with high tensions and tons of steam. She'll draw you into her taboo tales, breaking your heart before giving you the happily ever after.

Follow her on facebook.com/author.moonlight.muse

Check out her books on https://www.amazon.com/stores/Moonlight-Muse/author/B0B1CKZFHQ

Printed in Great Britain
by Amazon

43623707R00189